The Living Sword 3
The Burden of Legacy

Pemry Janes

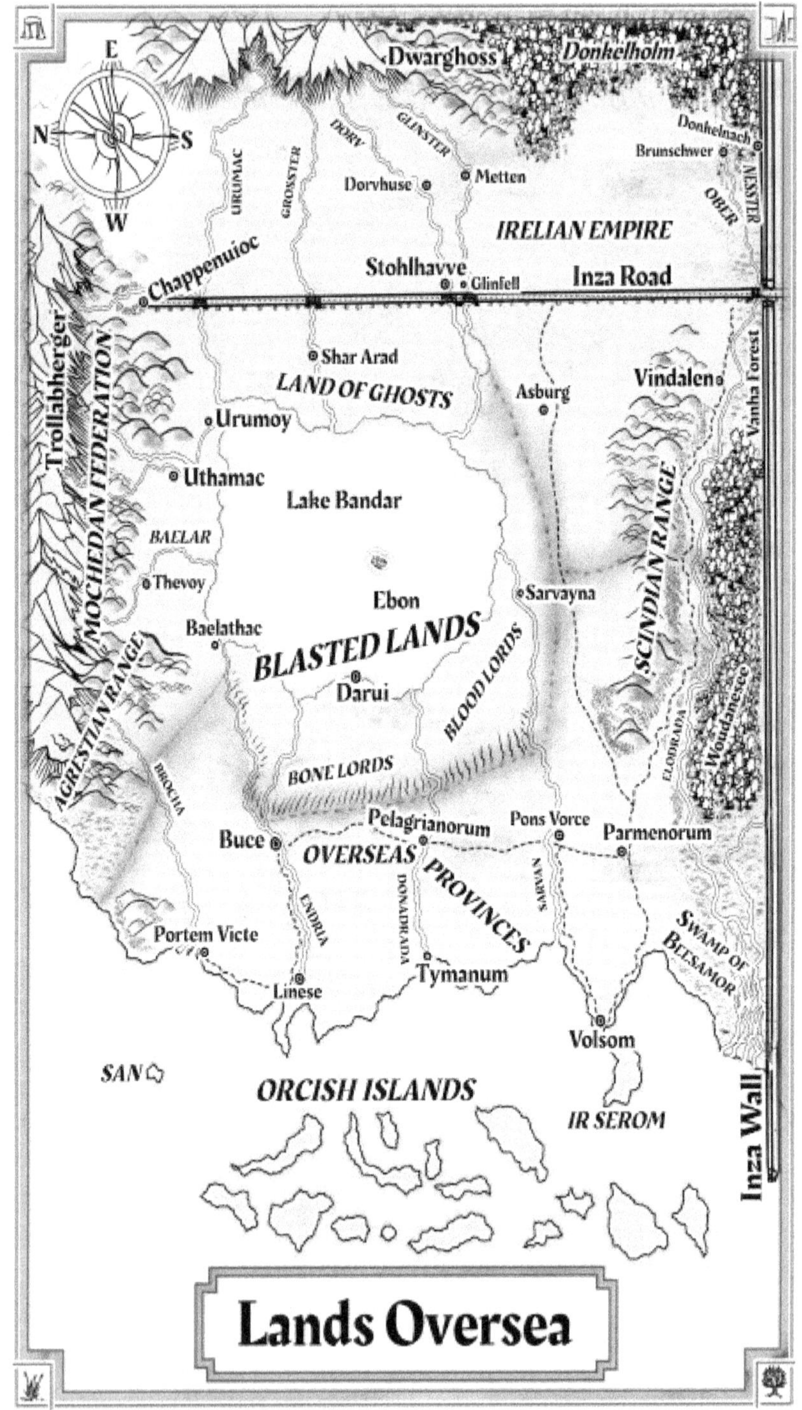

Lands Oversea

Chapter 1

Ghosts of the Past

"... AND SO I LOOKED THE demon in its eyes," Misthell said, using his magic to create a vapory image of the draconic demon's head staring down at the listeners. The hearths at either end of the hall were dying down now that dinner was over. The doors and windows of the lodge were thrown wide open to let a cool breeze blow through.

Misthell's illusion opened its jaws wide. "Pure hatred tried to strip me to the tang, but my steely resolve protected me and Silver Fang. We were all that stood between it and the helpless people of Glinfell. On my mark, Eurik launched his attack. And as it plummeted to the ground, I swung up to behead the creature!"

In Misthell's mirage, the creature fell apart, a hazy head rolling along an imaginary ground until it came to a stop before the living sword. Misthell rested against the frame of one of the cold hearths, the summer's heat more than enough to keep the room cozy.

A miniature army on horseback stepped into view. "But there was still the army of Duke Griffenhart. They advanced, but I sensed the fear in their hearts. So I told Silver Fang to lift my bloodied, battered self up high and I unleashed all my power upon them!" A small Misthell hung in the air, beams of light striking the army, which dissolved much like the demon had.

"And that, my friends, is how I and my friends saved the good city of Glinfell. You may have heard rumors already, but this is the truth."

One of the Chained Hunters grunted and blew out a bit of smoke before pulling his curved pipe out to point it at the living sword. "Don't know about all that. Ways I heard, it was a dragon. And methinks more praise should go to the warrior wielding the sword than the sword itself, however much it talks."

He got up, plucking at the mustache hanging from his upper lip. He wore no armor and his shirt was half-unbuttoned. When he got closer, the lingering scent of burnt dreamweed tickled Leraine's nose. "But fair's fair, it was a story well told." He gestured for her and Rock to follow him. "I'll show you to the armory."

Rock looked puzzled; his grasp of Irelian was poor and the Hunter's accent was quite thick.

"Thank you, Lieutenant Karrel," Leraine answered. She inclined her head as well, which Rock copied. "We'll leave Misthell here to keep your people entertained."

"Just so you know, you break it, you pay for the replacement. We don't run a charity here," Lieutenant Karrel said as he led them outside and across the yard to a small, stout building with a heavy lock on its door.

He left them standing outside while he retrieved the agreed items. The wooden swords weren't quite a match for their real weapons, the guard too big, the blade too broad. And the balance was off. But it would do.

Bidding them to have fun, Lieutenant Karrel went back inside. Given that it was still summer, the sun hadn't dipped below the horizon yet, even at this late hour. Still, the shadows were long as she and Rock squared off.

"I'm still surprised how quickly rumor spreads," Rock said, holding the sword in a high guard.

She mirrored his stance. "It may have had a helping hand. Do you not think it curious that it was the story most favorable to Griffenhart which we have heard these past few days?"

He frowned. "You mean?"

Leraine sprang forward, sword dipping down. Rock took the bait and left himself open for a stab straight to the chest. She jumped back out of his reach. "Concentrate. Not on the conversation, not on the weapon. On me. The weapon doesn't move, the wielder moves it." She switched to Thelauk. "You only need a few people to plant the seed, human nature will take care of the rest." One of Mother's sayings. It curled her tongue to agree with it, but their journey since Glinfell had proven her right. Again.

Rock furrowed his brow as he struggled to reply in the same language. "So ... Rozenbruk was right. Did he know?"

She shrugged. "Probably not the extent." Forward, again she raised her sword but this time followed through with the overhead strike. Rock caught it with a block, and Leraine pressed her lips together. His training with that stone magic left him with a certain mentality. Rather than deflecting, he sought to put his blade in the way of a threat as if it were a shield. Misthell would not appreciate that abuse if Rock ever tried to use the living sword like this.

The overhead strike spun around into a rising slice, block, cut to his left, block, cut right, block. "How did you know?" Rock didn't retreat when she relented, but moved in for a simple chop of his own.

She deflected the blow. Even without powering it with his magic, Rock could put some force behind his attacks. It left him open, though, and a moment later she laid the end of her sword in the crook of his neck. "No daughter of Raven Eye is allowed to be a mere warrior."

Leraine continued quickly, removing her blade. "Now, you need to be more fluid. I've seen you fight, I know you can do that. Don't simply be that mountain." She jabbed, and Rock struggled with a deflect. "A warrior can't afford to let some of her weapons rest." Jab. "The dead complain about a fair fight." Rock fell back. "Observe, adapt." She accompanied each word with another jab, and at last there was a change.

A shift in his gaze, his posture. Leraine felt the air stir even as she called upon Ghisa to quicken her own limbs. Their training swords blurred, filling the air with the *clack-clack-clack* of wood striking wood.

"Better," Leraine said with a grin as Rock pressed her. "But all you did"—cut, riposte, deflect—"was change approach." She stepped in, her body pressed against his, her hand blocked his elbow and stalled his strike. Leraine kicked one foot out from under him, unbalancing Rock enough that she could push him over. She planted the tip of her sword on his belly before his back hit the dirt.

He took a moment to regain his breath before taking the hand she offered. "You must use everything you have. In a real battle, when your life is on the line, it is foolish to do anything less."

Rock shook his head. "I would like to. I do not know how to use two kinds of *chiri*. Not at the same time. Not without paying a price. Crippling me to win one fight is a good way to die in the next one."

"Myself," Leraine said. "It is 'myself.' And I'm not saying to do that. But I know you can use the fighting style without the magic." She stepped back and brought up her blade. "Do that."

"I see." Rock frowned, looking down at himself as he shifted his posture and stance. "I have question. A question. You are ... at ease with the, uh, Chain Hunters. Not worried about leaving Misthell alone. Why?"

They crossed blades, their movements slow now. This was about figuring out how to move; ingraining them came after that. "You mean you don't know about the Chained Hunters? It's not in one of your books?"

He shrugged. "There was a little. About what they did, how the group came to be."

"The punishment for stealing under their roof is that they take the thief and stake him out in the Land of the Chained." Rock's eyes grew wide. "They use them as bait and they do free their soul afterward. It is half the reason why they continue to exist. Safest place to stay the night on the entire Road."

"That is ... harsh."

It was her turn to shrug. "It works. Now, from here you can turn the blade in. It is above mine and I will have a hard time defending against the strike. Yes, just like that." They pulled apart again. "However, we'll cross the Grosster tomorrow. From there, the journey will get more dangerous."

"How so? Are we not getting closer to Mochedan lands?"

"That is the problem. The horse people here will look at us with suspicion and hostility. They may think us spies, or thieves. We will have to be vigilant."

Rock lifted an eyebrow. "I may not have read much about the Chained Hunters. But a lot about the People and the horse people fighting one another. Especially along the Urumac."

"And much of that raiding is done by Falcon and Boar People. But horse people don't care to distinguish one of the People from another. Or admit that they give as much as they get." She pressed her blade and Rock teetered. "Too loose."

Rock regained his footing. "Have you ever gone on a raid?"

Leraine shook her head. "No, a warrior of Snake isn't allowed to until she has a child at least a year old. That was why I was in Linese."

"Looking for a child?"

She chuckled. "Now there's a thought. No, a mate. Someone to father the child. It is a tradition among my people. Not all do it. And very few travel as far as I have to find someone." She sighed and looked around, but they were alone. "In truth, I used it as an excuse to see the world. I thought there was nothing Irelith and I couldn't handle. She should have told me to grow up."

Rock was silent. A nightingale sang in the gloom. "You told me she'd seen little of the world before. Perhaps she, too, wanted to see more?"

Leraine froze and got a painful strike along her arm for her trouble. She hissed and forestalled his apology while rubbing out the pain. "Perhaps."

Eurik found that Silver Fang had undersold the hostility as they neared the Urumac. The Head Hunters were nice enough, but they wouldn't let them train any longer, and their guests kept their distance.

Other soldiers they met on the Road kept a wary eye on them as well. At least the neutrality of the Road held, and nobody tried to attack them. But it was strange to be looked at like that, not as an individual but as part of a group he had only the most tenuous connection to. It made him feel strange. Uncomfortable.

So it was with relief that Eurik crossed the broad river flowing underneath the Road. The Urumac had carved steep banks out of the landscape. There weren't a lot of other travelers on the Road and almost all of them had gathered in well-guarded groups.

A few of them were Irelians, dwarves, and even a group of lizarians. Their long heads bobbed back and forth with every step and they tugged along giant, long-legged birds with massive beaks. The birds, their wings too small to let them fly, were laden with goods.

But even the lizarians got less attention from the Mochedan on the Road than Eurik himself. Some of them spoke to each other in hushed tones. Maybe if his mastery of Dance of the Whirlwind had been greater, he could have eavesdropped. It took longer for him to figure out that their attention was on his sword as much as on him.

"Yes," Silver Fang said, guiding the horse by the reins. "I'm afraid you will have to get used to this."

"I can't look that odd to people." He would have preferred to speak Linese, but Leraine had used her native tongue.

"You think so?" The left corner of her mouth slid up. "It's true, there are those who don't follow our ways or forsake them. But they tend to leave our lands, instead of coming to them. And they wouldn't carry a blade like Misthell. He is ... unique."

"Glad you noticed," the living sword said.

She indicated a path of hard, backed dirt heading west. "I was referring to your design. Though I must admit, your personality is also weird."

"Well, thanks, I— Hey, what's weird about me?"

"You are a weapon that doesn't want to be used. A sword afraid of blood." They crossed the Road after a group of Irelian merchants, protected by Mochedan carrying large round shields and long-hafted axes, passed them by.

"Blood is very corrosive. I don't see you taking baths in acid." Misthell sniffed.

"You are exaggerating." She glanced over at the living sword. "And I cleaned you even while my own wounds were being tended to. Eurik has checked you every night since. You are fine."

"You don't know that. That demon blood could be a poison, waiting like a spider in its web. Waiting for the perfect opportunity to strike!"

Eurik and Silver Fang looked at each other and wisely kept their mouths shut while Misthell rambled on.

Chapter 2

Homecoming

EURIK TOOK A DEEP BREATH and half-closed his eyes to better enjoy the world. The sun's light easily burned through the few scattered clouds, and a stiff breeze came in from the southwest. The Road had been stifling on several levels, confining.

Sure, they'd stayed the nights off the Road; nobody with any sense would sleep on it. But most of those hours he'd spent asleep or busy doing something. Here, now, he could simply be and feel the world around him.

He didn't merely see the men—and a few women—in the fields reaping barley and the like, he felt them through the earth. He sensed mice scurrying through the stalks while snakes slithered after them. Worms and moles buried their way through the dirt beneath. Eurik felt a cart, heavily laden, move along the road, a herd of goats or sheep on the other side of the hill to the north. The world was full.

But this awareness of everything only served to blind him. He took a mental step back and opened his eyes again. Eurik studied the people they passed with more interest. What he saw didn't differ so much from what he'd seen so far. The fields along the road had hedges and banks to stop travelers from wandering onto them, much like they had down west. The crops in those fields were the same as well. Scarecrows were different, a tube of fabric tied to the end of a pole painted to resemble a snake.

The people, though, they did look different. The men didn't have beards or mustaches, their hair was as dark as his if not darker, and they wore it longer. They had the same coppery tan as Eurik. Their clothes were different, too: pants and sleeveless vests that had patterns stitched into them with colorful yarn and beads. There weren't many women in the fields, but they were dressed very much like the men.

After spending so much time with Silver Fang, he'd pictured a people of warriors, all of them wearing armor and weapons while going through day-to-day business. But that had been silly, of course, and he would have realized that if he'd thought it through. All of that would only get in the way if one was trying to milk a cow or thresh grain.

A group of young children ran past, bare legs and feet, swinging sticks and wooden swords. He noted with interest that none of them wore that braid the adults had. They barely looked at Silver Fang, but pointed at him and Misthell and talked to each other in hushed whispers.

They passed the settlement itself, which wasn't on the road directly. Instead, it stood off about a bowshot away on a low hill, squatting behind a thick wall of large stone blocks. Sharpened stakes stuck out at an angle at the foot of the walls, but others near the entrance stood straight up, and a couple of them had a lump of something stuck on top.

With a start, he realized he was looking at decomposed heads, human probably. Could be elf, orc, or dwarf—hard to tell from this distance—but all of them lived too far away to attack this place.

"Are those ... rule breakers?" He'd seen displays like this on his travels. Eurik could still remember the first time he'd seen a corpse hanging from a tree near Pons Vorce. He'd read about it all. But reading how they dealt with people who broke the law on the mainland was different from actually seeing it. Smelling it.

"Hmm?" Silver Fang's eyes had been on the road, about five steps ahead and a thousand years in the future. "Rule breakers? Oh, if you are trying to say criminal, drop the *voy*. But where are you seeing one?"

Eurik indicated the settlement and the stakes. Silver Fang shook her head. "No, those are *pochudanogic*."

They were talking Thelauk, but the last word he'd never heard before. "*Pochudanog*? Something to do with war, and spirits?"

"They are warder spirits. It was more common before the Truce. Those are enemies of the sept, their spirits have been captured, and now they serve that sept to ward off evil. And to warn other enemies of the danger of facing that particular sept."

Eurik frowned and looked at the heads again. "Didn't you disapprove of the Boudicians' use of spirits to protect their homes? How is this different?"

"How could it not be?" She looked to the south. Past the fields ran the Urumac, and beyond lay the Ghostland. "They used their own ancestors as if they were enemies, never letting go. Without a body, a spirit can't recuperate. Like a man you don't feed, they can only work so much before they falter. The shaman will keep an eye on the warder spirits and release them when their strength is spent. That is how it should be."

"And how do you know they're not criminals?"

Silver Fang gave a bark of laughter. "Who would honor scum in that way? Criminals, if their crime is such they are to be killed, their death is quick. Then their body is disposed of so that they can't be infested by a demon."

"I see." Eurik didn't quite know how to feel about this. The heads looked old. They certainly had been there for at least a year, though there was still some flesh and hair left. But this town's only neighbors were Mochedan and the undead across the Urumac.

No, the enemy might have come to them. And Silver Fang has warned me that the Truce only prevents clans and tribes from fighting each other. Individuals are on their own, literally.

"So how much longer until we get to Urumoy?"

"We'll not reach it today. Perhaps the day after tomorrow if we keep a good pace." She mounted her horse. "Try to keep up." She set off at a canter.

Eurik drew on the wind blowing through the stalks and let its *chiri* quicken his limbs. It only took five steps to catch up to her, another two to pass. "Try to keep up!"

Leraine guided Rock up to the hold of Silent Ice, one of her mother's allies. There was still daylight left, and it should be safe enough to camp out in the open. But here she could get a glimpse of the welcome she could expect back home.

Silent Ice's hold consisted of a single longhouse, its steeply sloped roofs sporting several chimneys. It had been built in a curve along the top of the hill that dominated the surrounding fields. Beside it, a barn stood made in a similar fashion with fencing connecting the two with a couple of smaller buildings to form a pen for the animals. The wall that encircled the whole thing was barely high enough to prevent Leraine from looking in if she'd been mounted on her horse.

She caught Rock staring at the warder heads and elected to ignore it. His reaction had been worse when he saw that lawbreaker back in Linese. He could be remarkably squeamish. The gate stood open, a sign of the peaceful times they lived in, though her approach had been noted, of course.

Two warriors strode out to meet them, and Leraine quickly spoke to Rock. "Remember, bow deep, don't speak unless spoken to, and don't unsheathe Misthell for any reason. Men aren't allowed to touch a weapon, but outsiders are exempted. To a point."

"I remember. You've told me this several times now."

There was no time to respond to that. The warriors had reached them. Both wore scale armor and casually rested their swordstaffs against their shoulders. "Ho there, who approaches the hold of Silent Ice?"

The other warrior elbowed her comrade. "Wait, you don't recognize her?"

The first warrior took her eyes off them. "Should I?"

"I'd say so. You do remember the demon slayer came through here a year ago? Then again, as I recall, you were in your cups at the time. I don't think you remember half the nights that month."

Finally getting a good look at their *draen*, Leraine recalled who they were. Sorrow Heart had indeed been drinking much that night, something about failing to court a man. And the one poking fun at her, now and then, was Mocking River.

Wait, what did she call me?

The other warrior swatted at the jokester's shins with the butt of her weapon, but Mocking River easily sidestepped the halfhearted strike. "Not that drunk. But there are forms to be observed. Silent Ice would have us both stand guard on the field in midwinter if we insult her honored guest." Sorrow Heart turned back to Leraine and planted her swordstaff's butt on the ground between her feet.

"I am," Leraine hesitated. This would make it real, if it was accepted. If not, the shame would be almost too much to bear. "I am Silver Fang, daughter of Raven Eye, who is daughter of Patient Adder. I ask for a place at your fire and a resting place behind your walls."

A grinning Mocking River sprang forward to clasp Leraine on the shoulder and almost dragged her into the hold. "You and your man are welcome! Light and rest will be yours. Now, you've got to tell me. How big was the demon? Big as a house? Cloud Dreamer bet me it couldn't have been bigger than the boulder over in Darkspar Forest."

"Oh, oh, I can answer that question!" Misthell rattled in his sheath, drawing the attention of Silent Ice's warriors.

I forgot to tell the sword to be quiet.

"Because I was there, you know. In fact, the demon wouldn't have been vanquished if not for me. My blade cleaved the demon's head in twain. Not that Silver Fang didn't help. Her and, uh, Rock!"

Mocking River blinked, then her grin returned. "Unless you sprang from your scabbard by yourself and flew at the demon on your own power, I'd say Silver Fang did more than help. But I could be wrong. I didn't know swords could talk either. So show me, oh sword, how you slew the demon of Glinfell and I'll listen to your tale of bravery and skill."

"Oh, I'll show you."

"No," Leraine said. "Misthell, you can entertain people during the evening meal."

"You're not the boss of me."

"Misthell," Rock said, "behave. We are guests and there's no need to boast. What you did was great enough."

Silent Ice's warriors eyed Rock carefully, Sorrow Heart nodding a moment later before returning her attention to Leraine. "Your man's got a head on his shoulders. And his Thelauk isn't half-bad. The son of outcasts?"

Leraine pressed her lips together. Rock was not her man, but men weren't recognized as independent in the Snake tribe. There were good reasons for that, of course, and they were flexible enough when it came to outsiders. But Rock might be staying with them for a time and in that situation, he'd need someone to be seen as in charge of him.

"We don't know, actually," she said. "His parents died when he was very young. He grew up among the san."

"The san?"

"Plant-men. You might have heard the story of Ash Flint and his sword Grasscutter? The creatures he slew were san, that's why his sword had that name."

"Oh, yeah, I heard the loremistress speak of him," Mocking River said. "Long time ago. I thought they were all gone though. Like griffons, giants, and Inza."

They entered the longhouse, Sorrow Heart bringing up the rear while Mocking River went forward to announce to Silent Ice who had arrived at her hold. She stood up, eyes wide at the sight of Leraine, and barely waited for Mocking River's voice to fall off before coming forward. Her daughters trailed after her, both of them only a little older than Leraine herself.

Silent Ice's hands enveloped her shoulders and she looked deep within Leraine's eyes before giving a single nod.

"Silver Fang is welcome in our hold," one of Silent Ice's daughters, Rime, said. Both of them had their mother's light blue eyes, but unlike their mother, no dark spirit had stolen their voices. Silent Ice had to let go of her to gesture, and Rime continued. "We offer you and your man salt and bread."

Silver Fang bowed to Silent Ice. The offer was symbolic, but very powerful. You could offer a traveler shelter and warmth, but it didn't obligate you to them beyond simple safety. Bread and salt, though, was the way to invite a guest, and guests had rights. They also had obligations. Relieved, she saw from the corner of her eye that Rock had bowed as well, a bit deeper than her, too.

"I am honored."

"No, it is we who are honored," Rime said, her eyes on her mother's flashing hands. "The tale of your heroism has spread far and wide."

Leraine's jaw slackened. "It has?"

Silent Ice smiled and nodded. "It has," her daughter said, this time speaking for herself. "You slew a real demon, Silver Fang. Few have done so since the Rift War and only a handful have faced a greater demon. They're calling you a new Two Fang!"

Perhaps Silent Ice caught some of her panic, because she took Leraine by the elbow and gently guided her to the table. And her next questions were of her journey and what she had seen. The small crowd listened silently as she described the Mountain Wall towering above the Woudanesee, and they hissed as she described facing her first elf, but it was at her description of the great city of Linese that they uttered disbelief.

The food they offered was simple fare, a pottage of peas, onions, and barley, enlivened by bits of chicken and thyme. They scooped it up with dark crusted bread while Misthell entertained everybody by regaling them with one story after another.

Thankfully, not her story. She nodded to Eurik across the room; he must have had a word with the living sword. From among his place with the men, he gave her a shrug. Still, this meal would end, and, judging from the looks she was getting from the women around the table, the story of Silver Fang and the demon would be told.

I should have gone straight home.

White clouds hung scattered across the sky, but neither they nor the wind offered any relief from the burning sun. Eurik felt a drop of sweat roll down his cheek and along his neck. He could try to generate some wind *chiri* himself, but the relief that breeze could bring wouldn't offset the effort he'd need to expend to do it in the first place.

The air was heavy with the scent of cut grain stalks. Yesterday, sheaves still stood in some of the fields they'd passed, but today all he saw were birds picking over the remains. A couple of bowshots away, a group scattered. He didn't see the snake, but he felt plenty of them slinking around.

To their left, Lake Bandar stretched out over the horizon. A few boats bobbed up and down on its waves, the people on them pulling in nets while more birds wheeled above. Other boats with billowing sails sailed toward or away from the docks built on the lake shore.

Not that he could see those docks, just the ends of them jutting into the lake itself. The walls of Urumoy hid them from sight, them and much of the rest of the city. And it should be called a city, though a small one compared to what he'd seen in the Linesan Empire.

The walls were interesting, both by structure and appearance. He'd felt it before when passing other Mochedan settlements. They were at least four steps wide, but not solid. The dressed stones he could see only formed the skin. The wall was filled with rubble, sand, and wood. The latter hadn't been placed haphazardly but laid horizontally across the wall on each layer of stonework, connecting the inner and outer wall.

This method made Mochedan walls not simply strong, but resilient. It would make bringing this wall down a lot harder, not that Eurik had any intention of doing so.

Eurik didn't know what the giant multicolored snake undulating along the entire length of the wall was supposed to do. It stood out against the lime-washed surface on which it had been painted. Perhaps it was only meant to impress.

He felt the activity within, even at this distance, the thrill or murmur in the earth that only several thousand people could produce going through their daily lives. Carts, piled high with straw and bags of grain, filed through the gate. Wooden watchtowers built on top of the wall on either side of the gate overlooked the crowd and he could see armored women standing under their roofs.

It must be nice up there. In the shade. Away from the heat that has soaked into the earth. Perhaps a hint of a cool breeze.

Eurik sighed and looked over at Silver Fang, who sat stiffly on her horse, eyes staring through the city, it seemed. "You're almost home." She didn't react. "Silver Fang?" Her saddle creaked; a fly landed on her hand holding the reins.

He looked around. Nobody was nearby, the sun was up, and the nearest crow was at least three bowshots from them. Still, Eurik spoke as softly as he could. "Leraine."

Silver Fang's head snapped around. Her horse danced away, and she had to spend some time calming her down. "Yes, Rock?"

"I said, you're almost home."

"Yes. It won't be long now," she said, looking once again at the gate of Urumoy.

"You don't look as happy as I would if I saw my home again."

"Oh, I'm happy." She didn't take her eyes off the city. "But we're about to face my mother. That is not something you should do without being prepared."

"How so?"

Silver Fang blinked and looked at him again. "Ah, it is nothing. Nothing that should concern you. I think. With luck, Mother will have little interest in you. Please, think of your own reason for being here. Even if your mother didn't live here, then she may very well have learned her art in Urumoy."

"Right." Eurik joined Leraine in staring at the city.

Chapter 3

By Accident

THE WARDER HEADS OF Urumoy were placed atop the gateway, keeping an eye on the easiest way for evil to enter the city. All knew evil spirits didn't like climbing or crossing large bodies of water. Leraine only gave them a fleeting look, but it was enough to notice one of the heads was much fresher; perhaps a month, maybe longer.

Before she'd left, Leraine hadn't imagined any wall could be mightier than the ones of her home. She knew better now, but only those of Linese itself truly surpassed them in every way. They passed through the outer gate and were waved in through the inner gate as she saw the news of her homecoming ripple through the crowd.

According to Silent Ice, Raven Eye had spread the tale of her battle with the demon far and wide. If she had known this would come from Mayor Rozenbruk's message, she'd have implored him not to send it.

Too many people hailed their new hero, though at least none tried to stop her. But they cheered her for a deed that was at least half done by the young man trailing behind her. It felt dishonest to be given sole credit. This hadn't been the plan.

Leraine had wanted to be called Silver Fang for avenging Irelith. She would have presented her blade and the fang of Irelith's killer to her daughters, speak of how she had fought the blooddrinker, and then claim her name. Instead, they hardly seemed to notice Viper wasn't with her.

She rode through the main street of Urumoy, dust tickling her nose as she breathed in the city's familiar scent. Urumoy didn't have paved roads. The only sewer was a ditch that ran through the middle of the settlement covered in most places by broad, flat stones. The city in the summer was a mélange of grit, sweat, soot, and the faint hint of shit. At least the wind wasn't coming from the lake or they'd be smelling the tanners as well.

When did I get so fussy? Leraine shook her head.

The street curved up to the north, leading to the market triangle and the longhouse of Raven Eye. The majority of the buildings in Urumoy were made mostly from wood; Raven Eye's was an exception. Some of the other exceptions flanked the triangle. To her right was the House of Lore, to her left the longhouse of Grumbling Storm.

The market triangle was packed with stalls and tables, while others sold their wares from blankets. She hadn't realized it would be market day today; that did explain most of the crowds filling the streets.

But it forced Leraine to slow her pace even as people made a path for her toward the steps leading to her home. Long before she reached them, people started filing out of the longhouse.

Warriors sworn to her mother led the way in their shining mail, the long blades of their spears glinting in the sun's light. Loremistress Blue Scale came out after them, the bronze rod of her office held up against her left upper arm.

Leraine's eyes widened as the last person walked out at a slow pace, leaning on a simple cane that she hadn't had when Leraine left. Even when she'd reached the top step and straightened up, her mother still leaned lightly on the cane.

Reaching the bottom step herself, Leraine dismounted and quickly whispered to Rock. "Keep a hold of Sniff and stay out of my mother's sight. Without looking like you're doing that."

She took a quick, deep breath before she jogged up the steps. Up close, if she ignored the cane, Mother looked very much the same as a year ago. Some silver streaks in her hair, but her eye was as dark and sharp as ever. Today, she wore an eye patch of dark blue, undecorated. That relieved one concern: Mother wasn't about to disinherit her.

With one foot on the step below the top step and the other on the step below that, Leraine bowed. "Mother, I have returned." *Perhaps I should have visited White Gale and Flashing Reed first.* But she knew that would only have been an option if she'd been able to enter Urumoy without getting recognized.

"Welcome, Silver Fang." Leraine felt a small weight slide off her shoulders. Silent Ice's welcome had told her Mother accepted her new name, but it hadn't been the same. "We've heard you've brought great honor to Urumoy by rescuing our allies from the folly of the horse people."

"I did what duty required of me." Truth be told, if her mother hadn't lost her eye to a spellsword, perhaps she would have been known today as Shadow Weaver. Best to keep her own words simple and hope not to be drawn into too many of Mother's plans.

"Words to live by. But you are too modest. And I see you brought guests. Come, boy, let me have a look at you."

Leraine's silver tooth dug into her lower lip. *So much for keeping Rock out of it.* It had been an idle hope.

Rock hesitated. Then he flexed his power, erecting a simple waist-high pillar from the ground with a hole in the top that he could use to fasten the reins. Murmurs spread as he walked up the steps.

Leraine grimaced. Her people didn't use horse people magic, but they knew what it looked like. What they'd just seen had been neither the power of the spirits nor what spellswords and wizards used. And that would draw interest, even if Raven Eye wasn't looking him over in front of a quarter of the people of Urumoy.

"I understand you two assisted my daughter in her heroics." It sounded benign enough, but she's spoken loud enough to be heard and the triangle amplified someone who spoke from that spot very well. "You are welcome in Urumoy. I offer you salt and bread."

Leraine closed her eyes before the crowd's reaction reached her ears. What was Mother playing at? Placing this much attention on an armed man, however much an outsider?

Rock hesitated, then bowed quite deeply. "You honor me." At least his Thelauk was decent, he'd even used the proper form of "you" when dealing with the head of a settlement of Urumoy's stature. She might have drilled him on that one. A lot.

"Not at all. And the offer of guest rights is for both you and Misthell. Though I fear neither will do a sword any good."

"That's all right," Misthell said. "I very much appreciate the thought. Maybe some good oil?"

She bestowed a smile upon them "I'm sure we can arrange something. And you, Rock? Will you be staying under my roof?"

"I . . . would be honored to do so."

"Yes, well. Just let my housekeeper know if you need your own place to sleep, so he knows where to put you."

Leraine didn't know what Mother was playing at, but she shouldn't let Eurik face her mother alone. "He prefers a solid platform on which to sleep." She took a deep breath and reminded herself to stay calm.

"Mother, I regret to inform you that Irelith the Viper has fallen." Leraine wondered who would take over the name now. Her rival, Ringing Blink, was older than Irelith. It could be some young warrior would yet outdraw her in the coming Truce Festival. "The blooddrinker that took her life died at my hands. And my tooth."

If her mother was going to use this for her own purposes, so would Leraine.

"Irelith died well. But come inside and tell me all about your adventures. We've held up trade enough as it is. Iron Bones, escort Rock and Misthell to Dandelion. I wish to speak to my daughter alone."

Leraine couldn't say she was surprised that her mother knew their names already. She might only have one eye, but she had many ears and mouths, spread far and wide. Silently, Leraine followed Mother as she hobbled into their home.

She did not speak, and neither did Mother, not until they'd passed the dividing wall that separated Raven Eye's private quarters from the rest of the longhouse and Swift Hop closed the door behind them.

The room smelled much as Leraine remembered, except for a new addition. Acrid, somewhat familiar, though it made no sense for her to smell it here. Perhaps Mother had taken a new lover?

"You got very lucky, Leraine," Mother said as she lowered herself with a grimace into her chair. Cushions embroidered with the geometric patterns of the dwarves depressed under her weight. "As it is, few speak of your flouting of our traditions. Criticizing the only living warrior of Snake who killed a demon is not popular today; not in Urumoy."

Leraine went to protest, but something else her mother had said caught her attention. "What of Demonsbane? Or Steel Cutter?"

"Demonsbane died last winter of fever. And Steel Cutter got into an argument with her new wife's second daughter. Blades were drawn and Steel Cutter's love for whiskey caught up to her. So you are it. Be glad, for it is half the reason you are still welcome in Urumoy."

Swallowing, Leraine focused on her breathing even as her heart thumped. "I did seek a mate, but found none worthy. And once

Irelith died, my duty to avenge her and return her blade to her family came first."

Raven Eye snorted. "Worthy? You aren't picking a thoroughbred here. Trust me, child, most men will suffice. Just mount them and get it over with. It is the rearing which matters. And that is only half the reason. Did you know that Bone Lord sent a lackey to negotiate your ransom when you had the temerity to get captured?"

"I broke free quickly."

"Yes, but while word of that took its sweet time coming here, I had to play nice and house that worm under my roof! And then he had the gall to call me a liar to my face when I informed him he had lost his leverage. At least his fate silenced some of my critics, for a time."

"The fresh warder head. I had wondered who it had been." Leraine hesitated, glanced at the cane Mother had placed next to her high-backed chair. "How are you?"

"I fell off my horse," Raven Eye said, answering the question Leraine hadn't voiced. "Broke my hip. Healers say it is mending nicely, but not fast enough for my taste." She felt around and pulled a long pipe from among the cushions and put something from a pouch into it. "Be a dear and fetch me a flame."

Leraine went over to the hearth where the fire smoldered and lit a small twig which she brought back to her mother, shielding the flickering flame with her hand. She lit the pipe and put out the twig with a quick shake, only to freeze when the first puff of smoke tickled her nose.

The smell was distinct, dreamweed. Mother had not been a smoker before Leraine left. Dreamweed put the user at a distance from reality. Useful against pain, but it dulled the mind.

Leraine watched as her mother's eyelid slumped just a tad and that famous eye lost some of its shine. "There's talk I have become old. That it's time for new blood. Your sisters were so clumsy in their first attempts, I could not step aside on sheer principle, and they've only gotten worse since. So eager for power, with no notion of what they want to do with it afterward."

"What have they done that you disapprove of?"

"Hmm? Ah, Anseri has cast herself as a traditionalist." Her mother sneered around her pipe. "You would have had her to thank for it if you'd found yourself banished from Urumoy."

Raven Eye exhaled a stream of smoke and Leraine leaned back as far as she dared. The silver raven's head in her mother's *draen* rested on her breast, its tiny black pearl eye staring at her while Mother's eye examined the ceiling. "Ferisha, though, is championing the cause of the Truce Warriors."

"Surely not." They didn't call themselves that, they said they were True Warriors of the People. And they advocated an end to the Truce and a return to free war. The horse people were divided, the soulless beset from every corner. Now was the time to seek battle and find glory and wealth. Leraine had to admit it had been an attractive idea once. Irelith had beaten the notion of glory out of her—literally, on occasion.

"Feh, at least they're trying. Can't say the same for you. What are your plans now, daughter of mine?"

"I intend to present Irelith's sword to her daughters, and proof of her killer's death. After that, help Rock with his search."

Raven Eye shook her head. "You have fame and the shadow of my lineage, yet that is the extent of your plans." She sucked in some dreamweed smoke. "What did I do to offend the spirits so? Cursed with daughters who have too much ambition, or not enough."

She held up her hand when Leraine opened her mouth to speak. "No, no, spare me the paeans to the simple life of a warrior. If you insist that is what you want to be, very well. I can make use of a simple warrior."

Leraine's teeth clicked together as she frowned at her mother. That had been unusually blunt. "Use me how?"

"Did I say that? No, you must have misheard. Your journey was long and it has tired you. Yes, you can go and recuperate. We'll talk tomorrow when you are rested."

She was sure that she had heard right. But Mother's eyelid sank further and talking to her when she was like this was even more disconcerting, so Leraine bowed and took her leave.

Leraine hesitated outside the room, glancing at Swift Hop. The warrior returned the look and the question died on Leraine's lips. Instead, she nodded to her mother's retainer and walked the familiar path to her own room.

Chapter 4
Caught

EURIK CLOSED THE DOOR to his guest room behind him with some concern. He hadn't seen Silver Fang since yesterday. Granted, the place was larger than someone might think when hearing the word longhouse. There were three floors, two of them divided by a double wall down the middle which separated the individual rooms from a common hall in which most of the daily activities took place.

They'd housed him on the second floor, among the warriors and clerks that served Raven Eye. He wasn't the only guest either; a dwarven merchant from the Dwarghoss was also staying under the roof of the ruler of Urumoy.

Straw mats on the wooden floor absorbed much of the sound of his steps, his and everybody else's moving through the hallway and into the hall proper.

"So you haven't told me yet what the plan is for today," Misthell said in Linese.

"Not sure yet. I want to talk to Silver Fang first, but I don't want to wait any longer, either. I'm sure I can find some blacksmiths, and one of them might have known my mother." They were getting looks; Eurik didn't know how many of them understood Linese.

Eurik saw someone he knew, at least by name, as he looked for a place to sit. Iron Bones was a massive person. She might actually be able to arm wrestle Captain Slyvair and win. He had some trouble guessing how old humans exactly were, but his best guess was that Iron Bones was a few years older than him.

The warrior's conversation ceased as she noticed Eurik's approach. "Yes?"

He bowed lightly. "Greetings. Would you know where Silver Fang is? I need to speak to her."

"Do you?" One of the others guffawed as Iron Bones smiled. "Eat something. Silver Fang will see you when she has the time."

Eurik hesitated. He'd prefer to insist, but his grasp of Thelauk wasn't perfect and Leraine had stressed how careful he needed to be. So he bowed again. "Let her know that I seek her if you see her. Please."

"Sure."

"If she's too busy, why not come by my room," another woman said. "I'm sure I can take care of your need." That set everybody off in a howl of laughter, and Eurik retreated.

"What was that about?"

"You," Misthell said before joining the women's laughter. However, lacking both a mouth and lungs, he could still speak while also laughing his hilt off. "You used *need* instead of need."

"I don't . . ." And then it hit him: the inflection, the emphasis on the second syllable instead of the last. "Ah, oh . . ." Blushing, Eurik got some food and sat down as far as he could from Iron Bones and her group. It didn't help.

It felt odd to Leraine to be walking around in something other than her armor or traveling clothes. Her outfit was sober, not much better than what others wore around the house. Yet she couldn't recall her pants being this tight or her vest so stiff. Perhaps months in their chest had made her clothes shrink?

Food had been waiting for her when she awoke; she hadn't even noticed someone entering and leaving her room. Leraine shivered and quickly checked to make sure none saw her shame. This was her home. She was among her own people again. To distrust them would be like one finger not working with the others.

Mother doesn't trust anybody.

She exhaled loudly and kept walking. Mother's duty required her to do things and contemplate the unthinkable to see their people prosper. But Leraine wasn't Raven Eye and had no desire to be. Not her.

"Little sister, I'd heard you had returned," a familiar voice spoke from behind.

Speak of the dragon . . . Leraine turned around and nodded to Anseri. "Sister, it's good to see you again as well. Though I will not be staying long. There is much left to do."

Anseri stopped her from turning away by placing a hand on Leraine's shoulder. "Surely it can wait. Unless it's about that man you brought along? Is he going to be the father, or your husband?"

Leraine took a deep breath. "Neither. He's a friend, and I have a debt to him, nothing more. I return without child from my search. Do you intend to do anything about that?"

Her sister blinked, then smiled, though it didn't reach her eyes. Anseri looked much more like Mother, with her dark eyes and prominent nose. But those eyes couldn't quite match Raven Eye's sharpness. It felt more like getting stared at by an angry bull. Scary, in its own way. "Has anybody given you any grief over your unproductive search?"

"Oh, no. They are too busy asking me what it was like slaying a demon. It can get exhausting."

Anseri shifted her hold to pat Leraine on the shoulder, but after the hand came down it rested there with a firm grip. "I'm sure. I'll see what I can do to get people to back off. But don't worry, the attention will fade fast enough. And I have your back when it comes to any shameful rumors that you abused our treasured traditions for . . . selfish reasons."

Ah, Anseri, subtle as a brick to the back of the head.

Leraine nodded. "Thank you, sister. It's good to nip such false gossip in the bud, since it would reflect poorly on our family."

"Yes, yes it would." Anseri's smile got a little wider. "Glad we got caught up."

As her sister left, Leraine decided that rather than risk another encounter like that, she'd best go to Irelith's daughters. Before Ferisha decided they needed a sisterly chat of their own, or Mother called Leraine to her.

I might be safe from steel blades here, but there are other kinds under Raven Eye's roof.

He'd tried, but there had been no sign of Silver Fang, and even when Misthell kept quiet they got a lot of silent attention. Eurik decided to strike out on his own. He had managed well enough in Linese, and Urumoy was vastly smaller. He knew what he was looking for and how to find it.

Standing outside the longhouse on the top of the short set of stairs, Eurik cast his senses into the ground. The earth *chiri* was restless, like trying to feel the surface of a pond when thousands of people were throwing pebbles into it.

But all those pebbles, all those throws, they had a rhythm. Fast, slow, deep, shallow. Many blended into each other to form a massive ripple, but it was still the same ripple. Eurik dug through the trampling of thousands of feet, hundreds of hooves, and looked for the steady thump of the blacksmith's hammer.

There, in the direction of . . . the river.

Eurik nodded to himself and descended into the bustling crowd. Many, almost all, were clearly Mochedan. A few Irelians, maybe from the Oathfellowship. Some, though, were pale and wore light mantles over their puffy jackets. Invariably they were escorted by skeletal guards, however much they were draped in cloth and steel to hide the fact.

People from the Land of Bone got few looks. Such visitors had to be a common sight here, then. Eurik moved away from the market and toward the river, following a broad road. He only paid half attention to the people around him, enough to avoid a collision. Much of his concentration was on the *chiri* beneath his feet.

"Ah, so we're heading for smithies," Misthell said.

Startled, Eurik glanced over his shoulder at the blade. "We are. How did you know?"

"We're looking for my makers, that's the point of this whole story. Also, there were at least two carts laden with iron bars and coal we passed heading the same way we are."

Looking past Misthell, Eurik spotted one of the carts in question. "Right. I should have noticed that."

"You're too focused on one thing. Or should I say, one Way. Why don't you try Dance of the Whirlwind to find what you're looking for?"

He hesitated for a moment as the people flowed around him. But these past weeks, what little time he'd had for training had been taken up by Silver Fang. And on the Road, even wind *chiri* didn't quite work as it should.

Taking a deep breath, he reached out only to have Misthell whistle sharply in his ear. Eurik flinched away. "What was that for?"

"Because you're starting wrong. The wind is motion, so if you're trying to become one with the wind . . ."

He sighed. He should know this and he did. "So must I." Eurik moved forward, arms hanging loose at his side, fingers lightly splayed, and felt for the flow of wind *chiri*. Though flow was the wrong word for the chaotic mess swirling around him, a chaos he added to with every step, every breath. On reflex, he closed his eyes to better concentrate on his other sense.

He tried feeling for the ringing of steel, of hammers striking hot iron. But the wind *chiri* shied away from his reach, his flow rebuffing those around him.

Eurik sidestepped a group walking toward them, their wake washing over him. A sharp flow snaked its way out of a tavern to his left, carrying a jaunty tune. Behind him an ox exerted himself, hot air blasting out with every huff.

Those flows he could feel, because they mixed and bounced off his own, but they also constrained his world. He pushed, wind ruffling clothes and hair, and he felt his perception expand. So did the chaos, new flows emerging within his flow while more flows beat at it from without.

The wingbeat of a lake gull, the wind blowing over the rooftops of Urumoy, hot air rising from a dozen chimneys, the staccato of a thousand voices whispering, speaking, hollering.

Eurik swayed, and a wagon wheel ground past his toes, almost crushing them. "Look where you're going!" Opening his eyes, he staggered away as he lost his connection with the world. Out of the flow of traffic, into a narrow, shadowed alley. The air hung in there, thick and fetid. His deep breaths only set him to coughing.

"What did you do wrong?"

"I—" Another cough. Eurik shook his head. "I don't know." Breathing through his nose wasn't better, only made the smell worse, but it helped against the coughing. "I tried to reach out to find the smithy, but I got swamped by the city. There was too much."

"Wind is not earth," Misthell said, his voice changing into a familiar one. One Eurik had not heard in months. "It is more like water, flowing from a place of abundance to one where there is absence. The wind dances to its own music, and you must dance with it if you wish to guide it to where you need it."

Eurik blinked until his sight stopped being blurry. "You talked a lot to *sesin*."

"Yeah. What, you thought I'd spent all that time in a box?"

Eurik shook his head. "Hard to imagine. I would have found you within a year or so if that were true. All I would have to do is follow the stream of complaints."

"You mean pointed reminders. Not my fault your fleshy minds leak memories like sieves."

"The san don't have flesh," Eurik said even as he closed his eyes again. Misthell's words—or Zasashi's—had sparked an idea. He moved his arms, connecting with the wind once more. However, rather than reaching, Eurik pulled.

He drew the wind to him, from the street and past him through the alley to blow out the other side of the warren of buildings that had formed this passage. And as the *chiri* flowed around him, he sampled the memories it carried.

There, the song of a messenger swift, here, someone plucked on the strings of his instrument to tune it. Conversations, the clinking of cups, geese honking, water bubbling, wood creaking—all of it passed him.

He didn't know what half the sounds were actually about, much of the voices too distorted to hear the words, but one of them was significant. A deep, rhythmic blowing, like the breathing of a giant monster.

The smithy on the island didn't use a bellows; they had no need for something like that when they could manipulate the fire itself, but Eurik had come across them in his travels. This was the sound, though louder than he thought it should be.

He plunged back into the streets of Urumoy and set out to follow the flow of *chiri* to its source.

Chapter 5

Sins of the Mother

LERAINE DIDN'T HAVE far to go; Irelith's house wasn't that far from Raven Eye's. It was a modest dwelling, nothing like the sprawling complexes some other families in Urumoy had. It curved slightly outward around a bump in the ground, the single tree that dominated its small soul garden peeking out from over the longhouse's roof.

That sight stopped her, her hand squeezing the scabbard of Irelith's sword. Leraine had said her goodbyes already; it wasn't the dead she dreaded to face. *But standing here does me no good, it only increases the shame.*

She let go of a shuddering breath and—with legs that trembled just a little—Leraine marched over to the door set in the left side of the alcove. Pulling at the cord hanging next to it, she heard the bell clang inside. A few more pulls and she let go, waiting for the door to open.

It didn't take long, but it opened with unexpected force. White Gale, Irelith's oldest, didn't look surprised to see her. To be expected. What wasn't was White Gale's snarl. "Get in," she said, looking past Leraine rather than at her, before getting out of the way.

"White Gale, I—"

"I will not repeat myself."

Leraine hesitated for only a moment before hastening inside. The door slammed shut behind her. White Gale stalked past her and Leraine followed her to the main hall where much of Irelith's family stood, waiting.

Flashing Reed, Irelith's other daughter, for once was not smiling. Her sister joined them at the foot of the low podium where the head of the family would sit. The rest of the family observed from the side.

Weathered Flint, Irelith's man, had his arms crossed and his lower lip quivered before he looked away from her. Irelith's son Violet still hadn't joined another family, and he looked so pale and vulnerable today. Flashing Reed's man, their young daughter, White Gale's husband, Dew, who held two babes in his arms—all of them were looking at her in silence.

Leraine swallowed a sudden lump away and with a quick prayer to the Great Serpent she approached and bowed before them, holding up Irelith's sword. "Irelith has returned to the mother of us all. She fell in battle, a true warrior to the end."

Silence filled the hall, only interrupted by a squirming baby. It took an eternity before a hand grasped the sheathed sword in between Leraine's own hands and lifted it up. At last, Leraine could straighten out.

As she did so, she retrieved the blooddrinker's fang. It was wrapped in a piece of fabric and had been so for months now. The cloth had become stiff from grime and had to be peeled away.

"I offer you proof that her killer has paid the full price for his transgression," Leraine said, offering the fang up. "He died by—"

A hand struck out, slapping Leraine's hands to the side and sending the fang flying. "I don't care," White Gale yelled. "The one who truly killed her stands before me."

Leraine reared back. "I . . . I . . ."

Flashing Reed stepped forward, joining White Gale with a hand on her sword. "She would be here if not for your selfish desire to see the world. You thought yourself clever, but we all knew. You abused tradition for your own pleasure, but it was our mother who paid the price for your transgression."

Leraine shook her head. "That's not what happened."

White Gale put a hand on her sister's shoulder. "Our mother may have treated you like a daughter, but we don't have to treat you like a sister. Leave."

Leave? Without attending the rites? As if I'm some stranger? "No."

Steel hissed before White Gale smacked Flashing Reed's hand back down. Her eyes never left Leraine. "It wasn't a request. From this day forward, this family cuts its ties with you. You and your mother. Now leave. There is no shelter for you here."

Her mouth opened and shut, but no words came. Closing her eyes, she took a deep, shuddering breath. Leraine didn't bow, didn't say goodbye or farewell. She turned around and walked through the hall that had been familiar to her and out the door.

It shut behind her with a very final crash.

As it turned out—and he should have guessed—Urumoy had more than one smithy, and Eurik had to square his shoulders as he faced the fourth one. So far, nobody had heard of a blacksmith named Ardent who'd left the Federation about twenty years ago.

It didn't help that he had no clue how old his mother had been, either when she left or when she died. And it was possible that she'd been born to parents who didn't live here in the Federation in the first place.

Silver Fang had told him about the community of Mochedan living in Pelagrianorum. There could have been one in Linese, or elsewhere. The thing was, he didn't know. And there was only one way to fix that.

He stepped into a dark cavern filled with noises, illuminated only by the red glow of several coal fires. The reason all these smithies had been placed next to the river revealed itself.

They used the river's flow to power bellows and hammers. But all of those wooden axles, gears, and leather belts combined with the normal sounds of a smithy to produce a racket that had driven Eurik out the first time he entered one.

Men and women worked the metal, sweating underneath their aprons. Men only worked on things like horseshoes, pots, pans, barrel hoops, anything that didn't have an edge. Even a kitchen knife was invariably forged by a woman. He'd visited three Urumoy blacksmiths so far, and in this fourth one it was no different.

The person in charge looked promising, a lot of gray in her hair and skin that looked like aged leather. She had to be old enough. Her arms were still powerful, and she easily lifted the heavy hammer as she demonstrated something to a much younger smith.

"There, see the difference in color. It's not absorbing heat equally because the iron's thicker here. Put it back into the coals, then get it to a more uniform thickness." She stepped back and handed the tongs over to her student, who did as she'd been ordered.

The older blacksmith puffed and looked around, catching sight of Eurik. He knew when she noticed the blade on his back, her thin eyebrows rose up. She stepped away from her anvil and walked over to Eurik. "So then, what brings Silver Fang's new buck to my little shop?"

Eurik bowed lightly first. "Greetings. I was hoping you could help—"

"Are you now? Well," she said, gripping his upper arm and giving it a light squeeze. "Got some nice muscles there. You any experience working metal? I know that sword wasn't your work."

"Uh, some. I was sometimes assigned to the island's smithy." He shook his head. He needed to get back to why he was here.

The woman, however, had wrapped her arm around his shoulders and was sort of marching him over to a nearby room that held a desk and a stack of papers. "Ir Serom? Can't say I've heard anything about their work. Now," she said, kicking the door shut behind her and sitting on the corner of her desk. "How far along in your apprenticeship were you before you decided to head out into the world?"

"I . . ." Eurik took a deep breath and willed his heart to slow down. "I am not here for work. I am here about my mother."

The left corner of her mouth rose up. "Now I know you're not mine. Only one who might have a kid growing up on the outside is Patient Eye. And you're a little too old to be hers."

He opened his mouth, then thought better. He needed to be concise and quick. "My mother was Kaite the Ardent. She was a blacksmith who left more than twenty years ago. I am looking for someone who knew her."

"A blacksmith named Ardent?" The old blacksmith leaned back, her eyes focused on the wall above Eurik. "Not here. With that name, she'd have grown up in the Copper Hills. Nearer to Fox territory than Urumoy . . ."

She stilled, then cursed. It was quick and Leraine hadn't focused on that part of the language, but her tone of voice told Eurik enough. "What? You know something."

The blacksmith let out a breath. "I do. Not many remember it happened . . . I was an apprentice back then, has to be more then twenty years ago now. I think. A juicy story back then but with Ardent disappearing people forgot." She gave Eurik a sharp look. "But some still remember. So you better not mention that name anymore and pray to the spirits that the news Ardent has a son doesn't reach them."

"What, why?"

She intertwined her fingers and rested her hands on her thighs. "Because your mother is a murderer, Rock."

Leraine found herself at a loss. She didn't want to go home right now, but the only other place she'd ever called that had just thrown her out with the understanding that she could never return. Instead, she wandered through Urumoy. Only to find herself stopped every ten steps by someone who hadn't seen her in a year and wanted to know what it was like killing a demon.

Nobody asks about Irelith, about avenging her.

She fled from the busy streets and out toward the docks jutting into the Dark Lake. The faint stench of the tanners and the fishmongers enveloped her but at least it was quiet here. Those who plied the lake for their livelihood were out there now. And those who came to trade docked farther to the west.

Closing her eyes, she enjoyed a little peace and quiet, but only a little. The wind rushing through the reeds was nearly always drowned out by the noise of Urumoy. Lake gulls screamed as they wheeled through the sky and fought among each other for scraps.

This wasn't how she'd pictured her return to Urumoy, not at all. But was her disaffection not childish? How many warriors had killed themselves striving for the recognition Leraine now received? Any sept would welcome her, any leader of warriors in Snake and beyond would offer gold and wine for the prestige of having Silver Fang the demon slayer at their side.

To be shown off like Griffenhart's paintings.

Her snort surprised her; the memory was bittersweet. Irelith had held her peace during the tour, but her dissection afterward of the scenes of battle depicted had nearly split Leraine's sides. And that story would never be shared with Irelith's daughters.

Irelith didn't blame her, she knew that. But that didn't mean White Gale was wrong. She had been selfish and her decisions had had consequences.

A wooden plank creaked and Leraine spun around, her hand going for a sword that wasn't there. *No, I'm not in enemy territory anymore.* She needed to stop feeling that, though it was harder to do when she saw her sister Ferisha approaching.

"Sister," Ferisha greeted her. "You've been hard to find." Leraine's sister's outfit was a little odd. She'd seen it several times today. The padded vest looked functional enough, but the worked copper plates affixed to it didn't really offer any additional protection. Just drew attention to the breasts and belly of the wearer.

But it sent another message as well, to wear any armor out on the streets of Urumoy when you were a member of the community. Especially to do so in this heat. So she'd seen members of the Truce Warriors, then.

A quick look around and she spotted a crow. An ill omen, as if she needed the warning. "Sister. I'm not hiding."

"Or doing a poor job of it," Ferisha said with a smile as she walked over to stand by Leraine's side and look out over the lake. "But this is a good place to gain some perspective."

Leraine kept an eye on her sister from the corner of her vision. "It is."

"The future presents itself with many options, many choices. Do you have an idea yet what you'll do?"

"My perspective, alas, is not yet wide enough. But perhaps you can help me there. How do you see the future? With the emperor of the horse people summoning demons and the emperor of the soulless increasingly angry with the People, it seems we are surrounded by danger."

Her sister smiled. "You've spoken to Mother. But that's the dreamweed talking. It has clouded her vision. The horse people are summoning demons, and it is up to us to put a stop to that. Forget the Linesans, they'll never do more than shake their spears and rattle their shields. It is the horse people that are a threat to us all."

"We are allied with the horse people of the Oathfellowship. You want us to break our given word?"

"Not at all. Not unless they prove as great a danger as the others. I never did hear what they did with the heart of the demon you slew."

Leraine looked away and rolled her shoulders. "When we left, the mages of Glinfell were arguing they should keep both. But the people of Stohlhavve demanded they share their bounty." She'd been sure she'd seen three, but between her injuries and the limited visibility it wasn't that hard to believe she'd made a mistake. It would have been better if there were none.

"It had two? Let's hope then that they don't have any accidents. But Mother will have an eye on them, I'm sure. She should," Ferisha said before breathing in deep through her nose. "But we're getting off topic. We were talking about you. The deeds of Silver Fang are on everybody's lips."

"Not all my deeds." Leraine couldn't hide a grimace after the words slipped out. "What of you?" This time, she managed to keep an impassive expression, though she cursed herself for a fool.

Why do I always end up a mumbling idiot around Ferisha?

Her sister, however, merely smiled wanly. "Me? Nothing as eye-catching as you. I've been working quietly to prop Mother up. All too many taste opportunity after her accident." She nodded. "In times like these, we need strength; strength like yours."

"The stories have been exaggerated. I didn't kill that demon all by myself."

"Do tell. As I understand it, everybody's just repeating Mother's words and well, you know her relation with the truth."

Leraine took a deep breath, then blew it all out. "When we saw the rift open, Rock ran toward the battle as swift as the wind. I had to get a horse. But without his ability to command the earth, without him lending me his living sword, I would have died."

"But you did deliver the killing blow?"

Leraine shrugged. "It was a team effort. Even killing Rik I didn't do on my own, I needed Misthell to save my hide or I would have been the blooddrinker's supper."

"Misthell?"

"That's the name of the living sword," Leraine said, turning back to her sister. She . . . looked a lot more like Mother than she herself or Anseri did, especially right now. Perhaps she should not have mentioned Rock, though she couldn't hide him either. "I hope you're not going to bother Rock. He's my guest."

"When have I ever bothered anybody? I would think the boy would appreciate being welcomed back home. He's clearly of our people, even if he didn't grow up among the People. Ah, one of his parents was Snake, right?"

Leraine hesitated, but knowing Rock, he was probably already asking around himself. No point in hiding it then. "His mother. Someone called Ardent. His father was a Puma. But they both died a long time ago." She looked a little closer at her sister. "I don't think he's interested in actually joining either tribe. I think his home is still back with the san."

"A warrior like that would be wasted in our tribe anyway. Unless our laws change, which may happen. Those aren't set in stone, after all, and the world is changing. Keep that in mind as you decide your own path."

Her sister nodded to her and walked back up the docks to two warriors who were dressed very much like Ferisha. They fell in behind her without a word being exchanged. The crow cawed as it flew away.

Chapter 6

Embrace

LERAINE HEADED FOR her sept's training field, located behind the longhouse between the soul garden's boundary hedge and the stables. Peace and quiet hadn't worked; perhaps swinging a weapon around and hitting something—or someone—would.

It shouldn't stir too many memories. Irelith had mostly trained her in her own yard or outside the walls of Urumoy. But she got a surprise as she neared the sand covered circle. There were about eight warriors there and only two hadn't stopped what they were doing to watch Rock.

He faced a pillar of stone that had to have been erected by him and attacked it with a speed only a few Snake warriors could hope to rival. The strikes were light; she could barely hear the impacts.

Misthell had been propped up against one of the posts that held up the rope that separated the practice area from the rest of the yard. "You sure you don't want me giving it a face? I can even have it appear to move, make it all more real."

"This is fine," Rock said, not relenting one bit in his assault. "It'd confuse me."

Leraine looked around again. Surely this was impressive but . . . she noticed the unease in more than one of the women. Rock might not be wielding a sword right now, but he was clearly demonstrating his skill as a warrior. And he looked a little too much like their men, their sons, brothers, and fathers.

Rock switched from punching to kicking. His acrobatics while he did that should have made the exercise impractical but given how fast he was doing it, Leraine wasn't sure she would be capable of capitalizing on that.

He finished by leaping up and pummeling the pillar with a staccato of kicks before landing on his feet again. He staggered back, breathing hard.

Leraine pulled up the rope as she ducked under it and entered the ring. "Tired already?"

Rock shook his head and kept quiet. She glanced at her fellow warriors, then nodded toward the pillar. "Get rid of that and I'll give you something more challenging to fight than an immobile object."

"I'm not—I don't think a lesson in the sword will work right now. It would be a waste of your time."

Leraine lifted up a single eyebrow. "I wasn't talking about lessons or swords." She took a ready stance. "A true warrior doesn't use weapons, she is the weapon. The sword, the bow, the spear, they are merely an extension of her ability. I might not be able to summon the wind or cause earthquakes with a stomp, but I don't need a blade to take you on."

A hint of a smile grew on Rock's face. "Unless I summon the wind or cause an earthquake."

"You'd be a poor guest if you destroyed my home just to win a spar." Her extended hand struck out, easily deflected by him. But he almost missed the real attack that came right after, having to step back and out of reach of her knee.

She was going to say something about holding back next, but Rock had other ideas. His movements sped up, forcing her on the defensive. At least, she judged that to be his plan but she felt no obligation to go along.

As she called upon Ghisa, Leraine's limbs quickened as well. First to deflect Rock's strikes, then to catch his arm as she spun around and put her hips into a throw. Keeping a hold of the limb, she wrenched it around and trapped it with her legs. They were both on the ground now, but Leraine had all the leverage as she pushed off against Rock's face.

"I've noticed you never go for a grapple," she said.

Rock grunted as she put the squeeze on. He resorted to Linese. "San . . . don't have bones. This . . . wouldn't work . . . on one of them."

Suddenly, the give was gone. It was like she was wrestling a tree, or a stone. He pulled his arm in and got up with Leraine still hanging off him. "Was actually a problem when they started teaching me."

"Do tell," Leraine said as she let go with her hands to reach for the ground. With her legs still clutching Rock, she now hung upside down. Rock hadn't straightened out yet so she could actually get her hands flat on the sandy ground to try and knock him over again.

But it was no use. With that stone magic flowing through his body, it truly was like wrestling a tree. So Leraine let go entirely and got out of Rock's range with a flip. He stomped forward, his stance solid and rigid.

"You normally start the Ways with Course of the River, but I simply couldn't make the connection. Or bend my limbs enough," he said as he flicked his hand out. A puff of sand flew into Leraine's face, blinding her.

Her hands moved automatically through Six Fangs Strike, reacting to sounds she could barely hear even in the silence of the ring. *It shouldn't be this quiet.* The technique didn't quite work, her fingers just about buckled even when they struck pressure points on Rock's arms, chest, and neck. But he still backed off, his foot scraping over the ground.

Moving to the side, she wiped the grit out of her eyes. "Sneaky. I approve."

"I wouldn't want to insult my host by not giving it my all."

"Then I shall do the same," Leraine said, pulling a training spear from the nearby rack and lunging at Rock.

She was still blinking some sand out of her eyes—his face was a blurry mess—but the jerky movement with which he backed off told her enough. Leraine pressed forward with quick thrusts, only for her fifth strike to hit a plate of stone that shot up from the ground.

The ground around her right foot stirring was her only warning. It gave way and with most of her weight on that leg, it was hard to get out. She resorted to striking the ground with the butt of her spear and using that to lever herself out of the trap.

Leraine didn't stay still but circled around. "I thought you were not going to stir the earth."

"I thought you said you were the weapon."

"I got five coppers on Silver Fang," Misthell shouted from his spot against a post. "Three to one odds. Who'll take me up?"

"Misthell, aren't you supposed to be rooting for me. And what's with those odds?"

"Sorry Eu—I mean, Rock. Silver Fang has the victory spirit and I have to go with the victor or I'll lose the bet."

"How do you—"

"Because I do not get distracted," Leraine exclaimed as she jumped forward and extended her spear fully. The wood cracked but Rock did take a step back as the air left him with an audible oof. She pulled the spear back even as she ran forward, whirling it around for a swipe at his legs.

The shaft shook and bucked as it impacted a small rock instead. Leraine whipped it around but Rock went on the attack. A clump of sand hit the spear's head, stopping it in an awkward position. Another clump hit her in the chest while more of it slid up her left leg, immobilizing her.

She brought up the shaft to block his punch, but it powered right through. Leraine bent backward, farther than she could have if her foot hadn't been trapped. The two broken halves of the spear she slammed into the sides of Rock's knees, then the crook of his elbow, his flanks, she kept on pummeling him.

With his arms up and his skin as tough as old bark, it didn't do much except keep him occupied. The sun was high in the sky and beating down on her. Even not wearing armor, she still felt sweat rolling off her back like a waterfall. Her lungs demanded air, her limbs ached. She knew she couldn't keep this up; she had to go for victory now or surrender.

Leraine chanced it, switching targets to the sand trap and cracking it loose with a strike on either side. She threw herself to her right, over a rising slab. But Rock wasn't done; a wave of sand picked her up and threw her away.

She rolled along the ground and bounced up, her back hitting a post and knocking the air out of her lungs. It cost her only a moment, but a moment was enough. Three spikes of sand and stone sprang up around her, trapping her.

Leraine sagged, the remains of the training weapons clattering to the ground. "So, feeling better?"

Misthell cried out in anguish. "Oh, come on. Can't I win just once!"

Rock was breathing hard as well. He gave a choppy nod. "And you?"

He pushed down with spread hands and the spikes sank away, as did everything else he'd done. She brushed off some sand as she got up. Misthell had shifted from complaining to arguing with Swift Hop, who had taken the living sword up on his bet.

As she looked around, Leraine saw that the audience had only grown. *Perhaps this hadn't been such a bright idea. This will only bring more attention to Eurik.* She nodded to the longhouse and switched back to Thelauk. "Come, let's get out of the sun and clean up. We're no longer traveling, might as well take advantage of the luxury."

He hadn't taken her hint and kept speaking in Linesan. "That sounds like a great idea." He stretched, then grimaced as he put a hand on his stomach. "You could have pulled those strikes a little more. I can make myself tough, but I'm not literally turning my flesh into stone."

"Better to suffer pain in training than death in battle. And I believe Misthell needs rescuing."

Rock glanced at Misthell and he smiled. "I'm sure he can talk his way out of it." He raised his voice. "I'll be back in an hour," he told the sword.

"Wait, Rock, wait a moment. Hey, don't leave me. I need you to pay her. Rock!"

Refreshed, Eurik joined Silver Fang in the upper hall. The bench she was on had enough space to seat half a dozen people, and only one other was using it right now. He was spinning yarn and keeping an eye on a couple of very young children playing with little wooden figurines of people.

Eurik couldn't suppress a wince as he sat down. "You really did not have to hit me that hard."

"Likewise," Silver Fang said, also in Thelauk. Even after a couple of months of instruction, just being surrounded by the language for a couple of days had done wonders for his grasp of it.

"I am sorry." But Eurik still felt like he was a child whenever he tried to hold a conversation in the language.

Silver Fang shook her head. "No, it is fine. You clearly had something on your mind."

He tensed as she reminded him of the thing he'd been trying not to think about all day. He finally had an answer, but he didn't like it. "And you?"

"What about me?"

Something in her words, how she held herself . . . "Something is wrong."

Silver Fang glanced at the man on the other end of the bench and switched to Linesan even as she lowered her voice. "Why would you say something is wrong?"

He went for a shrug, only to falter as his muscles protested. Much of it wasn't Silver Fang's fault. He'd been training for quite a while before she'd come along. "You threw yourself into that spar, same as me. You're usually very aggressive, very much like fire, but there was less thinking behind it. You just acted."

She let out a long breath. "Yes. I . . . am finding that my return is not as I imagined. White Gale, Irelith's daughter, renounced all ties with me. Me and Mother."

"I'm sorry?"

"I knew them, Rock. I trained with them, White Gale taught me how to ride a horse, how to fight on one." Her left hand went up and traced a cord in her *draen,* slowly drawing it out of the braid. She dangled the white and gray string in front of her. "And all that is mist now. Fading away under the morning's sun."

"They are angry at you about their mother's death?"

Silver Fang nodded. "They pointed out that I had abused tradition to excuse my travels throughout the land. That Irelith would not have been killed by a blooddrinker if she'd stayed here. They have a point."

Eurik hesitated, but only for a moment. "Someone once told me I can't be responsible for what others decide to do. That they aren't children and can take care of themselves."

She let out a bark of mirthless laughter. "So I did." She nodded. "And Irelith wanted to go, I know that. And yet, and yet. There are a hundred decisions of mine that would have led to a different outcome." Silver Fang dropped the cord. "What stings most is that I avenged her. I killed that blooddrinker and all everybody wants to talk about is how I slayed that scaleless demon. That, and—"

"And what?"

Silver Fang shook her head and leaned back, hands on her thighs. "No, I will not burden you with that. Some things must stay beneath the roof. But what of you?"

Eurik frowned. "What about me?"

"You never answered my question. What burdens you so? Ah, have you found no information on your parents? I can come along tomorrow. Perhaps some people will be more forthcoming with me."

Eurik tossed his head in what wasn't a shake or a nod, but something in between as he was caught between lying and telling the truth. But why hide it from Silver Fang? That there were things she couldn't share, well, that didn't matter. In the end, she truly was Mochedan . . . and Eurik wasn't.

"I did find some answers, actually. A blacksmith called Rolling Anvil had heard of my mother." It helped that they were still talking Linesan; few here would understand what he was saying.

Silver Fang's smile died before it had a chance to grow. "It wasn't good news."

"No. She killed, she murdered another woman. A drunken argument over something, who was the better blacksmith, or a man, Rolling Anvil didn't know. Then she ran away and ended up with the Immortal. That's what she'd heard, anyway."

Silver Fang shifted on the bench and put her head close to his. "You are sure? Perhaps this was not your mother. Who was the victim?"

"Ah, the dates Rolling Anvil gave lined up with what I guessed before. And there's not a lot of blacksmiths called Ardent. She only knew of the one."

"And the woman who was murdered? This is important, Rock. What sept was she?"

"The ruling sept of, uh, Caetiwo. A cousin of the leader back then. Rolling Anvil seemed to think they would still be looking for my mother. Should I let them know they can stop?"

Rolling Anvil told me to keep quiet, but why? I wasn't even born when the crime happened.

"No. Not now. Caetiwo is not as powerful as Urumoy, but when their leader speaks others in the tribe pay attention to her words. Her name is Fervent and you have a blood debt to her family."

"Me? But I wasn't even born when my mother—" It still felt a little odd to refer to anybody like that out loud, but that wasn't what stopped him. It was Silver Fang's expression, as if he'd been barking like a dog rather than speaking as a person would.

She shook her head. "That's not how . . . Right, grew up among plant-men. How to explain this. Yes, your mother has, or had, the direct blame for the offense. And I'm assuming the story you heard was true, so best not say what you were about to if the sept confronts you."

"I—"

Silver Fang held up a hand. "Let me finish. When a murder occurs, not a duel or a battle. When a murder happens, guilt flows from the murderer to her family and her sept. If they protect her, or she flees justice, then the sept has a debt to the victim's sept."

"I don't know what family she had, or has. Except for me. Uh, they're not going to want to kill me, right?"

"No, I'm sure it won't come to that." She pressed her lips together, her head twitched. "Don't worry about that. But as her surviving child you still have a debt. Less on account of being an outsider and a man, but not free of it. The matter will be put before the loremistresses and they'll decide how much . . . *galautik* you must pay. It is not money, it is . . . a fine. But there are many ways to pay. Ah, how much of that prize money do you still have?"

"I . . . don't think enough to pay for a person's life."

"We will figure something out. Until then, however, best you keep your distance and don't mention you are her son. The old ways are dying out, but they die hard."

Chapter 7

Face

"I CAN'T BELIEVE YOU left me with her." Misthell's complaining no longer elicited so much as a look from the others with whom he shared the table. "Do you know what they do with people who can't make good on bets here?"

"I don't," Eurik said. Their lunch was interesting. It was bread with preserved fruit jelly smeared on it. The bread was a little different as well. Until he'd left he island he hadn't considered that a word like bread could cover such a diversity. Then again, there were a lot of kinds of trees as well.

"You work off your debt," Misthell said. "She explained it all. And all the oil and polish I need to maintain my luster would just pile on top of it. I could have ended up being sold, traded and used in battle after battle. You'd never see me again."

Eurik furrowed his brow and looked at Silver Fang. "Is that true?"

She was already shaking her head with a light smirk. "No. Not over as light a debt as that, not when Misthell is a guest under this roof. And you can't sell people either, we're not the soulless. The debt can be bartered away, but there are limits to what you can demand of a debtor."

"I see." What mirth he'd had over Misthell's situation fled as he considered his own debt, as the Mochedan saw such things. What did it say that his mother had murdered someone? Had she actually done it?

Silver Fang looked up and past him at something. "Gliding Blade, good to see you. Is there something you need?"

"Not me. Raven Eye," a woman said. Eurik turned on the bench and saw she was older, a deep scar running from the corner of her mouth up her left cheek. The top of her left ear was missing as well.

Silver Fang got up. "Then I'd better see her."

"Not just you. This one as well," Gliding Blade said, looking directly at Eurik. Her blade and armor looked very much like what Silver Fang had been wearing at their first meeting. "Come." She didn't move until Eurik had gotten up, then she quickly left the hall and went down to the first floor.

Eurik looked at Silver Fang at his side. "Do you know what this is about?"

"No. Consider my mother's words carefully." She opened her mouth again, then closed it with a shake of her head. "Very carefully," she muttered. He wasn't sure he had been meant to hear those last two words.

They were led to a door with a raven painted on it in blue and white, with something black in its beak. He followed Silver Fang into the room, Gliding Blade remaining behind. A strange smell was the first thing he found inside.

Raven Eye herself sat in a large chair, on a heap of cushions with her cane loosely dangling in her right hand. She wore a different eye patch than when last he had seen her, red with the head of a raven embroidered on it. "Rock, Misthell, I hope you've found my home hospitable."

"Ah, yes. Thank you."

"Oh, think nothing of it," she said as the door closed behind him. "I've had worse guests, recently even."

Leraine twitched and knew that Raven Eye would have caught it. "What do you want, Mother?"

Mother gave her a look, both her real eye and the one on the patch staring into her. Leraine planted her feet apart and put a hand on her hip. "You requested our presence, and made sure to do so when we were in the upper hall for all to see. I'm not a fool."

"Are you sure?" Raven Eye let those words hang, but only briefly. "I wanted to talk to you. You and our guests. You might have missed it in all the excitement, but the Festival of Conclave is only three weeks away."

She had, actually. Not that Leraine was in any mood for a festival. So she shrugged. "So this is goodbye, then."

"Oh, I'm not going to Chappenuioc this year. Not with this hip." She spun the cane and pointed its tip at Leraine. "You'll be swearing Urumoy to the Great Truce this year."

"Me?"

But Mother nodded as if it made perfect sense, and Leraine was starting to see where she was coming from. A direction Raven Eye confirmed with her next words.

"Who else? Your deeds are spreading far and wide." No doubt on the wings of Mother's messenger swifts. "Having you swear the Truce will make good use of your newfound renown. Not like you were going to put it to any good use yourself."

Leraine carefully didn't look in Rock's direction. "Very well, I'll go." *And while I'm there, I can participate in one of the competitions as well. Unarmed or sword-stick. I'm not good enough with the bow.*

"Should I congratulate you?" Rock asked.

She gave him a shrug. "It is an honor."

"It's a little more than that," Mother interjected. "The Festival of Conclave is the most important event in the Federation and without the Truce, the Federation itself would not exist. We'd be back to a collection of squabbling septs and tribes. We'd drown in blood within the year."

Rock frowned at Raven Eye's words. "I must admit the books I read weren't clear on a lot of things. I think there was something about a festival at Chappenuioc in one, but they didn't use that name."

Leraine sniffed. "Oh, I'll bet they didn't. But the Festival of Conclave is its proper name. It's a celebration of our origins, of what it means to be People."

"Though those who are not are still welcome to participate," Mother said. "Indeed, horse people, short-people, sun-men, they've all competed in the Games, and some even won them."

Leraine regarded her mother and Rock; there was something about that explanation. *And why did she want him here if all she was going to do was tell me I'd be attending the festival?* "You want him to participate in the Games!"

Her teeth clicked as both Rock and Mother looked at her. Her mother shook her head after a moment. "Only to encourage him to join you. People from all tribes gather for the festival. It is quite possible for some answers to his questions to be found there."

Leraine shook her head vigorously enough that her *draen* swept over her shoulder and landed on her chest. "That is not wise." Then she hesitated, and decided to use a different argument. "He is still learning our language and our customs. It would be too easy for him to give offense among such a large crowd."

Mother scoffed and ticked her cane against the floor. "Please. He could mortally offend a Crocodile swamp-dweller and at best he'd be challenged to a duel outside the bounds of Chappenuioc. One to first blood. Or are you worried about something more complicated?"

She let out a sigh. "Of course you know."

"My ears and mind still work fine, whatever some may think."

Rock took only a moment longer to catch on, then he gave Raven Eye a hard look. "You know about my mother."

Raven Eye nodded. "I do. I even recall the incident. Well, of hearing of it. You are in quite a bit of trouble, boy. Fervent will hear of you soon enough and she'll demand restitution. The leader of Caetiwo can't afford to show leniency here, not that she'd be inclined to."

And would that news have any help reaching Fervent's ear? Leraine wanted to ask that question, but she couldn't. Not with Rock present. And Mother wasn't done.

"The gold you won in Linese might have been enough, but that's gone."

Rock's stance shifted. "How do you know?"

Raven Eye smiled. "Your clothes and boots are wearing thin. My daughter's new armor couldn't have been cheap. And your sword has a habit of losing his bets."

"I'm not that bad," Misthell said. "And most of my bets don't even involve money. Right, tell her Eur—ah, Rock. Tell her we're fine."

But Eurik's shoulders sagged as he let out a long sigh. Leraine balled her right hand into a fist, the one out of view of Mother. *How dare she. I invited Rock here. I promised him hospitality and now Mother thinks she can use him for one of her schemes?* She gave him a worried glance. Leraine knew him to be stubborn, too stubborn for his own good often enough. Surely even a few words from Raven Eye couldn't bring him down?

"I've yet to hear anything that convinces me my mother did indeed commit the crime," Rock said.

Raven Eye's smile only grew wider. "That's the spirit. Excellent. But that only buys you time, boy. Fervent will bring her case before the loretellers and she'll convince them of the right of her case. Your mother did you no favors by running away right after it happened."

Leraine couldn't stay quiet any longer. "No doubt you already have a solution."

"I do. Rock here is a skilled unarmed fighter. He'd have a good chance at winning that particular event at the festival. The prize would be enough not only to provide restitution but also cover his living sword's . . . habit. And the general expenses of living in a human settlement."

"I would be allowed to use the Ways in this competition?"

Leraine was already shaking her head. "It wouldn't matter. The Games are held within Chappenuioc. Horse people magic doesn't work there and you told me you had trouble with your powers on the Road."

"Is that so?" Mother tapped the cane with her fingers. They hopped from left to right like an anxious bird. "Well, it's just a thought. And whatever else, the festival remains your best opportunity to find someone who knew your father. I'll admit the name sparked no recognition from me. But there will be plenty of people from the Puma tribe there."

Rock grew still, his head turned down. "I'll need to think about it," he said, looking back up at Raven Eye. "If it is about money, I can think of other ways to earn it."

Her mother nodded. "Of course. Though you don't have long. Leraine and her party will have to leave soon. And while you are my guest, that protection only extends so far. But go, meditate, ponder. Talk to Misthell. Whatever you need to come to a decision."

"I need to talk to Mother about something else," Leraine said to him. "But I'll join you shortly. The training circle?"

He nodded. "Sure. See you there."

"I'm really not that bad," Misthell couldn't help but say one more time as Eurik headed for the door.

Leraine waited until it shut again before she spoke. "Why do you want him to compete in the Conclave Games?"

"Leraine, he's my guest. I just thought he could use a bit of advice. This is a complicated situation he finds himself in. Especially given that he didn't grow up among our people."

She crossed her arms. "Mother, he's not here now. You wouldn't be bothering with this if there wasn't some scheme. But Rock is my guest."

"Your guest?" Raven Eye lifted an eyebrow and glanced at the ceiling. "And here I thought this was still my house. Well, it's very nice of you to let me pretend, daughter."

Leraine looked away. "I apologize. But my point still stands. You mean to use him."

Raven Eye let the silence linger and settled a little deeper into the cushions. "The favorite to win this year's unarmed competition at the festival is a young man of the Wolf tribe named Dancing Spark." Mother levered herself up and forward. "He is also favored to take up the mantle in Thevoy as soon as Gray Mist steps aside. And it will be soon."

The cane thumped the floor as her mother got up and went over to a small chest. "He is easy on the eyes, charismatic, and not afraid to tell everybody that both Thevoy and the Wolf tribe must leave the Great Truce. And the winner's podium at Chappenuioc would amplify his message a thousandfold," she said as she stuffed some dried dreamweed into her pipe and went to light it.

Leraine pressed her lips together. "I'm not so sure Rock could win. As I said, his magic doesn't work properly on the Road. Chappenuioc will be no different."

Mother sucked deeply on her pipe and as she let out a stream of smoke Leraine could see some of the lines of her mother's face soften.

"Perhaps. It doesn't matter if Rock wins, really. I'm not even counting on his participation. It's a matter of throwing enough knives at your target, some will stick. Rock is but one more knife."

She stopped regarding her pipe and her eye bored into Leraine. "Now, does that strike you as a worthy endeavor? Stopping the destruction of our people?"

Leraine wanted to argue. But she'd noticed more Truce Warriors walking the streets of Urumoy since her return. And she'd heard rumors of brawls between them and some Traditionalists. That word hadn't been used a year ago. Lines were being drawn right through Urumoy and if that was happening in the other tribes . . .

She nodded and took a step away from the acrid, sweet smoke slowly filling the room. "Yes. Do you need me to compete then as well?"

Raven Eye sat down again. "You're better with the sword. You should play to your strengths, dear. And it's not like Dancing Spark is the only crow among our people." She made a shooing motion. "Go, practice, talk to your friend."

Leraine inclined her head. "Mother." She quickly left the room and took a deep breath of clean air once the door closed behind her. Then she headed for the yard.

Eurik could practically feel the hidden looks even as he did his best to concentrate on his other senses. He knew he'd draw attention, but he couldn't let that deter him from training. The wind was constrained here in Urumoy.

But it still blew. Standing on one foot on a post, he could feel it pluck at his clothes and ruffle his hair. It was getting a bit long. The wind carried with it the smells of the lake, and the smells of the tannery it had passed along the way. It held the cries of the lake gulls, the barking of dogs, the cheering of playing children, and the yells of hawkers.

Eurik tried to probe deeper. The wind had blown over the lake, but it hadn't started there. It had come from elsewhere. The impression was faint. Or his own senses not attuned enough. His arms moved as he drew more of the wind toward himself and tried to focus.

"I'm really not that bad. I win! Sometimes," Misthell said.

He wobbled on his post, the wind whirling out of his grasp. "Misthell . . ."

"I just . . . we're good, right? You don't— I mean, you're not a swordsman and I'm worth, like, a lot of money . . . You're not thinking of getting rid of me, right?"

Sighing, Eurik opened his eyes and looked down at where Misthell was propped up against another post. "No, I'm not."

"That's good, great! Yeah, I knew she was just trying to scare me. I mean, you."

"Misthell," he said as the sword kept rambling on. "I'm not going to sell you, but I'm not comfortable with how you're acting either. That you like to gamble." Eurik shrugged. "But you've been reckless lately and that's not at all like you."

"I don't know what you're talking about."

"When was the last time you complained about the dangers of combat, how easily you rust?"

"I did that yesterday, remember? You left me with that sneaky woman who wanted to make me work off my— You know."

"Your gambling debt. Yes, but you were worried you'd never see me again. About getting handed off from one person to another. You can tell me what's wrong."

"I think . . . that your memory is playing tricks on you. Must be from getting kicked around the ring so much by Silver Fang. Hey, Silver Fang! We were just talking about you."

Eurik sighed. "We're not done," he told the living sword in a low voice before spinning around by hopping from one foot to the other. "It was mostly Misthell talking. Everything all right?" he asked as he got a good look at her.

Silver Fang looked over the training women, mostly consisting of more mature children being instructed by older people. "I wonder about that. But mostly I question what the right thing is." She'd elected to speak in Linese and continued with that language as she met his gaze. "I did not tell my mother about Ardent."

He considered her words and the possibility that she was lying. Then, with a shake of his head, he hopped off the post. "I recall you once mentioned your mother has a lot of spies."

Leraine laughed. "Oh no, not spies. Mother has friends, people that share some news with her. An upstanding Mochedan leader does not have spies. Not among her own people, that is."

Putting a shoulder against a post she leaned against it and regarded him. "If you're thinking of following Mother's suggestion, I must warn you . . . it will not be as . . . safe."

"How so?"

"Fervent may be there on behalf of Caetiwo, or one of her sept, which is about as bad. You could keep quiet about your parents, but that will not be received well and run counter to your own aims. They can't simply kill you, not while you compete in the Games, not in Chappenuioc, but there will be hundreds of shamans and loretellers to pass judgment. I'm not one myself, I don't know what kind of penalties will be allowed. But a duel to the death isn't unheard of. It depends on how severe your mother's crime was."

"If she did it."

Silver Fang nodded. "Your skepticism may not matter," she said as she put a hand on his shoulder. "And many will find her cowardice wrong on its own."

It took Eurik a moment to catch on that Silver Fang was waiting for something. *Right, cowardice. That's an insult.* There wasn't any emphasis on such a thing among the san. Every san knew how to fight but they weren't warriors. What mattered was to act correctly, to do what was right. The hard thing to the san was to discern what that was.

To Eurik, fleeing justice was wrong but he didn't know if that was what his mother had done. Did she have an opportunity to prove her innocence—if she was—or had she left before the death happened? Everyone appeared to consider her guilty and worried about what to do about that, but to him that was the one thing he needed to know.

"I'll go. Your mother was right in one thing above all: this Festival of Conclave sounds like the best opportunity to find someone who has at least heard of my father. And perhaps I will learn more of my mother along the way. If that brings me trouble, it can't be any worse than having to face that demon," he said with a smile.

She considered his words, then nodded and returned his smile. "There is that. Very well. Then we best take this time to sharpen your skills. And there are a hundred things you must know or you will give offense."

Chapter 8
To the Festival

IN THE PRIVACY OF HER own thoughts, Leraine had to admit she'd thought it would simply be the two of them on the road again, as well as Misthell and perhaps a few others. And the road would be packed with other travelers making their way to Chappenuioc. So maybe it wouldn't be simply the two of them.

However, she hadn't considered the possibility that nearly half of Urumoy would be joining them. And with both her sisters part of it, even a couple of hundred people weren't enough to shield her from them.

The weather held up after they departed, though long ribbons of fluffy white clouds offered occasional relief from the heat. All of them rode horses, or a mule in a couple of cases—all except the man running beside her with long, loping strides.

It had already earned him plenty of teasing as more than one had offered to let him ride with her. At least a couple were clear that they weren't only talking about their mount. The jeering had abated, but the interest had not as Rock had easily kept up with their pace the entire day.

The sinking sun colored the sky an ocher red as they stopped for the night at the hold of Joyous Bell. She met them at the gate, which was barely open, so Joyous Bell could slip out. Her eyes surveyed their group. "There's a lot of you."

"One hundred eighty-seven," Anseri said. Leraine might have been chosen to represent Urumoy at the ceremony; however, leading this party had been left to her eldest sister. Not that Ferisha had accepted it.

"Though we don't expect you to let them all stay under your roof," Ferisha said, pulling up next to Anseri. "We simply seek the safety your walls offer."

Ferisha ignored the glare Anseri shot her. Her eldest sister turned her attention back to Joyous Bell. "This is my sister, Golden Tongue, and that is my younger sister, Silver Fang. I am Resting Python."

Joyous Bell sucked on her teeth, then spat to the side. "Raven Eye's get. Well, what do you got?"

Leather creaked, hooves stomped, and mail rustled at the insult. None truly put a hand on their weapon, thankfully. Leraine caught some movement on the low wall. It seemed Joyous Bell wasn't acting on impulse. But how to warn her sisters?

Anseri plucked a sack from her saddle and tossed it at Joyous Bell's feet, its contents clanking as the sack landed in the dirt. "Urumoy's gift to a gracious host."

Joyous Bell manipulated the sack with her foot, the bars of steel inside clinking against each other. "That'll come in handy. There's more and more thieves spilling out from the west this season," she said as she looked over their party once more. "Right, you lot can stay in my hold but I ain't as rich as someone's mother. So everybody except Raven Eye's daughters will just have to share with my pigs."

Leraine hesitated, but she felt more than one set of eyes on her. So she urged her horse forward to pass the gate after her sisters.

Entering the hold, it was easy to see the warriors who had been hiding on the top of the wall. They were still holding their bows and looked on silently as more and more of their group filtered in.

"We've heard of you," Joyous Bell said to Silver Fang. "So Raven Eye sends her most accomplished daughter to the festival as well."

Leraine inclined her head. "I only did what any warrior of Snake would do: aid an ally. I thank you for your hospitality." *Meager as it is.* The protestations of poverty rang hollow once she caught sight of the rich decoration on the warriors' helmets and the tapestries hanging inside the longhouse.

Joyous Bell's settlement was twice the size of Silent Ice's, and all the warriors Leraine could see were well-equipped. *Poor indeed.* But she was Urumoy's neighbor.

"Couldn't turn away travelers heading for Chappenuioc, now could I? But I should tell my people to wait until daybreak before herding the pigs. We don't want any of your people ending up on the butcher's hook." Joyous Bell let loose a bark of laughter that her household quickly joined in with.

Leraine did her best to keep her composure, and to not sigh at the gratuitous insult. *This is going to be a long night.* Joyous Bell thought herself a rival of Mother, but she was about as subtle as the pigs she kept bringing up.

I should have just rolled out my blanket under Rock's shelter. The company wouldn't be any less crude, even if they preferred to roll in the mud instead of slinging it.

Bringing up the slabs of compressed earth that would serve as his shelter for the night was easy. He did so on the edge of the group he was traveling with. Most of them were women and the men that had come along all seemed to be attached to one group or another.

Erecting the shelter brought him more attention, but he'd gotten used to that. Kind of. After slipping Misthell's baldric off his shoulder, he held the sword in front of him. "All right, looks like we'll be staying out here tonight. Do you—"

"Drop the sword," a woman said behind him as he heard wood ticking against wood.

Turning around, he was confronted by two armed and armored women from this settlement. One had her hands on her hips, a younger one with a short *draen* had been the source of the ticking sound. It was the arrow being nocked to her curving bow.

"Could you repeat? My Thelauk is . . . not great." And her accent had been a little different than what he'd gotten used to. Her l's dragged a bit.

She bared her teeth in a lopsided sneer. "Drop the sword, boy," she said, pausing after every word. "Now."

"I do not think he would like that."

"I would not. This place is filthy," Misthell said.

The bow went up, arrow now pointed at him though the string wasn't drawn. *Right, men aren't allowed to touch weapons around here.* After he'd gotten no comment about carrying Misthell around in Urumoy, he'd forgotten that this was a thing. But if he just dropped the living sword he'd be hearing about it all the way to Chappenuioc.

"This isn't Urumoy. We do things the right way here. Quiet," the older soldier snapped at the men who had set up their tent next to his. One of them had stepped forward to say something but now froze at the woman's glare. Her attention returned to Eurik. "Drop the sword and you might get it back when you leave. Drop it, or she shoots you."

Wait, she's going to steal Misthell? "No."

The speaker's eyes grew two sizes, the arrow wavered. "What?"

"Shoot me and get this over with." Eurik shrugged. But also frantically pulled as much earth *chiri* up from beneath his feet and into his body.

The bow looked different than the ones he'd seen before, a more elaborate curved shape with both ends bending sharply up so that the string rested against it. No way to know how powerful it was exactly, but the arrowhead looked sharp.

"There's no need," Misthell said. "I'm not actually a sword, you see. I'm a, uh, a horn. Yes. A . . . Linesan flathorn."

"I'm not going to argue with a man, let alone a talking sword."

"No, I'm a flathorn. Here, listen." Music began to emanate from the sword. It started as a high pitched tune he'd heard first at an inn in Pons Vorce, then it descended into a bassy hoot.

"Misthell—"

"I got this," the sword said in a low voice while the music kept going. "Is she buying it?"

"You tell me," Eurik said, lifting up the sword so Misthell's eye could see. The bowwoman reacted to the motion by drawing her bow. But the arrow slipped out of her grasp halfway through the draw and slammed into Eurik's chest.

Misthell's tune broke off as the archer stammered something that got drowned out by the older soldier's cursing as she wheeled on the archer. Eurik himself hissed and winced as he pulled the arrow out. *Not too deep. Still hurts.*

It barely bled as the arrow had hit a rib. He opted not to harden the blood, better to have it close off naturally. Instead he dropped the arrow as the archer's jaw dropped.

"What? Are you ignoring me?" The older soldier turned her attention back to Eurik, her eyes growing wide as she looked down at the arrow and then back up at what little blood stained his tunic. The fading light hid more and more, but not the fact that Eurik wasn't wearing armor. And had still barely been hurt by an arrow loosed from about six steps away.

"Looks like you both got lucky," another woman said, leading a group of armed soldiers toward them. Eurik recognized them as members of their traveling party, and they were led by one of Silver Fang's sisters. "If you'd managed to really hurt or kill a guest, Joyous Bell would have had to offer us your heads."

The archer gesticulated with her bow. "It was an accident!"

The older soldier grabbed her by the shoulder and cut off any more protests. Only after a hard stare and a twitch of her head did she turn her attention to the people who had come to Eurik's defense. "Your man is hardly hurt. And he's holding a weapon. The law is clear, Joyous Bell has a right to enforce it. Even with guests."

"Perhaps your old eyes strain to see much with so little light. Look again, he's not of the People."

The soldier snorted. "That doesn't matter. Horse men, even short-men, they give up their weapons while inside these walls."

"Excuse me, I can easily solve this." Eurik decided not to mention what had been said about keeping Misthell. Not when he received those two glares. Tempers were hot enough as it was. "Sorry, Misthell."

"Eurik, what are y—" A hole opened up beneath the living sword and Eurik dropped Misthell into it. Then closed it with a wave of his hand while pushing the living sword deeper with his other. He also firmed the soil around the blade so that no tunneling creature could easily reach Misthell. Not that the living sword would thank him for that consideration.

"There, I'll pick him up tomorrow. Problem solved."

Golden Tongue rocked back on her heels and regarded him with a raised eyebrow. "And your injury?"

Shrugging sent a prick of pain lancing through his chest, but he did his best to smile anyway. "Only a flesh wound. I am sure it was an accident. Anyway, it's getting late and I am getting hungry." He turned back to the older woman. "Do you need anything else?"

"Don't pull any other stunts, spellslinger. We're keeping an eye on you. Come on, you," the older warrior said as she shoved the young archer and stomped away. "You obviously are slacking off." The rest of her words were too faint to hear. Those on the wall and near the longhouse relaxed as well.

The group from Urumoy took a little longer to disperse, and when it did Golden Tongue came over to Eurik. "The shot was abysmal, but the arrow should still have skewered you," she said, pulling at his tunic and placing a finger near the wound.

Eurik set his jaw and could barely keep from cringing as that set off a fresh ripple of pain. "It did not. Could you stop poking the wound?"

"I'm not," she said, stepping back. "I heard you fought alongside my sister against the demon and about a spar you had with her back in Urumoy. Still, your ability is impressive when seen with my own two eyes."

Eurik shifted his weight, his face warming up. "Yes, well, thank you . . . for speaking to them. It helped." That wasn't quite what he wanted to say, but he was tired and Thelauk could be finicky. "I appreciate your help."

Golden Tongue grinned. "Bah, think nothing of it. Got to keep these people in their place. Can't have them bossing around our own. Or people who are with us. It would only give them ideas later on."

"They . . . were talking about keeping my sword."

She nodded. "See, got to keep a close eye or they'll rob you blind." Golden Tongue put an arm around him and squeezed his shoulder. "Come, join my fire. We'll get that scratch looked at and we can share a meal. Before I have to make nice with Cup of Venom. And maybe tell me something more about that magic of yours."

"Ah, I can do that. Uh, thank you?"

Her smile got a little more toothy. "Think nothing of it."

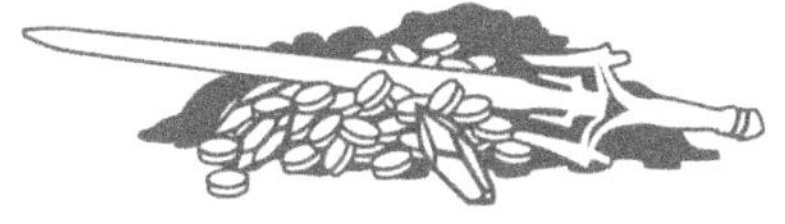

Leraine frowned when she met Eurik the next morning. "Where's Misthell? Please tell me you didn't let him gamble himself away."

He shook his head and looked back at the wall of Joyous Bell's hold. "No. There was an . . . argument. It got resolved, but Misthell will not be happy with me. I am avoiding the confrontation." Rock grimaced. "I can not do that any longer. Perhaps cover your ears."

He made a gesture, like grabbing something from a shelf and pulling it over to him. More of the group passed them by, but for some reason Golden Tongue stopped.

Leraine waited for her to speak, only to find that her sister ignored her completely to address Rock instead. "You didn't forget your sword, did you?"

"No, no. I am getting him now." He brought his hand up and Misthell emerged from the ground, held aloft by a crude arm of shaped dirt which crumbled away the moment Rock had a hold of him. "See."

"I'm sorry I used your real name. I know they don't like it." Words poured from the living sword in an unrelenting flood. "But you locked me up in the ground! I could hear things crawling around, I could feel them! They were hungry, Eu—Rock! And it was damp, too!"

"Misthell! Misthell! Please, calm down."

"What is this about hungry creatures?" Leraine stilled as Golden Tongue approached them. "When I saw you leaving the hold without it, I got worried. But I see you had not forgotten him."

Rock inclined his head. "No, I did not want to risk it in there."

"Wise. I wouldn't put it past them to argue just to waste our time. Though I don't think they would push it as far as they did last night. How is your injury?" Golden Tongue stepped closer to Eurik.

"Did something happen?"

"Yes, some of our host's warriors pestered your man here. I was settling in our people when I heard the commotion. They objected to Rock having the living sword. One of them shot him."

"Shot you?" Leraine said the words too loud, startling the riders nearest her and one had their horse step away from her before they got their mount back under control. "Where?" She looked him up and down and noticed that Rock wore a different tunic than yesterday.

"It is not so bad. Barely a wound."

"Yes, your magic is very impressive," Golden Tongue said. "Perhaps we can talk more of it tonight at our next stop. Until then."

Leraine waited until the other woman was barely far enough away before speaking. "You got into a fight serious enough to injure you and you weren't going to tell me?"

"It was not a fight, but an accident." Rock shrugged. "As I said, I barely have a wound and the problem was resolved. At least I think it was resolved."

She sighed. "Since nobody told me anything until now, I suppose it has been. Though my sister was absent for a lot longer than the time it would take to settle a small argument."

"She offered to bandage the wound after. It was not necessary, but we talked, we eat. Ate."

"Yes." Leraine shook her head. There was the impulse to keep silent, but her family seemed determined to involve Rock in their affairs. "Golden Tongue leads a group that advocates we no longer need the Great Truce. She might be more interested in what your powers could do for her and hers once they are free to attack."

"I have no interest in joining a war. Any war."

She put a hand on his shoulder. "We are over a week away from Chappenuioc. Be careful, yet respectful, and we'll get to the festival in one piece. I hope."

Chapter 9

At the End of the Road

SILVER FANG'S WARNING seemed overblown in the light of the days that followed. Certainly, Golden Tongue sought out his company, but it seemed harmless to Eurik. They talked about his travels, his life on San, and how a warrior of Snake was trained.

Silver Fang wasn't mentioned, not by Golden Tongue. And the conversation would always end up on some other topic whenever he brought up the topic of her sister. Either of them, really. There seemed to be a tension there between the three.

Today, however, the issue between what might be a new friend and his old friend was not at the forefront of his mind. He'd heard last night that they would reach Chappenuioc today and they appeared to be right.

They'd been back on the Road since yesterday. Around them the landscape quickly changed, farms and settlements giving way to manmade hills and erected stones engraved with images of people and animals. Ahead, the Road still threw up a haze that kept a traveler from seeing too far up its length.

The traffic on the Road had grown into a crowd, just about all of them heading in the same direction. They succeeded in making the final stretch of the Road feel oppressive, not helped by the earthen mounds looming over them.

Then the haze lifted away like a curtain and Chappenuioc sprawled out before him. It was a little hard to grasp what he saw at first, to make sense of the riot of colors snapping and fluttering in the wind.

People behind him didn't give him any chance to stop and take it all in, they all pushed to leave the Road and spread out over the circular plain that had appeared. The grass-covered mounds had been built at a distance from Chappenuioc itself. None of those ancient people had seemed to dare to erect their monuments too close to the place.

The modern Mochedan were different. A city of wood and cloth covered the entire place, spilling out from the Inza structure he could just make out underneath the scaffolding.

Eurik was so caught up with his examinations he didn't notice most of the rest of his traveling party had already left the Road. Only when Silver Fang spoke up from his left did he notice it was just the two of them surrounded by strangers. Some of them at least gawked like he had.

"Where did everybody go?"

Silver Fang led her horse through the crowd, one hand resting on its neck. "To the west. All of the tribes have their own piece of land around Chappenuioc, their own quarter. Ours, Snake's, lies past that of Boar. Outsiders have their own quarter; we already passed most of it," she said, indicating a couple of hundred tents to the right of the Road. They stood separate from the rest of the settlement and had clearly been put wherever their owners felt like. Just not too close to what the Mochedan considered their own territory.

"Should I go there as well?"

"No, you are our guest. You can stay in our tent. Now, come. It's been a long journey and I don't want to miss the opening ceremony. I think you'll like it as well."

"Right."

He followed her. They got closer to Chappenuioc proper, giving Eurik a better look. The stone pillars that lined the Road also lined the edge of Chappenuioc. Beyond them were even larger standing stones on which flat ones had been placed to form a ring of squared arches. And all of it was buried under wooden frames, ropes, and large stretches of fabric.

Chappenuioc was a tent city, in that it could be both considered a collection of tents or one giant tent. And much of the fabric was dyed and decorated with all manner of designs. Not only animals, but people and geometric shapes as well.

"Is this built every year?" He had to repeat himself, raising his voice to be heard over the din of a hundred songs and a thousand conversations.

"Yes and no." Silver Fang shook her head. "It used to be that only the shamans and loretellers were allowed to live here. But it became impossible. It would take months to set everything up and then break it down again. So they allowed others to stay so they could maintain everything and from there it just grew and grew."

"I see." But he could also see that not everything was ready yet. People were still hoisting up canvas in places and between the notes of flutes, drums, and string instruments Eurik could hear the pounding of hammers.

"They didn't abandon all propriety. It is still forbidden to use stone for construction within sight of Chappenuioc," Silver Fang said. "And just about all who come to visit will live in a tent or lean-to."

Moving along, Eurik noticed that the various quarters as Silver Fang had called them were clearly separated. Their borders marked with banners and statues of animals. They passed a group which used kites shaped in the form of a bird, tied to tall posts. After that came posts with climbing ferrets carved into them.

Snake had something similar, though he could see one or two of the kite-snakes he'd seen in the fields used here as well. They'd caught up with the rest of their group, but Silver Fang stopped him and quickly pushed him behind her horse.

"What is it?"

"Do you see that banner? The yellow one with a blue adder strangling a rooster."

It took him a moment, there were so many. Just looking for yellow fabric only cut it down to about a fourth or fifth of all the pieces of fabric that had been hung up. "Right, yes. I think I do."

"I don't see her. But that is the banner of Caetiwo. Fervent is already here."

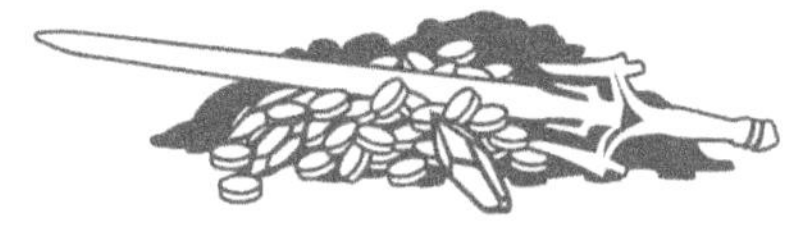

"You are in luck," Leraine said in Linesan as she ducked into her chamber. "Perhaps. Fervent has come to the festival but she is not here at the moment. She went to see the loretellers in the Inner Circle."

"I don't see how this is a good thing." Rock looked around the small space they would be sharing. The walls billowed in the breeze. "I didn't come to see only this. And perhaps it will be fine. How would she know who I am?"

Misthell beat her to it, rolling his single eye. "Yeah, because humans don't talk at all. Nope. Not like you've drawn any attention during this trip either. Nah, you're fine. They've probably all forgotten about you. Not me, of course. I'm unforgettable. But you're just the guy who carries me."

Rock rubbed his forehead with the tips of his fingers. "Fine, you made your point. Still, how many will know who my mother was?

I took your advice," he told Leraine, "I haven't mentioned her at all since we left Urumoy."

"That might only delay the inevitable." Leraine left unsaid that her mother might have helped matters along. There were things one couldn't say except behind closed doors under one's own roof. "But you are right, remaining here won't help at all. It will only make it easier for Fervent to find you if she does come looking. So instead, we'll head for the Inner Circle ourselves."

"I have no desire to go find this Fervent."

She shook her head. "We, by which I mean you, need to go see the loretellers and shamans. They'll need to rule about your abilities and whether you may use them in the Conclave Games. And one of the ones from Puma might know of your father." Rock still hesitated. "Come, the crowds will be a far better place to hide."

"Right. I am . . . not that comfortable with that many people."

Leraine frowned as she considered Rock. He hadn't seemed uncomfortable back in Linese and that city held far more people than Chappenuioc even during the festival.

But there, his abilities were not diminished.

Before she could say anything, though, Rock took a deep breath and got up. "I will have to get used to it." He pulled the baldric over his head and settled Misthell in his customary place. "Lead the way."

"You can't bring Misthell with you."

"What? Why not?" Misthell narrowed its eye. "I can be respectful around important people. I think. I haven't had enough practice, really. Which is why I should come along, so I can practice being all formal-like."

"Only the guardians are allowed to be armed within the Circles," Leraine said. "And you are a weapon."

"And I don't think you'll convince them you're a Linesan flathorn," Rock said.

"Maybe a lute then?"

That got a laugh out of Rock, for some reason. But he also shook his head and placed Misthell on a stand he drew from the earth. "You'll stay safe here. And we'll be back as soon as possible." Yet he hesitated.

"If you worry about someone stealing him, don't. We are in my people's quarter, within the pavilion reserved for my sept. Any thief would have to get past a hundred well-trained warriors. And Misthell would not go quietly."

"I sure wouldn't."

"Right, lead the way," Rock said.

Leraine moved quickly, not stopping when others hailed her. Few did in truth, too tired from travel and too excited at being here. She led the way, following the curve of the Outer Circle and up a staircase built up against one of the tall standing stones that formed the Outer Ring.

The lintels on top formed the base for the buildings here, constructs of reed, wood, and fabric. The pathways, however, were built out from the lintels and creaked and groaned as hundreds walked over them. The ropes that gave more support were taut and sang in the wind.

Four rope bridges connected this upper level with the one on the Inner Ring. Only a few used them but it wasn't much quieter. The sounds from everywhere else still reached here, and Leraine could hear chanting and singing as well.

The Festival of Conclave hadn't started yet—it would be a few more days—and not all preparations for it could be done physically. All shamans and loretellers received at least some of their training here, with a few exceptions, and it sounded like that training didn't stop just because there was a party going on outside.

Everything here was of more substantial construction, plastered walls with thatched roofs to keep out the worst of winter weather. Between the multilevel buildings she could see plastered walls preventing anybody from looking into the center of Chappenuioc. They'd been painted in vivid colors with scenes from the first Conclave.

They passed the Wolf racing against the Hare, Hawk and Falcon chasing the traitorous Crow, Dragon leaving Chappenuioc to head south to go his own way. But Leraine had more of an eye on the carved door frames; she was looking for one in particular.

Eurik felt a little uncomfortable walking along this walkway suspended as much as twenty paces or more above the ground. Wood as dry as this still had some earth *chiri* in it, enough for him to sense that not a single piece of metal had been used in the construction of anything nearby. There'd been some in the first ring, but not so here.

It was easier to tell because just about everybody wasn't wearing armor or weapons, including Silver Fang. All the metal he sensed on her was her fake tooth and a small knife on her belt. They passed a group of people queuing up in front of a building, the second such queue they came across.

"What are we looking for?"

"Ah, the *pedaethoc* of the unarmed combat competition. The door frame should show Snake, Bear, Lion, and Ibex wrestling with one another."

"I'm not familiar with that word. *Pedaethoc*? Something about spiritual home?"

"Not quite. A horse person would call it a temple," Leraine said, using a Linesan word instead. "Though that wouldn't be accurate either. But it's the closest thing. Really, a *pedaethoc* is more for the shamans. Though it is not a house for people, not just people."

"I see." He didn't, not at all. "And an ibex?"

"A mountain goat. It has large, curved horns. Not as big as the ones kept by dwarves, however. And there it is." She pointed at a building with a queue of about twelve people in front of it. The building itself was painted white with blue on its frame, including the door.

"I'll come along," Silver Fang said. "I can't speak for you, but I'll be able to explain."

They joined the queue and didn't have to wait long for it to move up, though the person who came out was a surprise. It was Slyvair, a new left arm glinting in the sun.

Chapter 10

Of the World

"I WASN'T EXPECTING to see you here," Eurik said in Linesan.

The old orc grinned. "And I didn't expect you. Are you joining the tournament?"

Eurik nodded. "Yes. I'm hoping it will help my search, and it's always a good idea to hone your skill against others. Especially when it's a friendly competition." His lips twisted in distaste as he recalled all the times he'd had to fight for his life. All of them since he'd left the island.

"Not that friendly." The orc looked at a few of the others waiting ahead of Eurik and Silver Fang. "But what search?"

He frowned; had he never told the orc what he was doing on the mainland? "I'm looking to learn more about my parents. The san found me with their bodies, but I have no memory of them. All I have is their names, thanks to Misthell."

"Ah. Yes. If you are looking for a lot of Mochedan in one place, there's no better time or place than right here. And you, Silver Fang? Competing as well?"

"I am, though not the unarmed event. I will have a better chance in the stick fighting." She eyed Slyvair's new arm. "The dwarves did quick work."

"Yes, Master Ghajir was grateful I kept his wares safe during a siege. Even a brief one. That and the bonus I got from Mayor Rozenbruk, and I had enough to finally get back into fighting shape."

"But will they let you compete in the unarmed event with a metal arm?"

"They didn't," Slyvair said. "It was worth the attempt, but I knew it was a long shot. No, you'll be facing me," he told Silver Fang, "while Eurik here will not have to fear a rematch. At least in this tournament."

Eurik looked around; he didn't notice Perun. "Will anybody else of the Gored Axes compete?" He didn't think the child would, but Hanser, perhaps. Given that there was a prize, he would guess at least some of the mercenaries would fancy taking their chance.

But Slyvair shook his head. "They've gone to visit friends and family while I got my new arm. That didn't take as much time as I thought, though, so I took the opportunity to come here and test it out."

"And Perun?" Leraine had the same thought as Eurik, then.

The orc gave out a booming laugh. "He was off the moment I turned my back to him. So yes, he's down there somewhere." Slyvair waved in the direction of the Outer Ring. "I just hope he remembers he has money to buy what he wants. He sometimes still forgets." The last said so softly Eurik could barely hear it.

Slyvair tossed his head. "But I'll leave you to it. I got some last-day training to get in myself. I have a reputation to defend." He gave Silver Fang a nod. "I hope to meet you in battle." Then he looked Eurik up and down. "And you, I hope you've learned a few things."

"Try not to lose too quickly, old warrior," Silver Fang replied.

"I'll surprise you," Eurik added.

"Good, good. Until then." Slyvair walked away, the walkway booming with every step of his long legs.

"Wasn't expecting to see him here," Eurik said. "What do you think the odds are for a conqueror of the Cider Duel to win this thing?"

"Not that good. He is skilled, but not a young sun-man," Silver Fang said, switching back to Thelauk. "He'll do better than a horse person—too many rely on their magic. But People can use the assistance of the spirits." She gave Eurik a sideways glance. "Remember that. You'll need every bit of power you can call upon just to make it an even fight."

"So you've said. Several times now."

"Yes, but that skull of yours is so dense, it's hard to say when something finally sinks in." They exchanged a bit more banter as the queue moved up, until finally they could walk into the building's dark interior. No mage lights here; they wouldn't work. Instead, polished bronze mirrors did their best to spread the light falling in from windows high in the walls throughout the room.

Several people sat or stood within, none of them dressed quite like any other Mochedan he'd ever met. With the exception of some of the women he'd seen coming in and out of a building across from Silver Fang's home.

Their *draen* were hidden by striped shawls draped over their heads like hoods, flowing down their shoulders to cover most of their arms as well. They all had bronze rods. Most had them tucked into their belt. The ones who didn't either held it in their hand, or in one case, had left the rod lying on a table next to an opened book.

Going by Silver Fang's description, that was the person they were supposed to talk to. Eurik examined the rod closer. It had a spiraling groove going up toward the head, which was the head of a strangely massive deer with large, proud antlers. Perhaps it represented one of those fabled elk?

The shaman looked from him to Silver Fang and back. "Yes?"

"I'm . . . Rock. I'd like to join the unarmed combat event of the Conclave Games." He'd considered using his real name, as one of his father's friends might hear it and wonder if they were related. But while non-Mochedan were obviously allowed to compete, Eurik was sure they'd share Silver Fang's unease at hearing his real name. And most would have known his father by One Claw.

"And where are you from, Rock?"

"Ah, the island of San. Do you know it?"

"It sounds vaguely familiar."

"He grew up among the plant-people," Silver Fang said.

"Ah, yes. I remember hearing some stories." The shaman tapped her chin. "But I am not familiar with them. To what spirit do the san belong?"

"Spirit?"

"Yes." She made an expanding gesture with her hands. "Some may forget, but these contests are held to emulate what the Great Spirits once did. But that doesn't work if a contestant represents nothing. That is why the soulless are barred from competing."

He could guess why Irelians were allowed to compete with that logic. "What of orcs, then?"

"The honey bee."

Eurik blinked. "Bee?"

"Yes. If you consider the way their people function and their love of fermented honey, what other Great Spirit would fit better?"

That . . . makes sense. Sort of. I could see how an orc matriarch is like a bee queen.

"But you are not an orc," the shaman continued. "And there's no such thing as a floral spirit. Well, some great trees may harbor a simple one." She looked over at another shaman, he was speaking to a few young men. He'd tucked his fluted rod into his belt. "But even a little one isn't enough."

Eurik didn't know what to say. The san didn't identify with any animal in that way. They mostly ate meat, but weren't picky on what kind. He could try some sort of scavenger animal—given how they liked their meals—but none came to mind. Well, crow could work. But Mochedan really didn't like crows.

Silver Fang had been very clear about that in one of her lessons. Something to do with the Great Spirit associated with them.

"The world!" Both Eurik and the shaman looked to Silver Fang at her outburst. She cleared her throat. "The san are attuned to the spirit of the world. That has to be a Great Spirit, right?"

The shaman shook her head with a snort. "Just because the world is big, doesn't mean it is a spirit. Places and things can have a spirit, yes, but they are simple things. Great Spirits can only form a connection with something more alive."

"But the world is alive," Eurik said. "It breathes, its heart beats, its life flows through its veins."

The shaman squinted at him. "I've communed with the spirits for twenty years. I think I would have noticed being surrounded by a giant spirit."

"Perhaps some proof would be in order," Silver Fang said, giving Eurik a look.

He considered it. Easier said than done. In here, wind *chiri* was nearly nonexistent and earth was little better. Building up the wind would take time, more than the shaman was perhaps willing to give. His eyes fell on the rod.

If this were anywhere else, all he'd have to do was gesture. But there wasn't enough earth *chiri* in the wood to form a connection. Eurik gestured at the rod. "May I?"

"If you damage it, you will have to pay for a replacement," the shaman said with a smile that showed a lot of teeth.

"I haven't made a mistake like that in years." He didn't need much contact. A single fingertip was enough and he became aware of the entire object. Bronze, hollow, old. Handling and cleaning had worn away at the rod, made its grooves shallower. One of the antlers had broken off at some point and been reattached.

"It wouldn't be the first time it was damaged," Eurik said. "It's been cared for, probably older than you. Certainly older than me."

The shaman barely lifted her left eyebrow. "Nothing about its weight, its color perhaps?"

The rod came up with his hand. He spun it lazily as he turned his palm up and levitated the rod. "No."

She hummed. "I can see that sort of trick in the Outer Ring. And those gleepeople can sing and dance as well."

"So you want to see something more?"

The shaman nodded.

"Very well." Eurik squeezed and the rod bent into a circle with an audible squeak. The metal groaned as the stag opened his mouth and tossed his antlers about. The shaman jumped in her seat at the noise and her hand went up. "Don't worry, your, uh, rod is fine." Spreading his fingers, he returned the rod to normal and floated it back to the table. It landed with a *tick* and rolled right into the shaman's snatching hand.

She ran her fingers over its length, examined it by holding it up and looking along its length. "Still straight, and I don't feel anything wrong." Her gaze returned to Eurik. "And certainly not horse people magic. Still, ruling that something like a World spirit exists is not something I can do on my own. I'll put it before a *tidaechanek*. Come back tomorrow to hear our ruling. Ah, who were your parents?"

He could take the safe route and simply give Zasashi's name. The san had raised him, if the word parent meant anything more than where you came from. But he was here to find out exactly that. Eurik only had to risk the nebulous consequences of Fervent learning the son of Ardent was here.

"Zasashi raised me . . . but I'm the child of One Claw and Ardent."

The shaman made a note, asking another question as she did so. "And their tribes? Were they People?"

"Ardent was of the Snake tribe. One Claw, supposedly from the Puma tribe. But I have no certainty on that. Not yet."

"One Claw certainly sounds like Puma to me. I'll accept it provisionally. We'll see if anybody recognizes it. And that's assuming you'll be allowed to compete."

"I'll come back tomorrow morning to learn your decision. If you'll excuse me," Eurik said, giving her a bow.

"I'll need to sign up as well," Silver Fang said. "Could you wait for me?"

Eurik gave her a silent nod even as he turned around to walk out. He took a deep breath once the door had shut behind him. Then he headed for the edge of the walkway and looked out, his hands resting on the railing.

He considered what to do if he were denied. It would actually be an advantage as much as anything. Less chance of drawing both the wrong and the right attention.

The great sheets that had been fastened between the Outer and Inner Ring rippled in the wind. Eurik stood almost right above a gap and could see people below in the Inner Circle. They were standing on a platform and wore strange outfits combined with outsized helmets fashioned into the likeness of animals. A crowd squatted before them. A few stray notes made it up, combined with a voice too indistinct to be understood.

Ah, they're acting out a story.

One had feathers on his arms and flapped them about as he walked. With that head, Eurik guessed he was a crow. Or a raven. The crow hopped over to someone clearly meant to be a wolf. Wolf took a swipe and Crow made gestures, slowly approaching before pointing at two others off to the side of the platform. One was a rabbit, the other . . . looked like the turtles that sometimes swam around San. Except the "shell" this person wore was high domed.

Both waved their hands about as the wolf began to stalk toward them. Crow hopped up and down behind Wolf, then turned toward a chest.

"I apologize for not thinking of it before," Silver Fang said, startling Eurik. "I hadn't considered that you might be thought of as a soulless. I should have, since none of the stories of the Great Spirits ever mention the san."

"It's fine. I hadn't guessed myself, not after seeing Slyvair." He glanced down. Crow had something in one arm and was being chased around the stage by Wolf and Hare. "Either I'll be allowed to compete, or I have more time on my hands to ask around about my father. Everything went well with you?"

Silver Fang nodded and they began to walk back the way they came. "Yes." She looked down at where he'd looked. "Oh, I've always liked that one. Watch— No, I shouldn't spoil the story. We could go down there, it would be better when you can actually hear what the actors say. But this story is coming to its end."

True to her words, the chase ended as Crow crashed into Turtle. Something shiny and round dropped to the floor, scooped up by Hare as Wolf snapped and chased Crow off the stage. The cheering and clapping easily reached them up on the Ring.

"We could watch one story. I don't want to leave Misthell alone too long."

"Yes, that would probably be best. But there should be some plays out beyond the rings, though they won't be as good. We can take Misthell there."

Eurik gave her a look. "Do you think Misthell will sit quietly through a story told badly?"

She considered it, then smiled. "No. But neither would I."

Chapter 11

Confrontation

LERAINE AND ROCK SLOWLY made their way back out of Chappenuioc and along the outside of the Inza structure to Snake's territory. Slow, because the crowds had only grown and many stood still to watch this or that performance.

Rock himself stopped when he caught sight of a warrior whirling a doubleblade around. The size of a quarterstaff, its polished steel reflected the sun as it spun around and around.

"She is impressive," Leraine said. The warrior was part of the Wolf tribe, judging by her *draen* and the cut of her vest. Her leggings were so tight they had to hinder her movements. "But this is for show. There's a reason Two Fang is so renowned. She was one of the Nine Saviors and one of the few to truly master the use of the doubleblade. It is not a weapon fit for war."

On the platform, the woman leaned back so far that her toes no longer could reach the floor. She used the doubleblade for support, point digging into a seam in the platform as the blade itself bent. Then she twisted her wrist and the blade sprang back to true, launching the warrior into a whirling leap.

"So then she learned it to show off?"

"There's always a few who dream of being the next Two Fang. And not just members of my own nation, either." Leraine didn't add that she'd had such dreams herself. But she'd had no talent for the doubleblade and Irelith had been right, too. Better to find your own path than to try and walk down someone else's. She chuckled. "Or they want to show off."

Three assistants began throwing small objects at the Wolf warrior. She didn't stop for a moment, cutting through each and every one of them. Explosions of color covered both the stage and the nearest onlookers as they burst. Those covered in the bright powders cheered the loudest.

Leraine herself didn't stint on showing her own approval as the warrior wrapped up her act by throwing the doubleblade high into the air. One of the assistants threw a wicker target her way and she caught it. It had been turned into a shield and she brought it up above her head, right in time to have her weapon land in the center.

"That was well done," Leraine said as they walked away.

"It was impressive. Dangerous, too. That last part could have killed her as she was practicing it."

"There are a lot of things that can kill you. To show fear . . ." Leraine grasped for the words, as she'd never had to explain this to someone before. Even horse people, even soulless understood! She knew Rock was brave, reckless even. He'd intended to face a greater demon all by himself. But he also had no shame when he showed his fear to her.

It was such little things that reminded her Rock had grown up among a people that were truly strange.

Rock opened his mouth, though he remained silent for a moment longer and gave a quick, small shake of his head. He switched to Linesan. "What is the difference between being afraid and cautious? I know there is one, but do you . . . worry that others might mistake one for the other?"

"It happens. But while some may be quick to accuse others of cowardice, people will dismiss them if your past deeds show that you are not."

"And we've taken some really stupid risks," Rock said with a nod.

"Not that stupid. We survived. Won, even!"

He looked at the ground. "Not everything."

Ah, right, our failed rescue of those taken by the elves. "Even the best don't win every battle." Irelith had told her that, and she had not believed. *I didn't think Irelith could lose.* But lost she had.

"And that doesn't worry you? That there is going to be another fight, another battle. And that we won't win that one?"

"I will give it my all. What more can I do? And what of you? Are you worried about the competition? That you will not stand a chance without the full use of your magic?"

He sighed at her choice of words, but what else to call that power of his? "It won't be easy. If they're as good as you, I'm in real trouble. But you're awfully sure that they'll let me in."

She shrugged. "They will, or they will not. No use worrying about something that is out of your control." *And Mother is sure to work her own brand of magic underneath the surface.*

They finally reached the area assigned to Snake, but a large crowd had gathered on its edge. On its own it wasn't strange, since there were people gathered to watch one performance or another every ten paces. But this one was unusually large and they could see a small creature fly off into the air. It looked like a goblin, except with wings and red skin. A glowing arrow smaller than one of Leraine's throwing spikes pierced it and both burst into a shower of sparks.

Both of them came to the same conclusion. "Misthell."

They gave each other a wordless look and made their way through the crowd. Leraine could hear the living sword before she saw him. "Alladan yelled his defiance, his bow singing the death of every demon that dared to show itself."

Ah, he's telling the Cyclus of the Nine. He won't be running out of material any time soon, then. The Nine's final adventure that had closed the rift at Ebon alone could fill an afternoon and evening. Judging by the lines she heard, this wasn't that saga. This was one of the tales of Alladan Ironbow, though not one she'd heard before.

"The last of the villagers had fled, but still Alladan stood in their way. The demons flowed around him, thirsty for his blood, hungering for his soul! They died yearning, but the noose closed around Alladan ever tighter."

Two spears had been stuck in the ground, their shafts crossing to form a brace for Misthell. He'd been pulled from his scabbard, but a folded piece of fabric had been placed between him and the ground. Before him, ground had been sectioned off by using more spears and a rope to tie them together. And hovering above the living sword, the small figure of Alladan was surrounded by crawling and scuttling demons—his metal bow glinting in the light of the afternoon sun.

"But even as hope gave way to defiance, a cry rose up. For the great hero had heard of Alladan's valiant stand from the villagers, and he rode into the army of demons, Flect flashing, Punct stabbing."

And indeed, a miniature Sharlaten rode in, his two swords slashing and stabbing. Together, the two broke the demon army and sent them fleeing back to the broken land of Evenau. The images faded away.

"Thank you, thank you," Misthell said as the crowd clapped and shouted. "Please, give me a coin if you can. Sword polish isn't cheap!"

And indeed, a woman was going around holding up a shallow basket and Leraine could see coins landing in it. She could hear them clink against money already in it. *Wait, that draen. That's Still Pool!*

Leraine held her peace until the woman reached her part of the crowd. "What are you doing?"

"Collecting on Misthell's behalf. He lacks the hands to do it and I'm getting a tenth of the take. Not all of us are rich, Silver Fang. I'd like to bring back a nice scarf. This is an easy way to get that money."

Rock finally joined her as the crowd thinned. "Well, if you don't mind," he said to Still Pool before turning his attention to the living sword. "You could have told me you were going to do this."

"Wasn't planning to. Wait, hold on." The sword raised his voice. "Folk, I'm taking a break. But come back in an hour or so and I'll tell you the tale of Alladan and the champion of Volsom. A tale of romance, betrayal, and sacrifice! Tell your friends!"

More coins landed in the basket. Much of it was copper, but Leraine could see the glint of silver in the growing pile. Eurik ducked under the rope and squatted in front of Misthell so he could look the sword in the eye.

"Then what brought this notion on?"

"Eh, I heard somebody tell the story of—not important—and really, he tried to tell. It was so bad, E—Rock. I just had to put a stop to it. So I called out, got ignored. Then Still Pool came along and she was kind enough to carry me out. I got into this argument. He had the nerve to think I didn't know how to tell it properly. Just because I'm lacking hands! And a face! Well, I showed him!"

"And how did that end up with you here, entertaining a crowd and asking for money?"

"If you can do something well, you don't do it for free. Resting Python told me that."

"Did she now?" Rock glanced at Still Pool as she came back with the basket. It clinked and sagged with each step. It must hold enough coin to cover Misthell's gambling habit for quite a while. Or buy him a lot of sword polish.

"She did." Still Pool put the basket down and started sorting the coins. "You and me, we have to worry about survival. And relying on the wrong person is a good way to end up in a bad way," she said, giving Leraine a look.

Leraine, in turn, refused to look away and bit down on a hot reply. Here and now was the wrong moment to have that argument. "And so you only consented to assist Misthell in exchange for a reward."

"Yes."

"Well, Misthell obviously did enjoy this," Rock said. He looked over his shoulder at the people who lingered, then back to Misthell. "So I take it you want to stay here, then?"

"Are you going somewhere?"

"I want to try and find someone who knew my father. My best bet is visiting where the members of the Puma tribe are staying. Ask if anybody there knew One Claw."

"Right, sure. If one of the ladies will stay here to help me with the donations?"

Leraine carefully didn't look at Still Pool as she quickly answered. "I can stay." She gave Rock a shrug. "They'll be more likely to answer your questions without me there anyway. Just remember to be polite, and if they bar your way, don't press the issue."

"I know, I know. Your lessons were quite clear. All right, I'm off. Still Pool, thanks for helping Misthell."

"Oh, it wasn't a problem. In fact, Silver Fang here can go and have some fun. Like I said, I can use the money."

"I see."

"Just go, Rock," Leraine said, staring at Still Pool, who met her gaze with her usual placid calm. "Still Pool and I will hash it out with Misthell."

Proving once more that he'd missed half the conversation, he just nodded and left with a casual goodbye. Perhaps she was too harsh on him. He had been looking forward to finding out more about his parents and now that goal was within his grasp. Hard to have eyes for something else when you could see the long longed-for end.

"Hash something out?" Still Pool pocketed her share and straightened out. "Don't know if that's needed."

"Enough." The word cracked like a whip. Leraine took a deep breath and eased her voice. "Enough, Still Pool. I don't know what you think you are doing. Or what my sister is thinking. But leave Rock out of it."

"Uh, what's going on?" Misthell's eye shot back and forth.

"Nothing you need concern yourself with," Leraine said.

"Indeed, there is nothing going on." Still Pool nodded along.

Leraine returned it, not trusting her voice right now.

"Yes, so how about it, Misthell? We're partners, or do you think Silver Fang here will do a better job of it?"

"I've already visited the markets. You haven't."

"But Still Pool needs the money to buy something," Misthell said. "Unless you have enough?"

"Sadly, not yet."

"Oh, well, uh, then maybe I'll keep working with Still Pool. If that's okay?" The living sword gave Leraine a furtive look. In some respects, the blade was more perceptive than Rock. In some very limited respects.

Leraine let out a long breath. "Very well. I'll . . . do some training for the event. Good luck, Misthell. Still Pool."

Eurik made his way along the outside of Chappenuioc, undaunted by the multitude of people now that he had access to his full senses. His worry lay behind him. Eurik wasn't sure he should have left. The way both had stood, it felt more like they'd been ready to draw swords, except they hadn't been carrying anything more than daggers.

He would have liked to pry, but Silver Fang had made it clear that he had to be careful about that. Eurik would still have done it if it was just her, but there'd been people watching and he barely knew Still Pool.

She'd accompanied Golden Tongue on the journey here, but if they'd exchanged more than a hello or goodnight, Eurik could not recall. And Golden Tongue had been speaking to Misthell without him around.

He shook his head. Silver Fang would be fine. So would Misthell. So he turned his thoughts to what lay ahead. Rehearsed the words he would say. He had to get it right.

Up ahead, he could already see his destination. Large wooden pillars with climbing pumas carved into them denoted the area reserved for that tribe. Getting closer, Eurik saw that wooden panels had been placed in between most of the pillars as barriers. These weren't only carved, they were painted in vivid colors and showed large felines and armed warriors bringing down armored knights riding their horses.

Approaching the entrance, he caught the attention of two men standing guard. One of them set down a jug before gripping his quarterstaff more securely. "Ho there. What you business 'ere?"

It took Eurik a moment to parse the words. Their pronunciation was different from what Silver Fang or that shaman had used, emphasizing different letters than what he'd heard back in Chappenuioc. *So that's what Leraine had meant about being marked as Snake.*

He bowed, a little more than necessary if he had it right. "Greetings. I am looking for someone who knew my father."

"Your father?" The speaker looked at his fellow guard. That one rolled his broad shoulders in a shrug. Their *draen* were on the back of their heads, so low they draped over their back between their shoulder blades. "You don't look like one of us, boy. You sound like you got a forked tongue."

"I learned Thelauk from a warrior of Snake and I grew up among people who were not People. My parents died when I was very young."

"Then how do you know your da?" The other guard slurred his words. Concentrating, Eurik could feel an unsteadiness to the man's footing through the subtle shifts in the earth *chiri*.

"The sword he made with my mother has design features of the Puma tribe."

They looked him over, obviously looking for this sword.

"I don't have him with me. He wanted to stay and earn some money."

The slurring guard, the one who had been holding a jug, come to think of it, guffawed. The other man shook his head and hefted his quarterstaff. "Right. Get lost, you drunk."

He lightly jabbed it at Eurik, but he'd drawn earth *chiri* into himself on reflex. It bounced off Eurik without moving him a hair's breadth. Frowning, the man tried again to move him.

"I'm not drunk," Eurik said.

"You're drunker than me," the slurring man said. "Here, you're not doing it right. Got to put your weight into it." He placed his staff against Eurik's chest and leaned into it, only to stumble when that failed to move Eurik as well. Then the drunken guard proceeded to stare at the end of this quarterstaff like the reason for his failure was written there.

The other guard sighed. "I told you not to drink so much." He turned his attention to Eurik. "And you, get lost."

Eurik wanted to argue, wanted to force his way through. But that was Rise of the Mountain, the Way of earth. He could do it, but angering these people would not get him what he wanted. Letting go of earth, he took a step back. Eurik would follow Dance of the Whirlwind. Give way and come at your target from a different direction.

Come back with Misthell and hopefully meet a pair guards who were willing to listen.

Chapter 12

Judgement

THEY HAD TO WAIT A few hours the next morning before someone from the shamans came to collect Eurik. Silver Fang came with him and together they made their way through Chappenuioc once more.

However, they didn't end up in the same place as last time. This was a more open area in between two buildings. There was an awning above their heads, giving some shade. Fifteen people sitting in chairs, each one wearing the shawl and bronze rod of a shaman, awaited them. Each of the chairs had a carving of an animal's head at the top of its backrest, one that matched the head of the rod of the person sitting in that chair.

There's a shaman from each of the tribes here. Leraine was right. This is more than just a decision on whether I can compete in a game. He only recognized the one who had interrogated him. She was sitting to his left, four seats from that end of the half circle.

Eurik bowed to them. "You've made a decision?"

The one sitting in the center wasn't the one to speak. Instead, a shaman two seats over on the right leaned forward. Above him, a sort of massive dolphin bared its teeth. "Not quite. We have debated the matter, but agreement is hard to come by. Only one of us saw any evidence and while none here would doubt her word," the shaman said, one person seated to his left shifting in their seat as the speaker paused.

He spread his hands. "We need to see the evidence for ourselves. I'll volunteer my *vipaen* for the demonstration." He held up his rod. The figure on top wasn't simply a head, but the full body of the creature. It was some sort of massive dolphin, a killer whale if Eurik recalled right. It had been years since he read Lollandros' bestiary.

"And what will that prove?" Another shaman gave Eurik a glance, but her attention was mostly on the one who had volunteered. An elk's head decorated her chair. "Magic can take many forms. Horse people, people-eaters, sun-people, short-people, dragons. All have their own type of magic, but none are like the blessings the spirits provide us."

"That's not entirely true," someone else said. "The dragons, for one—"

"There is no need to repeat this discussion," the original speaker said with a loud voice. Then he spoke more softly and gestured toward Eurik. "Especially with an audience that is waiting on our decision."

"Perhaps a different demonstration is in order," Eurik said, thoughts racing.

The one in the elk chair regarded him. "And what would that prove?"

"You wish proof that I am connected to the world. But the world is not just the earth we stand on. It is the wind around us, the waters of the rivers and oceans, the fire that brings us light and life. As I said, I am a student, I don't know all the Ways." He would likely never be a master. It took more than a human's lifetime to learn enough. Zasashi had told him not even a master knew everything.

But Eurik had learned a thing or two since leaving the island. He moved his arms. Up here, the wind had room to move and whatever dampened the wind *chiri* on the Road wasn't present here in Chappenuioc itself. The air stirred, the canopy fluttering rhythmically in time with the motion of his quickening limbs.

"But I can rise as the mountain, I can dance with the wind." A maelstrom of wind formed between Eurik and the seated shamans, faster and faster. Eurik felt his hair ruffling, the shamans had to put a hand on their shawls to keep them from getting plucked right off their heads.

He drew the *chiri* into himself and spun around. He danced with the small tornado. His heart beat fast, a laugh on his lips as the freedom gave him wings.

"Enough!"

He noticed Silver Fang first, holding herself upright by digging her fingers into one of the supports of the building next to this open area. The shamans likewise had ducked into their chairs and were holding on tight to both their shawls and their seating.

Getting a hold of himself, Eurik slowed down. He at least knew better than to just stop and let the built-up *chiri* go wherever. Most of it he blasted off into the wide open sky in between the rings.

"You may decide that what I do is not proof of a world spirit," he said in the sudden calm. "But as I have told Silver Fang, what I do is not magic."

The shamans looked at each other, and the one in the elk chair stopped rearranging her shawl. "I don't know what that was, but I'm reluctant to tie it to a spirit. Still, if he can use it within Chappenuioc . . ."

The tallest among them—sitting in a chair decorated with a bear—extended his hand to her. "What else can work here?"

"What I would like to know is if he can affect the stone of Chappenuioc." The words of the woman in the wolf chair caused all discussion to die as the gathered shamans looked at Eurik.

He shook his head. "No. Whatever the Inza used, it's not of this world."

Everyone leaned back in their chairs, except the one in the elk one. "You say that, but how do we—"

"Enough, Sharp Prong," the woman seated across from her said. Her chair had a horned sheep on it. "We've discussed this more than enough. We even had the loretellers here to recount nearly forgotten tales of the plant-people. I'm satisfied that there is evidence of a world spirit. Perhaps this is not a great spirit, but if it is strong enough to grant power like this to someone, it doesn't matter." She turned her attention to Eurik. "Though I must urge for a stipulation that this competitor is not allowed to use this spirit's power externally. If he uses the wind to blow his competition away, he's out of the games."

Sharp Prong looked around and sat back herself, her arms crossed. "Very well. We have spent enough time on this."

"Good." The voice was threadbare, barely a croak. The person in the center chair had wrinkled hands, and long, stringy gray hair spilled out from under her shawl. She was the oldest here by far, had to be. On top of her chair, the long head of a crocodile leered at everybody. "I'm relieved to hear we can finally vote. Those in favor of recognizing a world spirit, of whatever status?"

Many held up their rods. Sharp Prong was not among them, neither were four others. But apparently it wasn't enough, for the old shaman merely nodded. "The existence of a world spirit has been accepted. And on the matter of whether this competitor may use his spirit's power to affect others in the competition?"

Not a single rod went up. "I thought so," the Crocodile shaman said. "This is the judgment of this *tidaechanek*. You may compete, young man. But your spirit may only aid you, not hinder others. You can tell Bitten Fin here which events you wish to compete in. This *tidaechanek* is dissolved."

Nearly all got up and left, the old shaman requiring the help of a young man who had stood off to the side. Bitten Fin turned out to be the one in the killer whale chair. He approached them, with a noticeable hitch in his step.

"I just realized," Bitten Fin said. "We didn't actually ask if this world spirit of yours can affect you rather than the world around you. All the great spirits can, yes, but we'd never heard of a world spirit before."

"There is no issue there. Using the Ways to enhance one's own body is one of the simpler techniques." Though using earth *chiri* was going to be difficult within the rings. He'd have to rely on wind instead.

"Good, good. Well, come on. I understand you were looking to compete in the unarmed combat event?" He headed down the walkway, his limp barely slowing him down.

"You go," Silver Fang said. "I have something to discuss with the shamans here."

Eurik waited a moment longer, but she gave no sign that she was going to tell him what it was about. "All right. Uh, I will meet you back in Snake's Quarter then."

He only needed to jog a little to catch up to Bitten Fin. The killer whale shaman hadn't slowed down and only gave him a brief glance when Eurik came up to him. "So yes, I would like to fight in the unarmed event. But I would also like to compete in the Three Games."

"Excellent. Too many these days only have eyes for the games where there's a chance blood will flow. But the Three Games is what the Conclave Games started with. They were even their own individual events, back then."

"I did not know that."

Bitten Fin shrugged. "History now. They've been relegated to the first day of the Games. The other four are now solely dedicated to fighting. Ah, what am I complaining? Better they do it here to celebrate what binds us than out there breaking the Great Truce."

The shaman turned his head to follow two Mochedan wearing something like armor. Though the leather wasn't boiled and the metal on it was too thin to offer much protection. Eurik had seen more and more of that style since he'd arrived in Chappenuioc. Garments that resembled armor, or basically were armor.

"If only it were enough." Bitten Fin jerked his head. "Enough. Come, we'll get you written up. I'm sure you will want to prepare yourself."

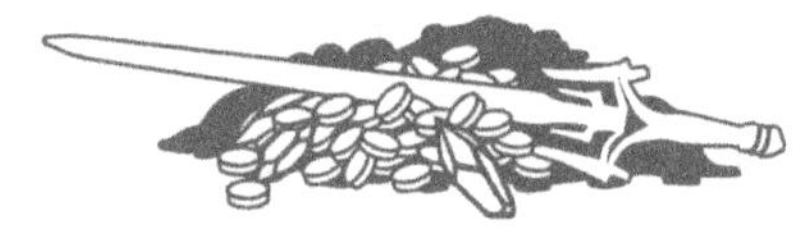

Leraine took a deep breath and followed the Snake shaman. She was in a discussion with some of her fellows, so Leraine stayed back at a respectful distance and waited for an opportunity. It came when the shaman bid the others goodbye and turned around with her arms crossed. The lines of her face deepened with disapproval.

"Well? You've been hounding my steps long enough. Spit it out."

Leraine averted her gaze. "I apologize. I didn't wish to disturb."

"So instead you waste more of my time."

She bit down on another apology. "I wish to dedicate a trophy to the spirits."

The shaman regarded her. Leraine wished she knew who this was. Probably not Urumoy or she would have had to have gone to Chappenuioc before Leraine's time. The shaman's *vipaen* would offer no clue and shamans didn't have *draen*. They belonged less to the tribe and more to the Great Spirit. Supposed to, anyway.

"Ah, yes, the girl who slew a greater demon. Silver Fang." Her nail traced the head of her *vipaen*. "Fine. Let's get this over with." She muttered some more things after she'd turned away, too low for Leraine to catch.

As Leraine followed, doubt beset her again. Was this the right course? Certainly, White Gale and Flashing Reed had spurned the offering but they might still reconsider. Eventually, at some point in time.

Except they had shunned her. Their door had remained closed when she'd come by, and none of them had come to the festival. No, any reconciliation would be long in waiting, if it ever came.

They passed into the inner sanctum, the center of Chappenuioc. High above, beams and planks made from ancient Rott Ruus trees formed a pointed roof. And filling much of the floor were the sacred statues of the Great Spirits. Those that still had tribes to take care of them were adorned with gold and silver jewelry, sparkling with jewels of every color. Their wood shone, polished daily.

Those statues that represented lost tribes, like Hawk, Turtle, Mouse, and Rabbit were not neglected. But they lacked the rich adornments and they only had one small altar each.

The shaman, who had still not told Leraine her name, ignited an oil lamp and led her down a winding set of stairs to the ground level.

The smell changed. The acrid smell of wood polish disappeared, so did the fragrance of wood dust. The aroma of the burning oil couldn't hide a moldy scent mixed with the sharp smell of rust. The smell thickened as they shuffled into the dark, cluttered chamber that had been divided up like a cake.

"Now let's see. It has been a long time since someone wanted to dedicate a demon's parts to the spirits. That thing went out of fashion with the Rift War. Good thing too, something foul clings to them still. Those horse people can't stop fooling with things they can't control."

"I'm not here for that."

The shaman whirled around. "What? Then why did you have me go down all the way to here? And you told me you wanted to dedicate a trophy to the spirits," she said, pointing a long finger at Leraine.

"Yes, the tooth of a blooddrinker. He killed my teacher and I avenged her death. But her daughters—"

Squinting, the shaman looked her up and down before nodding. "Right. Well, that's better." She turned away. The light playing over rusted weapons and rotting shields. Pitted armor buried under a thick carpet of spiderwebs reflected the light weakly. Gold and silver shone in the light of the lamp, gems glittered.

"There are demon hearts here, then?"

"Yes. This place holds trophies from every conflict. Elven knives, spurs from when the horse people first arrived, banners captured when the soulless first came to our shores. Many of those have fallen down since. And over there a mirror captured from the Traitor-Mage himself," the shaman said, pointing at one of the rooms. "Two Fang herself brought that one in. In truth, half of what's here is because it's the safest place to keep it. Which honors the spirits in another way, for they love the world as much as we do, or more."

The shaman approached one of the doors, blew dust off of a plaque stained nearly completely green, then moved on. "Ah, here's the one. Show me the tooth, girl, and tell me how it was obtained. Who did it belong to?"

"It belonged to a blooddrinker called Rik. No, his name was Sharverik. He worked for a Bone Lord called Merin. He wanted a living sword and tasked Rik with acquiring it. We happened to be there when the blooddrinker made his move. He killed Irelith."

"And you killed him in turn?"

Leraine shook her head. "No. I . . . I used the owner of the sword as bait. But instead, I got captured. I escaped and, together with Rock, we took on Rik and this bone construct of Merin." The flickering flame and darkness hid the shaman's face. If she'd noticed Rock's name in the tale, Leraine couldn't see it.

"He let me borrow Misthell, the living sword, and I took on Rik. But in the end," Leraine said, bearing her silver tooth, "I killed him with this. Rik was arrogant and thought nothing of the lives of others. Only his own fun." She spat the last word out. "Irelith was worth a thousand of him. But all I can offer is this." Leraine retrieved the fang from her pouch and held it up.

The shaman raised her right hand, waving her fingers over the fang as she softly chanted. Even before she announced it, Leraine could tell it had worked. The fang shivered in the palm of her hand, though not in a way that she could see.

"It has been accepted." The shaman walked over to a shelf and picked up another clay oil lamp. She lit it using her own and offered it to Leraine. "It will show you its proper place. Go."

Leraine looked around, then at the fang in her hand. The glimpse of the shaman's expression put a stop to any thought of asking her for a direction. "Right."

Walking around her, Leraine looked around for a clue. The level had been divided up into a number of rooms arranged around a central chamber. That chamber itself had piles of stuff lying all around. Some of the doors were closed, others weren't. Through the cracks, she saw more dust and spiderwebs with ancient relics buried underneath. Shelves bowed with age and weight.

The fang in her palm kept shivering, but she noted that the intensity grew and waned. She retraced her steps, the shivering grew. She stepped back, it slackened. *The shaman did tell me it would show me its proper place.*

The shivering led her to a shut door. Opening it wasn't easy. The hinges had not been oiled in a long time, the door itself barely fitting in the frame. Not until she set down her lamp and pulled with both hands and her full weight did it shoot open.

Leraine glanced at the shaman, but she hadn't paid attention to her struggles. The shaman instead was examining a nearby chamber. Relieved, Leraine picked up her lamp and took a step inside.

Her steps kicked up dust, a spiderweb tangled itself into her short hair. Nobody had been in here in some time; months, years even. But there was a path through the clutter, an old trail through the dust on the floor and the webs.

She passed a chest with one half of its lid caved in. Within, dull daggers and rusty axe-heads lay in a jumble. On a shelf, a helmet with a crest rested right next to a skull nearly twice its size. Broad, with large tusks, it took Leraine a moment to place it. A troll's skull, unusually large.

Leraine wondered about the story behind that one. Did anybody still remember it? It would have been an impressive hunt, a fierce struggle. But why had it been dedicated to the spirits?

The fang jumped in her hand, but when Leraine looked at it the fang laid perfectly still. Yet it felt like it was dancing on her palm. She extended her hand and slowly moved it about, only to jump herself when something crashed. It hadn't been in this room.

"Everything all right?"

There was no reply. "Shaman? Can you hear me?"

"Yes! Just some mice."

Leraine had a hard time hearing the reply between her own coughing. She'd inhaled some dust with that last shout. "I see."

The shaman didn't ask if she was all right. Breathing through her nose, Leraine struggled to focus on the fang. On the way it felt in her hand. It led her to a shelf in the back, a little box in between a shriveled hand and a flute she recognized. She'd seen them only from afar, but the bone flutes of the elves had left an impression.

Leraine nearly put the oil lamp on the shelf, then gave it a closer look and thought better. Setting it on the floor, she worked in deep shadow to lift the lid of the box open. There were a lot of teeth within, yellowed with age. Some had fading blood stains.

"I thank you, Ghisa. Without you, I would not have returned home safe. Without you, I would have failed to avenge Irelith. Irelith . . . I'm sorry I wasn't there at the soul garden for the ceremony. Do not worry about us. They miss you, as I do. This rift between us will heal. I hope."

A deep breath, and she let go. Leraine closed the lid, only to twitch when the sound of another crash broke the solemn silence.

Heading out, she called out. "Do you require help?"

It took a moment for the shaman to respond. "No, no." Something fell, setting off a series of metallic clattering and crashing. "I need some light. I dropped my oil lamp."

"Of course." Leraine didn't need to ask where the shaman was, the noise told her where to go. And if in doubt, all she had to do was look down at the tracks in the dust.

She couldn't smell smoke, at least. Didn't see the growing glow of a blazing fire. Much of the structure was wood, but the floor was made of the Inza's eternal stone. What did waft toward her was the penetrating scent of oil as she entered the right room.

The shaman stood not far from a large mirror resting at an angle against the wall, the broken pieces of the lamp at its feet. The shelves here were thick and she recognized the spiky lumps on them. None were the same, all had a slightly different color, but Leraine recognized them none the same.

The center of the room had a pile of weapons and armor, more than a few showing strange signs of damage as if they'd been melted. "Is everything all right?"

"Yes, of course it is." The shaman walked over to her. "As I said, mice. Are you done here?"

"I have dedicated the fang." Leraine frowned as some instinct warned her. Of what, though? Looking over the room, she didn't see movement. She didn't hear any mice. Didn't smell them. But there was a lot of stuff in the room, lots of places for such vermin to hide.

"Good," the shaman said. "Then you can go. I'll need to clean this mess up and secure everything again." She held out her hand for the oil lamp.

"I can help," Leraine said, handing the lamp over. The sense of wrongness did not abate.

The shaman shook her head. "Not possible. Can't risk desecration. So, go. Have fun at the festival." And she gave Leraine a smile. "Enjoy yourself."

Leraine nodded. "Can you escort me to the stairs, then? You have the only light now."

"Fine. But hurry up. I have other things to do."

They headed out. Leraine couldn't shake the feeling, not even when they left the room filled with the demon hearts. Was it her imagination or was the shaman acting strangely?

"There's the stairs. You can find your own way out from here."

Leraine turned around to thank the shaman but she was already turning away. *Didn't she wear her vipaen on her right?* But she could see it clearly on the shaman's belt, on her left. And the coils wound their way down the *vipaen* instead of up.

She glanced at the layer of dust around them. Their own footsteps she could see, and the fading trail of other supplicants. No paw prints, though. No sign of mice. "On second thought, I can't let you clean up the mess alone. I am to blame for you being down here in the first place."

"Kind of you, but the answer is no."

"I can hold the lamp for you. That would make your work easier."

The shaman tossed her head and let out a sigh. "Fine. Come on then. You have wasted enough of my time already."

Leraine hesitated. She sounded fine. Was her mind playing tricks on her? The shaman was waiting for her to head back first so Leraine hastened past. The shaman wasn't offering her lamp to her though.

"Do you have anything to mop the oil up with?"

"Some rags," the shaman said. "They're in the same room."

Leraine tensed at every step, her body expecting an attack even as her mind doubted. Yet her liver told her she walked into danger. "You haven't told me your name this entire time. Have I done something to offend you?"

"No. Though wasting my time does annoy me. There, behind the pile. Not too far from the mirror."

Leraine stepped forward only to jump and roll. Her mind caught up a moment later to what her senses told her. A foot scraping, fabric fluttering, a fist ruffling her hair. She came out of the roll, only to stumble when her heel hooked on something lying on the ground.

A quick glance nearly cost her. For what she saw made her forget her situation for a moment. Someone was lying there, a corpse judging by the angle of the head. But those clothes, her face, it was the shaman.

A growl was her only warning. The shaman—who had to be someone or something else—had put the lamp on a shelf and lunged for Leraine while she was distracted. Leraine fell back, then tried to block the next strike.

She grunted as her arms went numb and she was forced another step back. The power in that swing had been inhuman. And the technique had been wrong. This murderer wasn't using the arts of her people.

Leraine retreated, calling upon Ghisa to quicken her limbs and ducking out of the murderer's grasp. "Who are you?"

"I'm her," her assailant said, pointing at the body at her feet.

Another distraction, but Leraine had found her footing. This lunge she didn't block, she deflected. Her own counterattack slammed home, hitting the side of the false shaman's neck, then under the arm.

Leraine's opponent had felt the blows, she knew it. The murderer's hiss, the way her limbs had twitched, but her return palm thrust had still knocked the air out of Leraine's lungs.

"Your kind truly is annoying," the murderer said, cracking her neck. "Always screwing everything up. You can't even die when I need you to." She advanced, every punch and strike made Leraine's arm shake.

Leraine fell back, angling to leave the room and slip into the darkness. But something else bothered her. *The room is filled with weapons. Why isn't she using any? It can't be respect for the spirits or she wouldn't have snuck in here and killed a shaman.*

They left the room, but the murderer kicked the door wide open so that light spilled out from the opening. Between that and whatever filtered through from the floor above Leraine found herself in deep shadow rather than true darkness.

With a sweeping motion the murderer took off her shawl and tossed it at Leraine. She stepped to her left and plucked the fabric out of the air. The murderer swung through the shawl and the spot Leraine had just been with her *vipaen*.

A snap of the wrist and the shawl curled itself around her left forearm. It wouldn't do much to protect against a *vipaen* swung in anger, but it was better than nothing. "What are you after?"

"Oh yes, let's take a break from your imminent demise so I can explain my greatest secrets to you." A quick lunge to test her defenses, but Leraine backed away, deeper into the dark. "Do you really think you're getting out of here alive? Or maybe you hope someone else will come along if only you stall long enough?"

"Then how about introductions? I'm Silver Fang." Her foot caught on a shield, setting off a small avalanche.

Her opponent took the opening and swung again. Leraine gritted her teeth and deflected the blow with her left arm. Even without taking the full brunt of the blow and through the layers of rolled up fabric, pain shot up her arm.

Leraine stepped into the opening and punched the impostor in the throat. The murderer gagged and reeled at the blow, but her own hand snapped up to grab at Leraine. She pulled her arm back just in time and jumped back. Her opponent pursued, only to stumble and curse at the old treasures now littering the floor.

"I'm nobody," her opponent said, holding the *vipaen* low.

They were shadows in the dark now. The central chamber was fairly large, but the entire center was a mountain of metal that shifted whenever either one bumped against it. It became hard to judge the distance, where their opponent's limbs were.

Leraine danced on the edge. Her opponent was a lot stronger than her. If she ever got her hands on Leraine, it would be over. But every mistake, every time the dedicated gifts to the spirits fell or got stepped on, it all worked in her favor. This continued ruckus had to attract attention.

But the noise also made it harder to tell what her opponent was doing. And in the end, the dance ended. Leraine punched, missed, and a blink later a crushing grip closed around her forearm.

Teeth bared in the darkness. "Got you." The *vipaen* came down. Desperate, Leraine counterpunched and hit the fist holding the rod before it could hit her.

The impostor growled, only to freeze as they both heard a new sound. Feet running down the stairs, a voice calling out.

Leraine bared her silver tooth. "What was it—" The *vipaen* came around. Leraine just managed to bring her arm up to shield her head but the blow still sent her into the central pile. Dazed, her arm screaming, Leraine fought through the pain. Light lanced her eyes.

When she could finally see and think again, Leraine saw no sign of the impostor. Only a confused shaman crouched over while someone else held an oil lamp.

Chapter 13
Drying Tinder

EURIK TOOK DEEP BREATHS, trying to center himself, trying to stay in the now. Yet he couldn't help but glance up at the people watching from the top of the Outer Ring, and at one in particular. Silver Fang had turned up last night with severe injuries. A bone in her left arm had been shattered. In her right they'd been merely cracked.

At least those I could heal. I could do nothing for the rest. It must have something to do with the commotion that day. But nobody wants to tell me what that's about. Not even Leraine.

She'd gotten into a fight, but with whom? Why?

Eurik shook his head and shifted his attention to the people around him. Like Eurik, they were preparing for the race, though each did so in their own way. Some hopped from foot to foot, shook their limbs out, or rolled their shoulders and neck. Others stayed still, or talked to one of their competitors, and yet others waved at people on the walkway up above on the outside of the Outer Ring or in the stands built up against the pillars that encircled the entirety of Chappenuioc.

Between the mass of people and the buildup of Chappenuioc, the wind down here was constrained. So like some others, Eurik had to keep moving to make sure enough wind *chiri* rushed through him.

The sound of a massive gong boomed through Chappenuioc, quieting everybody as they looked over at the old man standing on a bridge that connected the Outer Ring with a tower built around one of the pillars. He raised one hand up, then chopped down, and the gong fell silent.

"People! I welcome you all to the 324th Conclave Games. All of you are here to honor the Great Spirits, whether you compete or not! And this I implore you to remember. All of you are children of the Great Spirits. Whatever differences there are between us, so there are between the spirits. And like them, we come here in peace!"

His words stirred the crowd. A thousand hushed conversations rose up, and together they were enough to nearly drown out the shaman's next words.

"And so in peace, we begin! Competitors, on your mark!"

No explanation of the rules or how long the race is. Good thing Leraine already told me.

They had to run along the Outer Circle of Chappenuioc three times. First to reach the finishing line won. Which meant those in the back of the group, like Eurik, were in a bad spot.

"Get set!"

Silver Fang had also told him that a bit of elbowing and shoving wasn't against the rules. But if he touched the standing stones of Chappenuioc or left the Outer Circle for even a second, he was out of the race.

He bent his knees as he drew more wind *chiri* in and the world slowed down.

"Run!"

Leraine met Rock's gaze and pressed her lips together. He deserved to know, but the shamans had forbidden it. After they'd found her and she'd been able to tell them what had happened, they'd searched the sanctum.

It hadn't been long before they'd found Tense Coil. That had been her name. Her impostor had killed her in the room with the mirror. A demon heart had been placed nearby. They thought it had been what her murderer had been after.

But how had the killer managed to get into the holiest of places? How had she managed to look and sound like Tense Coil? Anywhere else, the obvious answer would be magic. Not here. But there were more forms than just what was practiced by the horse people and the soulless. Could Rock's kind disguise someone?

Well, I can't ask. And how did she get down there, anyway? I should have heard her come down the stairs. Or Tense Coil should have; she was closer to the stairs.

She hadn't paid attention to Sated Resting Panther's opening speech; it had been a mistake. Something he'd said had caused a stir, because people were actually talking though the renowned loreteller wasn't finished.

For a moment, Leraine held her peace. But ignorance now could cause far more embarrassment later. Best to swallow a little bit of dishonor now. She turned to her sister Ferisha. "What did he say? I hadn't caught everything."

It was Anseri who answered, though. "He told the Truce Warriors to stop trampling on our most sacred traditions."

Ferisha turned on their sister. "He did no such thing. Sated Resting Panther merely reminded all of us that the Truce is not what binds us. Some of us forget that," she said, staring right back at Anseri.

"And some of us must have smoked too much dreamweed if that's what they heard," Anseri shot back.

Leraine considered pressing for the shaman's exact words, but the way her sisters descended into their argument convinced her it was a lost cause. Their respective followers were busy staring daggers at each other as well. *Mother thinks those two are merely using those factions. I'm not so sure. This division even in my own family, it's dangerous.*

Sated Resting Panther couldn't miss the stir his words had caused, but he continued as if it had done no such thing. Leraine almost missed the start of the race because of that. The runners set off, a mass of people who jostled for position while those in front tried to separate themselves from the pack.

A few managed, others disappeared into the greater crowd of competitors. Rock, though, could do no such thing. He stood out, even at this distance. He didn't speed up as quickly as he'd done back in Glinfell, when he'd raced for the wall. But he was making progress, ducking and weaving. Then he was out of sight.

Leraine sat back. Her sisters had stopped speaking to each other and were making a point of ignoring the other's existence. So instead, Leraine eyed the rest of the crowd. They'd searched for Tense Coil's murderer and had found no trace. Even the shamans of Wolf had been stymied; the impostor had smelled just like the deceased shaman as well.

There were thousands here for the festival, but even in that great mass a fleeing Tense Coil should have been spotted. She had been, right up until she'd reached the Inner Circle. After that, nothing.

And the most likely reason is that she dropped her disguise. Or used a new one.

Leraine worried it was the latter. Because if it was, they had a murderer here in Chappenuioc that could potentially wear anybody's face. Could be anybody. And they didn't know what she wanted.

Yes, the demon heart they found next to the body was a clue and they'd posted extra guards on the sanctum. But what if the murderer had other things she wanted? Like revenge on the person that had spoiled her plans?

Her back itched and Leraine resisted the urge to readjust a weapon not at her side.

Finally, the mass of humanity dispersed as each runner moved at their own pace. Eurik evaded an elbow, startled another as he rushed by them. The wind *chiri* grew, stirred to life by every person in the race.

Eurik took in as much as he could, though not all of it. Drawing in too much would be like pouring too much water into a cup. All it did was spill out and create a mess.

Leraine was right. Two runners in front of him got tangled up, each so consumed with hindering the other that they didn't notice they were slowing down. *This race is not just about going fast.*

Many seemed to move slow to his enhanced senses. A tangle of them blocked much of the path. Going around wasn't an option, not without getting caught in the mess. Deep breath, the *chiri* rushed and howled, scraping his nerves.

Eurik leaped.

The crowd pointed and screamed as he flew through the air and over the heads of the group of runners. The ground came rushing at him and he didn't bother trying to stay on his feet. He let his legs buckle and rolled over the ground only to push off and get back on his feet in a single smooth motion.

Free to run, he increased his pace again. The runners in front of him now were the real competition. Their legs moved as fast as his own. Whatever spirits they called upon granted them great speed.

He didn't know much about how that worked. He'd seen Silver Fang use it, but she'd refused to talk about it. *Another secret. How am I going to find some answers if they hoard them all like a dragon does his treasure?*

Eurik noticed the distance between him and the rest increasing, the *chiri* within him wavered. With a quick shake of the head, he pushed off thoughts of Silver Fang and all the things she didn't tell him. He couldn't worry. Not now. The wind was careless, free. He had to be the wind.

The roar traveled through the crowd like a wave, rising as the first of the runners passed them by. The first few were members of Wolf, Puma, Falcon, and a single Elk. Then came Rock, with a few others falling farther behind.

She frowned and got up to her feet, as most others had done. "You can go faster! What are you waiting for?"

Leraine had little hope Rock would hear her over the hooting and screaming of everybody else. Yes, supposedly his magic enhanced his senses as it did everything else. But the crowd was very loud.

Then Rock raised his hand in her direction and quickened once more. "That's it!" She kept standing even as Rock disappeared from view. She wasn't here just to cheer him on. Members of her own tribe were running in this race as well, both from Urumoy and elsewhere. One was a man, even.

Ghisa did not lend itself easily to running. When a warrior sought the aid of their Great Spirit, they almost always could only call upon the aspect that they had the most affinity for. And all Great Spirits had their own set of aspects.

With Ghisa, speed usually came in short bursts or lightning fast reactions. Leraine prided herself on her deep connection to the first snake, but it was a more general connection. More like that of a shaman, though nothing like their command of it.

If I'd joined this race, I'd be like those unfortunate ones.

And they were unfortunate. The last of the competitors huffed by as the crowd started their own competition. Theirs was to see who could come up with the best insult for those who had clearly overestimated their ability.

Leraine simply sat down rather than join in. They stood no chance, yes. But they were here to honor the spirits. That, if nothing else, should be respected.

Eurik's lungs screamed, his legs ached. He'd just finished the second round, only the third and final one to go. But he'd never had to use this much wind *chiri* for this long.

He dodged around a swipe by a competitor. He and two others were still fighting over first place. And fight was the right word as hands, elbows, and shoulders were employed to try and knock someone else back.

Arrogance. Why did I think nobody else could keep up with me? I should have realized these spirits the Mochedan use are capable of great feats too. The Ways don't make me invincible. I'm no master.

And more trouble appeared up ahead. They'd caught up to the stragglers. To Eurik, they practically stood still and they all passed them before they knew what was going on. All but one, who got pushed into one of the stragglers by a woman with several teeth threaded through her *draen*.

Eurik nearly stopped at the sound of breaking bones as they slammed into the unyielding Inza stone. A glance back showed him some people already leaving the crowd to help the fallen. And it wasn't like he could do much here, cut off from earth *chiri*.

He let the wind carry away that concern as well and faced forward once more.

They came around the bend, weaving through the slower runners. Leraine got to her feet, everybody did. "Go, go, go, go!" "You can do it!" "Wolf!" "Puma!" "Elk!"

But none cheered the runner in a solid third position, nipping at the heels of the two just in front of him. None but her. "Run, Rock! Run!"

One of the two in front looked back at Rock, maybe worried he was getting too close. He shouldn't have done that because the other took that moment to pull at his trousers and she yanked them down. It didn't slide down much, but it messed up his pace.

It also caused him to almost collide with Rock if he hadn't jumped over the runner. Then they were across the finishing line and they slowed down. "YES!"

He hadn't won, but coming in second in any of the Conclave Games was a feat worthy of celebration. Rock nodded to the winner. Leraine thought she was from Wolf though it was hard to tell from this distance and angle. Could be Boar as well.

However, the one who came in fourth after he'd had his pants pulled down in front of everybody—the one who clearly belonged to Puma—stalked toward the winner with a snarl. His shouts were garbled but still audible.

He's not going to attack another contestant? Not here? Not now!

If he wanted to, he didn't get the chance as Rock put a hand on his shoulder. That didn't calm the Puma down, but it did redirect his anger. He tried to shove Rock, who stepped back. This caused the Puma to stumble and laughter began to bubble forth from the people watching it all unfold.

Roaring, the Puma went for a clawing strike at Rock, only to have some of the judging shamans pounce on him instead. He stumbled as they worked their will upon him, a rope snaking out from around one of the shaman's waists to catch him and pull him away.

Leraine wanted to dismiss the incident. People got worked up. Some trained for years just to compete here during the festival. But then there were the groups of Truce Warriors walking around, daring everybody. And that murderer who could wear the face of another. It all felt like this year's festival was dry tinder, just waiting for the spark.

Chapter 14

Caught Up

EURIK WATCHED AS ONE after another failed to clear the bar. The stone toss event had been a straightforward affair. Contestants had to throw a stone the size of an apple as far as they could. It had been the only event where he could use earth *chiri*, drawn straight from the heavy stone they provided.

It had been a balancing act, too much and the stone would have disintegrated, not enough and his throw would have fallen far short of what many of his competitors were managing. But he'd gotten through that event with a respectable distance of eighty-four paces, though the best had neared a bowshot.

So it came down to this third event, jumping over a wooden rod suspended between two poles to see who could jump the highest. Touch the bar, or fail to get over it, and you were out. Already the competition had been whittled down to him, a couple of people who had done very well in stone toss, as well as Springstep and Rending Snarl. Those two had been the ones to come nearly to blows during the foot race, and neither had appreciated him butting in.

This wasn't the only group competing. There were three more around the Outer Circle. So there was no guarantee that beating everybody here would get him a win. He'd have to push and go for as high a jump as he could manage.

Rending Snarl ran at the bar, tucking in his legs he cleared the bar that already hung past Eurik's head. The man fell into the thick sack on the other side, so big it had to be shoved back into place by six people after every few landings.

One of the shamans gave Eurik a nod, he was up next. He jumped up and down, then ran at the bar. Not on a direct route, but a curving one that gave him a few extra seconds to build up the wind *chiri* that carried him over the bar.

Leraine held her breath as the bar moved, threatening to fall. Then it did, accompanied by groans and cheers as the Puma pounded the cushion. The rumors floating through the crowd told her his name was Rending Snarl, and he'd been a favorite to win this event. Had been, until Rock. Now he was out, and seeing how people were drifting in from the rest of the ring, this was the final competition.

Rending Snarl's head snapped up in the direction of the two who had cleared the jump. One was Rock, the other someone from Wolf. She'd won the running part. The member of Puma leaped off the cushion and rushed at them, yelling . . . something.

People rose up; they could see what he intended by his expression, his hands raised up and readied to claw them. But the shamans could tell as well and they stepped in.

A rope snaked out from one, wrapping itself around Rending Snarl's waist. The rope went taut, vibrating. Rending Snarl's charge slowed down, but it didn't stop. The shaman's feet scraped over the ground as he leaned back, trying to use his weight, but even that wasn't enough.

Rending Snarl finally noticed the rope, but instead of stopping he struck at it with his nails. The rope didn't snap, but it was clearly frayed. Another rope jumped out, wrapping itself around the crazed Puma's calf.

And he had to be crazed, it was obvious to all. Rending Snarl turned to the shamans trying to restrain him, only to falter as a third approached him chanting a revocation. With his connection to his spirit suppressed, he wasn't much of a threat anymore. Relieved, Leraine sank back down in her seat.

The shame will fall solely on Rending Snarl, then. Trying to attack fellow competitors, twice, even the shamans! Who could claim that it had been a transgression by Puma as a whole when he is obviously beyond reason. Still, this should not have happened in the first place.

Obviously, the shamans had figured that Rending Snarl would behave after being warned. They had been mistaken.

Leraine looked over the crowd once more. The sun was dipping below the Troll Mountains, but there was still enough light to see details. Details such as the divisions between not only between tribes, but within them. Groups of Truce Warriors, with their armored clothing, held themselves apart. Was it her imagination, or did some of them not look happy at Rending Snarl's capture?

Eurik watched them take Rending Snarl away. Springstep stared at their fellow competitor as well, then shook her head and turned to Eurik. "Now the battle is between you and me."

"Why do you say that?"

She gestured at the crowds. "The others have stopped. Haven't you noticed everyone gathering here?"

Eurik looked around, and it wasn't hard to spot it now that it had been pointed out to him. There had been a crowd before, but now people had squeezed themselves wherever there was space. He could nearly hear the wood groan under the weight. More crammed the lines below, and the stairs to the upper level were filled as well.

"I hadn't noticed."

Springstep hummed. "What do you say we stop with the pegs. Have them raise the bar by a hand and decide this now."

She won the race, but I think I threw a little farther than her. But several tossed their rock a lot more. Including Rending Snarl. And I don't know how high the others jumped. Beating her here might not mean I win the event, but it would help.

He shook his head. He wasn't here to win. The goal was to get his name out there in the hopes that someone knew his parents. But if winning helped with that . . . Fervent was almost certain to be in this crowd as well, but if he let that stop him then why was he here at all?

Springstep lifted her chin and sneered. "Very well. I—"

"That was not my answer," Eurik said. "I actually agree. Let us settle it here and now." *While there's still as large a crowd as possible.*

She hesitated, then nodded. She waved over a shaman, who came over to them. "Yes, Rending Snarl has forfeited." He sniffed. "He can't step foot in Chappenuioc for a year so he wouldn't be able to accept any prizes anyway."

"Thank you, honored one. But that was not what we wished to talk about. This—"

"Rock."

Springstep tossed her head. "Rock and I have agreed to a challenge. We would like you to raise the bar by a hand. And a hand again, if we both clear the jump."

"Is that so?" The shaman stroked his beard with two fingers. He was the first Mochedan Eurik had ever seen with one. He himself didn't need to shave at all. "I will confer." He spun away and walked over to the shamans by the bar.

Springstep let out a long breath. She looked Eurik up and down. "Where are you from, Rock? It is a strange name. Not horse people. Have the shamans let a soulless compete?"

"Rock is not . . . the name I use when I am not with the People. I grew up on San. With the plant-people."

"Plant-people? Then which spirit do you represent?"

"The world."

"The world? That's imposs—" Springstep frowned, then glanced at the jumping bar which was being raised by four pegs. "Obviously not. No human could hope to match me without aid from the spirits. Not here in Chappenuioc. Very well, Rock of the World. May the greatest spirit triumph."

"May the greatest spirit triumph."

Springstep was up first. As before, she mumbled with her eyes shut as she geared up for the attempt. The words turned to near-growls right as she opened her eyes again, and Eurik could swear her eyes flashed yellow right as Springstep began to run.

Much like Eurik himself, she took a curving path to build up a little more speed before she jumped. Springstep arced over the bar with her legs trailing, then came down and landed on her back on the cushion, which folded around her.

Eurik had to wait a while for Springstep to extricate herself and for the cushion to be moved back into place. He would have preferred a longer approach, but the starting position was fixed. Instead, he jumped in place to build up some wind *chiri* around him.

The shamans didn't react to his antics; they'd gotten used to them. At their signal, he took off. The wind whipping past carried scattered shouting from the onlookers. Focusing it all in one moment of time, he expelled all the *chiri* within him and let it launch him into the air.

He tucked his legs in as far as he could as he reached the apex of his jump. *I did it. Next round will—*

Eurik felt the tug, at his feet, at his heart. Even over the crowd and his body hitting the cushion he could hear the bar hit the stone floor of Chappenuioc. Cheering turned to groaning, which quickly got drowned as others screamed in exultation as their favored champion had just secured her victory.

Eurik himself just lay there on the cushion. He wasn't going to be winning this. He just hoped it would be enough for a spot on the podium. Not that it hadn't been fun, but he'd entered this competition to get his name out there: his, and his parents'.

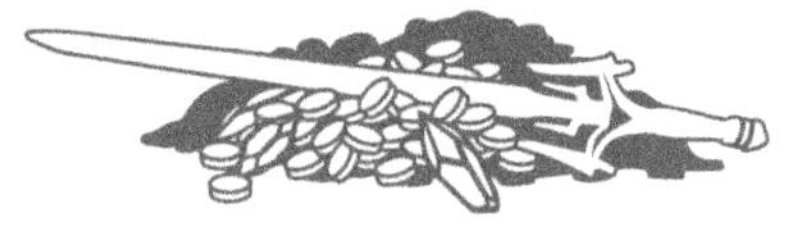

It took time for the shamans to tabulate the outcomes and figure out who had won the Three Games. Rather than waiting with her sisters and the rest, Leraine made her way down to Eurik. It wasn't easy, the crowd had grown and many were on the move. It would have been easier to climb down the outside of the stairs rather than using the steps.

Eventually though, she reached Rock. He did justice to the name she'd given him. He was a solitary boulder in a flowing river of humanity. Nobody approached him to congratulate him; they were all here for someone else. Almost everyone.

"Rock," she said, inclining her head. "You did well. Though some of those jumps looked a little awkward."

He scratched the back of his head. "Yes. I had not practiced the feat beforehand. I did not think it necessary." Rock shook his head, a small smile on his lips. "I still need much training."

"More," she corrected on reflex. "Never mind, much works as well. I'm surprised, though. I didn't think arrogance was one of your failings. Stubborn, foolish, ignorant, yes. But not arrogant."

Rock looked down at his feet. "Are you sure you didn't forget anything there?"

"Also courageous, generous, and intelligent. Sometimes you're intelligent," Leraine added when Rock looked up at her.

He looked in the direction of a pavilion that had been set up. All the shamans had disappeared inside and its entrance had been closed so that nobody could see their deliberations. A contingent of guards made sure nobody got too close. Not that anybody would dare to.

Just like nobody would dare to attack another competitor in full view of the Great Spirits and everybody?

"Do you think I made it?"

"Hmm?"

Rock nodded at the pavilion. "Do you think I got into the top three? They're the people who go onto the podium, right?"

"Yes. Those are the ones who will be named before the crowd. First place receives a golden statue, second place one of white gold, third gets a statue plated with silver. It's the same prize as the other contests."

Rock looked around. "But fewer people attend the outcome."

Indeed, all around them the crowd flowed away to the Inner Circle or out of Chappenuioc proper, drawn to the sound of music and the smells of food and drink. What remained was perhaps half of those who had actually attended the Three Games. More than a few were escorting those who stood no chance to reach the podium so that they could drown their sorrows.

"Look on the bright side. Fervent may not be here either."

"I'm of two minds on that. I have no desire to defend a person I've never met against a charge that might actually be true. I don't know. I don't remember her. But even through her victim, or her family, I might learn a little more about my mother. Is it . . . strange to feel that way?"

Leraine let out a breath. "I don't know. I never felt any need to learn much about my father. And that is the only one of my progenitors I don't know much about."

"Oh? Who was he?"

"A horse man. A wandering spellsword. Mother was taken with him, for a time. His name . . ." Leraine searched her memory. It had been over a decade since Mother had talked of him. Their affair hadn't lasted long. He wasn't happy with staying in one place for so long and she usually grew bored with men just as fast. "Betram, or Bertram." She shrugged.

Rock tilted his head to the left a little. "And you were never curious? About what happened afterward? Does he even know you exist?"

"I have no idea. I don't even know if he still lives. For all I know, he was with Griffenhart's army. I think his family had land near the Glinster." Again, a shrug. "We don't consider the father as significant. Most of the time. Girls are often raised by mothers, aunts, or even uncles. Fathers take care of the boys, with the help of uncles. But what of you? Do the san have families?"

Rock shook his head. "No, not like humans do. They don't need to have sex to procreate. I don't think they can. The san have successors that they train. But each generation is close. I suppose you could consider them brothers, or sisters. San don't have genders."

Any further discussion was forestalled by the emergence of the shamans. Fifteen of them filed out and walked in a line onto the podium where one stepped forward. Up on the Outer Ring, someone rang a large gong three times to silence the last few talkers.

"The first day of the Conclave Games has come to an end. The competitors brought much honor to their spirits, competing as they once did. The scores have been tabulated. It was close. I call to the podium, Copper Huffer, son of Amber Blaze and Brown Bristle.

Rock, son of Ardent and One Claw. Springstep, daughter of Bloodclaws and Dashing Mist. Come and be lauded."

She slapped Rock on the back. "You did it! Well done." Leraine had to shout over the applause to be heard. She gave him a little push and he made his way to the podium, head bowed and cheeks flushed.

Rock stood awkwardly on the podium, next to a grinning Springstep. Copper Huffer towered above the both of them, fists held high. Leraine could place him now. He'd come in only sixth or eighth in the race, but he had won the stone toss with a comfortable margin. He must have done well in the jumping contest as well.

The cheering died down quickly when the shaman indicated he needed silence again. "Do not think anything less of yourself if you have not made it to this podium. All of you, contestant and attendee, honor the Great Spirits by participating. We keep the memory of the Conclave alive through these games. Still, like in the first Games, some rose above others."

The shaman stepped back and another stepped forward, carrying a silver statue. It was small, no taller than Leraine's hand, and had few features. Man or woman, young or old, clothed or nude. Hard to tell. The shaman walked over to Rock and presented it. "For the World Spirit."

That set tongues waggling. It was easy to tell what spirits Springstep and Copper Huffer represented, but Rock had no *draen* nor did he dress like one of the People.

The shamans ignored the hushed whispers rising from the crowd. Another walked over to Copper Huffer, while another went to Springstep. The white gold statue went to Copper Huffer, while Springstep received the golden one. She'd won the Three Games and by extension, so had the Wolf tribe. At least she wasn't a Truce Warrior, unlike Copper Huffer.

Eurik paid little attention to Springstep and her words. She spoke of gratitude and honor, but he was more interested in the crowd. He couldn't see everybody's reaction when his parents were announced, but was anybody paying more attention to him than to Springstep right now?

Looking around, he saw that it did look like some were paying attention to him. Though was that because of his parents or the "spirit" he represented. He'd have to be deaf not to have noticed their reaction at the shaman's announcement.

Finally, Springstep finished and it didn't seem either one of them was expected to speak. *Good. I . . . would not know what to say to all these people.* The idea alone made him uncomfortable.

Stepping off the podium he met Silver Fang again. "Third place. But it got you what you wanted," she said.

"Yes. Though I'm not sure it was enough. I—" He noticed movement out of the corner of his eye. A woman approached them. Her draen was on the left side, like Silver Fang's, though she wore a leather vest with metal plates decorating it and a padded linen shirt underneath that quite a few people wore.

"You," she said. "I heard the shamans say your parents were One Claw and Ardent. What was their tribe?"

Could it be? Had this strategy already born fruit? "They were from different tribes."

Silver Fang laid a hand on his arm and spoke up. "Perhaps this is a conversation held best at another time. My friend had to give it his all. He is tired, and famished." That was true, though he hadn't told her so yet.

"This won't take long. Was your mother Ardent? Of Caetiwo?" Her eyes bored into him. One hand flexing, the other on the knife on her belt.

Hope blossomed in Eurik's chest. *Does this woman know my mother? Except she doesn't look that much older than me. Would she not have been a child when my mother left?* Before he could ask the question, though, Silver Fang spoke up again and stepped forward.

"Sept leader, allow me to introduce myself. I am Silver Fang, daughter of Raven Eye."

The woman's smile had a lot of teeth. "Oh, I know who you are. I've heard plenty of your . . . great accomplishment." Then she sighed. "Fine, fine. I'm Fervent, daughter of Stern Anvil. There, happy. Now, how about your companion intro—"

Another woman, hair gray as steel and with a large scar on the right side of her face, took a hold of Fervent's arm. "Fervent, something's—" Fervent ripped her arm out of the older woman's grip. The scarred person grabbed Fervent's arm again and pulled her toward her.

A few quick, whispered words broke Fervent's stare and she gave the weathered warrior her full attention. "What? Are you sure? Where . . ."

Silver Fang pushed Eurik away and cut him off before he could ask what she was doing with a shushing sound. He soon could neither hear nor see Fervent, only then did Silver Fang speak. "That was close."

"Why did you prevent me from answering her? Yes, I recognized the name. You were obvious. But I have this now," he said, hefting the statue. "The idea was that I could offer that to end, to stop . . ."

He grimaced and switched to Linese. "To end the hostilities between us. That's half the reason I agreed to this plan. And she obviously knew something of my mother."

"If you had offered that, she would have tried to murder you then and there."

He frowned. "How could you know that?" Though thinking back, he realized her grip on the knife had been very tight. Like she was trying to strangle the hilt.

Silver Fang looked back and at the people talking to each other. "It was obvious. She stood ready, she'd called upon the Great Serpent. She was actually poised to murder someone standing on the holy stone of Chappenuioc!"

"Wait, someone else got murdered?" The person that had spoken was an older man with a long *draen* that reached his shoulder blade. He'd been talking to a few others, but had spun around at Silver Fang's words.

Silver Fang herself froze at the man's words. "What do you mean, someone else?"

"You hadn't heard? Someone killed a shaman, Inkpaw of the Fox tribe." His gaze slid over to Eurik. "It must have been an outsider. Shouldn't be allowed to set foot in Chappenuioc."

This time, Silver Fang didn't come to his defense. In fact, she looked pale.

Eurik turned away from the man. "Are you all right?"

"I . . . yes. I just . . . hadn't expected that. Come, we best get back."

Chapter 15
A Hard Trial

THE NEWS WAS ON EVERYBODY'S lips when they reached Snake territory. The living sword was the only one who could speak about anything else. "Hey you two. How was it? Did you win? Did anybody die? I mean, other than that shaman. Come on, give me details."

Leraine shook her head. "Show some respect, Misthell. And take it seriously."

"Yes, I'd gathered from your earlier words that it was unusual," Rock said. He spoke in Linesan. Leraine wasn't sure that was a good idea, given that she'd overheard more than one speculate that an outsider must have killed Inkpaw.

"Unusual?" She refused to speak Linese. Not here, not when others could hear and wonder what they were talking about. "I . . . you'd have to ask the loretellers if this has ever happened before. Yes, people have been killed within Chappenuioc. Sometimes during a contest, accidents happen. Sometimes, passions run too high. But they are cast out, their bodies buried, their spirits severed."

Leraine dared not elaborate on that. It touched on secrets not to be shared with those not People. She shook her head. "A terrible fate. But one of us would have to be truly mad to even attempt to kill a shaman."

However, there was someone, something, that had done exactly that only yesterday. It must have been the same culprit. It was better than another answer. However, nobody but the shamans knew of that murder. People's suspicions would be focused elsewhere. This would only put more logs on the smoldering fire.

Nothing to be done for that, not by her. Instead, she turned to their own little problem. "I think it's best if you stayed with the other outsiders. Fervent will no doubt look for you and she knows who I am."

"I do not like running away," Rock said, switching to Thelauk as well. "Best to face a problem and deal with it."

"I can't disagree. But your ability to create walls and the like might be very useful in the Outsiders Quarter soon."

Rock frowned. "How so?"

Right, he had little experience with humans. "In case some decide to take justice into their own hands. A wall should at least delay them and perhaps prevent a tragedy."

"Ah. I . . . had read about that. But how do you know the killer is not an outsider? How will I know they are, uh, an angry group?"

She gave him a look. He wasn't that bad at reading people. But perhaps he wasn't asking how to recognize angry people. "If there are no guardians with them, you can be sure it is not sanctioned by the shamans."

Rock nodded.

"And I can help too," Misthell said. "I'm great at distractions. I razzle, then dazzle, and it'll be dawn before they realize what happened."

"Yes. It couldn't hurt. I think," Rock said.

"Come, I'll help you gather your belongings. I'll also talk to the shamans, find out if Fervent has approached them about you. But first we need to find you a safer place to stay."

The Outsiders Quarter lay along the Road on its north side, farther away from Chappenuioc. It didn't look as nice as the other quarters either. No worked wooden panels or colorful fabrics, only wooden poles driven into the ground twice the height of a human at a five step interval.

The dwellings within were a mishmash of wagons, lean-tos, and tents. Some looked like the ones Ghajir and his caravan had used, others were more like pointed cones or rectangular pyramids.

The only sizable open spaces were pens where a variety of animals were held. From the ordinary cow, pig, and horse to more exotic species such as a bird taller than Eurik but with very small wings. Its beak looked quite dangerous and each had a leg shackled to a steel rod in the ground in the center of their pen.

"Not much room left for someone to put down their sleeping mat," Eurik said. He watched a lizarian throw a dead rat at the giant birds; one snatched it out of the air and bit it in half. "There are people here from beyond the Wall."

"Yes," Silver Fang said. "Outsiders may not understand the festival's true importance, but they can grasp what an opportunity for trade it is. Come, we'll try to find Captain Slyvair. Perhaps he has room to spare."

It took a while to find someone who knew the orc. He did stand out with his dwarven-forged arm and bald head. It was on their way to his tent at the south end of the Outsiders Quarter that they ran across him.

"Eurik! Congratulations on ending up on the victor's podium."

Perun, however, stomped over to him. "You cost me five coppers! You threw like a girl!"

"What?"

"If he threw like a girl, he would have ended up in first place," Silver Fang said at the same time.

Perun gave her a look, then sketched a shrug with his shoulders. "Maybe. Don't change the fact that if he'd done as he was supposed to, I'd have won big. Did you know the odds on him winning?"

"I did not. Not that I would have bet on Rock anyway. I knew he was not there to win."

The boy's eyes grew a size, then he turned back to Eurik and shoved him. "What the hells? What were you thinking?"

"Please calm down. I just wanted to get the names of my parents out. I'd hoped someone knew them." He grimaced. It had worked, after a fashion.

"But you're not here for that," Slyvair said. "Or to celebrate your third place." He gave Silver Fang a look. "Are you kicking him out?"

She shook her head. "His plan worked, but not as he wanted. His mother . . ." Eurik sighed and motioned for her to continue. Keeping it a secret seemed less than useful at this time. "Stands accused of murdering the mother of Fervent. She is the current leader of Caetiwo. And she is attending the festival."

"And now you're hiding from her." Slyvair crossed his arms. "Yes, she wouldn't kill you within the Inza structure. They have very strict laws against violence there. Even the guards must take solemn vows and use quarterstaffs. Still, how far will she go if she learns you're here?"

"I don't know. She might have been on the verge of breaking those laws when she confronted me."

"In the heat of the moment, perhaps," Silver Fang quickly said. "But with some time for her liver to settle, she will do the smart thing. Go to the shamans and demand justice. Just killing you when you are a guest of Urumoy would put her sept at odds with ours. It risks breaking the Great Trust. But Fervent may need some time to realize that. Best to give her that time."

Slyvair frowned at Silver Fang. "You could think of no other place to stay?"

"There is another reason," Eurik said. "Silver Fang worries about the people here. A shaman was killed within Chappenuioc and some of the Mochedan suspect—well, someone who isn't Mochedan."

Slyvair bared his teeth and growled deep in his throat. "I'd heard something about that. But I thought it an exaggeration. That someone had merely had an accident. How serious is it?"

Silver Fang looked around. "Perhaps we should talk of this somewhere more private." She looked down at Perun.

The boy squinted. "You're not sending me away. I can hear whatever you want to talk about. I can keep a secret."

Slyvair rested a hand on Perun's head. "You sure, boy?"

"Yeah." He ducked out from underneath the orc's large hand. "I'm not a child. I'm thirteen now!"

"Well, then. We'll retire to my tent. Come."

It was a short walk. Slyvair's tent wasn't very big, however, and got more cramped with four people inside. The orc and his ward sat on their sleeping mats while Eurik took a seat on the ground at the back of the tent. Silver Fang squatted near the entrance, eyes downcast.

"There's a little space to our right. You could fit one of those stone shelters of yours. If I decide to let you stay here," Slyvair said. He turned his attention to Silver Fang. "Now out with it. You know something about this murder and it is obviously serious."

"I suspect. I . . . worry." Her jaw worked but no more words came.

Slyvair huffed. "Well?"

Silver Fang twined her fingers and pressed her thumbs against one another. "I don't know much of this murder, I have no special insight in this murder. But I worry it may form a pattern."

"Your broken bones!" Eurik reared back, his cheeks heating up as three pairs of eyes stared at him. "Sorry, I should not have spoken so loudly. But Silver Fang, something happened yesterday. I healed the fractures in your arms, someone struck you with great force. You refused to speak about it."

"You healed me, yes." Again, she fell silent.

"You are usually more forthright, girl," Slyvair said. "Now we have to drag the words out of you. And you speak carefully. Have your priests ordered you not to speak?"

"Shamans, Captain Slyvair. Priests serve gods and my people have no need for their sort." Silver Fang said nothing more.

"One day you must explain to me the difference. Hmm, but you wouldn't have us retire to my tent if you didn't intend to tell us anything."

"Oh, it's a riddle," Perun said. "You . . . you can't talk about something. But you want to warn us?"

Silver Fang tapped her thumbs together.

Slyvair let out a short bark of laughter. "Following the letter of the command, but not its spirit." He sobered and plucked his lip with his right hand. "We only traveled together for a short while. But you struck me as one who held her own honor very high. You must be very worried to skirt around your people's laws like this."

"This wasn't the first shaman who was murdered," Eurik said. It made sense. Whatever had happened yesterday, it had happened in the heart of Chappenuioc. Few books had gone into detail about this place, but all agreed that no outsider was allowed there. And Silver Fang had gone in the company of a shaman, one he didn't recall seeing afterward. Nor was she one of the shamans judging the contests.

"Someone's killing off Mochedan priests—shamans—during their most important festival," Slyvair said. "Yeah, I can see why they'd want to keep that below the surface. And you caught the murderer?"

Silver Fang made a motion with her head. It could be a yes, or a no.

"The murderer caught you," Perun said. He grinned when Silver Fang bobbed her head.

Slyvair leaned forward. "But the injuries you sustained were the ones you'd get if you'd fought back. You got a look at the murderer. You know who they are."

Silver Fang, however, shook her head after hesitating.

Perun's frown deepened. "But how can you fight someone and not know what they look like? That don't make sense! Oh, unless he was wearing a mask. Was he disguised?"

"Hey, you already had your turn," Misthell said.

"But I made a right guess! So I get another."

"That's not in the rules."

"Yes, it is."

"No, it's not."

"Is too."

The living sword's words rang out. "Is not!"

"Misthell!" "Perun!"

Slyvair and Eurik looked at one another. The orc looked away while he muttered an apology.

"I should go," Silver Fang said and she turned halfway toward the entrance. "All I can say is that you all need to be careful. I do not know what will happen. But I worry things will grow worse and that the people here may become a target."

She went to leave, then hesitated and looked back over her shoulder. "I'll speak with the shamans myself, find out if Fervent has approached them yet. And . . . be prepared for an attack from an unexpected direction."

"Thank you for warning us," Slyvair said. "I'll not let Perun out of my sight again."

"But I—" A single glance from the orc and the boy's teeth clicked against each other. He looked away, arms crossed. "I can take care of myself."

Eurik got up as well. "We are not the ones you should worry about. You will be alone."

But Silver Fang shook her head. "And that is where you are wrong. I am surrounded by my sisters. I have not been safer in some time. Until tomorrow. Fight well."

"You as well." He'd actually forgotten about the next contest.

Should I? No, the plan holds. Get as many people as possible to hear my parents' names and hope someone will recognize them. Other than Fervent. The combat events are the most popular, so they remain my best chance. And with all eyes on me, I should be safer. Right?

Chapter 16
Test of Mettle

THE FESTIVAL WENT ON. One, or even two murders did not deter the shamans. In some ways, it only made it more important that they continue. And as the hour of the next event drew near, even talk of Inkpaw's murder and speculation on who was responsible gave way to talk of who was favored to win the armed and unarmed combat events. But talk of the former did not disappear.

Leraine was glad she had not agreed to meet Rock and the others somewhere before it started. She hadn't really thought about it, but it turned out Fervent had set someone to follow her in hopes of leading her to Rock's location. She wasn't very good at it, or maybe everything that had already happened had Leraine on edge.

She stopped and glanced back, made sure to be obvious about it. The girl spun around, trying hard to look like she was examining a dwarf's wares. Yes, not great at stalking prey through a crowd.

Leraine set off once more. Both events were held at the same time, on podia that ran along the length of the Outer Circle. One podium would hold unarmed bouts, the next one for armed combat, and the next unarmed again, and so on.

She'd been assigned to the Pangolin podium. An auspicious sign, only slightly below being assigned to the one dedicated to Ghisa herself. But that one was to be used for unarmed combat in these preliminary rounds.

Craning her neck, she searched for the right banner and found it flapping in the stiff wind that blew through Chappenuioc today. It carried the chill from the mountains in the north and gave warning that summer was giving way.

She didn't see anybody she knew. Rock would have naturally been assigned elsewhere and it looked like the same was true for Captain Slyvair. Leraine spared one glance for the two squaring off right now. A man from Boar and one from Orca, both armed with a wooden sword and a small shield. They wouldn't be facing someone with a spear until after the preliminary rounds.

Their stance, the way they held their weapons, showed they were well trained. But how often had they truly faced off against someone who aimed to kill them? That question she would only know once they got into it. For now, she took the time to check her own equipment.

The weapons were the property of Chappenuioc and wouldn't be distributed until the match started. But their protective clothing they had to acquire themselves. It was the reason why the armed combat competition tended to attract those who could afford it.

Leraine left her padded jacket open for now. Even with the chill breeze it would be too warm. Same reason she carried the open-faced helmet under the crook of her arm. The trousers weren't padded, just had a double layer of linen. All of it had been dyed green, yellow, and blue: the colors of Urumoy.

A combination of a cheer and a groan erupted, but all Leraine saw when she looked up was the Boar warrior staggering away. The Orca warrior was on the ground, covering his face.

"Silver Fang of Urumoy," one of the presiding shamans called out, pointing to her left. Then she gestured to her right. "Trollbane Oak of Auchariuc."

Even before she caught sight of her opponent, Leraine cursed her luck. It didn't stop her from fastening her jacket and donning her helmet. But why did a Trollbane have to be her first opponent? You couldn't get that name unless you'd killed more than three trolls.

The man that stepped up could have some troll in his ancestry. Easily a head taller than her with broad shoulders. His lower lip hung on his right side where a troll's claws had left a nasty scar. His *draen* told her he was Bear. He came onto the podium with his arms raised up, propelled by the cheering of the crowd. A local favorite.

Must be nice.

The shaman who had called them forth stayed in the middle of the podium, while two others came forward to present sword and shield to the two contestants. Oak's sword wasn't any longer than hers, but those arms would give him the edge in reach.

The sword was a simple length of polished ash with a disk of the same material that functioned as the guard. The shield covered little more than the hand and was thick. It wouldn't be the same as her preferred dagger, but she'd trained with this setup.

"Are you ready?"

"I am," Leraine said, stepping forward. Oak did the same. No, he swaggered to the line painted on the stage. Still, she did the right thing and gave her opponent a bow that almost forced her to take her eyes off of him. Oak gave half of that.

He is insulting me. Deliberately.

She blew out her anger. This was not the time or place for it. The insult could very well be intended to make her sloppy. She'd done much the same not so long ago. But there was a time and a place for a tactic, and this was the wrong one. Judging from some of the sounds from the people watching, he'd offended not only Leraine with that display.

"The first to get three blows, first blood, or force their opponent off the podium wins," the shaman said. "If I call a point, you stop. If

I call out a winner, you stop. If your opponent surrenders, you stop. If you strike your opponent afterward, you are out of the Games for the next nine years. Or longer. Do you understand."

That last part was new. A consequence of Rending Snarl's behavior yesterday?

The shaman's eyes bored into Leraine, not relenting when she nodded. "Yes." That word finally released her and the shaman turned his gaze upon Oak. He quickly said, "I understand."

"Then begin." The shaman stepped back as he said it.

Both brought up their weapon and buckler, but neither moved from their spot right away. Leraine had gone for a high guard. Shield arm extended, sword arm bent with the blade angled above her head. Oak had tucked his buckler in more with the sword resting against it, ready for a stab.

Leraine opened her soul to Ghisa entirely and the world relaxed. It all moved a little slower, more obvious. When Oak moved, so did she. His weapon slid along her buckler, which had appeared in its path. But the power behind that stab could not be denied. The buckler twisted in her grasp and she had to lean out of the way as the sword kept going. Her own arm came around at the same time, slamming into Oak's wrist before he could pull back. He didn't flinch.

"Point, Silver Fang!"

Both froze, Oak only had to take one step back to return to their starting positions. It wasn't just his arms, his strides let him bridge greater distances in one quick motion, too.

The Bear gives him great strength. I cannot try to block any of his strikes with just my buckler or I'm out entirely.

She gritted her teeth as she brought the buckler back into position. Oak caught her discomfort and bared his teeth. "A lucky hit."

"I only—"

"Begin!"

No waiting this time. Oak brought his sword around for a swing at her side. Right fist behind the buckler, she slammed the small shield into it. The shock traveled through her arms while Oak's sword bounced off. Leraine turned block into a stab but he threw his head back.

Another swing, overhead. Sidestepped.

Not using his buckler?

Oak swung through trying to get his sword back into position while thrusting the buckler in her direction. But it was not a practiced move. All it did was offer his other wrist as a target.

"Point, Silver Fang."

Oak roared, but retreated. So did Leraine, after a moment. The shaman had barely stepped back for the third round when Oak pressed forward. He swung his sword around in a tight pattern, it whistled through the air.

Leraine hissed, but she had to retreat. She could dodge, but by the time she could get close enough, that sword would come back around. She turned her retreat into a circle, she had to if she didn't want to end up tumbling off the podium.

Right. He's clearly used to fighting trolls and the like. With a proper shield and an axe. Or a spear. Lots of power, but not used to an intelligent adversary. How to use this?

The Bear warrior took a sudden, big step forward and brought his blade up. Leraine went for a block, no other option left, but her arms buckled and the wood slammed into her side. Gasping for breath, she staggered.

"Point, Trollbane Oak!"

"Might want to give up. Or you'll be going to the healer instead of the loser's bracket," Oak said.

He is used to being the hunter. That's what I'm doing wrong.

"How about . . . you? Will . . . your ego . . . survive?" It hurt to breathe. But with every exhale, the pain slackened. By the time the shaman told them to resume, it had become a dull throb that flared when she brought up her buckler and sprang forward.

Her blade licked out, high, low, high, low. Oak brought his buckler back up, for a moment he lost sight of her. The blunted point of her sword dug into his belly and the air rushed out of his lungs. Leraine caught a hint of breakfast, spiced flatbread.

"Point, Silver Fang. Winner, Silver Fang of Urumoy!"

Leraine bowed to him, Oak didn't. Or he couldn't come out of his bow, depending on how you looked at it. Giving her buckler and sword back, she walked off the podium with her head held high.

Hopefully the rest won't give me this much trouble or I'll be one big bruise by tonight. Wonder if Rock is doing any better?

Eurik danced with the wind, slapping a punch away and chopping the upper arm right after. His opponent shrugged it off, like she had everything else. He kept moving, ducking, evading, attacking.

This was his third fight of the day and sweat glued his shirt to his back. The morning had started off refreshingly cool, but the sun had burned through the clouds and he'd been fighting this woman for what felt like hours now.

His first two bouts hadn't been this difficult. But this Iron Sow took everything he threw at her and kept going. The fight would only end if one of them was knocked out, any part of their body touched the outside of the square, or they gave up. How was he going to do that to Iron Sow?

She went for a grab, Eurik dodged.

Iron Sow moved slow to him; the whole world did. But he couldn't get enough power behind his attacks to get through whatever defenses her spirit gave her. If only he could access earth *chiri*, this fight would be over. He could have overpowered Iron Sow and simply thrown her out of the square. Instead, it was him who was in constant threat of being pushed out.

Eurik jumped back to put some distance between them. The wind ruffled the clothes of the referees.

"I don't recognize your style," Iron Sow said.

She made no move to close the distance, but Eurik had to keep moving or lose the wind *chiri* rushing through his body. "It's not Mochedan."

She grunted. "Strange. You move too fast for it to be natural."

"I dance with the wind." The breeze that carried the memory of the white tops of the mountains up north flowed past him. And perhaps that was his answer. The wind came in many flavors. Rather than pelting Iron Sow with the whirling blows of a storm, perhaps he should be the sharp blow of a gale.

"But this ain't a dance!" Iron Sow rushed him.

Eurik met that charge, then jumped clear over her. He had to balance this right. Landing in a crouch, he stopped moving for the first time this match. Eurik drew in the wind *chiri*. It had already stopped building up, and in the blink of an eye it would slip through his grasp entirely. But for a single breath, it all concentrated in him.

Iron Sow skidded to a halt and turned around when he uncoiled and launched himself at her. He threw his arms forward, not in a punch, but a push. His opponent couldn't miss the move and braced for it, but she'd set herself to resist a fighter; a human. His palms slammed into her and the full force of the mountain wind rushed from his hands into her. It picked her up like a leaf.

Arms flailing she sailed into the crowd. Eurik was still. It had been a gamble, putting it all in one move. If Iron Sow had been strong enough to resist all that force, if she'd evaded the blow, if he'd timed it wrong, he would have had nothing left to fight her with. Given Iron Sow's skill, that small window of vulnerability would have cost him the match.

The judges looked from her to him, then at each other. One nodded, then the other. "Winner, Rock of San!"

There was some cheering and applause, but as Eurik looked over the hundreds—thousands even—watching him and others compete he couldn't help but feel alone. He didn't see Leraine, or Slyvair, not even Perun. These were all strangers.

He bowed to the crowd and made his way off the platform. He needed to think. If he didn't come up with something he wasn't going to make it through the next day.

Chapter 17

A Safe Bet

ROCK LOOKED TROUBLED as he emerged from the crowd. It wasn't difficult: as the day had progressed the people watching had segregated themselves, leaving spaces open between them. They had fractured not only by tribe or sept either. The Truce Warriors were easy to pick out, and the others had to be so-called Traditionalists.

"Hey," he said.

"Hey. Were you victorious?" He gave her a nod, though it was stiff. And the way he held himself . . . "You had a hard time of it, I see."

"So did you. There's a hitch every time you breathe in."

Leraine grimaced. Her side and arm flared up as if Rock's words banked the pain—like it were a slumbering campfire. "A few looked to try and cut with a blunt, wooden sword. It didn't work, but it's not pleasant. Nothing is broken," she said, waving away Rock's hand.

On the podium, the victorious Wolf strode back to his supporters while the Crocodile shot him a furious glare. Those supporters wore the garments of Truce Warriors, and not all were Wolf tribe. Indeed, one was Snake.

"Evident Spark of Urumoy." Joyous Bell's daughter stepped away from them and jumped up onto the podium. "Slyvair of Volsom." The mercenary captain thumped up the steps. Unlike Evident Spark, he did not wear much in the way of protection. His new left arm gleamed in the sun.

"You are still in?"

Leraine looked down at the boy; she hadn't noticed Perun getting so close to her. "Yes."

"So far," Rock said right after.

Perun nodded. "Good." His face scrunched up. "The . . . kaptin . . . he wants to fight you." He glanced at Rock. "Does not want you losing too fast . . . too." His Linesan continued to improve.

"And I see Captain Slyvair has done well as well," Leraine said. Indeed, the sun-man looked uninjured. Then again, who ever heard of a bruised sun-man?

Still, Perun swelled. "He don't need magic. He just better."

"He is good. Still, some of the people I fought didn't just rely on their magic," Rock said.

"You see. Watch."

On the podium, Captain Slyvair greeted his opponent. Evident Spark, however, did not. Leraine pressed her lips together at the fool girl's disrespect. It was worrying to see her own experience was not an isolated incident.

Girl? She's a year older than me. But she's not acting like it.

Evident Spark's limbs moved with the flowing grace that Ghisa's aid granted. She held the buckler fully extended and moved it lightly. Leraine recognized her intention, another sign Evident Spark underestimated her opponent.

Captain Slyvair didn't fixate on the shield and slammed his buckler into hers as he pressed forward. Evident Spark swiped at his leg, but the older sun-man parried then swept his blade up. If it had been steel, he would have lopped Evident Spark's left arm off with that move. As it was, it earned him a point while her fellow Snake warrior stumbled back, cradling her arm.

They returned to their starting positions. This time, Evident Spark took Captain Slyvair more seriously. The sword blurred and spun in her hand as she attacked, the sun-man needing to use both buckler and sword to defend himself.

"Yes, your captain is very good," Leraine said. "But he is still but flesh. And flesh falters." The end came quickly. Evident Spark fixed his sword with her buckler just after he'd blocked another strike. It left him open and Evident Spark chopped at his leg. Given their disparity in height, it was the best target available.

"Point to Evident Spark!"

"Lucky hit," Perun said in Irelian as he crossed his arms. Then he started shouting in encouragement in the same language.

The third clash ended in three strokes. Evident Spark tried to use her speed again to dominate Captain Slyvair while the sun-man sought to counter. He tried to stay in contact, turn it into a wrestling match. But Ghisa made Evident Spark too fast and the moment her blade slipped away from his buckler its slashed across his right arm.

"Luck!"

Leraine bestowed him an amused smile. Evident Spark was not her favorite person in the world, though that was more because of her mother than anything. But there was still some pride—however reluctant—that one member of her tribe and sept was doing so well.

However, that amusement died when she saw Perun's glance across the podium to something on the other side, or someone. She didn't recognize him, but his *draen* told her he was Falcon, and the gold he'd used therein spoke of wealth. Not the markings of a leader, though. A merchant then, one who prospered.

But why is Perun looking so nervous?

On the podium, the combatants clashed once more. Captain Slyvair had the right idea: make Evident Spark react to him instead of the other way around. It wouldn't counter her speed, not quite, but there was power behind those swings that Evident Spark struggled to stave off.

"Yes! Yes! Get her!" Perun jumped up and down.

Evident Spark caught the sun-man's blade with her own and her buckler. She slid her blade up in a counterstroke which in turn got caught. Captain Slyvair pushed it away and lunged forward. She threw herself to the side and struck.

The shaman extended a hand down the middle of the podium. "Simultaneous hit, no point!"

"No!" Perun turned to her. "He hit first!"

"I could not see from this angle," Leraine said. "Evident Spark dodged, so it must have bought her a moment. But the shamans have a better view." Certainly Captain Slyvair didn't seem perturbed by the pronouncement.

"But he must win!"

"There is no guarantee. Evident Spark is well trained and she has the Great Serpent to aid her. The odds favor her." As she said that, and saw Perun cast another furtive glance, a suspicion reared its head. "Perun, did you make a bet?"

He shrugged. "Maybe." The boy looked at Captain Slyvair. "He supposed to win."

They squared off again, this time Captain Slyvair fell back when Evident Spark surged forward. He stayed out of range, baiting her to chase him around the podium.

"Stand and fight, you co—" Evident Spark's shout turned to a yelp as the sun-man stopped and lunged at her. She almost didn't get her buckler in position and her own slash only hit air. Her fellow Snake warrior pressed forward but Captain Slyvair resumed his retreat.

He can't keep this up. She's already trying to herd him into a corner.

He had noticed that himself and feinted to his left, then sprung forward, slashing at Evident Spark. So focused had she been on attack that the idea of defending took precious time to take hold. Too long, her clumsy block fell apart and Captain Slyvair's wooden sword thwacked her on the shoulder.

"Point to Slyvair!"

"I wasn't aware people were betting on these fights," Rock said.

"Of course they are . . . Let me guess. Betting is another thing the san do not do."

He shrugged. "Not much to bet with. They—we—have no need for money or much in the way of wealth. Our houses, I suppose? What would you do with two houses? You can only sleep under one roof at a time."

Perun sniffed. "Said by someone never been poor. I will not be. I am going to be rich!"

Leraine looked at the merchant again. He looked tense himself. "How much did you bet?"

The boy didn't look at her, his foot scraped over the ground. "It . . . I bet big."

She squinted. "How much, Perun? More than you have?"

"Mebbe."

"Ah," Rock said. "What happens if you lose more than you can pay? I know you can lose your freedom in Linese and Irelia."

"The same is true here. Especially when the debt is owned by an outsider."

"He going win." His command of Linesan faltered as he hunched his shoulders and set himself against the future. A future that arrived now as Captain Slyvair and Evident Spark exchanged blows for the last time.

Clack, clack, clack. Slyvair grunted, bending forward as Evident Spark's sword dug into his stomach. But her knees buckled under the blow on her shoulder. A hushed silence descended upon the crowd as the three shamans conferred. Their shawls hid some of the discussion, but the gesticulating of one of them told Leraine it was not an easy decision.

"He won, he won, he won," Perun said.

Rock said nothing, but shook his head when their gazes met. One moment later one of the shamans turned away while the other crossed her arms. The third stepped forward and waited for a heart beat longer before pointing. "Point to Evident Spark. Evident Spark of Urumoy wins."

"No!" Her hand landed on Perun's shoulder before he could rush the stage. "Let go. Let go of me!"

He'd returned to Irelian and Leraine answered him in the same language. "He fought well. It was a close thing."

"You just say that cause she's one of you. Same as the—" He faltered under her stare.

"It's not a wise thing to suggest the shamans are biased. Especially during the Conclave Games. Especially when there is no evidence of that. Now, here comes Captain Slyvair. Did he even know you wagered on the outcome of this fight?"

Perun looked away. She only caught a mutter but she could guess what word Perun didn't want to say.

But nothing more could be said on it, as the sun-man had good ears and he'd caught sight of her and Rock. "You fought well, Captain Slyvair," she said, switching back to Linesan.

"Yes, it was a close thing," Rock said.

"Not close enough." Captain Slyvair shook his head and raised his new left arm up. "It responds well, but a few weeks training is not enough to condition a limb of flesh and blood. I should have figured it would not be enough for one of steel and crystal either."

"And the skill of your opponent had nothing to do with it?"

He gave a tired chuckle. "It's not the skill that made the difference. No offense to your people, but some of the fighters in this competition are not that good. They've had training, yes, but they lack experience."

"We've had a peaceful few years."

Captain Slyvair nodded, but his attention had turned to Perun who had said nothing and wasn't even looking at the sun-man. He put his hand on the boy's head. "Buck up. I'm not out of this yet. And I never thought I could win it all anyway."

At that Perun finally looked up. "Yes, you can!" He still wasn't using Linesan. "You're the best! You don't even need magic to beat spellswords! These beastlies—"

"Perun!" The sun-man's voice cracked like a whip. "What have I said of such words?" He leaned in, casting a shadow over the boy.

"It's all right. I'm sure he meant nothing by it," Leraine said.

Rock said nothing as he couldn't follow the conversation. His Irelian remained quite poor.

But Captain Slyvair grunted and shook his head. "No, that's even worse. You say what you mean or you don't speak at all. And what have I said about disrespecting an enemy who has beaten you?"

"It says worse things about yourself." Every line and motion of the boy spoke of sullen resentment. "Because they were good enough to beat you."

"And?"

"No such thing as a fair fight."

The sun-man gave a sharp nod. "Just so. You'll almost never face an enemy that is your equal in skill, in gear, in strength, in power, and a hundred other things. You do your best to bring the odds in your favor and this time, I didn't do enough. But winning is not about defeating the enemy, it is about getting what you want. And I wanted—no, needed—practice."

Leraine decided not to speak of Perun's bet. Still, when they headed out for a bite to eat she turned to Rock. She did make sure to speak in Thelauk. "First Misthell, now Perun. You wouldn't be so foolish as to bet on the outcome of my matches, right?"

"No. I leave the betting to Misthell. And he is earning his keep these days. When I left he had a whole new audience to entertain over at the Outsider quarter."

"And you're not worried about someone stealing the unattended living sword?"

"Not sure. How long do you think before they'd try to return him, you think?"

Nibbling on her lower lip, Leraine hummed. "A day?"

He grinned. "Surely not. Given how valuable he is, they'll hold out for at least two!" Rock shook his head. "But no, I'm not worried. I set him up next to a merchant. He agreed to guard him in exchange for some of the money Misthell earned. And pulling him out of the little stage I made for him would take a pickaxe."

Music drifted through the evening's air. From his seat on the bench Eurik could just see the one producing it. He had a long, fairly flat wooden box lying on its back before him with nearly a dozen long strings. The man plucked at them and notes sprang forth.

The food was good as well. Salmon baked in clay with several herbs, it just about melted on his tongue. This, he could get used to. Leraine's elbow dug into his side and Eurik finally looked away from the musician. "Yes?"

"I asked how you were feeling about the next round. The competition will only get tougher." Thankfully, it wasn't happening tomorrow. They were giving the competitors a day to rest and recuperate. Instead, there were archery competitions and a game called spear-tossing. That one involved throwing and catching blunt spears.

He gave out a sigh. "What can I do? I'm still learning Dance of the Whirlwind. If I had access to earth, I could switch. But trying to use a Way when you don't have access to the right *chiri* while you're facing, well, someone like you, that's not going to work. Maybe if I could bring a stone and set it in the corner. Or wear jewelry during a fight. Yes," he said before Silver Fang could. "I know the rules. That's not going to work."

I could absorb earth chiri outside Chappenuioc and then carry it inside. But it wouldn't be easy and I'd lose it quickly if I used it. And I'm not good enough to combine the Ways yet so I'd have to lose it all if I wanted to use wind.

He became aware of someone approaching just as Silver Fang looked past him, her eyes growing nearly two sizes when she caught sight of something. It was a shaman, a familiar one. Yes, she was one of the people who had decided if he represented a world spirit. Sharp Prong, that's what the rest had called her. She was accompanied by several guards and they were coming right at him.

"Rock, son of One Claw and Ardent," she said.

"Uh, yes."

Sharp Prong's lips twisted and she held up her bronze rod. "Is your mother Ardent, daughter of Reed Dagger, once of Caetiwo?"

"I don't know."

"You don't know?" She made a noise in the back of her throat. "Don't get clever with me, boy. You claimed parentage, how could you not know? Or were you lying?"

"No. But I only have a name and that she was probably a blacksmith."

"Right, well, we'll sort this out, then. But not here. Come along. And I hope this is the last trouble you'll give us. We've got more important things to deal with." Her gaze strayed toward Silver Fang before snapping back to focus on him.

"Yes. But could we make a detour? If we want to clear up who my parents were, I do have a witness. Of a sort."

"Yes, yes. Best we round them up as well. I don't want to have this take all evening."

"Thank you. Ah, but he's not allowed into Chappenuioc."

Sharp Prong waved her rod under his nose, nearly stabbing it into his face. "What? If he is a criminal, an oathbreaker, then his testimony is worthless anyway."

"No, his kind is not allowed into the rings. He's a sword."

"What?"

Chapter 18
Taken In

THEY DREW ATTENTION as they made their way into Chappenuioc. Misthell wasn't helping with that, as he insisted on a running commentary on everything he saw. "Will you look at that. What keeps them upright? And look at all that fabric, thousands must have worked to make all of it. Is this where you fought?"

"Not quite. I fought over on the stage marked by a standing bear." Misthell was the only friendly . . . face here. He'd placated Slyvair and Perun, told them not to worry and that he'd resolve this soon. As for Silver Fang, she'd accompanied him back to the Outsiders Quarter, but then had left to go get Blue Scale, a loremistress who had come along from Urumoy.

One of the guards carried the sword over her left shoulder. Her right hand gripped a cudgel and she'd take a step away whenever Eurik got too close for her liking.

There were fewer people here in the Outer Circle. Mostly they were cleaning up. The Mochedan respected Chappenuioc, that was clear even to him, but litter and sand found a way. Misthell's voice wasn't drowned out by the partying, and many of the sweepers stared as they passed them, up the Outer Ring and over to the Inner Ring.

The sky was dark. A waxing moon, accompanied by the first stars, illuminated the rope bridge with its pale light. The awnings cast much of the inner parts of Chappenuioc in deep darkness. Looking down, Eurik wondered if the murderer Silver Fang had warned them about hid in there. Or were they off mingling in the feasting crowd?

He shook his head. That murderer wasn't his concern right now. Finally, he found himself in front of a row of seated people once again.

There were only five of them and they didn't have the shawls or rods of shamans, though just about all wore some jewelry. A ring or two around their fingers, or a bit of silver threaded through their *draen*. One had a bronze pin closing a short cape richly decorated, while another wore a thin plate of gold shaped like a crescent moon on his chest with a wolf chasing after a crow depicted upon it. Sharp Prong gestured at Eurik. "I present to you Rock, son of One Claw and Ardent."

One of the seated people—the armrests of his chair ended in snarling cats—leaned forward to get a better look at him. Oil lamps of glass and bronze had been hung from poles, providing light for the group. The fabric above their heads rippled and clapped in the stiffening wind.

Thanks to that light, he had a clear picture of Fervent's expression as she stared daggers at him. Next to her, another woman stood. Maybe a loreteller? They didn't stand out like the shamans. Apparently it could be read from the *draen*, but how to read one of those was one of those secrets Silver Fang wouldn't tell him.

"So you didn't run away like your mother did."

Should he defend his mother? What if she had done the deed? Eurik just didn't know. He didn't know her. But he knew himself. "Was there a reason?" Regardless of what Ardent had done or not done, he wouldn't be afraid. Not of this.

"Testing Fork," one of the loretellers said, the one in the middle of the row. By coincidence, this one was both old and a woman, just like the last time he stood in judgment before a bunch of seated people. The snake on her chair told him something. There were a lot of things a man wasn't allowed to do or be in the Snake tribe. Including becoming either a shaman or a loreteller.

"Kindly remind your *rangtauk* that she is here to prove her case. Judgments are reserved to the court." The word she used wasn't quite that, though it basically meant that in Linesan. Justice was a more happenstance thing in this society. Coran of Pelagrianorum's *On the Nature of Law* had devoted several chapters on the various Mochedan tribes and how they differed.

And none of that is going to help me here. The book's over a century old and things change. I just have to stall for Blue Scale to get here. And remind myself that it is my mother who's on trial here. Not me.

Testing Fork inclined her head. "Of course. No such disrespect was intended, Steel Cobra." Her voice was smooth, almost like it could slide into a song at a moment's notice. "But I must also correct you. The case was proven twenty years ago. The question we put before you is whether this . . . outsider is indeed the offspring of Ardent. And to have him tell us where the murderer is."

"Objection," Misthell said. "I dispute that assertion."

"Why," Steel Cobra said, cutting through the living sword's words, "is there a sword here? And why is it talking?"

Sharp Prong shifted her weight. "It's supposedly a witness. I thought it best to bring it along if it was true."

Steel Cobra shook her head. "Well, that is in your power. Though can we call a possession as a witness?"

"We can," another loreteller said. He sat in the bear chair, his feet dangling off of the ground. "Slaves can testify to facts. They are only barred from giving evidence that would exonerate their master. That's precedent that property may participate in a trial."

"Well, then," Steel Cobra said, giving Misthell a harsh look. "Be silent until you are called to testify. This is not some soulless trial with lawyers and juries." Those two words were said in heavily accented Linesan.

She turned her attention back to Eurik. "You say you are the son of Ardent. Did that Ardent live in Caetiwo twenty years ago?"

"I don't know. I only know my mother's name through Misthell here."

"Misthell?"

"Still think we should allow that to give testimony?" someone else said, laying a hand on the Bear loreteller.

And Eurik dearly wished he could have had words with his parents right then and there. Relying on a witness whose name was basically Liar wasn't going to do him any favors here. "I didn't pick his name."

"Right." Steel Cobra gestured at the guard holding Misthell who stepped forward. "Very well . . . sword. You claim that this young man is the offspring of One Claw and Ardent. How do you know this?"

"I am glad you asked," Misthell said, his voice ringing out. "It all began in blood and storm, some seventeen years ago. I woke up—"

"What? No illusions? I had heard you drew crowds with your illusions," the loreteller wearing the big golden necklace said.

"Well, if you want, I could liven up my testimony."

"That will not be necessary. Your words should suffice, or not," Steel Cobra said. "Continue."

"You su— Right, where was I? Yes, as I said before I got interrupted, I awoke one bloody, stormy night out at sea. The salty spray—"

"We are not here for stories," Fervent said, only to fall silent when the seated loretellers stared at her.

Then Steel Cobra nodded. "You are not here to apply for an apprenticeship, sword. Let us stick to simple facts. What is your connection with Rock and his parents?"

"Ruin my performance, why don't you. Some people have no appreciation for my art. Fine, fine. I was made by One Claw and Ardent nineteen years ago in Vanha Forest. Rock here is their son."

The loreteller in the puma chair spoke up before anybody else could. "This One Claw, he was of the Puma tribe?"

Running feet pounded on the walkway and Eurik saw Silver Fang drag a huffing Blue Scale along. She gave him a nod while Misthell answered a couple more questions about his father. Though why the interest in him? Had this shaman known him?

"I see they've started already," Silver Fang said.

"Sort of. They're asking Misthell questions right now to see if my mother is the right Ardent."

Blue Scale couldn't stay upright and clutched her left side with her right hand. "Is . . . that . . . in . . . question?"

"I am not sure she is. Probably?"

"Right. Do we . . . want to fight them . . . on this?" Blue Scale straightened out as her breathing grew less laborious. "I don't recommend it."

Fervent was whispering something in Testing Fork's ear as well. The loreteller nodded and stepped forward. "We are not here for this One Claw. It is clear they met after the murder. So instead, I'd like to know what this . . . blade knows of its other creator. Ardent, daughter of Reed Dagger."

"Didn't know she was the daughter of Reed Dagger," Misthell said. "Or where she was from. I can show you what she looks like and that's it. My creators didn't impart their own life stories to me, and I woke up unplanned."

"That can work," Testing Fork said. "I knew her. And her victim."

Blue Scale stepped forward. She did something with her voice; it had a whole different quality than when she'd spoken to him. "Please, let's not jump ahead here."

"Blue Scale," Steel Cobra said. "You're defending the boy?"

"I am."

"Hmm. Good. Having to suffer an outsider blunder through this process is bad enough when we don't have more important things to worry about." She slashed with her hand and Fervent's teeth clicked shut without having uttered a word. Steel Cobra nodded. "Good. Now, your description."

A figure appeared before the seated loretellers. A woman perhaps a hand shorter than Eurik. Brownish hair cut short, like Silver Fang, with a *draen* that had a little iron hammer hanging from it. It wasn't a statue; there was life to the image. It gave the impression of strength, a fighter, a maker of things. There were scars on her arms and her face, her nose a little crooked.

I never did ask Misthell what they'd looked like. Why hadn't I?

"I'm satisfied," Testing Fork said. "The scars, the particulars of her *draen*. This sword has shown us Ardent, daughter of Reed Dagger. Now tell us where she is!"

"Oh, I thought I'd been clear on that," Misthell said. "Both she and One Claw died nineteen years ago. It's what awakened me."

Fervent balled her fists so tight they nearly turned white. "Then the son will answer for his mother's crime!"

"That's what we're here to determine," Blue Scale said. "I've heard accusations, I've heard murder, but what is the evidence? What was the crime?"

"Oh no," Steel Cobra said. "We are not going to hold an entire trial tonight. We'll reconvene tomorrow and sort this all out." She fixed Fervent with her gaze. "If you've waited for twenty years, you can wait another night."

Blue Scale extended a hand in Eurik's direction. "Rock is a competitor in the Games."

"In the unarmed combat event." Sharp Prong smiled. "The next round will be held the day after tomorrow. He has plenty of time."

"Good. That's settled, then."

"We request that he be held," Testing Fork said. "We wouldn't want him to . . . leave like his mother did."

Blue Scale turned to her opposing loreteller. "He has no reason to flee."

Steel Cobra scratched her cheek and sighed. "Where is he staying right now?"

"The Outsiders Quarter," Sharp Prong said.

"Right, then we'll hold him here. No, I don't want to hear it, Blue Scale. Unless someone else here has a better idea."

The other seated loretellers shook their heads. "What about the sword?"

"I can take care of Misthell," Silver Fang said, joining Blue Scale's side. "Rock is my friend and he's lent me the blade in the past."

"When you needed to slay some monster," Misthell said. "You're not planning on slaying one tonight, right?"

"I will give any I encounter a chance to surrender. If only to avoid your complaining afterward."

"All right then. You stay strong, Rock!"

"I'll be fine." He had wanted this to be over with. Now he had to wait another night? But it seemed his desires or wants held no weight here.

Silver Fang laid a hand on his arm. "We expected this much," she said softly in Linesan. "Do not worry too much. Whatever you may have read, we are not savages. You will not be punished instead of your mother."

"I don't know that I want my mother to be known as a murderer. I'm . . . the only one who can defend her. But I don't know her."

If they had been san, he would very much bear responsibility. He would be the next generation of Ardent and as such, considered much the same. He wouldn't be executed or anything like that, but their line would end. They would be forbidden from creating a new generation. Just as Chizuho had been.

"I'll speak with Blue Scale," Silver Fang said, having switched back to Thelauk. "I will see you tomorrow."

"Tomorrow."

The guard carrying Misthell accompanied Silver Fang and Blue Scale as they left. Many did. Only some of the guards as well as Sharp Prong and Fervent remained. "How did Ardent die?" the latter asked.

"Must I remind you of the law, Fervent?" Sharp Prong said before Eurik could answer. "You can't interrogate the party you accused without any loretellers present."

"It does not matter," Eurik said. "And I don't quite know the answer. At sea, after barely surviving a pirate attack. I don't know if they died of injuries, or simply hunger and thirst. All I know is they kept me safe."

Fervent bared her teeth. "So she did suffer? That's something. And if she ended up among outsiders, then no proper burial either. Well, that does help." She looked him up and down. "And you speak so calmly about your parents' death. If they mean so little to you, then why claim them at all? You already knew Ardent was a murderer."

"I am here to find out who they were. Where I come from. Until I left the island, all I had were names. It's not that they don't mean anything to me, it's . . . I don't know what they mean to me. Now," Eurik said turning to Sharp Prong. "Am I put into a cell?"

"Not quite," the shaman said. "But yes, the hour grows late. Fervent, you may leave. Don't return to the Inner Ring until the sun has risen again."

Fervent bowed and walked off with long, sharp strides while Sharp Prong and the remaining guards led him in the other direction. They followed the walkway until they squarely faced north. The peaks of the Trollabergher were silhouetted against the starry night.

"You'll be staying in there," Sharp Prong said, indicating a wooden frame that had ropes on top leading to a long wooden beam.

It took a moment for his tired mind to make sense of what he saw. A cage, about two and a half steps big in every dimension. The beam and the ropes must be used to hoist it up. "It could be worse." At least he'd be able to draw some comfort from the winds blowing through Chappenuioc. If they'd locked him up down below in an air-tight room he'd be cut off from the world.

"I suppose. The sky is not promising rain tonight. Go in."

An iron lock clicked shut after he did so, Sharp Prong deposited the key in a pouch on her belt then turned away without another word. None of the guards remained behind either, except a pair who operated a winch that dragged the entire cage up very slowly.

With the cage swaying, Eurik had to grab hold of one of the bars to steady himself. It got worse when the entire wooden beam swung out so that he hung over the Inner Circle. One other cage of the four he could see was in use, the occupant snoring loudly.

That wind ruffled his clothes and Eurik shivered. *They could have given me a blanket.*

Chapter 19

Visits

WITH MISTHELL RESTING against her shoulder, Leraine bid Blue Scale a goodnight and returned to her bed. That had been her intent, anyway, if not for the one person she didn't want to see right now suddenly stepping into her path.

She swallowed her first response. "Is there something you need?"

Anseri crossed her arms. "Shouldn't that be my question? I heard your friend got himself into a lot of trouble."

"This wasn't unexpected."

"Not unexpected?" Anseri took a step closer. "Your friend stands accused of the murder of the mother of the current leader of Caetiwo." She prodded Leraine with a finger to punctuate her sentence. "Do you have any idea the problems this creates for our tribe?" Another prod. "Do you even care, or are our problems something else that is beneath the notice of the great warrior Silver Fang?"

Leraine pushed her sister away. "His mother was accused. That is it. Not even our oldest laws hold the child equally responsible for crimes committed by the parent before that child was even born!"

"Your . . . friend might have some power. I've seen it with my own eyes. But it's not worth driving a wedge between Urumoy and Caetiwo."

Leraine let the anger roil in her liver, then exhaled it. "I'm not abandoning my friend."

Her sister shook her head, lips twisted in disgust. "Mother might indulge you over this, but Mother's days as leader are coming to an end. You should think carefully how you welcome the next dawn." With those words Anseri turned and stomped away.

"Thank you, for not speaking during that," Leraine said to the living sword once Anseri was out of hearing range.

"Eh, I'm not dumb enough to get in between that. And don't worry, I'm real discreet. Eurik won't hear about this from me. But how about you? You're going to be okay?"

"I will be fine," she lied to Misthell. "And despite her words, it is not decided yet who will lead after my mother. Which may not happen for many years. No, we should worry about Rock's trial." And other matters of which she was forbidden to speak.

"All right, if you say so. But if you need some help, or want to blind your sister with a surprise ball of light, I'm your sword."

Leraine nodded and ducked into her room. The thin walls of wood and canvas did nothing to stop the sounds and smells of celebration that permeated the place. But all Leraine wanted right now was to sleep. Even when it would bring tomorrow.

Meditation turned out not to be so easy. The wind flowed freely between the bars and all around him, but Eurik was still trapped. The disparity made it hard to connect. And whenever he moved, it sent the cage swaying.

Walking around was even more impossible. The cage was large, but not that large. And in the dark it was too easy to misstep, he'd found that out the hard way. As if summoned by the memory, the pain in his foot flared up again.

Maybe I should try sleep instead?

Eurik opened his eyes, looked to his left. The other prisoner still snored away. And the sounds of music and singing drifted over from the Outer Ring of Chappenuioc and beyond. They were faint, many of the fires had been put out as the hour grew late. The smells of roasted meat and boiling soup had disappeared entirely.

Movement in the dark drew his attention, a pair of guards making their rounds. They carried no lights and their footfalls on the wooden walkway were soft, but their armor reflected what little light there was. They spoke to one another, though Eurik couldn't catch what they spoke of.

He and the other prisoner barely rated a glance as the two guards passed. The next patrol would come by soon enough. Eurik had seen enough of them come by to get a feel of the schedule by now. The guards disappeared into the deep dark shadows the buildings on the Inner Ring cast.

"You don't look like much."

The voice was unexpected and familiar. A figure, a shaman, stood by the winch of the cage, his shawl hiding his face in shadows. Eurik had met many shamans these past few days. Which one was this?

The shaman laid a hand on the thick rope. "Hanging like ripe fruit, begging to be picked."

Eurik frowned. *I know this person, but . . .* He started. "Rending Snarl?"

"You recognize me?" The hand now held a knife. "That is a problem." He shook his head. "But I was curious. I had to see you for myself. And then there is the opportunity . . ."

He sounded like Rending Snarl, though also very different. There had been simmering anger even at the start of the event and it had built up every time something hadn't gone right for Rending Snarl. At the end, he truly had been snarling more than speaking.

"Are you trying to kill me?"

"Thinking about it."

"Why? The contest is over. My death will not give you my spot or my prize." He'd have to lunge for the door of the cage. He wouldn't be able to open the cage until he'd laid hands directly onto the lock. But once out, using wind *chiri* would be no problem and he could get onto the beam. Rending Snarl would not be able to cut the rope quickly enough to prevent it. Probably.

Rending Snarl's shoulders shook as he laughed softly. "You're an outsider as well. Maybe I want you dead for the same reason Springstep died. Spite."

Eurik's calm shattered. "You killed Springstep?"

His head turned to the Outer Ring. "It doesn't sound like they've found the body yet. Believe me, you'll know when they do. Its body was displayed for maximum effect."

Things came together. "You're the murderer. The one that's been killing shamans. But . . . what reason would you have to kill Inkpaw? Or . . ." He faltered as he couldn't recall the other shaman's name. Had he heard it?

Still, the question remained. Why would Rending Snarl do this? The person he'd interacted with seemed so different from the man now speaking to him.

"You know? But they've kept Tense Coil's death a secret. Ah, of course. The other one, your friend."

"You're not Rending Snarl." The conclusion arrived only after he'd spoken the words. "You sound like him, but don't speak as he did. And Rending Snarl wouldn't draw this out, he'd just cut the rope." Rending Snarl was many things, but he had shown no signs of patience.

"Yes, but who else would want you dead? Ah, I must have been hired by Fervent, then."

"No. Why do that when the rules are getting her what she wants? And why would Fervent pay you to kill Springstep?" Was Springstep dead, though, or was that another lie? What was Rend—this person—doing? Was he playing some sort of game? "And we've been over this already. You can't kill me just by cutting that rope."

"But if you escape, it'll be free to hunt you down and kill you. No waiting around and hoping. Which brings me to a question I have. Why are you here?"

"You seem to know a lot about me already. You should know that, then. I haven't hidden that I'm looking to find out more about my parents."

"No, no, I mean why are you in that cage? Why go through this trial?"

Eurik tilted his head to the left. "Because they believe my mother committed a murder?"

The impostor made a throw-away gesture. "Bah, why would you care? See, what is Ardent to you? What connects you to it but the fact that it gave birth to you?"

"I . . . I don't know. But she is my mother. That's important."

"No, it's not. It is a tenuous connection even for humans who were actually raised by their parents. But you weren't. So why not renounce this stranger? Why burden yourself with their failures? Why limit yourself like this?"

Eurik weighed the words, his own and this stranger's. "I don't see it that way. It is not a burden. Ignorance is. I don't know what my parents are to me, who they were. I don't know what I missed. I . . . I also think that my *sesin* worried there was no place on San for me. Maybe he was right. But I don't know if there is a place for me here. Among these people."

Belatedly, Eurik considered the wisdom of revealing such thoughts to a self-confessed murderer.

The person that wasn't Rending Snarl scoffed. "Why would you want to? These ignorant, arrogant fools will destroy themselves. For all the effort they've put into building their world, they're even more eager to tear it down. They hardly need our push. You're better off throwing away what little humanity may have clung to you. You'll live longer, for certain."

"What are you?" Eurik had caught a glimpse under the hood in the moonlight as he had gesticulated. The features, they had been those of Rending Snarl. But he wasn't him. And the way he spoke of humans, as if they were something other.

If he intended to answer, the impostor didn't get the chance. Soft footfalls heralded the arrival of the next patrol and when Eurik glanced back, the walkway at the cage-winches was completely empty.

He considered calling out, but would the guards believe him? What would he even say? But Eurik could not pretend this hadn't happened. Forgoing sleep, he resumed a meditative posture and tried to connect to the wind once more.

Soon enough, yelling and screaming broke the peace.

Chapter 20

Witness

LERAINE SAT ON THE bench, her eyelids heavy with sleep and all too aware of the only other person she shared her seating with. Anseri acted as if she wasn't there, her lips a thin line of disapproval.

Leraine rubbed one eye, trying to clear it. This was important. Rock's future could very well be decided by how the loretellers ruled. But there was more going on.

Springstep had been murdered last night and her corpse found hanging from the rafters near the podium on which she'd accepted her triumph. Some of Springstep's tribe had tried to get the person most people thought responsible. Of course, the Pumas had not wanted a bunch of Wolves to enter their territory and a brawl had ensued.

Nobody had died, thankfully. But it had taken several shamans and a quarter of all the guardians to break it up. The commotion had interrupted her sleep, and going back to bed while the peace of Chappenuioc might rupture at any moment hadn't even crossed her mind. Judging from the yawns and bleary eyes, most had agreed with her.

For now, however, that peace held while everybody sought Rending Snarl. He'd disappeared, confirming his guilt to many. But not to Leraine and the shamans. There was another suspect: the impostor, the murderer of Tense Coil.

Murdering shamans was bad enough, but this last one seemed aimed to light the kindling within the Federation. If this kept up, Mother's plan would be useless. If the tribes went to war here in Chappenuioc, more than the Truce would break and it would happen before the Conclave Games had concluded.

Silence fell and Leraine realized Testing Fork had finished her speech. She tried to remember what exactly had been said, but her mind drew a blank. At least Blue Scale seemed more awake, nodding and stepping forward with her fingers entwined.

"I mean no disrespect to my fellow loremistress, but I do believe she's getting ahead of herself again. Rock doesn't deny that Ardent is his mother, the same Ardent who was once a blacksmith in Caetiwo. However! However, simply because she left to learn how to make living swords from the Immortal after a murder occurred does not mean she did it."

Blue Scale turned to her opponent in this trial. "You spoke eloquently about how Caetiwo suffered. What debt the murderer owes. I agree that justice must be done. But before punishment must come guilt. I ask you to show us, show us all, the strength of your case. Rock may be an outsider, Ardent was not. She is owed a measure of respect."

"Certainly," Testing Fork said. "Though it has been over twenty years and I had little time, I have found a few who can attest to the events. Including myself, as it so happens. I will show that Stern Anvil was killed by Ardent over a matter of little import. I will show exactly how much respect Ardent, formerly of Caetiwo, is owed. None at all."

"Right, then," Steel Cobra said. "Let's get on with it. Who are you calling as your first witness?"

"Ambiguous Coin. She is a niece of Ardent and knew her well. She can attest to the relationship the . . . accused had with her victim. I mean, the victim," the loremistress said when Blue Scale opened her mouth.

She beckoned forth a woman in her late thirties. Judging from her clothes she was a trader. The golden ring in her *draen* studded with a single little emerald spoke of success. Or the appearance of it.

Eurik stared at the woman walking over to Testing Fork. A niece of his mother. That made them family, right? He had to think hard exactly how they would be connected, and why hadn't she approached him?

Is she my aunt? No, no, that would be the sibling of a parent. She's a . . . child of that sibling. A niece then? Though, how do Mochedan count such things?

Ambiguous Coin showed little interest in him, even now. She stood before the seated loretellers, right hand on her hip, and her *draen* jingled with every motion of her head. Blue Scale asked her to tell everybody what she knew of Ardent and Stern Anvil.

Ambiguous Coin shrugged. "I knew a little less than others, since I was still a child at the time. But they both liked to think themselves the best blacksmith of Caetiwo. And both accused the other of sabotage. Tools went missing, that had to be Stern Anvil. Someone had smeared shit all over Stern Anvil's anvil, must have been Ardent. That went on for a couple of years."

One of the loretellers leaned forward. "Did it ever escalate to actual confrontations?"

Ambiguous Coin nodded. "Yeah. Every few months they and their apprentices would get into a screaming match which ended in a brawl. Nobody died in those, and I know the old *rangtauk* would try to settle the problem after that. And that kept the peace for a week or so." She shrugged. "Then it would start up again."

Another loreteller spoke up. "And who would start it?"

"Does it matter?" Blue Scale said. "The witness admits she only knows what was widely known. Or believed."

"It may, or may not," a third loreteller said. He twisted the ring on his finger around. "We can circle back on the matter if necessary. I'd like to hear more about the events leading up to the murder of Stern Anvil. Had the *rangtauk* intervened again, or had these incidents escalated into violence?"

Ambiguous Coin looked up into the sky for a moment. "I think things had heated up. Yes. The shit thing had happened maybe a month before. Then the *rangtauk* decided her retainers needed new armor and she gave the task to Stern Anvil. Ardent didn't like that, not at all. I remember her getting real drunk several nights before the murder. I think her smithy was in trouble."

"And what of the day in question?" Testing Fork said. "When did people find out what had happened to Stern Anvil?"

"Not right away. She went missing, actually. People went looking for her and it took hours to find her."

"And where was she found?" Testing Fork faced away from Ambiguous Coin.

"A barrel behind Ardent's shop."

The questioning loreteller spun around. "And where was Ardent?"

"Gone."

Rock's cousin had done him no favors with her testimony. Blue Scale had done her best, but all she'd managed was to show that the women's conflict had waxed and waned for years. The incidents leading up to Stern Anvil's murder had not been an outlier in that history.

Now, though, the loremistress was on the attack herself as Testing Fork herself testified. Leraine listened as she explained how they'd reconstructed that night. "We retrieved Stern Anvil from the barrel in which Ardent—I'm sorry, I should say the murderer—had stuffed her."

"Testing Fork," Steel Cobra said. "If you must resort to rhetorical trickery, try to use something better than what we've all learned in the first years of our apprenticeships. Treating us like simpletons will not help your case."

Testing Fork bowed deeply. "I apologize. No insult was intended."

"You will not be warned again. Now, continue."

"Yes. Stern Anvil had been clubbed to death by a hammer or some such. All the wounds were on her back, back of her head, between the shoulder blades, lower back. It looked like an ambush, but it wasn't a robbery. She still had some coins in her pouch."

Blue Scale motioned toward Testing Fork. "And you found her behind Ardent's smithy. So naturally you looked inside for clues."

The loremistress from Caetiwo shifted her weight. "Yes. The place was spotless. All the tools clean. The ones that weren't missing, that is."

Blue Scale waited a little longer after Testing Fork had fallen silent. "And how did you know Ardent had left?"

She let out a breath. "Her room above the smithy was a mess. Clothes were missing, her money chest empty. And her horse wasn't in the stables either. Guards confirmed she'd left but a few hours before, heading west. That false trail threw us off."

Testing Fork's gaze glided over the assembled loretellers. "We did more digging, including through her books. Ardent had debts she couldn't pay, not without the job of outfitting the *rangtauk*'s retainers. Our conclusion, at the time, was that Ardent had lured Stern Anvil to her smithy and killed her there by surprise. Then left before the deed could be discovered, or the debts were called in. It fit the facts we had," Testing Fork emphasized.

"Forgive me, but I believe you are confusing facts with interpretation. Tools were missing. Well, a blacksmith would take her tools with her if she decided to leave. And if she left because of debts, why kill Stern Anvil?" Blue Scale raised a finger. "Put another way. Killing Stern Anvil before she could do the work would have saved Ardent since then the assignment would go to her. The facts you have presented would make sense of one part but not the other. And you can't honestly tell me that a settlement like Caetiwo has but two blacksmiths?"

"They were our best," Testing Fork said.

"But with both Ardent and Stern Anvil out of the way, one of these lesser blacksmiths got the job. Didn't they?"

Leraine took a moment to gauge Fervent's mood as Testing Fork nodded. She didn't look happy, not at all. Blue Scale was doing good work, sowing doubt. But there was only so much she could do with a murder this old.

"But then how do you explain the note found in Stern Anvil's pouch?" Testing Fork's voice was smooth, the perfect example of an innocent question.

Blue Scale froze, then directed a deep frown at her opponent. "What note?" She bit off the words.

"Ah, yes, I'm sorry. I was going to tell you, but you asked another question. There was a scrap of paper in her pouch. The water in the barrel had run out much of the ink, but what could be read showed that it was an invitation to visit Ardent's shop. Her family told us that she had received a note that evening and that she'd left shortly after. Nobody saw who delivered the note."

Fervent relaxed, gritted teeth disappearing behind a hungry smile. Leraine directed her worry at Blue Scale, who held herself well. No sign of worry there, but loremistresses were trained actors.

"And how does this prove that Ardent was indeed the one who murdered Stern Anvil?"

"It looked like her handwriting."

Blue Scale chuckled. "I've had to deal with blacksmiths' handwriting before. It's barely legible. And here the paper had been soaked, the ink must have been dripping off the scrap."

Testing Fork's nose went up as she straightened to her full height. "My mentor was certain. Sadly, she died some years ago. But who here can dispute Measured Flute's judgment?"

That name stirred some of the loretellers, though Leraine herself didn't recognize it. No surprise there, she'd never paid much attention to those telling the stories. Her head was too filled with their words and the images they conjured.

"I am." Blue Scale's voice cut through, tinged with humor. "I am disputing it here and now. Her skill is well known. My own mentor used Measured Flute's investigation of the murder of the *rangtauk* of Uthamac to instruct me in the finer points of the art. But we don't have her or the note you spoke of to see for ourselves whether she was right."

Leraine tried to guess how much that argument swayed the loretellers, but much like Blue Scale, they knew how to give away nothing they wished to hide.

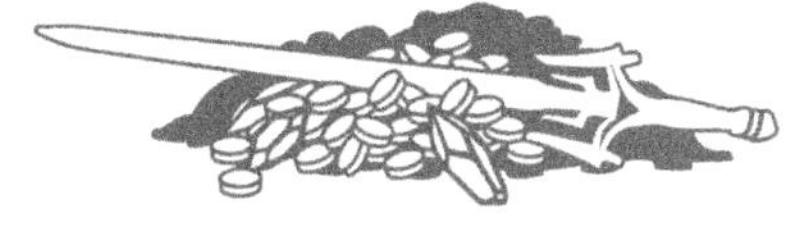

Eurik blew out a breath. The trial was over, the part where they argued and dueled with words anyway. The judges had retreated deeper into Chappenuioc leaving the rest of them to wait and wonder.

He'd joined Blue Scale and Silver Fang, but was too antsy to sit. "So where do I stand?"

Blue Scale let out a long sigh. "We'll know soon enough. If they don't come back soon, then we have a chance. Time was against us here. I offered another version of what might have happened, but none of us will ever know what truly happened. Barring intervention by the spirits themselves."

"But likewise, Testing Fork could do little to disprove your words," Silver Fang said.

The loreteller nodded. "Yes. But I didn't know Measured Flute had been the one who'd done the investigation. Arguing she made a mistake . . ." She made a gesture with her right hand. "It was the only path I saw. But you must prepare yourself for a judgment of guilty."

"I'm not sure that would be wrong," Eurik said. "The truth is, I do not know that she didn't do it. And if she did murder Stern Anvil, should that not be said?"

Blue Scale blinked several times while Silver Fang shook her head. "Only you . . . Perhaps, from the perspective of Fervent and her sept. If your mother truly killed Stern Anvil. But for your mother to be judged a murderer, one who fled justice, it will reflect on you. How others treat you."

"I just thought there would be a penalty, a price I had to pay?"

"At a minimum. But Fervent or someone else may petition a *tidaechanek* to remove you from the Conclave Games. Honor travels both up and down the generations. Your mother's dishonor is your dishonor."

"But I am not a Mochedan." He struggled to find the right words, but Blue Scale's Linesan was quite poor and he didn't want to exclude her from the conversation. And his own Irelian wasn't any better.

Luckily, Silver Fang understood what he was trying to say. "That helps and hinders you. It is understood that you don't fully grasp what proper behavior is. But there aren't that many obstacles to treat you harshly either. No family to shield you, or allies."

He crossed his arms. "Us being friends doesn't count?"

Leraine took care not to glance at her sister, still sitting on the bench. "It counts for less. It has gotten you this trial. And an advocate," she said, indicating Blue Scale who inclined her head. "If you had come here alone, there's a very good chance the loretellers would have left the original finding stand and thrown you out of the Games and Chappenuioc. After that," she trailed off looking behind Eurik.

He glanced over his shoulder. Fervent and Testing Fork were on the opposing bench, speaking with Silver Fang's sister.

"After that," Silver Fang said. "I think Fervent would have followed with some of her people. I think highly of your chances, though the Road would not have helped. But defending yourself might only compound your problems."

"That's not right."

Blue Scale hummed. "Yes. I'm not sure Fervent would risk you getting away. Better to demand a high *galautik* and take you back to Caetiwo to put you to some unpleasant, dangerous work."

"That's not what I meant," Eurik said.

"I know what you meant," Silver Fang said. "But you must understand. If you seek to connect with your parents, then you seek to connect to all of us. You can't pick and choose." She hesitated for a moment. "But I am glad you are here. I, for one, am comforted that there's someone here I can trust."

Right, there was a murderer going around. One that had come to visit him. This wasn't a good place to talk about it, but he shouldn't delay it any longer. "I heard a commotion last night. Did Springstep get murdered?"

"You heard, then. Yes," Blue Scale said. "And Rending Snarl is missing. Quite a few have made the obvious connection." She shook her head. "There hasn't been a murder here in years, now two in as many days. I preferred it when the momentous events were safely in the past. Now, there's something building."

He hesitated, but what good would keeping quiet do? Silver Fang hadn't, though she'd been told to. Eurik did have to remember not to hint at that in Blue Scale's company. "I got a visit last night from someone who . . . looked and sounded as Rending Snarl did."

Blue Scale's eyes narrowed. "Explain."

Eurik gathered his thoughts, and the words he'd need to express them. Or as best as he knew how to. "I thought he was Rending Snarl, but . . . he did not act right. His words were . . . not what I remembered. Of him."

Blue Scale shook her head a little. "You are claiming someone is stalking Chappenuioc and using magic to take on the appearance of others."

Next to her, Silver Fang bared her teeth. "He is. What did it say?"

Blue Scale shifted her attention to her fellow Mochedan. "You would trust his words even in this? He's claiming someone is using magic within the confines of Chappenuioc! Why would you simply believe that?"

"Because not all magic stops in Chappenuioc," Eurik said. "I can use the Ways. Yes, I've always said that they're not magic and they're not. But I am using . . ." His command of Thelauk faltered here. "Never mind. Misthell can use his abilities without issue. So some powers do work."

The loreteller leaned back. "That is concerning. So this murderer visited you in confinement? How? Even looking like Rending Snarl would not have helped. The guardians should have stopped them. And why?"

"He, it, wanted to talk to me. It was curious. And it wore the shawl and the rod of a shaman. It must have disguised itself as one."

"That . . . could work. Well, it would have a better chance than at any other time. There are many shamans—and loretellers—visiting at the moment. The guardians would not be so surprised to see one they did not know. And reading the *vipaen* in the dark would be difficult."

Silver Fang leaned in. "Did he tell you why he's killing? What is he after?"

"It seemed to hate people. No, it used the word humanity. It was looking to push us to destroy ourselves? And referred to persons as "it." I don't think the murderer is human."

"And you waited until now to tell anybody?" Blue Scale hissed. "This is important. It must be some angry spirit then. A most powerful one. The shamans can calm it or destroy it, but only if they know what they are dealing with."

"I wasn't sure anybody would believe me," Eurik said. Though the defense sounded feeble to his own ears. He'd known people had died; Silver Fang had nearly joined their number. But he'd been afraid and . . . distracted. Distracted by his own small concerns.

"At least you didn't wait even longer," Blue Scale said. "Right. I'll let the shamans know after the verdict. With luck, they can act before anybody else dies."

"Perhaps," Silver Fang said, her forehead wrinkled from deep thoughts. "Perhaps."

Chapter 21

Consideration

THEY HAD TO WAIT FOR quite a while longer. It gave Leraine plenty of time to ponder what she'd learned. Blue Scale's conclusion should be right. She knew more of such matters than Leraine did. Far more.

And yet . . . and yet it did not sit right with Leraine. Going over the events of that day again, it hadn't felt like she'd faced a spirit. No, she'd faced something with a body of flesh and blood. Or something close enough to that.

But that claim brought her right back to problems she had no answers to. What was the murderer? How had it gotten in? And how could they stop it?

Those questions took a step back when Anseri finally returned to their side and sat down. "What were you talking about with Fervent?"

Anseri regarded her and let the silence stretch out. Leraine got the point she was trying to make, that she didn't answer to Leraine. But the thing was, Leraine didn't really care about that right now. "I will not let you sell out my friend."

"Oh, I know. But someone needs to make sure this doesn't go any further. Someone has to preserve peace and make sure we don't find ourselves isolated within our own bleeding tribe." Her teeth clicked as Eurik glanced over at them. Lowering her voice, Anseri continued. "So I went and did what was necessary. What a leader of our sept must do. I made nice with that truce breaker."

"Now who's making relations worse?" Leraine murmured. "She's a Truce Warrior, but they're not talking about breaking the Great Truce. Just . . . stopping it."

"A small distinction." Her sister let out a breath. "But . . . an important one. And it wouldn't do for Fervent to hear my words, it would undo everything."

A glance over at Fervent told them she had not. The leader of Caetiwo had taken up pacing behind the opposite bench, her gaze locked on the entry from which the judging loretellers would emerge. Any moment now.

The sun approached the peaks of the Trollabergher when they finally came back to announce their verdict. One loreteller looked unhappy, another plopped himself into his chair with all the grace of a sack of grain.

Steel Cobra's face was drawn. "Right, we've decided. If the parties would present themselves before this tribunal." Both Fervent and Rock stepped forward, flanked by Testing Fork and Blue Scale. Rock glanced at the *rangtauk*; she gave no hint she knew he was so close.

"This matter has proven to be a real pain," Steel Cobra said. "So much time has passed. And the person suspected of the deed has been dead for nearly as long. None here dispute Measured Flute's skill, but she herself always argued that the conclusions of an investigation had to be tested. In this case, time has tied our hands."

Does this mean they will wash their hands of the matter? Simply let Rock go on his way? That . . . would cause problems. One look at Fervent confirmed that.

"However, Stern Anvil deserves justice. But what would that look like? It is that question that has vexed us today." Steel Cobra gave her fellow loretellers some pointed looks. "Stalled us. Testing Fork presented a logical case, based on available facts. She does credit to her teacher. Yet Blue Scale's alternative interpretation of events cannot be disproven by what we know. So, we have decided not to convict Ardent of Caetiwo of the crime of murder—"

"NO!"

Silver Fang's liver had jumped at the words, and Fervent's shout. *Has Blue Scale truly done it?*

Fervent stomped forward a single step, jabbing back in Rock's direction with a pointed finger. "You can't let filth—"

"Silence!" Steel Cobra's voice cut through Fervent's words; her eyes flashed. "I've had just about enough of you, girl. You are a *rangtauk*! Act like it! Now step back and not another word, or you can hear our judgment from Testing Fork tomorrow. After you've cooled off in a cage for a night."

She wasn't done? Then Rock and his mother were not free and clear. Fervent, too, appeared to have caught on as she bowed very low with her cheeks reddening as she slinked back.

Steel Cobra waited one more moment before giving a firm nod. "Where was I? Ah yes, we can't find Ardent of Caetiwo guilty of plotting and committing murder but the weight of evidence has convinced us that she had a part in Stern Anvil's death. And so we find her guilty of killing Stern Anvil of Caetiwo."

Rock sagged a little. In his place, Leraine would be shamed at the black mark on her family's honor. But he didn't think in those terms. Did that make it worse, or easier to bear?

"Which brings us to the matter of punishment," the loreteller to Steel Cobra's right said. He was Bear. "Ardent is dead. The circumstances are murky, though suggest she died with honor. But her spirit has not been laid to rest according to our customs. Some have argued that this would be more than enough punishment for the crime we've found her guilty of, but punishment has a greater goal than merely the perpetrator or perpetrators. It is a reminder to all that criminals do not prosper."

He leaned forward, one hand on his knee. "Fervent, *rangtauk* of Caetiwo, daughter of Stern Anvil. What punishment would you demand for Rock of San, son of Ardent?"

More than one person stirred. It was unusual for a court to ask that question. Especially when the other judge had told the accuser to keep her mouth shut just before. Fervent hesitated, then inclined her head. "I am no judge. I have no training in law. All I ask is that Ardent's family feels the pain she inflicted upon mine. That they make up for the years stolen from us."

The loreteller made a sound deep in his throat, then turned his attention to Rock. "And what do you argue. What can you offer?"

"I . . . do not know. I do not understand fully the pain of losing a parent. I never had them. I have no memory of them. That is why I came here. To . . . gain memories of them." Rock moved his hands as he went on. "I can imagine the pain of never seeing the one who raised me. I do not know if that is the same. But it is . . . great."

Rock turned to address Fervent directly. "I am sorry for your loss."

Leraine froze. *Please do not offer the prize right now. That would be a mortal insult.* She could barely cover the sigh as his next words did not mention that.

"But I don't understand you, or your people, well enough to know if I could make good your loss. If it is possible."

Thank the spirits. For once, he's not so dense and ignorant.

Fervent took a deep breath, her lips twitched. "Words won't suffice." She turned her body away from Rock and faced the loretellers fully. "Let us take him at his word. My sept has been robbed of a life. Let the son of Ardent repay with his life. Serving in our mines for twenty years should do."

"I think not," Blue Scale said. "Precedent is clear. A child of a criminal can only inherit half the guilt of the parent. And in this case, Rock has inherited even less. All his parents gave him was a name. They taught him nothing of our people. Not our language, our customs, our laws."

The loreteller on the far left knocked his ring on his armrest. His *draen* and his chair both screamed Wolf. "You're not arguing that ignorance of the law should shield someone from it?"

"Of course not. My argument is that as Fervent suffered the loss of her mother, so did Rock. Even more so, he lost his entire heritage. Would any here argue that is not a greater loss?"

The Wolf loreteller frowned. "Simply because a criminal suffers misfortune, it does not follow that they should be let off."

Blue Scale threw her arms out. "But if that misfortune follows from the consequences of their crime? And falls on others? Like their children? Should that not be taken into account?"

"That is dangerously close to arguing that the spirits have already punished the criminal," the Bear loreteller said. "Which is a matter of the shamans."

"I merely argue that Rock inherited little in the way of assets or family. So why should he inherit the full amount of Ardent's guilt?"

The loreteller of the Ibex tribe quirked her lips. "Ah, an argument of fairness. But then, what is fair? In your opinion?"

"A *galautik*. Its weight to be decided by you."

Fervent's teeth clicked shut and she gave Testing Fork a furious glare. "That will not be enough. How can we even be certain he would pay? His mother fled justice before, and he's not even People."

"He is competing in the Conclave Games as we speak. He already placed third in the Three Games," Blue Scale said. "You should be aware of that."

"Yes, well, you can't suggest he'll pay simply by winning. No outsider has won the combat events in living memory."

"Not true," Steel Cobra said. "I was very young. But there was a lizarian that did just that." She laughed. "Unless you don't consider me quite alive anymore?"

"No, of course not. Still, my point stands. It is unlikely," Testing Fork said. "And how would Rock pay if he failed? He is a wanderer. With little ties to anybody, and the only possession of note is his living sword. Though that would be fitting payment. It was made by Ardent, and it is a life, of a sort."

"No," Rock said. "He is not mine to give away. That would be . . . wrong."

"I care not for how you feel about it," Testing Fork said. "The sword is yours. The only thing that could approach how we treasured Stern Anvil."

"If it is treasure you wish, I can provide. Inside Chappenuioc it has been hard to show, but I can sense through the ground. Move rock and earth. Bringing up its wealth is not hard," Rock said.

"Truly?" Steel Cobra lifted a single, thin eyebrow. "So easily? Then why haven't you done so already?" She looked him up and down. Leraine had to acknowledge Rock was dressed somewhat shabbily. The fabric of his clothes had worn thin in places, especially the trousers. His boots especially showed the wear and tear from walking more than halfway around the Valley.

Rock tilted his head to the left. "I've had no need."

She shook her head and gestured at Leraine's friend. "Well, I'm convinced of one thing. He truly was raised by those who are not People. If you speak the truth."

"He does," Leraine said. She got up and stood next to Rock. "I've been traveling with him since we met in the great city. We've sneaked through the Land of Bones in a tunnel he made and camped in a fort he raised from the ground every night as we traveled through the Barren Hills."

"Silver Fang," the Bear loreteller said. "You will vouch for this outsider's word, then?"

She didn't hesitate. "Yes. I don't know what stories have been told of . . . my victory, but Rock here was vital in our fight against the demon. It was his powers that brought the demon out of the air so that I could actually strike at it."

"I hadn't," the Wolf loreteller said. "His part was downplayed in the tale I heard. Very well, a *galautik* in gold or silver it is." The other loretellers nodded, though the Bear loreteller hesitated. He was the last to agree.

"If memory serves," Steel Cobra said, "the *galautik* for the life of a blacksmith is ten *daiphon* of silver."

"Don't forget that she was a member of an important sept," the Bear loreteller said. "Twelve *daiphon* would be better."

Rock frowned, they hadn't really talked about weights yet. Leraine did some calculations in her head and leaned over to whisper in his ear. "A *daiphon* is little less than half a Linesan pound. It's ten *phon* which is the most basic weight merchants use."

"So twelve daiphon would be six pounds of silver? No, less than that."

"Don't forget that the young man only inherits half the guilt, half the galautik. Six daiphon of silver, and if Rock manages to win the combat competition, the prize should easily cover that. If Fervent doesn't want to wait much longer for restitution."

The loreteller from the Boar tribe shifted in her seat. "I'm not comfortable with treating the prize of one of our most sacred events as a means of payment."

The Bear loreteller barked a laugh, slapping his thigh. "Tell that to everybody else, then. Half of them already have a buyer lined up before the Games begin! Bah, but enough, there's still some daylight left and I'd like to see who's winning the spear toss. I'm in favor, place a *galautik* of six *daiphon* of silver upon Rock for the death of Stern Anvil."

All the others voted in favor and soon after just about everybody left. The loretellers with some eagerness, Fervent with a snarl and a huff.

"So, that's it, then," Rock said.

Leraine nodded. "More or less. No doubt Fervent will press for harsher measures if you are anything but prompt in paying. But that shouldn't be a problem?"

He shook his head. "No. Still, I feel . . . sad. From here on out, people will hear that Ardent killed someone. That she is a criminal. Was. And I will never know if it is true. I . . . don't know what I feel. What I should feel."

Leraine placed a hand on his shoulder and squeezed. In truth, neither did she.

Chapter 22

The Enemy Within

EURIK SET OUT TO RETURN to the Outsiders Quarter. He longed for the steady presence of the earth to settle his mind, but that also reminded him. If he wanted to pay this fine, he needed wealth.

Taking it from the ground should be no problem, except the local area lacked any he could sense. Winning the competition could also give him that, but he was fighting with a hand tied behind his back.

"Are you ignoring me?"

He blinked and realized that Silver Fang had been talking to him. "I did not mean to. What did you say?"

"You're going the wrong way. The shamans we need to talk to are over there," she said, pointing at a building on the Inner Ring.

"About that, will you not get into trouble if I do? I'm not sure I'll be able to hide that you warned me."

"That is for me to worry about." She reminded Eurik of a san at that moment. Face immobile, the tones of her voice hiding much. "This is too important. They must know what is stalking Chappenuioc. Or more people will die, and not only at the spirit's hands."

"We don't know that it is a spirit. Why would a spirit need a knife?"

Silver Fang's gaze drilled into him, then she laid a hand on his arm and took a step closer. "I will be fine," she said softly. "They can't fault me too much if the spirit basically revealed itself to you anyway. And as I'm not an outsider, I have more protection than you have. Now, come, let's warn them."

He let out a breath and nodded. Perhaps she was right. Perhaps he worried over nothing. And this . . . facechanger did need to be stopped.

Silver Fang exchanged some quiet words with a guard then they were ushered in. Though getting him in required some not so quiet words as the other guard used his staff to bar Eurik's way. "They'll want to hear it directly from him. You could have him wait out here, but then you'll have to make the shamans wait while you fetch him later. Well?"

The guards exchanged a look, then one sighed and they removed their weapons from his path. "Very well. Come on, then."

They were led past the entrance hall and up a flight of stairs. The building felt a little wobbly to Eurik. It creaked as the wind hit it. Upon reaching the top of the stairs, Eurik saw that this top floor was much as the hall below. Open, with a few alcoves against the left and right walls that were partitioned by way of wicker screens. Light filtered in through windows in the back, the shutters hinged on the top and were propped open by the use of two staves.

The guard motioned for them to stay there, then walked over. Though there were several chairs and tables, only one was occupied. The shaman looked up when the guard approached him. Eurik knew him. Bitten Fin had been there when they'd decided if he could compete. He couldn't hear what they said and Eurik saw no reason to eavesdrop.

Instead, he concentrated on his breathing and went over what needed to be said. And said in a way that didn't give away Silver Fang's prior warning.

"Silver Fang, Rock," the shaman said as they were finally allowed to come over. "You had some news concerning . . . Springstep's murder?" Bitten Fin looked from him to Silver Fang and back. The guard didn't stay; he went down the stairs again. Eurik could hear and feel her footsteps through the floor.

"Yes," Silver Fang said. "Rock told me he was visited last night while he stayed in the cages."

"I'd heard about your court case. I was sad to learn you were involved in it." He shook his head and frowned. "But how does your mother's trial concern our present tragedy?"

Taking a deep breath, Eurik explained. How someone that looked and sounded like Rending Snarl, but was not him, paid him a visit in the night. Threatened to kill him, revealed what he'd done.

Bitten Fin prodded, trying to discern what words exactly had been said, though Eurik had to admit more than once that he couldn't remember them. Still, the essence had been hard to forget and some things the killer had said couldn't be forgotten.

Finally, the shaman relented and leaned back in his chair with a grimace. "This is worse than we thought."

"This isn't good news? We now know what we are dealing with," Silver Fang said. "We can even see some of its intentions now."

"Can we?" Bitten Fin shook his head. "Ah, of course, you are thinking of Hathadaewu the Face Stealer. You think we're dealing with a spirit from the Before-Time."

"We're not?"

Again, the shaman shook his head. "Of course not. There's a reason it's called the Before-Time. Those spirits can't exist in this world anymore. And their thoughts are too alien; they don't understand those of flesh and blood. You spoke to something which understands us well enough to exploit our weaknesses. Our divisions."

"If not a spirit, then what could it be?"

"Ah, now if I had all the answers I'd be out there cornering the murderous *phracto* right this moment. Still, this does help. If the pattern holds, then we should be looking for Rending Snarl's body. And finding out where that is may tell us much."

He gave Silver Fang a look and she fidgeted. "I will not ask how much you know, Rock. Some things I don't need to know. Would be best if nobody knew. I'm not going to assign you guardians. I don't have any to spare and it might give the wrong impression."

Bitten Fin levered himself out of his chair, then rubbed his leg. "If this impostor approaches you again, be cautious. Try to stall for time and attract our attention. It might not have shown all it can do."

They both agreed that they would be careful. Eurik hoped that Silver Fang meant it. She all too often threw herself into danger without a second thought.

Leraine headed for Snake territory, barely aware of her surroundings. Bitten Fin's conclusions were bad enough. She'd been certain she knew what they dealt with. She'd heard the story of the face stealer and how Bishint managed to steal its greatest treasure. Not that she thought it was Hathadaewu itself they were dealing with, but a lesser spirit related to them. Not so.

But at the moment her mind was more occupied with Rock's parting words. He'd wondered why it had first appeared within the inner sanctum. There would have been easier and better targets anywhere else.

But there is something in the inner sanctum you can't find anywhere else. All the trophies dedicated to the spirits.

Silver Fang stopped in the middle of the path. Someone bumped into her but she paid them no heed, nor the hot words thrown her way.

What if stoking our anger, breaking the Great Truce, is not its goal?

But what was it after, then? Simply to steal something from the inner sanctum? Taking a mental step back, Leraine acknowledged that an outsider would see it as a great collection of wealth.

This can't be about something as simple as riches. Can it?

Was that the plan, then? Cause enough chaos to draw the guards protecting the inner sanctum away so they could steal . . . what? Not just gold or jewels. Both could be stolen from those visiting the festival with far greater ease. Some of the items held within were magical in nature, like the mirror of the Traitor-Mage.

And what had Tense Coil said? Half the items were dangerous? Perhaps it's not wealth this murderer seeks, but power.

Leraine set out once again, though not back to the shamans. She could be right, she could be wrong. Either way, the goal remained the same. Stop this thing from murdering more people. But how could she find someone who could be anybody?

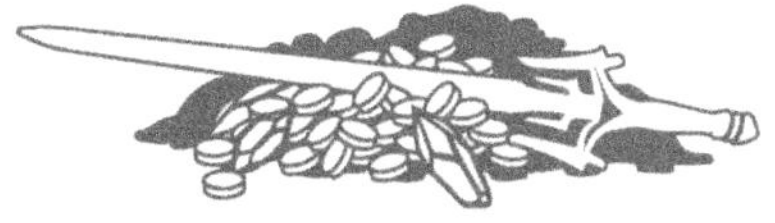

Eurik sat down with a weary sigh. The Outsiders Quarter was a little quieter today, a little emptier. Well, quieter away from his shelter, as Misthell at the moment was voicing his displeasure.

"You're sure you're not going to have to give me away to that Fervent person? Absolutely, completely, totally, surely sure?"

"Surely sure?"

"Yes, it's double sure. Are you?"

"Yes. I made it clear I'm not using you to settle a debt. That I don't own you. Though they won't see it that way."

"I asked you to reassure me." The living sword's single eye drooped. "How, how did her sword look like? Well taken care of? Does she like to go hunt demons?"

"Misthell . . . I haven't seen her sword. I don't know." Eurik shook his head. He'd already assured the living sword that that wouldn't happen. Had done so multiple times, but getting some ideas out of its mind was next to impossible.

"Oh. Well, you better win this competition then. I'd cheer you on, but they don't allow my kind in there. So, get on with meditating. Center yourself, look within to—"

"Misthell," Eurik said sharper than he'd intended. Continuing in a softer voice, he closed his eyes and deepened his connection to the earth beneath him. "I know how to meditate. What I need isn't a greater connection to the Ways. I need some way to get around the limitations this place puts upon them."

"Right."

With the sword falling silent, Eurik focused on quieting the turmoil within himself. The mess with his mother, the murderer operating with impunity and with some interest in him, the danger his friends were in. None would bring him a solution.

He could use Dance of the Whirlwind, but his understanding of Rise of the Mountain remained far greater. Yet that was the Way he couldn't use within Chappenuioc. Well, not entirely true. There was some earth *chiri* there, disconnected little pockets in the metal and stones some carried around; like pools of water after a rainstorm.

But those were out of reach, no use to him when he was walking through its streets or over its hanging walkways. Perhaps he should fashion some sort of bracelet or ring for himself and pack it with earth *chiri*. It wouldn't solve the challenges he faced in the competition, if it worked.

No better time to test that.

Eurik slapped a hand flat on the ground as he cast his senses deep into the earth. He sifted the various layers and seams for its heavier, sturdier elements. Then he pulled them up and let them wrap around his finger and his wrist. Both circlets consisted of a dark material with glimmering veins and streaks of orange and blue.

He drew in more *chiri*, it flowed like thick lava up his legs and through his chest. It poured down his arm and into his new ornaments where he packed it in, pushing until the ring and bracelet felt twice as heavy. It wasn't a true weight; another person wouldn't have noticed a difference. To Eurik, however, it was both that and more.

Eurik made his way to the Road. The Outsiders Quarter was set some distance away from Chappenuioc proper, but practically next to the Inza Road. He wondered if that was for convenience, or so that non-Mochedan could quickly be ferried away from their holy city.

Holding up his right arm to inspect his work one last time, Eurik took a deep breath and flushed the earth *chiri* out of his body, into the ground below before severing himself from the world. He waited for a heartbeat, two, three, four. The *chiri* in the ornaments didn't flow into the sudden void. It sat there, heavy . . . slightly vibrating?

Stepping onto the Road itself was still uncomfortable, like finding your ears stuffed with wool, floating in a still pond, or waking in the dark of night. But he could sense the *chiri* in the rings and gently, he tried drawing on the one around his finger.

Fresh strength filled his hand and traveled up his arm. Distributed over his whole body, however, it wasn't that much. One good punch, a few moments of stonelike toughness, that's all the little ring could hold.

He drew from the bracelet as well and went through a short movement pattern, blocking and attacking a couple of imaginary adversaries. It was better, but he could already tell that he'd have to adapt his normal style. He'd have to use Rise of the Mountain in bursts rather than a steady, implacable advance. Not a boulder rolling down the slope, but an earthquake.

Though as he stomped about, Eurik noticed something. His steps felt odd, the Road felt slippery, springy. He'd already used up nearly half of what he'd brought with him, but he could get more *chiri* by stepping off the Road so he tried something. He gathered what energy still remained and concentrated it in his legs, then pushed it down into the direction of the ground.

He wasn't ready for the results. Eurik felt himself lift off the ground. Not much, but enough that he fell forward and only just caught himself from landing face first.

How? What? He pushed himself back onto his feet. *Most of the earth chiri is gone, it went somewhere. But . . . it pushed me too.*

Eurik shook his head. That had been odd, but now was not the time to investigate. His idea worked, he could bring earth *chiri* into Chappenuioc. But how did that help him in the competition? He held up his arm and examined the bracelet. They looked fine, ready to be used once more. But he still couldn't bring them with him onto the fighting platform.

The only jewelry you're allowed to wear is a draen and I'm not Mochedan. And I can't think any place on my body that I could have this and not cause a problem.

It wasn't intended as a weapon or armor, but it would work like that. Eurik wouldn't want to hit this with his bare, unprotected hand. There just wasn't any place on the body where that wouldn't be true to some extent.

Wait, on the body. But what if I didn't bring it with me?

Chapter 23

The Knife at Your Throat

LERAINE FELL BACK AS her opponent unleashed a flurry of blows that she only barely caught with her buckler and sword. She should be focusing on this, this fight, this enemy in front of her. But other thoughts wouldn't go away. They kept rearing their ugly heads and crying for attention.

She didn't even notice the hit itself, only the call of the shaman let her know that she was two points behind now. The sting came when they reset their positions. Not from the hit, but that confident sneer of her enemy.

Enough, you're not going to lose like this. Remember Irelith's lessons. Focus on the knife at your throat, not the army a day's ride away.

Leraine and her opponent moved as one. For a moment, there was no threat, no murderer, no family. The moment was neither long nor short; it was as long as it lasted. Right up until Leraine pushed her enemy's weapon out of the way with the buckler and struck at the exposed wrist with her wooden blade in one motion.

"Point to Silver Fang."

The satisfaction Leraine felt at wiping that smile off of her competitor's face was not in keeping with the spirit of the festival. But she was still behind. Celebrate after victory was secured, not while trying to achieve it.

Leraine raised her blade again. *The knife at my throat.*

Eurik sailed through the air, the crowd quickly parted to give him an unobstructed look at the bare stone of Chappenuioc's surface. Failure and more laid heavy on his stomach, but right now he needed to worry more about not breaking any bones.

He'd lost, so he didn't have to worry about breaking rules then. Sailing through the air generated more than enough wind *chiri* for his needs, he spun in the air and pulled the winds along. They gathered between him and the ground, pushing against him. Not enough to stop his fall, but it slowed it down to the point that he could make a neat landing on his feet.

And this was the first bout of the day. But I still have a chance. One chance.

"Victory to Snap Gap," the shaman said, gesturing at the man who had moved like greased lightning.

Eurik shook his head lightly and got up onto the platform to bow to his opponent. "I did not see it coming. Well fought." And quick too: the shaman's signal to begin had still lingered when he'd found himself lifted into the air.

Snap Gap shrugged and said . . . something. Maybe that it had been a good fight? His speech was barely recognizable as Thelauk. Certainly Snap Gap's lips quirked in a smile, showing several teeth that had been filed into points. Then he turned away, gave Eurik a lazy wave, and left.

With a sigh, Eurik did the same. He wasn't out of the competition yet, but this made things a lot harder. He rubbed his stomach. *Didn't even get to try my solution. Would it have helped there?*

Probably not. Losing wouldn't be the end of the world, he could pay the fine with the aid of the Ways. He'd have to get closer to some mountains for that, though. He'd already checked and there hadn't been any precious metals or stones near Chappenuioc. At least, not close enough for him to sense.

Zasashi wouldn't have had that problem. A master's sense of the world far outstripped his. But they weren't here, and this was Eurik's problem to solve. That was why he wouldn't ask Silver Fang for help paying either. This was the consequence of his decision, so he should bear it.

Walking past other platforms, he looked out for Silver Fang and Slyvair. She was at the wolf platform and the orc should be fighting under the killer whale. He saw wolf, but no Silver Fang. Her bout must have finished already.

"Watch it!"

"I am. Especially you murderous lot."

It happened in front of him, two people standing within arm's reach while people gathered around them. Except, no. They were gathering behind the two in separate groups while the way those two held themselves was easy to recognize. Eurik had seen similar postures during the fights.

"You dare?" The one who'd told the other to watch it shifted his weight.

That other wore a padded vest, though Eurik doubted the soft leather offered much real protection when it left the arms exposed up to and including the shoulders. It had the design of a blue bear standing on two legs on its front.

The people behind him wore similar garments, or thin leather with metal fixtures that probably offered even less protection even when it was clearly made to resemble armor.

"Dare?" The one with the blue bear gestured at everybody. "We all know who's responsible for the murders these past few days."

"You are!"

Four guards slipped through the crowd, made easier by the fact that those people had divided themselves in distinct groups with space between them. Very few people stood alone, like Eurik. The guards brandished their staves and shouted for everybody to get going.

For a moment, everybody held their ground. Then the ones wearing armor retreated, though not before the one who had mentioned the murders spat on the ground.

"I had hoped that the news that Rending Snarl wasn't responsible for Springstep's death would ease the tension," Silver Fang said from next to him.

Eurik didn't jump, he didn't. And she couldn't tell his heart was galloping, though quickly slowing down to a sedate pace again. "I—" He cleared his throat. "I didn't know it had been announced. Have they found him, then?"

Silver Fang's lips twisted. "No. So many doubt it is true. It is not helped that they haven't revealed who, or what, is truly behind all this."

"I don't know how much it would help. Knowing that anybody could be this murderer. Wearing the face of someone you know, perhaps." The thought came that he couldn't be sure this was Silver Fang.

"Accusations could do far more damage than this thing has done." She shook her head, a quick, sharp motion. "I won my first fight. It was closer than I'd liked. How did you fare?"

"I lost." He grimaced. "It was quick."

"You are facing the best the People have to offer. But you are not out of the competition."

"Not yet. But maybe I should be."

She put a hand on his arm. "What's this? I've not known you to quit even when it was wise."

"I'm not that bad. But . . . I'm here to find out more about my parents. It hasn't worked and I can spend my time better by helping to find the killer." He hadn't even tried the Puma quarter again. With all this going on, he knew they wouldn't treat him any kinder. But perhaps if this murderer was caught . . .

She looked around and led him away from the crowd, deeper into Chappenuioc. "And how would you go about that?" Silver Fang asked once they were away from anyone else being able to overhear them.

"I . . . have no idea."

She squeezed. "I share your frustration. I would love nothing more than to hunt this murderer down. But I can no more see beyond its disguise than you can. And have you already forgotten the *galautik* you owe to Fervent?"

"No, but that won't be a problem." He let out a long breath. "I was actually thinking of using myself as bait. The murderer has already shown interest in me, so maybe they'll try another conversation if I'm alone and vulnerable again?"

She started to pace. "I've had a similar thought. I've been trying to figure out what it is after. Certainly, it has shown interest in you but I don't believe that was its reason for coming here. I think it's after something held within the inner sanctum. But the question would be, what?"

"I take it there's a lot in this inner sanctum?"

Leraine stilled, then a quick bob of her head. "The trophies and spoils of generations of Mochedan. Centuries, really. Battles, wars, hunts. But why try to steal from the inner sanctum? It is well guarded at all times. There are easier targets to steal from, even here."

"Which means they can't find what they're after anywhere else? Or at least, those places would be even harder."

Silver Fang paused in her pacing, then resumed. "Yes. But what?"

"Something old? You did say some of the stuff there is centuries old. Is there any system to how these trophies are stored? If we assume that, uh, Tense Coil interrupted a thief, then whatever was near the body would be a likely target."

"I didn't see everything. But . . . there were a lot of demonic related items in the room. A mirror belonging to the Traitor-Mage of Bandar Ebon, remains of demons." She frowned. "There was a demon heart lying right next to her body. I thought it had fallen there, knocked off its perch during a struggle."

"Are they that rare? Merin used one to power his bone construct, and they're fighting over a pair of them over in Glinfell right now."

"Yes, but there's many— What do you mean, a pair? The demon we slayed left three demon hearts behind."

"No, Slyvair only mentioned two." Eurik had been talking to the orc last night about this and that. Anything but his own problems. While hearing of the troubles Glinfell and the other cities of the Oathfellowship were dealing with wasn't that enjoyable, at least they had the chance to resolve them.

"If they are after demon hearts," Eurik said, "that raises the question of why."

"Nothing good, which is enough of an answer for us. We need to talk to Captain Slyvair."

She didn't wait for his reply before plunging back into the crowds of Chappenuioc, leaving Eurik with no other choice but to hurry to catch up.

Leraine knew she'd failed. She knew how dangerous those things were, but she'd been too drunk on victory, on survival, to care what happened to those demon hearts. She'd heard they'd been secured and that had been good enough for her. She'd trusted the horse people of Glinfell not to repeat the mistakes of their ancestors.

As it turned out, she couldn't even trust her own people to learn from their past. All around her she could see the tension, the cracks, and the fraying of the Great Truce.

Now, she had to wait as Captain Slyvair fought well against an Elk warrior of middling skill. He pressed the sun-man, overcommitted, and Captain Slyvair took advantage. A sidestep, a well-placed slash into the back of the knee followed by a hard stab in the back.

A softer touch would have counted for the point, too, but this way his opponent would be hampered by the pain. A small advantage, but of such small bricks victory could be built.

Not that victory was assured. Not until the Elk lost his head and threw caution to the wind. He tried to substitute aggression for skill and paid the full price for it. Not long after, Captain Slyvair descended the steps and met them.

"Don't take this wrong, Silver Fang, but I'd hoped to face something better than that."

"Yes. But a win is a win. I'm sure you'll face a greater challenge in your next fight."

"But we're not here to congratulate you," Rock said. "I mean, not just that."

The sun-man's eyes narrowed. "Then what is this about?"

"Not here," Leraine said. They spoke Linesan and there was no telling who of the people around her could understand it as well. And a poor grasp of the tongue could be even worse. "This is a delicate topic."

She looked around. "Where is Perun?"

"With Misthell," Rock said. "Slyvair told Perun to guard him."

"I did not think it wise for him to be alone right now. No offense meant, but something is growing between your people."

"You . . . are not wrong. Come, we can talk more freely elsewhere."

Captain Slyvair followed her to the Outer Ring, up the stairs, and into a narrow alley between two feasting halls. They'd still need to keep their voices low; the walls here were thin and they could hear drunken revelers shouting over the music. If one drew away to take a piss, she might overhear them.

The sun-man crossed his arms, his metal one covering the other. "Now, what is this about, exactly? Another revelation?"

"Of a sort. Is it true the Glinfellers only recovered two demon hearts?"

"Yes." Captain Slyvair turned his head a tad to the right. "Why do you say only two?"

Leraine closed her eyes. "I saw three after the demon died." Mother would not have made that mistake.

"You were injured, you suffered a bad blow to the head. Humans don't recover so quickly."

"I know what I saw. But the reason that's important is that I think the murderer stalking Chappenuioc is after them as well. It killed Tense Coil among a trove of demonic remains, and I found a heart right next to the body."

Captain Slyvair scratched his chin with a gleaming claw. "I don't know if it's connected, but with what's going on here . . . Guild Master Haversen died that day. Not during the battle. They found him hanged in his bed chamber. The rest of his household had been slain. There was a confession with him in which he took responsibility for the state of the city's armory and granaries."

"Do they know who did it?"

Both her and Captain Slyvair looked at Rock. "Let me," she said when the sun-man opened his mouth. "Rock, he did it. He killed his family, then hanged himself. At least, that's what it was supposed to look like." Leraine returned her attention to Captain Slyvair. That way she didn't have to see more of her friend's expression. "You think it's this same murderer?"

Captain Slyvair shrugged. "Possible. If you are right about the interest in demon hearts. And that third heart."

She let out a breath. "I'm not sure. I thought the killings here served a goal. But what you described, killing the entire family is excessive. Especially for someone that can impersonate people."

"Excessive or thorough."

"And he despises humans," Rock added.

Captain Slyvair nodded. "If this . . . impersonator enjoys killing. Then he'd indulge himself whenever he has an excuse. Though what is his excuse here?"

"That is the other reason I wished to speak with you. If its goal is getting demon hearts, then—"

"Bait," Captain Slyvair said, giving her a toothy smile.

"Yes. We let it believe it has succeeded in drawing away the guardians. Best way to do that is to actually have the guardians leave."

"And have some who aren't guards and so should be able to escape his notice close the trap instead. But we'd have to get inside your holiest of holy places for that. Will your holy men and women allow that?"

"I . . . don't know."

A laugh bubbled up from deep within Captain Slyvair's chest. "I look forward to seeing the clash. And the fight, should you prevail."

Leraine drew herself up. "Then I have your assistance?"

Captain Slyvair's mirth receded and he thumped his chest with his flesh fist. "I will stand with you. My axe will fell your enemy."

Chapter 24

Baited

"THIS WAS NOT NECESSARY," Sharp Prong said, eyeing Eurik and Slyvair.

"I disagree." Bitten Fin shifted his position. He sat on the only chair in the stuffy room.

Light filtered through little gaps and seams in the wooden structure, reflecting off the gold and silver to turn total darkness into concealing gloom. The scent of oil mixed with the sharper smell of a glowing slow match.

"This is the best plan to end this now," Bitten Fin said. "And if it doesn't work, there should be no harm. At least the increased presence of our guards in the Outer Ring and quarters will ensure the peace there."

"But why let outsiders into the inner sanctum? We could have handled this ourselves." Sharp Prong rolled her *vipaen* in the palm of her left hand with her right. She kept her voice down to a hushed whisper. They all did. And fell silent with every loud creak or thump.

"And risk alerting our quarry? Even if we restricted this party to shamans alone, there's too great a chance the killer would learn of this trap. He's impersonated one shaman already."

"You would have done this without me?" She made a cutting motion with her bronze rod. "You'd rely totally on these . . . three?"

223

"We will not let you down," Silver Fang said. "And I assure you that both Captain Slyvair and Rock are honorable warriors. But, Bitten Fin, are you sure about keeping some of the guardians at their posts? It may decide to kill them rather than go around them."

Bitten Fin let out a long sigh. "It can't be helped. It would look far too suspicious if nobody guarded the inner sanctum. I've set it up so that there are plenty of gaps in the coverage. I made them so obvious I got complaints about that. We have to hope the temptation will prove too much for the killer."

Silence fell once again in the room. They weren't right next to what they believed the murderer's goal to be, but instead held a post closer to the stairs. They'd been waiting for some time now, and the tension ratcheted up at each false alarm. The person coming down the stairs stopped at the level above, that plank groaning was the wind.

Eurik's eyes were half-closed as he stirred the air with his fingers. Wind *chiri* drifted through the cluttered chamber, allowing him to perceive where everybody and everything was. The practice helped keep his mind occupied, but it couldn't keep him distracted.

Slyvair squatted nearby, inspecting the axe he'd been lent. A crescent blade set directly onto the handle. The other side had a wooden block carved into the rough shape of a ram's head. He didn't join the discussion, hadn't said a word since they settled down to wait.

"We will see," Sharp Prong said. "But I warn you, Bitten Fin. If this does not work, if these outsiders take but a pebble from the inner sanctum, you will find yourself replaced and I will call for a harsh punishment. There are limits to your *airhophir*."

Eurik perked up. "I'm not familiar with that word."

The shaman sniffed, then continued speaking to Bitten Fin as if Eurik had said nothing. "Heed my words."

"I am fully aware of the task assigned to me and what I have to do. You should be glad that I let you come along," Bitten Fin said.

"Let me? I thought you at least wise enough to know you could not have stopped me." She stopped fiddling with her *vipaen*. "And you're the one who volunteered—"

Someone came down the stairs and they all fell silent once more. But this time, it didn't stop. The person came down all the way to the ground floor. It was harder to hear them walk over the stone. Flint struck steel and fresh light slipped underneath the door.

"Wait." Bitten Fin's voice was soft, Eurik only heard it because he strained to catch any sound right now.

Eurik drew a bit more wind toward himself, maybe catch some hint of who had come down here. It carried the scent of oil, the click of a sword in its scabbard swinging about. *Is this the killer? He'd have to be impersonating a guard, then. They are the only ones who could walk around with a sword without rousing suspicion.*

It would be a good choice with all the guards moving about. Every time the schedule had changed back on the island, there had been confusion as well. And that had been with a small group, not dealing with thousands of angry people and a string of murders.

He considered letting them know his suspicion, but the light was shifting; the new arrival was on the move. The light spilling in grew stronger; nobody in the room dared to move, and the tension only jumped when that person stopped.

Did he notice something?

Maybe not, because he started moving again. He spoke to himself. Was he counting? At three he stopped, so did the light for a moment before it flickered and steadied. A door screamed like a cat losing a fight, the hint that he was going for the right room.

That had been Sharp Prong's work, though Eurik didn't quite understand the mechanisms behind it. He hadn't sensed anything different in the metal when he'd brushed against one, yet now they behaved as if they hadn't seen a drop of oil or use in years.

"Wait," Bitten Fin repeated. "We need to be sure what it's after." He pushed himself off his chair.

"Oh no, you stay here," Sharp Prong said. "You are not a young hunter anymore. Leave the capture to us."

He hissed between clenched teeth. "I'm not that weak." A muscle in his cheek vibrated as he put more weight on his left leg. "But very well, you can take the lead. Now, let's go." He picked up the slow match and their own oil lamp, but did not light it.

Their door opened quietly, Silver Fang in the lead with Sharp Prong right behind. Both Eurik and Slyvair waited a moment longer. Eurik knew he couldn't match his friend's ability to move without making a sound and Slyvair must have felt the same. Bitten Fin had more confidence and was two steps behind them, after which Eurik and Slyvair followed.

His heart thumped in his chest. Deep shadows hid much of the floor and it only took one coin or bowl getting underfoot to alert the murderer. That, it turned out, wasn't the problem. Light spilled out from the open door, casting shadows on the walls and banners hanging here and there. But that light was moving back to the door.

He emerged just before Silver Fang and Sharp Prong could reach the door themselves. He wore the armor of a guard, sword and club worn on his belt while he held up an oil lamp with his left hand. The murderer stopped, surprise so clearly written on his face that even Eurik couldn't miss it.

"Shaman, what—"

"Save it," Bitten Fin said, lighting his own lamp. "You're not fooling us." He stepped forward, passing in between Sharp Prong and Silver Fang.

"Bitten Fin, stay back," the former said, but he dodged her touch and got even closer to the murderer. He was ignoring their plan.

"I only want to know—*phracto*'s got a heart!" Bitten Fin leaped at the thief, knocking him back. The thief's head bounced off the solid doorpost and both oil lamps shattered against the wall next to them. Flaming oil covered the wall, dripping down even as the dry wood caught fire.

Bitten Fin gave the hungry fire one look. "Alert everybody! We have to put out that fire!"

Silver Fang and Slyvair ran for the stairs, Eurik stopping after the first step as he thought better. "I can slow it down." *Maybe.*

Sharp Prong shook her head. "I'm not leaving you alone with this thing."

"Fine." Bitten Fin hauled himself and the impostor away from the growing fire. It was hungry and hopped from the wall to the nearest banner hanging from the ceiling. There was plenty of light now, reflected by the heaps of gold, silver, bronze, copper, and iron objects; anything not encrusted by rust.

Whirling his arms over his head, Eurik drew the wind toward him and away from the fire. In some ways, fire was almost alive. It could starve, for it needed food; it could freeze, for it needed warmth; it could suffocate, for it needed to breathe.

Anywhere else, he would have opted for smothering it with sand or stone. But that was not an option here, so he would have to draw the air away instead. Prevent fresh air from reaching the fire and let it smother itself with its own exhalations.

This would have been so much easier if I'd followed the Path of the Sun.

A useless thought. There was a reason for the order of Ways. Each person was different. Came to understanding in a different manner. His would end with fire. If he would but live a century more.

The flames surged, crawling toward the ceiling and the ashes of the first banner drifted to the floor.

If fire doesn't end me first.

But his idea worked. The flames diminished as a dome of smoke enveloped the wall. That smoke swirled along with the whirling wind. Eurik felt sweat drip down his back as he struggled to keep the two separate. But it was working.

A commotion to his right put a crack in his concentration. Sharp Prong staggered, clutching her side. She'd toppled a pile of bronze armor gone green with age. Blood seeped through her fingers. The impostor already lay on the ground with his throat cut, and Bitten Fin drew a bloody knife back for a throw.

Time flowed differently when wind *chiri* quickened your senses and let your thoughts fly fast like the wind. *Why has he betrayed us? No. The killer. Here comes the knife. Stop it? Sharp Prong is alive. Knife halfway. Can't switch, no time. Don't forget about the fire. Catch!*

His right arm dipped and plucked the knife out of the air. It was of simple construction with a blade shorter than his hand and an undecorated wooden handle. His whole body spun around. Eurik couldn't stop for a moment or he'd lose a hold of the winds and the fire would roar back to life. He just had to buy some more time. And while he'd never practiced it, Silver Fang and the killer certainly made it look easy. So he threw the knife right back.

Boosted by the wind, it whirled through the air in a blur, only to bounce flat off the murderer's chest. He caught it before it hit the floor and charged Eurik. In a blink or two, the false Bitten Fin was on him, slashing with the knife, punching, kicking.

Eurik dodged, the wind letting him keep pace with his assailant. But he didn't just dance with the murderer, the fire still lived. A palm thrust to the murderer's shoulder only rocked him back a little, a kick blocked instead of deflected left Eurik's leg numb. Dance of the Whirlwind wasn't cutting it against the false Bitten Fin, but if he tried using his reserve of earth *chiri* he'd lose control of the fire.

End this. Now.

Taking a chance, Eurik steered the racing winds away from the fire and into his opponent. It picked him up and threw him across the room, but in the moment that he extended his arms the murderer sliced a fiery line across his left arm.

Heat belched forth; unbreathable air punched Eurik in the face and sent him staggering. He lost his grasp on the winds and the fire came back. Not so fast—it had charred much of the wall—but it hadn't been starved fully.

Backing away, he set himself to try and fight the fire once more. But Eurik caught movement from out of the corner of his eye, Sharp Prong stirred; she was still alive. A moment of hesitation, then he hastened over to crouch besides her.

He laid a hand on her face and sent his senses out. Wasn't easy, since the human body was a mix of *chiri* and water dominated. But blood held a sprinkling of earth, and bones were a steady framework to guide his search.

The knife had gone through arteries and had hit the lung. Blood wasn't just leaking out, it was flowing into that lung. There was a . . . bubbling quality to Sharp Prong's breathing. But he could fix this.

Eurik hadn't considered he'd be using them for this, but it should work. He focused inward—on the three heavy stone pills sitting in his stomach—and pulled the earth *chiri* out of one of them. He guided the energy into the shaman's body.

There wasn't enough to simply strengthen everything, he had to be more targeted than that. Half went to promote the production of blood, to replenish what had been lost. The rest Eurik used to take hold of the blood that had gotten into the lung and everywhere else it wasn't supposed to be and pull it back. Not all the way back into the arteries. Instead, he compressed and hardened the spilled blood to plug the holes.

He had to take care not to damage anything else when he did that. Not easy when his left arm began to itch where he'd been cut. As if that itch had conjured the cause, the false Bitten Fin appeared.

Eurik tensed, but couldn't move without interrupting his work and wasting the limited earth *chiri* he had. But the murderer barely gave him a look as he shielded his eyes and plunged through the fire into the room.

He's not here for me. But that's not my problem right now.

Concentrating on Sharp Prong again, he finished sealing her wound. It would be uncomfortable, but she wasn't going to die. He coughed and realized that although she wouldn't die from the stab, other dangers could kill them right now.

We have to move.

Shifting his position, he brought his arms under her shoulders and legs, tried to. His left arm felt like all the muscles had turned into water. His heart was beating faster and struggled against his attempt to calm it.

A glance at the arm shattered what optimism he had for Sharp Prong's chances, and his own. The veins leading away from the cut—and some of the flesh itself—had a grayish tint. And the shaman's heart hadn't eased off its pace either, even though she wasn't losing any blood anymore.

How could I forget? Silver Fang uses poison. Easy for him to get a hold of.

The false Bitten Fin rushed out of the room and ran for the stairs, stairs on which a lot of other feet were running. Eurik could hear them coming. Help was coming, but would it be in time?

Chapter 25
A Matter of Time

LERAINE LED THE WAY down, the heavy bucket twisting and swinging with every bounding step. Captain Slyvair was right behind her, a bucket in either hand while everybody else came after with only one bucket or just a jug.

The heavy smell of burning wood and choking smoke met them, carried up by a warm wind. But they were armed to face this enemy. It wasn't the first time Chappenuioc had faced fire and they had not only water, but sand to combat it.

And Rock can use that to stop this. I just hope the murderer hasn't used this to try and escape.

Nobody was coming up the stairs, that should be a good sign. She did find Bitten Fin at the bottom of the steps, hunched over and clutching his stomach. "Hurry! The murderer is dead but it almost killed Sharp Prong. Put out the fire!"

He kept shouting, hurrying them along as they ran. The fire was out of control, spreading out over the walls and even the ceiling. The flames gave more than enough light to see Rock crouched over a fallen Sharp Prong even through the haze of ash and smoke.

"Rock! We have sand! Can you put out the fire with that?" She hacked a cough.

Her friend looked up and shook his head. "No! You have to go catch Bitten Fin! He's the murderer!"

Leraine faltered, holding everybody behind her up for a moment before they started rushing around her. Of course, they hadn't understood. Eurik had been speaking Linesan. Her mind grappled with the words as well, then her gaze fell on the still form of the guardian, his throat cut and blood no longer flowing. With a snarl, she dropped her bucket and ran back the way she'd come, Captain Slyvair hot on her heels.

Behind her she could hear the hiss of water hitting the fire. She'd have to leave that to them and Rock.

It was a small relief that Silver Fang didn't question him; she simply accepted his claim and acted on it. That left the fire and the poison. He'd done what he could for Sharp Prong, but it had taken all the earth *chiri* he had to find the poison and draw it out along with the blood it had mingled with.

The people Silver Fang had gathered ignored him in favor of the fire. Jugs of water were splashed over the banners and walls; others threw buckets of sand. The latter could only work on ground level flames, but they gave him something to work with.

He struggled to his feet and staggered over as the itch worked its way up his arm. He'd had enough for Sharp Prong, but not himself. The ones who had thrown their load on the fire now raced back to get more, while a few scooped up the buckets Silver Fang and Captain Slyvair had dropped.

"Don't throw them," Eurik said, only to be met by incomprehension. Right, he needed to use their language. "I need.

I can put the fire out. With sand." It was hot down here, he was sweating and his heart beat against his ribs.

No, that's not the heat.

They walked over to him, but not fast enough and he wasn't steady. Impatient, he plunged his hand into the bucket and drew out the sand, then used a couple of tentacles of the stuff to siphon the other two.

It tempted him. He could siphon the earth *chiri* out of this sand and heal himself. But then he couldn't use it to put out the fire. Without *chiri* the grains would fall apart. His left arm flopped as he turned and sent the sand out.

It connected with the piles of sand that had smothered some of the fire, adding it to its mass before it attacked the flames that had withstood the splashes of water. It covered every bit of burning wood and cloth in a blanket of sand, suffocating the flames before moving on.

And as the sand sought out the last of the flames, the itch crawled into his chest. The sand fell to the ground, so did Eurik. His knees hit the unyielding Inza stone as his right hand clawed at his chest.

People spoke, shouted. A hand on his shoulder. "Poison. I have—" He didn't know what language he used as he finally lost the struggle and the itch became white hot pain squeezing his heart.

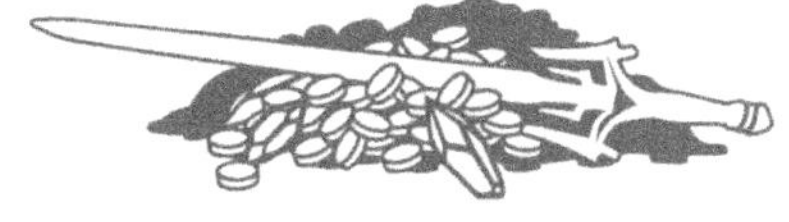

Leraine ran up the stairs, but she wasn't the only one. She caught a glimpse of Captain Slyvair behind her, and up ahead she could hear more people coming down. This quick response was great: it would save much of the inner sanctum. But it also masked the murderer's flight.

She gambled that it wasn't going to hide. That it would try to use speed and its head start to evade pursuit. The gamble seemed to be the right one when she came across the shamans' students still sorting themselves out. Someone had obviously plowed through them. Like she did now. "Make way! Coming through!"

She resisted the temptation to pull her club out to threaten them. It wasn't needed anyway. Though now what? Had it kept going, or tried to hide on the level below the entrance to throw them off? But why risk getting cornered when it had what it wanted and an unobstructed path out of Chappenuioc?

Leraine kept going, only to stop in the fresh air. *Where did it go? Left, right, forward? The nearest rope bridge, or maybe down a ladder?*

Captain Slyvair moved past and threw himself down, his good ear to the floor.

"What are—"

"Quiet," he hissed. The sun-man shifted his head. "There, running, away from us." Captain Slyvair pushed himself up to his feet with a single heave and ran.

Leraine didn't question it and followed. He led them to the outer walkway of the Inner Ring and went to the right. Evening had turned to night, the cold air burning in her lungs. She finally had the time to consider her failure.

How long had it impersonated Bitten Fin? How had she not noticed it wasn't a Person? Was it going to get away with its crimes?

Finally she spotted a dark figure holding something. The height was right too. But they weren't running, they were talking to someone else. The two heard them coming; one glance and they did run. That was good enough for Leraine. The second one had to be an accomplice. Why else would they run?

"Stop!" She had no hope they'd listen, but it might draw a guard's attention. "Murd—"

Someone ran out of a corridor and collided with Captain Slyvair, shoulder first. The impact sent the sun-man off the walkway and through the railing. He somehow managed to grab the edge of the platform with his right hand rather than falling to his death.

The attacker acted quickly, already drawing a hidden sword and swinging it at Captain Slyvair's fingers.

Leraine herself had been a mere three steps behind the long-limbed sun-man, close enough to act. She pulled out her club and swung to interpose it. Rather than having his fingers sliced off, the club rapped him on the knuckles as the blade collided with her weapon.

Now she had a moment to think, to take stock. But that only brought fresh shock. The blade hadn't been hidden, it had been coiled. The few warriors that used the segmented blade were nearly all members of her own tribe. They were rare and expensive. Her sisters were the only wielders she personally knew.

She tried to read her enemy's *draen*, but a bird mask representing the raven hid much. Leraine did get a glimpse of the back of Raven's head. So not Wolf, Ferret, Fox, Orca, or Puma; not likely to be Elk either.

Raven pulled back, Leraine already bringing her own weapon up before she realized that her enemy was retreating out of range. *She's stalling!* Leraine didn't know why—it was the wrong move given their respective weaponry—but Irelith had told her not to waste time when your opponent made a mistake.

"Why are you helping that thing?" Leraine pressed forward with an overhead strike. Raven had to support her blade to deflect. "Defile the most sacred place of our people!" Her next swing Raven sidestepped and Leraine had to duck the counterattack.

Her opponent didn't let up and Leraine struggled to keep the segmented sword away. What training she'd had with staff and club had been years ago. The weapon had runes carved into it that let her connect to it much like with her own sword, but the same was true for Raven.

Her enemy's segmented blade struck like a viper, coiling around her staff when she blocked and nearly taking out an eye as the tip nicked the corner of her forehead. She had no choice but to give ground. And with every moment wasted thus, the murderer got a greater lead. "You should wear a Crow mask. Own your treachery."

Her hand on the hilt tightened and Raven lunged. Leraine couldn't help a hint of a smile as she deflected the blow and went in for a counterstroke. But Raven had kept a better awareness, her back-swing slicing through several of Captain Slyvair's fingers even as she blocked Leraine's blow with her free arm.

Raven fell back with a gasp of pain. But Leraine did not press her advantage right away. Raven caught on and gave the hanging sun-man an exaggerated look. Then she ran off, as if she was daring for Leraine to pursue.

I . . . I can't.

The staff clattered to the ground so she could seize Captain Slyvair's wrist with both hands. "Don't," he said. "I'm fine. Fall probably won't—"

"Shut up." The words escaped past gritted teeth. Every muscle in her body strained at the heavy weight, the awkward angle. "Not. Letting. You. Die!" Finally she pulled him up enough that he could grasp one of the railing's supports with his metal hand and then it got easy.

"Go, go," Captain Slyvair said even as he pulled himself back onto the walkway. "I'm fine. Go!"

"Right." Leraine picked up her staff and started running, but every muscle protested and her lungs burned. She pushed through, eyes darting this way and that, looking for Raven, looking for the murderer.

Instead, she came across a pair of guardians coming the other way over the walkway. Leraine ran over to them. "Quick, did you see Bitten Fin? Or a woman in a raven mask?"

But instead of answering they backed away and leveled their staffs at her. "Stop it right there!"

"Drop the weapon," the other one said.

"What are you doing? I have permission," she said, before remembering that that permission had been granted by the fake Bitten Fin. No, Sharp Prong had agreed, more or less. "I was chasing the murderer. It looked like Bitten Fin. Did you see him?"

The guardians grew unsure, but their weapons didn't waver and they kept an eye on her. "Did you notice a limp?" one asked the other.

That guardian frowned, before giving a slow shake of her head that picked up speed. "I . . . don't know. I don't remember."

Leraine ground her teeth. "You're wasting time. Either help me or get out of my way."

Before they had a chance to decide, someone came around the bend. She could feel the vibration of his footfalls even before Captain Slyvair came into view and he wasn't slowing down. "Out of the way."

She didn't know who he meant, but a second later she got the idea. Throwing herself flat against the wall, the grizzled sun-man rushed her by and threw his arms wide to catch both of the guards.

They were good, they had to be if they'd made it into the order of holy guardians. One thrust low with her staff fully extended to trip Captain Slyvair, the other spun their staff around in a horizontal block and took a step forward. They were good, but Captain Slyvair was better.

He jumped over the thrust and kicked out with both legs, hitting the blocking staff. Captain Slyvair came to a stop in midair, all his forward power transferred to the guard who stumbled back and over his partner.

Leraine noted this in passing, already running after the sun-man when he'd jumped. She hopped to the side, over Captain Slyvair. Another hop past the entangled guardians and she had a clear run again. Judging by their words, they'd encountered Bitten Fin. She could still catch him.

Somewhere behind her, she could hear a bell being rung. More and more of the Inner Ring was roused to action as people shouted and ran. Another bell picked up the alarm and carried it further.

All good things, if anybody knew what was going on. But nobody did, and she didn't have the time to spare to explain it to them as she passed bleary-eyed shamans, hoarse loremistresses and other loretellers, but no guardians. The false Bitten Fin had sent those away to patrol the outer areas of Chappenuioc, all part of its plan.

A rope bridge came into view and a figure was hurrying across it to the Outer Ring. Leraine's grin had a lot of teeth as she found some hidden reserve and ran a little faster. She wouldn't get to the false Bitten Fin before the murderer could enter the Outer Ring, but she'd be close enough to make it a chase rather than a search.

It knew it too, looking over its shoulder as the bridge swayed when she jumped across and over the hand rope instead of taking the extra moments to run around the post. The murderer gave up any pretense of being Bitten Fin, no hint of a limp as it ran with easy, bounding steps.

Leraine ran after it, only to stumble as someone called out behind her. "Fang!"

Raven stood at the end of the rope bridge, segmented blade poised above her head. She waited until she was sure Leraine saw her before she swung, cutting all the ropes in one motion.

Time seemed to slow down. Leraine was trapped, too far from either side to find safety. No, that wasn't quite true. Her spirit pleading for Ghisa's aid she turned back and sprinted after the murderer. It reached the Outer Ring with one final jump a moment before the bridge gave way under Leraine's feet.

She threw herself forward, grasping, clawing for a solid hold on the wooden boards as the entire bridge swung down. The end of the bridge ripped through an awning and crashed into a platform, splinters the size of daggers flying through the air.

Now dragging along the ground, it slowed the rest of the bridge down so that it didn't quite hit the framework of the Outer Ring with the same force. It still slammed into the wooden skeleton of Chappenuioc. And so did Leraine.

Her vision turned black for a moment, her head ringing like a bell. Her nose throbbed, dripping blood into her mouth.

Broken, again. Still alive. But that voice. No.

Leraine shook her head and immediately regretted it. Looking down brought another wave of nausea and her vision swam, but she couldn't keep hanging there. Even thinking of shifting her grip hurt, and her arms shook at the notion of climbing.

Squeezing her eyes repeatedly, she finally saw that the ground wasn't too far off. Even better, the bridge didn't hang straight down but had a sort of curving slope. She could simply let go and slide down.

Her slide quickly turned into a tumble, Leraine could only tuck her head in and endure as she rolled to a stop in the middle of the Inner Circle.

I'm out of the competition. Doesn't matter. And was that? No. I need to get up. Can't lie down. Come on. Get up. Get. Up.

"Raaah," she croaked as she used an elbow to push herself up. Only to collapse once more, spent.

Chapter 26
New Plan

EURIK EMERGED FROM oblivion with a vile taste in his mouth, a lingering ache in his arm, and a heavy weight on his chest. It was the weight that drew his attention. It belonged to a stone smoothed by the patient hand of a river. Earth *chiri* still flowed from it into him, replenishing his strength.

With a deep breath, he drew all the energy into himself in one go. The stone crumbled into smaller and smaller pieces which slid off him as he drew himself into a seating position.

"As I told you," Silver Fang said. "Rock can gain strength from the world to aid in his recovery."

"We'll see how much," someone else said. It took him a moment to recognize Sharp Prong's voice.

He opened his eyes and immediately had to shield his eyes against the light. He was somewhere in Chappenuioc; the lack of earth *chiri* all around him told him as much.

"It would have worked better if he'd been away from this place," Misthell said. "Morning, Eurik, it's really good you're still alive. And not just for me. It's good for you too."

"Yes, good . . . morning to you too, Misthell," Eurik said. He opened his eyes again, just a little. "What happened. Did we catch the fake Bitten Fin? And what happened to the real one?"

The silence that followed did not bode well. Their expressions confirmed as much.

"He's dead," Slyvair said. Sharp Prong gave him a look and he batted it away with his hand. A hand that was missing fingers. "I see no point in dancing around the matter. We got fooled."

Silver Fang was injured too, fingers wrapped in bandages. Eurik noted Perun was here as well, holding Misthell.

"He got away, then," Eurik said. He swung his legs off the bed and tested their strength. "How are we going to find him?"

"Oh no," Silver Fang said, crossing the room to push him back down. "We will speak first of your recklessness."

Slyvair guffawed. "Ha, pot meet pan."

Silver Fang ignored him. "You didn't tell me you were poisoned. It nearly cost you your life. And now you want to jump out of bed and act like it didn't happen. Heartvice is not something to be shrugged off so easily."

"Perhaps you should let me examine him first," Sharp Prong said. Guiding Silver Fang a step back, she addressed Eurik. "We can answer your questions as you answer mine."

Eurik nodded, after a moment's hesitation. That did sound reasonable and he honestly wasn't sure how long he'd be able to stand before his reserve of earth *chiri* ran out. He gave another look toward the sunlight streaming in. "How long have I been out, anyway?"

"A night and half a day," Slyvair said as the shaman placed her fingers here and there, plucked at his eyelid and told him to show her his tongue.

"Shouldn't you be at the competition, then?"

"Rock, we're all out of the competition."

"Oh."

"Don't you try to apologize as well," Slyvair said, pushing off from the wall and holding up his mangled hand so that everybody could clearly see it. "This will be healed in a couple of weeks. I'm not that old yet. And as for the tournament, I competed to test myself. I was never good enough with sword and shield that I could win against the best of the Mochedan."

"Right. And no, no lingering pain in my chest. Some in the arm," Eurik said in response to the shaman's question. That prompted Sharp Prong to prod and squeeze the limb, asking if that hurt. It didn't, much.

Silver Fang sighed. "I'm out as well, unfortunately." She looked at her hands. "But not all may be lost. Whatever its intentions, the face stealer did quell some of the unrest. There were no incidents last night and no fresh murders. That is, other than the guardian's. And the news of what happened here has given everybody's anger a new target."

"Not like we could have kept the devastation hidden," Sharp Prong said. "But it was Bitten Fin who advocated we hid what we knew. To lull the murderer into complacency, to catch out someone who knew too much. He had convincing arguments, now I wonder if he'd already been replaced. How blind have I been?"

She shook her head. "You have recovered." Sharp Prong gave Eurik a hard stare. "And . . . thank you for saving my life. I felt some of what you did. I recognized the poison, but not in time to counter it." She stepped back and rearranged her shawl.

"Right." Eurik pushed himself to his feet, a tremor of weakness running down his legs before he steadied. "And you saved me, I take it. So thank you."

"My contribution was small," Sharp Prong said.

"She has also told Fervent to go away," Silver Fang said with a hint of a smile. "She came by this morning—as soon as you didn't show up for your first match—to demand you be placed in her custody."

The shaman shrugged. "The girl should know better than to interfere with someone under my care. And shouldn't have needed a reminder that she is no loreteller. Her word is not law! Bah, they let anybody become *rangtauk* these days."

Eurik tried to thank her, but the shaman interrupted him as he got started. "I suggest you stop now. My life is no small thing and I do not appreciate anybody claiming otherwise. I will know when that debt is paid. Not you."

"All right." He didn't know what else to say. He was at a loss in general. "What do we do now? The murderer will be long gone by now. He got what he wanted." And the only people he found who knew his parents were Fervent and Ambiguous Coin.

"Maybe," Slyvair said. "Nobody's been allowed to leave since last night. He might not have had the opportunity. And he's not acting alone." His gaze went from Silver Fang to Sharp Prong, both looking away at his words. "He has an accomplice. At least one."

"There's no evidence it's anything more than a single traitor!" Silver Fang hissed and relaxed her balled fists, shaking them. She turned to Eurik. "But yes. We chased the face stealer, and it was talking to someone. Then we were attacked by someone in a raven's mask. That one probably was Mochedan."

Slyvair quirked a brow ridge. "Probably?"

"Fine, she had to be. She wielded a segmented blade as only one of us could. She also cut the bridge while I was on it. That is how I got injured."

"She wasn't so gentle with me," Slyvair said, showing off his missing digits again. "But this is good news! One person who could be anybody is near impossible to find. But three—one of whom used a weapon I know is an oddity even among these people—that's far better odds."

"I don't know," Misthell said. "I wouldn't bet on us here."

"Even better," Silver Fang said. "When was the last time you took a winning bet? And . . . I do not like it but Captain Slyvair does have a point. A traitor will be easier to find."

"But not by you," Sharp Prong said. "This is a matter for Chappenuioc to resolve. And you," she told Eurik, "still need to regain some strength. So don't even think of sneaking off to perform some idiot heroics. Actually, that goes for all of you. None of you are in fighting shape."

"I'm glad you noticed," Misthell said. "I've been telling these people to be more careful but they just won't listen. I'm just not cut out for this life of action and adventure."

"As you command, shaman," Silver Fang said, inclining her head.

Eurik thought of objecting, but he was in the Inner Ring at the moment. The mere thought of having to make it all the way out of Chappenuioc before he could draw on more earth *chiri*, made his legs tremble. "Could you bring me another stone?"

"Of course." Silver Fang inclined her head. "I'll come around this evening. If that is all right?"

Sharp Prong nodded. "Yes, I'll let the guardians know to let you pass."

Leraine felt like a coward. She should have said something to Sharp Prong, to Rock, to Captain Slyvair, yes, even to Misthell. The living sword complained like a coward but when battle was joined he was a true ally.

And that it is only a suspicion is an excuse. I just don't want it to be true.

Yesterday, there had been a sharp tension brewing beneath the surface of celebration and merriment. But that surface had receded now. Walking through Chappenuioc on her way to the Snake Quarter, she found many giving her searching looks. Measuring how much of a threat she'd be. Was she the crow?

The armed and unarmed competitions were still going on. She passed Dancing Ember himself, in the process of demolishing some poor Falcon. Some in the crowd cheered, and all of those wore the not-quite armor of Truce Warriors.

No chance now of Mother's plan working. But maybe it won't matter.

There was some music, but it only added to the tense, somber atmosphere and nobody stopped to listen. Judging from their baskets and bowls, few bothered to gift them either.

From the Outer Ring onward, she came across guardian patrols. Not the pairs of past days but groups of five, always within earshot or sight of one another. People got out of their way, which was easier because there were fewer people out and about.

They hadn't left, that much was clear when she passed the Boar quarter. It was packed, with triple the guards on its entrances which kept an eye on anybody who got close. Even a fellow tribe member was stopped and asked some question before she was allowed to pass inside.

Something similar happened to Leraine herself when she reached the Snake Quarter. Four guards, all from different septs stopped her. Thankfully, one was from Urumoy. "Good morning, Mere Scratch."

"Good morning, Silver Fang. You were missed last night."

"Yes. I was involved with last night's incident."

"Of course you were." Mere Scratch shook her head. The fine lines of the scars crisscrossing her face moved as she gave Leraine a wan smile. "Well, we've taken some precautions because of that. Can't have a whatever sneaking in."

"And how do I prove that?"

"By telling us the true name of the Great Serpent."

Leraine looked around. "Here? In the open?" Her heart pounded. Yes, it was a clever answer to the question of finding out who was the impostor. Still, to speak her name out it in the open where others could hear went against all practice and tradition.

"Good reaction," a warrior from Uthamac said. "But we still need to hear you say her name."

Leraine glanced around one more time. "Fine." But she leaned in and whispered it into Mere Scratch's ear. "Ghisa." And shivered as the word passed her lips. For a moment, she felt naked.

Mere Scratch nodded. "Right, you can pass. Before you go though, did you bring any weapons with you to Chappenuioc? Armor?"

"Just my sword. Do you need me to take a turn guarding the quarter?"

"No. Just keep it within reach while you're here. Just in case."

"I will." Leraine took care not to show how concerning those words were. *Is this just in case the murderer appears within the quarter? Or are they expecting trouble from their fellow Mochedan?*

"Ah, did you see my sisters? Have they gone out?"

"Golden Tongue did," Mere Scratch said. "Her and about ten others. Resting Python didn't pass through here." She shrugged. So Anseri might still be in the quarter.

Thanking her for the information, Leraine entered the quarter and navigated its crowded passages. Many here were armed, some even wore some armor. Yet it felt a little better here. Less suspicion rested in the eyes she met, someone laughed. But her own mood only grew darker as she entered her own room and belted her sword on.

Not that I'll need it. I won't.

Her first try was Anseri's quarters, but they were empty. So were Ferisha's, but that she'd expected. Asking around only told her that Ferisha had indeed left the quarter. Leraine took that opportunity to get some lunch as well, only to regret the decision.

Instead of asking others where Anseri was, it was Leraine who got swamped with questions. How had she gotten injured? Had she really fought Tense Coil's murderer? Could it really imitate people?

Her soup had gotten cold and left a sand-like residue on her teeth when she finally got around to eating it. Then she had to use half her cup to wash the residue away. The taste hadn't been great either, but she made no comment when she returned her bowl to the cook. Wasn't his fault she hadn't enjoyed her meal much.

At least one of her questioners had been able to steer Leraine in the right direction. Anseri was holding court in one of the upper rooms of the Great Hall. That Great Hall was sitting on the outer edge of their quarter, acting as a solid boundary wall and a fallback position should the unthinkable happen.

The Great Hall was not used to house anybody. Nobody ever slept in there. It was used for storage and the leaders of the septs could gather inside to decide matters that impacted the entire tribe.

But that hall on the ground floor was closed, the doors bound shut with ropes and wax seals on the knots. There weren't many people in here, mostly men carrying out supplies to feed the ravenous horde that had descended upon Chappenuioc and now didn't want to go out to eat or drink.

Halfway up the stairs, Leraine realized she was stalking. Her feet barely making a sound, her sword pushed out of the way so that it wouldn't bump into anything.

Useless. I'm not trying to ambush anybody.

But she couldn't get herself to stop as she moved up the corridor. The quarter was outside of Chappenuioc proper and so mage lights could be used to light the corridors and rooms of the Great Hall. But with so few using it right now, only three illuminated the long hallway. Entire stretches were steeped in darkness, with one exception. A closed room at the end where light spilled out from underneath the door.

Getting a little closer, Leraine heard the familiar voice of her sister. "I know, I know. And I agree, we can't wait around while the Truce Warriors forge ahead. But the shamans have been clear, maintaining order in Chappenuioc is their responsibility. And we can't act without their blessing. Well, not outside the quarter. Which is why we're questioning everybody coming in."

"It's not enough," someone else said, others making noises of agreement. "We can't wait around and let them dictate the pace. We should strike, before they do."

"I think you're overestimating how ready they are. And to act too fast risks shattering the very pact we seek to preserve. No, now is the time to prepare."

Leraine hesitated, then resolutely knocked and opened the door. Twenty-three women turned to her, a few readying to draw their weapons.

"Sister," Anseri said. "You either had a great night, or a terrible one."

"Few had a good night last night." Leraine eyed the others. A few of them looked to Anseri for guidance. The rest kept their attention on Leraine. They shifted as she took a step inside the room, as if an enemy had entered their presence.

Am I different? I hold my tongue, rather than speaking openly.

"True. Very true. Were you looking for me?"

"I was." Leraine deliberately ignored the rest and approached her sister, making sure to keep her hand away from her own sword. "Did you see our sister this morning?"

Anseri blinked. "I . . . did. Yes. Not that we spoke." She narrowed her eyes. "Why do you ask?"

Leraine spotted it. A segmented blade wrapped around Anseri's waist like a belt, the hilt on her stomach. But the decoration didn't match her memories of last night. Relief staggered her; she had to fight to regain her balance and it left her limbs a little weak.

Anseri reached her side to support her right after. "Are you . . . Everybody, my sister and I have family matters to discuss. We'll talk later."

"I'm fine," Leraine said. But she said nothing about the rest. It would be better if they didn't hear her words. They filed out quickly, only bidding Anseri goodbye and not her. A small insult, not one to take notice of in these circumstances.

"You don't look fine," Anseri said when the door closed. "Now what is this about? Why do you want to know where Golden Tongue is?"

"I . . . was involved in last night's events. I confronted the murderer of Tense Coil. It had an accomplice. A woman that used a segmented blade." Leraine swayed.

Something's wrong. This weakness . . .

"Did you think it was me? Or our sister?"

Leraine shook her head. "Something's wrong. I'm . . . I think I've been poisoned." Her mind settled on lunch, the perfect opportunity. She'd been crowded, distracted. The soup hadn't just gone cold.

"Oh, that's nothing to worry about. It won't kill you."

Leraine finally caught on to her sister's words. She pulled away and grasped for her sword. But her hand knocked into the hilt instead of getting a hold of it, and she couldn't pull out of Anseri's tightening hold. "But. You?"

"I didn't think you'd come right to me. It does make this easier. Now, stop struggling. Just go to sleep. That's it."

Leraine struggled as her sister shifted her hold, but she felt so weak. Darkness crept in from the edges of her vision, narrowing it to a point. "Scaleless traitor."

From up at the end of the tunnel, Anseri's voice echoed down in an incomprehensible mumble.

Chapter 27

Listen

EURIK LOOKED UP FROM the book Sharp Prong had provided him. The light was fading. It wasn't evening yet, but twilight was rapidly approaching and he could detect the first hint of dinner's preparations. But no Silver Fang.

He tried to return his attention to the story of Hassajj Boudhadhi, better known as Stonespeaker. One of the lesser-known Nine, but knowing what he knew now about the dwarves' connection to the Ways put his deeds in a new light. Yet he found his thoughts wandering.

When he heard someone approach he put the book away, only to be disappointed when Sharp Prong entered the room. "You don't have to give me that look," she said before looking around. "So she hasn't come by yet."

"Not yet." Eurik got up from the bed. There was still a lingering weakness, but he managed to stand and walk without assistance.

"She probably found the nearest deadly danger and threw herself at it," Misthell said. "I'm surprised nothing's on fire yet."

They both directed a look in the living sword's direction. "What, just saying out loud what you're thinking. She's got a knack for getting into sticky situations where she needs me. I have the scratches to show for it."

"I told Silver Fang to stay out of our affairs," Sharp Prong said. "Suggesting that she would ignore our commands is an insult. One that would land you in much trouble if you weren't an object. Instead, the burden would fall to your owner."

"I'm sure Silver Fang wouldn't mind it. She knows Misthell and how much he means what he says."

The living sword rested against the wall at the foot end of the bed. "And what's that supposed to mean?"

"That you could use some new material?" Eurik turned to Sharp Prong as Misthell shouted. "Still, he's not entirely wrong. You have heard nothing?"

The shaman shook her head and adjusted her shawl. "No. Though I do have other duties to attend to."

Eurik nodded and looked out the entrance and over Chappenuioc. Various banners and awnings rippled as the wind toyed with them. He was a little worried, but Sharp Prong had to be right. She was fine and he was just trying to not think about the future.

But that future was coming quickly. His purpose here was done, he wouldn't find anything more on his parents. His next best source of information would be in Puma lands. Eurik didn't know quite where they lay—somewhere in the west, close to Linesan lands—or how big the territory was.

He knew it was far from Leraine's home. If he went there, he would have to go alone. Even here, where all were supposed to be at peace with one another, there had been hostility between the tribes. It was clear to him Silver Fang would not be welcome even if she wanted to accompany him. But did she?

Silver Fang had come home and her people were in trouble. In the short time that he knew her, she had not once hesitated to do what she saw as her duty no matter how dangerous it was. So he knew what her answer would be, but was he still expected to ask?

Now that was a harder question. Silver Fang had done her best, but her people were still strange to him and could be sensitive about the strangest things. He had no desire to offend her, but what would be worse here? Forcing her to give him the answer they both knew she had to give, or treat her as a stranger he hardly knew?

Wait, why am I thinking so hard on this? Aren't shamans supposed to council people on questions? Or was that priests?

"I see some color has returned to your cheeks. No stiffness in the limbs," Sharp Prong said. "You've recovered well enough, even without more aid from your magic."

"It's not magic." The words were a reflex by now. "Sharp Prong, could I ask you a question?"

"Tell me, does that sound as dumb in the soulless tongue as it does in Thelauk? If the answer is no, you have already transgressed. Bah, yes, you can ask. I make no promises on any answer though."

"Right." Eurik still hesitated, then plunged ahead. "I came here to find out more about my parents. It hasn't worked. Not well. So I intend to go to the Puma tribe to find someone who knew my father."

Sharp Prong hummed. "I know some shamans there. I can give you a letter that will open some doors and secure you a roof over your head for a night. But you may not get many answers. Your speech is clearly Snake, and there's a well-nursed grudge between the two tribes."

That hadn't been his question, but that last part drew his attention. "How so?" If his father and mother had some inherited feud between them, how had they ended up together? How had he come to be?

Misthell piped up. "You got a day?"

The shaman sighed. "Your sword isn't wrong. It is a long tale. But since I do not have a day, I'll simply say that it's from when they both lived side by side, before the Rift War and the Great Truce. And being apart hasn't done anything to wear away that hostility. If you want to know more, you'll have to ask a slitherer or a stalker."

"Or me," Misthell said.

"Slitherer? Stalker?" This was the first time Eurik had heard anybody refer to members of the Snake or Puma tribe as such.

She gave him a hint of a smile. "Words not to be used to their faces. Or where outsiders can hear. And I'm sure they've got their own word for my people, too. Please do not tell anyone I used those words. I'm supposed to be above such things." She let out a long sigh.

"Of course. However, I didn't intend to ask for aid. It was about asking to accompany, not you. I am not saying this right. I . . . I do not know if I should ask Silver Fang to come along. I know she has just returned home after a year's absence and it's obvious she has duties. But would she take it as an insult if I simply assumed her answer? Am I supposed to pretend I don't know it already?"

"Ah." Sharp Prong stroked her chin. "Not asking wouldn't be an insult," she said slowly. "Though I always council against assuming . . ." She looked away for a moment before returning her attention to him and cleared her throat. "Yes. Ah, you weren't planning on just leaving without telling her your plans?"

"No. I was going to say goodbye."

"Good, because simply disappearing would have been wrong. Can never know what outsiders think is acceptable behavior. Some of it is just insane. Right. I recommend you let her know a few days before you intend to leave what your plans are. I make no pretense to know Silver Fang, so I have no idea what she'll do. And I've just been reminded that we all know less than we think."

Eurik nodded slowly. "Wise words."

"Yes. I've been known to find some from time to time." Sharp Prong looked outside. "I think it might be best to get some dinner now. Perhaps she's been delayed and will come after she's had her own evening meal."

"Perhaps." But that didn't sound like Leraine.

Snippets of awareness pricked her mind, threads that helped Leraine to pull herself out of the murk of oblivion. A sour taste in her mouth, rough rope scratching her wrists, the scent of a soup laden with slices of sausage, wood scraping against wood.

I've been captured. Again. Who . . . Oh no.

Memory finally returned. Recalling Irelith's training, she did her best to fake unconsciousness and relied on her other senses to feel out her surroundings.

There were ropes around not only her wrists, but her legs, chest, and head as well. The last two tied her to a round beam while her hands were tied behind this wooden pillar. Her sword had been removed, so had the escape kit she kept with her. Irelith had always told her that the one time you needed a file would be the one time you decided not to bother with it.

But she'd been taught by Irelith too.

Chancing a deeper breath, she discerned other smells underneath the soup. A mélange of foodstuffs, dust, and earth. Through her eyelids there was light, but it was soft and very steady.

Mage light. I'm in a cellar then, probably underneath the Great Hall itself. Haven't been moved far.

The one guarding her wasn't too far away, and in front of her. She'd have a good view of Leraine then, but not the rope tied around her wrists. If only she'd had something to use. Spreading her fingers, Leraine felt around. Maybe something had shattered down here. A pottery shard would cut through her restraints with enough time.

"So how long are you going to keep this up?"

Leraine did her best not to flinch, or to freeze up. Kept her breathing steady.

"It's not going to work," her sister said. "We've both been trained by the Viper, Leraine."

She gave up on pretense and shot her sister an angry look. "You were only her student for a year, Anseri."

Anseri held up her curved spoon. "Two years." She sat on a stool, a mage light resting on a box within her reach which cast their shadows on the wall to Leraine's left. No sign of Leraine's blade. "And I'd say I learned more than enough." Her smirk was as infuriating as ever.

"So you were the one underneath the raven mask."

Her sister had been setting her bowl away, but she froze at Leraine's words and then slammed it down. "Crow's luck! I thought you'd figured it out. You mean you weren't looking to confront me?"

Leraine tried to shrug, but there wasn't much give in the ropes. "Either you or our sister. I thought it made sense for it to be Golden Tongue. But I wasn't sure."

Anseri trailed her fingers through her hair, pushing the locks away from her forehead. "Got a little hasty then. Ah, it doesn't matter. In a way, it made this easier."

"Yes, about that. What is this? Why am I not dead?"

Her sister's eyes widened and her mouth worked. "You thought I'd kill you?"

"You tried last night."

But Anseri shook her head and smiled. She had the sheer gall to smile! "If I wanted to kill you I wouldn't have risked that warning before cutting the bridge. You're family, Leraine. And family should stand together."

"You're also supposed to stand with your sept, your tribe, your people. Instead, you betrayed everybody and broke our most sacred laws."

Anseri flinched and looked like she'd bitten into something sour, but she shook her head. "I did break the law, yes. But betrayal? No. What I'm doing will save us, all of us."

"And what are you doing? You and that . . . thing." Leraine held her breath. She doubted her sister would fall for it, but she was out of options. Keeping Anseri talking, finding out anything, was the most she could do.

Her sister stood up and started pacing. "I know what you're trying to do." Leraine froze. "You and mother." *Wait, what?* "I even agree, up to a point. Ferisha has hitched her horse to a wagonload of idiots. Breaking the Great Truce won't free our people to reclaim what we've lost. Instead, we'll spend more time fighting each other than the horse people and the soulless. We'll lose."

Her sister stared at the wall across from Leraine for a long moment. "The People do need unity. But words alone won't do it. We need a threat, a common enemy. Something to fight for, or against. And I'll provide that."

Anseri turned to face Leraine, hands crossed behind her. "Once that mirror demon has escaped Chappenuioc and brought the demon heart to its masters, they will use it to open a new rift."

Leraine stared at her sister. "Are you mad? A rift would render our lands lifeless!"

"*Tss.* You think I'd help them if they wanted to do it anywhere near the People's lands?" Anseri shook her head. "The fools think they can control this rift, use it for their own purposes. So they'll open it in their own lands." She sneered. "They're wrong, of course."

"If you know that, then why help them?"

"You don't see it? Think about it. Once they lose control and a new Rift War begins, our people will join together to stop the demons. And with the horse people reduced to wandering bands of survivors, we can reclaim what they stole so long ago. After that, we can deal with the blooddrinkers, the necromancers, the soulless. We can finally finish off the elves and reclaim our islands from the orcs. The Valley will be ours again, as it was promised to us by the Great Spirits."

Leraine studied her sister, the gleam in her eyes as she beheld the future in her own mind. "You don't want to be *rangtauk* of Urumoy. You want to become *ogirangtan*." There hadn't been a war leader in generations. Even during the Rift War the People couldn't agree on one.

Anseri thinks she can pull it off now? Is she mad?

But Anseri merely shrugged. "And why not? I have more support than you think, and not just in Snake. My . . . useful idiots have a lot of connections I've been making full use of. Some of them actually believe in their promises, but they'll come around when it all goes horribly wrong. I would have to take a new name," Anseri said, rubbing her chin. "Resting Python is just not a good name for an *ogirangtan*."

Leraine decided to ignore that last bit. Either Anseri was more like Mother than even Mother had known, or she was deluding herself. That did lead to another question. "Why are you telling me all this?"

"I thought it obvious." Her sister crouched down. "I want you to join me. Your reputation will be invaluable. If you publicly agree that I'm the People's best chance against the demons, it will sway many. And privately, neither Mother nor our sister will make a fight of it if you support my bid to become head of the family."

That did it. Leraine burst out in laughter.

Anseri rocked back on her heels and frowned. "Did I say something funny?"

Leraine realized she'd messed up, again. Her mother would have remained calm, appeared interested, lulled Anseri into a fall sense of security. And only then would she have struck.

I'm stuck. Literally. She grinned and Anseri's frown deepened. *Oh well, might as well be fully honest.*

"Honestly, I don't know where to begin. How about that you think Mother will give up power without a fight? That you're a great leader? Or that I would dishonor myself by allying myself with a murderer?"

Her sister's expression flickered through a series of emotions as she shot up and a hand went to the hilt of her segmented sword. Anseri huffed and her hand fell to her side. "You still think that you're one of those heroes in the stories." Her sister shook her head and picked up the mage lantern. "But this is reality, Leraine. Ponder that in the dark for a day. Perhaps thirst and hunger will shatter that delusion."

Anscri walked around her and she could hear the creak of wood. Didn't sound right for stairs, it had to be a ladder. The creaking stopped after a few steps, the light still shining from behind.

"I don't want to kill you," Anseri said. "But I won't let you stand in the way of what must be done either."

Her sister didn't wait for a reply and finished climbing up the ladder, taking the light with her. A trap door fell into place with a heavy thud, a bar ground into place, then light footsteps died away.

Leraine felt around, finally finding a gnarl on the beam that she could reach with her bound wrists. Wasn't very sharp—just a rough patch—but it was better than nothing. Pushing off with her legs she twisted around the beam so that she could align the ropes around her wrists with the gnarl and started running them along it. Back and forth, back and forth.

This is going to take forever.

Leraine considered the possibility that she'd still be bound when Anseri returned. Could she lie? Pretend to be cowed?

Who am I kidding? I've never been that good at lying. And what of Eurik? Does Anseri have plans for him as well? No, that is a dumb question. Of course she's got plans.

She worked the ropes faster, though her arms already protested.

Chapter 28

Deception

THE WARM EVENING MEAL had restored his strength, but it had done nothing for his worry. The sky was still light, though the sun had dipped behind the Trollabergher. Yet of Silver Fang there was no sign.

"I'm sure she's fine. I mean, last time you came to her rescue, she'd already rescued herself," Misthell said. "Remember?" Eurik held the sword by the scabbard as they crossed the Outer Circle. It earned him more than a few stares, though once they saw the person at his side they tended to direct their attention elsewhere.

Sharp Prong's gaze roamed over the thin crowd, tapping her bronze rod. "More importantly, why must you be the one to come to her aid? You are still recovering. I will not have you undo my work the same day. If you fall ill, or collapse, you're on your own. There are limits to my gratitude."

Eurik glanced at her. "Not going to argue she's fine? That she wouldn't interfere in your affairs?"

The shaman pressed her lips together before answering. "She's late. Too late. Obviously something has delayed her. I will not say that she has gone against my express command, not without evidence. But something must have happened. I'd like to know what that is. That's all."

Eurik nodded. He hoped that it wasn't anything serious, but that hadn't been the case so far on this journey. At last they passed the standing stones on the edge of the vast Inza structure, the giant stones casting them in shadow as he finally stepped foot onto something other than Inza stone.

He inhaled the earth *chiri*, circulating it through his limbs and driving away the last vestiges of weakness.

"You should take care not to become too reliant on your magic," Sharp Prong said.

"Not magic. And you shouldn't think of it as something external. It's not. The Ways are the world, and we are part of the world. It's the separation that's harmful. Ah, I don't mean to insult your choice of living here."

"Hmm. It's not an insult, just ignorant. There's more than one world and they're not so separate. But mired in this one, it is easy to lose sight of that. To forget we are more than flesh and bone."

"But the world is more than that."

"Yes, yes, I heard your explanation before the *tidaechanek*. And I can hardly complain too much when it is that . . . not-magic that saved my life. Still, you should take care. All life is merely passing through this world. None of us can stay."

"Unless you're the Immortal."

"Him, yes. There's a debate on how . . . alive he is. And whether he truly is immortal rather than long-lived."

Eurik already regretted bringing that man up. His words still rankled and they only grew worse given the current situation. Had he known what was going to happen? Had his own presence made things worse?

"I see Snake's area," he said, pointing. "There are quite a few guards."

"Yes. All the tribes posted more warriors at the entrances of their quarters. And they're only letting people in who can prove they are who they say they are. If you think I can get you past them, you are mistaken. My authority ends at the posts."

"I'll manage," he said. He squared his shoulders and marched to the group of armed and armored women. They spotted him right away, a few stepping forward and spreading out.

"Halt, outsider. You're not getting in."

"I'm looking for Silver Fang. From Urumoy."

"We know who she is," another said, the left corner of her mouth raised in a smile.

"Good. I'm her friend. Rock, from San. We were supposed to meet, but she never came."

The one who had spoken looked at some of the others, who shook their heads or shrugged. "She did not pass through here while we were on duty, Rock of San. Though we've only been here since the evening meal. You can ask at the other entrance."

Eurik considered it, then shook his head. "She was supposed to meet me before dinner. If she left on time, the people there wouldn't know anymore than you. I need to know if she's in there, or whether I should look for her elsewhere. Can't I look with an escort?"

"No. We have no way to be sure you are who you say that you are."

He gestured at Sharp Prong, who stood a few steps back. She'd tucked her rod into her sash. "And I don't suppose having her affirm that I am who I am will work?"

The guard bowed lightly to Sharp Prong. "Apologies, shaman. But it will make no difference."

"Hold on," Misthell said. "You, the one hiding in the back behind that scary-looking one. No, the other one." That didn't clarify it for anybody, not until two disembodied hands appeared to point at a young woman with short hair. She held a swordstaff, but also had a broad quiver on her hips with an unstrung bow tied to it. That detail tickled Eurik's memory.

"She knows us," Misthell said. "Tell them why I ended up sleeping in the dirt all night. For which you still haven't apologized. Do you know how filthy that place is? You people keep burying your shit in it." The blade shuddered in his scabbard.

The woman shrank into herself as everybody looked at her. "I don't . . . It wasn't my fault." She gestured with her weapon. "He should have just handed you over. It's the law!"

"Oh, I want to hear this," the guard who had denied Eurik's request said, grinning. "Did this man give you trouble, Little Slip?"

Little Slip's hand tightened around the swordstaff and her cheeks burned. "No!" When she said nothing more, others started to chime in, calling on Little Slip to tell the story. She tried to fend them off, but they pressed.

All of this was a waste of time. If Silver Fang was in trouble . . . he considered marching through the guards. Pillars of earth to clear a path, shield him from any arrows. Or just dig his way in. But if they were on their guard, he wouldn't be free to search the area. He'd have to dodge or fight, wasting more time.

"If she doesn't want to tell the story, I can," Misthell said. "And not just tell. I can make the encounter come to life." Between Eurik and the guards, figures about a third of the size of the real people appeared.

"No, I'll do it!" Little Slip ran forward, swiping through the illusion with the butt of her swordstaff. "Not like it's a long story. Or important. That boy came in with a group from Urumoy. Silver Fang was in that group. But he carried a sword within our *rangtauk*'s walls. I backed Humming String up when she went to confiscate it. He got difficult."

"Well, Humming String was talking about keeping me. And I almost had you fooled into thinking I was a flathorn."

A few chuckled and Little Slip raised her voice to drown those out. "You did not. Not for an instant."

"It seems one of us can vouch for your identity," the first guard said.

"Oh, but we haven't gotten to the good part yet," Misthell said. His one eye peered at Little Slip. "Shall I tell them, or were you getting to that?"

She inhaled sharply through her nose, teeth clenched even as she spoke. "I had an arrow nocked. There were some other men there who were getting riled. Then . . . my hold . . . slipped."

It occurred to Eurik that her name might have been something else until recently. Silver Fang's words from a few months ago had hinted at that: that you weren't necessarily the one who decided what it would be. And Silver Fang had not been Silver Fang when they met. Little Slip might be quite angry with him, then.

Now they were all openly grinning or chuckling. The one who appeared to lead this group asked the follow-up question. "Who did you hit?"

Little Slip said nothing, only pointing at Eurik. He shrugged as their attention shifted to him. "It wasn't a full draw and I sort of was expecting it. So I stopped it."

"Stopped it?"

"My arrow bounced off his chest, barely drew blood," Little Slip said, glancing at him. "He has power."

"An accident, no harm done. And Misthell was fine, even after a full night buried deep in the ground. Don't let him convince you of the contrary. But he's all I have left of my parents, and he's my friend. I couldn't just hand him over."

The leader shook her head. "You almost broke guest-right, and they still let you come to the Festival of Conclave? I'd have you dig pits for a year, even if the guest had demanded you offer penance."

"For drawing blood, that would be a finger," Sharp Prong said. Those fingers shifted on the shaft of her weapon as Little Slip hunched her shoulders.

"So," Eurik said quickly. "Is that enough? Can I come in and look for my friend?"

"No, our orders are clear," another of the women said. "We can't allow an outsider in, even if he's proved that he's himself."

The leader shook her head. "No, we're just supposed to make sure people are who they say that they are. Outsiders aren't specifically forbidden."

"But—"

"Are you calling me a liar?"

The guard—wearing newer armor than what the others wore, now that Eurik took the time to note such details—opened her mouth. Then clicked it shut and averted her gaze. "No, no. Still, an outsider roaming around the quarter in these times is asking for trouble. Allow me to escort the boy around."

"A good suggestion, but I think we should give that task to someone more deserving. Do you think you can keep him out of trouble, Little Slip?"

"Yes." Little Slip gave him a hard look and jerked her head. "Come on then."

Eurik turned to Sharp Prong, who already shook her head. "I'm going to talk to the guardians patrolling. They might have seen her. We don't know that she never left, after all. Good luck on your hunt."

"Ah, you as well."

Sharp Prong walked away without another word. Eurik looked after her, only to have a wooden staff hit him on the shin. It didn't hurt, earth *chiri* still flowed through his limbs, but there had been some force behind it.

"Don't waste my time," Little Slip said. "You wanted to get in so badly, go."

He wanted to argue, though not sure what about. He did want to get into the quarter, as he was worried about Silver Fang. Shaking his head to dislodge that useless impulse, he walked in with Little Slip following two steps behind.

His first and only destination was Silver Fang's room. It was really the only place he knew in the place. If she wasn't there, he'd try some of the neighbors and hope to get lucky. He found himself watched the entire way, and not just by Little Slip. Conversations would fall still, and some stopped their work until they saw Little Slip behind him. Just about all the women wore a weapon or two, mostly swords, long knives, or a couple of daggers. Armor was a lot rarer.

Finally, he reached Silver Fang's room in the large pavilion and drew back the curtain. Everything looked neat and in its place. No sign of a fight. He extended his senses into the floor, but found little. Nothing buried, or swept up. The chest was a little lighter than he recalled. Dropping to one knee, he touched the iron lock and it clicked open. Inside, there was a collection of clothes and some other supplies. But no sword.

Little Slip shifted her grip on her swordstaff. "Hey, what are you doing?"

"Tracing her steps. Her sword is gone, she didn't have it last time I saw her. So now we know she did reach her room."

"Well . . . you'd better lock it back before we go."

"Certainly." He studied the chest's contents closer, but if there were any clues hidden inside, they eluded him. Closing it back up, he gave the rest of the room another look, but nothing else jumped out at him.

Her neighbors weren't in their rooms either, which left him standing outside the pavilion considering his options.

"What makes you think she's still here?" Little Slip asked. He turned to face her and she rolled her left shoulder. "If something happened to Silver Fang, it would have happened outside. Plenty of enemies. Not to mention that disguising murderer."

"She has a point," Misthell said.

"She does. But retracing her path has to start from where we know she was. Now, we know she was in her room. So . . . where would she go from there?"

"Food? I mean, she left in the morning and humans do need to eat a lot," Misthell said.

"There is a tavern nearby," Little Slip said after a beat. "You could ask there."

"Sounds like a plan. Please, lead the way," Eurik said.

Little Slip lifted her chin and pointed to the south. "It's in that direction. Look for the placard with a rattler drinking from a cup on it. Can't miss it."

He wondered what a rattler was, exactly, but he got the impression Little Slip wasn't in the mood for more explaining. He had a direction, and part of a description, it should be enough.

Navigating through the warren of tents and stalls—half of them empty—he discovered that a rattler was some sort of snake with a peculiar tail. It had wrapped its body around a tall cup and its tongue extended to lap some of the drink up.

Unfortunately, that was about all he learned from this tavern. The barkeep did recall serving Silver Fang lunch, but didn't know where she'd gone or when she left. Just that a lot of people had wanted to talk to her. But if she left with any of them, he couldn't say.

Thanking the man, he left. Standing outside the large tent, he took a deep breath and considered his next course of action. Wandering around hoping to stumble on a clue in this big mess was an option, but he could do better.

"Could you tell me where the center of the quarter is?"

Little Slip narrowed her eyes. "Why do you need to know that?"

"It's the best place from which to search the entire quarter."

Her frown deepened. "You're not casting any spells on our territory."

"It's not magic, and no. I'm going to draw the winds to me and listen to what they carry. Sounds, smells, that sort of thing. If Silver Fang is here, or someone mentions her, I'll notice." That was the theory, anyway. And if she wasn't here, or dead . . .

"So . . . the center of the quarter, if you please."

She glanced to her left before shaking her head. "You only have permission to look for Silver Fang. You didn't mention you were going to use magic to do it."

"It's not magic!" Eurik had had enough. Little Slip had barely been helpful and he shouldn't be wasting time.

"It really isn't," someone else said. Turning to his left, Eurik recognized her as Silver Fang's sister. *Resting Pity? No, that's not it.*

She inclined her head toward him. Behind her, several men were carrying something large and heavy covered in cloth. His senses easily made out the silver used in its construction. "Rock, I'm surprised to see you here. I thought you'd found lodgings in the Outsiders Quarter."

Python, that's it. Resting Python.

"I have. I'm here looking for Silver Fang. We were supposed to meet some time ago, but she didn't show up. I'm having a hard time retracing her steps. Have you seen her today?"

Resting Python hummed and glanced at Little Slip. "And what's your business here?"

Little Slip rolled her right shoulder. "I'm here to keep an eye on him. We can't have an outsider wandering around the quarter without a guard."

"I'm surprised they let you in at all," Resting Python said.

"That's because of me and Little Slip here," Misthell said. "On account of her shooting him. By accident."

"Ah, yes. That was you." Little Slip averted her eyes and her face flushed under Resting Python's attention. "I did see her," Resting Python said, returning her attention to Eurik. "Hours ago. She left the quarter right after, so I'm afraid you're looking in the wrong place."

"Did she tell you where she was going? Was she alone?"

"Yes, to the last question. And it didn't come up. But you shouldn't worry, Silver Fang can take care of herself."

Those words struck Eurik as strange. He couldn't help but glance at all the armed people; all the armed women, that is. The men walking and working in view wore neither armor nor weapons, save for a few short knives.

Resting Python seemed an exception, but he could feel the daggers hidden on her person and a strange sword wrapped around her waist.

"Wait a moment, is that a segmented blade?" Misthell asked.

He caught it, a tremor in the earth *chiri* as Resting Python shifted her weight even as her expression did not move a hair's breadth. For just a moment, she'd readied herself for a strike.

"It is," Silver Fang's sister said, placing a finger on the hilt. "I prefer something more subtle. I, for one, trust my fellow sisters to hold to honor." She gave Little Slip's swordstaff a once over.

"Not why I ask," Misthell said. "I heard what happened last night from Silver Fang. She fought someone with a blade like that. So why did she want to see you?"

Resting Python's eyebrows shot up. "Are you accusing me of something?"

"Please answer the question," Little Slip said.

She gave the younger woman a smile. It wasn't a friendly one, not at all. "Are you making some sort of accusation? Of me?"

"That's not answering the question," Misthell said.

Resting Python sighed. "Fine, fine. She wanted to know where Golden Tongue was. Our sister," she told Little Slip. "She didn't tell me why, but now I know. When we were younger, we had something of a competition going on. Trying to best one another at this or that, including the use of the segmented blade."

Misthell rolled his eye. "Still think there's no reason to worry? Figures Silver Fang went looking for the one working with that face stealer. Especially if she thought it was her own sister."

"Wait, hold on," Little Slip said. "What are you talking about?"

"We helped set a trap last night for the murderer of Springstep and the others, the one that can look like other people. We thought we were, anyway," Eurik said with a shake of his head. They'd been had. "The face stealer set a fire and escaped with a demon heart."

He might be revealing more than he was supposed to, but he was getting sick and tired of secrets. "Silver Fang and Slyvair went after him, but he had help. A woman in a raven mask. I didn't know she had an unusual weapon too."

"One used by two daughters of Raven Eye," Little Slip said.

"I hate to think Golden Tongue would stoop so low as to work with something that would break the peace of Chappenuioc, murder shamans." Resting Python shook her head and let out a long breath. "But all the Truce Warriors have gotten—"

"Watch what accusations you throw about," Little Slip said. This time, she didn't look away when she met Resting Python's gaze.

The latter inclined her head. "Yes. Still, Silver Fang went looking for her. She's your best lead to find her." She hesitated, then turned to the men still carrying their cargo. "Go ahead and meet up with Still Pool. She knows where this needs to go. Let her know I'm helping Silver Fang's friend to find my sister."

"Of course," one of the men said. He bowed to her, and Little Slip thought that one was shallower. Then they were off.

"We best head out as well," Resting Python said. "I know Golden Tongue has been spending some time in the company of Dancing Ember so we should try the Wolf quarter first. You can leave as well," she told Little Slip, who shook her head.

"I'm under orders to guard this man."

"While he's here. But we're leaving and I can make sure he doesn't do anything he shouldn't during the brief journey out of the quarter."

"Actually, we should head for the center of this quarter first," Eurik said. "I want to make sure she's not here first. Since we're here already."

"Why? Oh, yes, your magic." Resting Python nodded to herself. "But what makes you think she could be here?"

"Well, you didn't actually see her leave the quarter. Right?"

"I did not," she said slowly. "Though I'm sure we'd have heard if something happened to her here."

"I'm here now. Having to come back if your lead doesn't pan out will only waste more time."

"I see. How would this work?"

"I'll call the winds to me. They can carry sounds like her voice, or someone mentioning her name, from several bowshots away."

"I see. That is a powerful ability. You would be able to find her quickly, if she was here." Resting Python nodded again. "Very well. But if you need access to winds, perhaps the lookout on the top of the Great Hall would be a better place?"

She pointed at the large building sitting on the outskirts of the quarter, a dark shape silhouetted against the darkening sky. There was something sticking out of the roof in the center, a little tower with a domed roof on which a pole sat. Tied to that pole was one of the wind catchers in the shape of a snake he'd seen everywhere since coming to Mochedan territory. It rolled and undulated as the wind picked up.

"That could work. It looks to be open."

"Good. Well then, we're heading for the Great Hall," Resting Python told Little Slip. "You can go."

"I'm not under your command, Resting Python," Little Slip said. "And I already told you. I am not to leave Rock here unsupervised while within the quarter. No exceptions."

They stared at each other for a moment longer, then Resting Python inclined her head. "Very well. You can lead the way, then."

Little Slip shot Eurik a look. Silver Fang's sister clapped him on the shoulder. "I have questions for Rock, so he'll be walking beside me. Is there a problem? Not sure you can manage to navigate our way there?"

"No. I'm sure I can manage." Little Slip spun around and marched in the direction of the Great Hall.

Now Eurik was certain he was missing something in the conversation. Like back on the island, when san spoke to each other. Some of the sounds in the san language his ear simply couldn't pick up on. Except these two were human, like him, and still he missed something.

Chapter 29
Out of the Dark

TIME HAD BECOME A NEBULOUS concept down here in the cellar, measured in frayed strands and aching muscles. Leraine became very familiar with the ropes that bound her. The rope was clearly old, crud had worked its way between the twisted strands and some of the fibers had already come loose. They must have taken the first coil of sufficient length and thickness they could find in one of the Great Hall's many storage rooms.

That was the only reason she had a chance. Even then, if they'd bothered to post a guard or have someone check her from time to time this wouldn't have worked. Leraine didn't know why they hadn't done that.

It could be carelessness, excessive caution, or they were too busy with other matters. At this point it didn't matter. She just had to make use of the opportunity.

So she kept working the rope against the wood even as her arms protested every motion and her body shivered at the pervasive cold radiating from the four corners of the root cellar. If she could see, Leraine was sure a cloud of breath would be visible with every exhale.

It wouldn't be long now. She could part her wrists wider and wider every time she pushed down. Not long now.

Resting Python stayed close as they walked, not that there was much room in the narrow passage that Little Slip had chosen. "You had questions?"

"Hmm? Yes, I did. How much has my sister told you of what's going on here?"

Got to be careful here. She's told me things she shouldn't have.

"What she could, I think. I don't know if she's told me everything she knows, if that makes sense. I know I'm an outsider, people have made that very clear. So I know there are things she can't tell me."

"That is true, but not quite what I asked." She lowered her voice and got a little closer. "I meant about this business with this murderer. And its accomplices. Did she tell you she suspected a member of her own family? Our sister?"

She'd been told to stay out of it, but Eurik wasn't about to tell her that. "I'm not sure what was talked about this morning. I, uh, I was poisoned."

"He almost died," Misthell said. "Very inconsiderate of him. He never thinks of how his death could impact me."

"You'd miss him?"

Eurik already knew where the living sword's answer would go.

"Oh yes. Where else will I find a human whose first instinct is to not draw me in a fight? It'll shave decades off my life if he dies too early. None of you fleshies appreciate just how delicate and vulnerable someone made of metal is."

Eurik thought better than to argue. As long as Misthell was talking Resting Python's ears off she wasn't asking him uncomfortable questions.

Triumph and relief filled Leraine as the rope gave way at last. But while her arms cried out for rest, she couldn't afford to. The first binding was the hardest, but she wasn't out of this yet. Gritting her teeth, she pulled her arms around and then out of the squeeze of the binding around her torso.

Leraine sweated while her teeth chattered and her fingers were numb. She had to push and squeeze hard before she could feel what they were doing. The rope holding her head in place went easier, and the one binding her ankles together took moments.

But when she tried to push herself to her feet, Leraine found herself falling back and hitting her head against the beam. Lights flashed in front of her eyes and she had the sense that the world was spinning.

The cold or the dregs of the poison? One won't get better waiting here, and what time do I have? Anseri said that the mirror demon hadn't left yet. I've got to get out of here and tell someone. If it's not too late already.

Using the beam for support, she clambered to her feet. Though there was no light, she closed her eyes anyway as she tried to picture the root cellar in her mind. Her foot on the rope that had bound her legs, that told her what direction she'd been facing. Then the ladder was that way.

Leraine took careful steps, probing with her foot before committing to the step. She let go of the beam only when she had no other option. She swayed the moment she did, her lips were cracked and dry. Nausea bit the back of her throat. But every step felt a little better. With every step, keeping her balance became easier.

Unfortunately, so did disappointment as she confirmed that her sister had pulled the ladder up after her. Risking it, she pushed herself up to her tiptoes and reached out, laying her hand flat against the rough wooden planks of the ceiling. Feeling around a bit, she was sure she'd found the hatch. A push confirmed it was barred from the other side.

Silent, not daring to move, Leraine listened. But nobody came to examine the noise. They'd truly left her here to her own devices.

With all these supplies. Should have studied under Irelith a few more years, sister.

What they hadn't left, though, was a light. That slowed things down as she had to walk slowly. And Leraine still bumped into barrels and crates. Her first goal was the source of the chill pervading the root cellar. And it had a source, she could feel it get colder with every step as she neared one of the cellar's corners.

Her fingers encountered a rough metal cage, with something inside. Leraine hissed as she yanked her hand away. It had felt like she'd touched a hot kettle. The finger that had made contact with the cold stone was stiff.

Leraine trapped the numb finger in her armpit. As warmth and feeling returned back to it, she started pushing some of crates over to the hatch.

The Great Hall reminded Eurik of some of the greater houses he'd seen on his travels through Mochedan territory. Except not a single piece of stone had been used in its construction even as it had been built on a grander scale. Three stories, stretching nearly a third of the length of the outer border of the tribe's territory here in Chappenuioc.

Mage lights hung here and there to drive away the evening's growing darkness, illuminating not only the roads but also the painted carvings of every exposed beam and timber of the Great Hall.

"And that's why I think I should have been a musical instrument," Misthell said. "Nobody goes around banging two lutes, or flutes, together. People take care of their instruments. Keep them safe from the elements in cases."

"That's . . . an interesting way of looking at things," Resting Python said. "But it appears we are here. Come, we'll use one of the side entrances. It would be best if you weren't seen entering the Great Hall at a time like this."

Resting Python took the lead, guiding them to a small door in a building that had been attached to the Great Hall. Inside, she activated a mage light which she handed over to Little Slip. "Are you sure you want to waste your time babysitting us?"

"There's no shame in doing one's duty. Even when it involves escorting babies. If that is the case, of course," Little Slip said with a smile.

Resting Python returned the smile. "Thank you."

Little Slip's smile died out. "For what?"

"For being so true. Come." Resting Python laid a hand on Eurik's back and gave him a gentle push. "Let's not waste any more time."

The stones clicked as she plucked the cold stone out of its cage and plunked it into the bucket. Even with a rag between the stone and her hand, Leraine felt the cold burning her skin. But this was the last one. They rattled in the wooden bucket as she carried it back over to the spot below the hatch.

At least she could see something now. Rummaging through the various sacks, baskets, crates, and three barrels in the root cellar she'd found a packet of candles. One of them now sat burning on top of one of those barrels. Compared to a mage light, the illumination it offered was poor, but it beat stumbling around in the dark any day.

Leraine emptied the bucket on the crate lid she'd laid on the floor and swore she could feel the temperature drop through her boots. She retreated behind the crates she'd piled up high next to it and picked up the broom handle. She set it against the crate on top of the precarious tower.

Did I estimate the distance right? Will they break? How far will the frost reach?

A deep breath did not dispel those questions, but it quieted them. A lot could go wrong with this plan. But her next best option was to wait here for someone to check up on her. That would take too long. She might already have run out of time.

Her heel dug into the packed dirt as she pushed, only to fall to her knees as the handle's end slid up and away. Leraine tried again, same result.

The angle is too steep, maybe it would work with a lighter crate but I need all the weight I can get. Right, then I need to change what I can.

Wrestling one of the barrels over, Leraine stood on it and tried again trapping the handle's end in the upper lip of the crate. That took care of the slipping, but when she pushed it wasn't the crate that moved but the barrel on which she stood.

Leraine kept her balance as the barrel wobbled back and forth. She only dared to hop off when it had come to a rest. So now she had to brace the barrel.

At this rate, I'm better off trying to dig my way to another root cellar. The Great Hall is supposed to have several.

Leraine didn't dare to use the last barrel off in the corner, so she tried it with sacks of grain and beets. It seemed to work; the barrel only moved a little before the crate slowly toppled forward.

That's it, that's it! Go, go, oh shit, jump!

Leraine threw herself away. Away from the crates, away from the cold stones shattering. There was a flash, a hiss underneath the dying echoes of cracking stone and splintering wood. It bit her arm and plunged the cellar back into darkness.

Resting Python directed them to a broad set of stairs, Little Slip still in the lead. Eurik hesitated at the foot as he felt a ripple through the earth *chiri*, really more like a shiver.

"Something the matter?"

"No," Eurik said to Resting Python. He didn't feel anything else. Just that one impact. But it was hard to tell with all this wood in the way. It was like trying to feel with thick gloves, or hear a song with wool stuffed into your ears.

It could have been anything, really. A blacksmith working his trade, someone setting a heavy load down with little care. Except it had felt . . . cold. That had been an odd sensation. Earth rarely felt warm or cold, not unless you dealt with extreme temperatures. Like the ones in the vicinity of a volcano.

Eurik looked down the stairs. "Just on edge. I've already had two run-ins with the murderer. I guess I'm waiting for the third."

"You are not alone," Resting Python said. "Is that the reason you're worried for my sister? The demon slayer can handle a single foe."

"I suppose."

Resting Python huffed. "Come, let's get up to the roof. You're worried, yet also the one wasting time."

"You are right." He followed her up the stairs. "And you are not worried, then? Not even a little?"

"No. Well, perhaps some. My sister can get into a lot of trouble. The embarrassing kind. I remember when we were both children, she would—"

"Would what, sister?"

Eurik spun around. They'd just reached the top of the stairs and he only had to take one step back the way they'd come to find Silver Fang standing at the bottom of the steps. The right sleeve of her tunic was mostly gone and the revealed skin a raw red. What remained of the right sleeve looked oddly stiff.

"Silver Fang!" He went to approach her, but the next thing he knew he found Misthell held against his throat by Resting Python.

Leraine knew she'd made a mistake even before Anseri acted. She stood right next to Rock, who carried Misthell in his hand. Her sister drew the living blade and stepped behind him in one smooth motion. Leraine moved, already too late.

Dumb, dumb, dumb. I should have ambushed her, not confronted her.

Anseri pressed Misthell against Rock's throat. "Don't." She dragged him away from the stairs and angled him slightly away. This obstructed the advance of the other warrior with them. So she wasn't with Anseri then? "You, don't move either."

"Get your hand off me," Misthell said. "I'm not your sword. When was the last time you washed that anyway?"

"Oh, be silent. I don't know what possessed your makers to create a squeamish weapon," Anseri said before directing a baleful look in Leraine's direction. "I don't suppose you'd tell me how you got out?"

Not seeing an opening, Leraine could only play for time. "You left me alone in a stocked cellar for hours. Without a guard." She pinched a bit of her tunic's shoulder. It snapped off like it was glass. "Of course I got out." She dropped the piece and took another step up the stairs.

It hadn't been so easy. The broken cold stones had turned half the cellar and its contents brittle. Leraine herself had barely avoided a similar fate.

Her sister dragged the blade to the right, just enough to draw blood. Rock grimaced, but didn't say anything else. That look of concentration—he was using his magic, then. Or power, or ways, or whatever he wanted to call it.

Anseri had gotten lucky; any other blade and Rock would already be turning the tables on her. Was their location a hindrance? No stone or earth up here, but how much of a problem was that? And even if Rock could work his magic through the wood, she knew how sharp Misthell was. It might not be enough.

"Please, don't do this," Rock said.

"Already begging? I'm disappointed. Sister, from your stories I gathered this one had some courage."

"More like a reckless disregard for his own safety," Leraine said. *We're of the same mind, then. Good.* "But he's also soft. He's begging because he doesn't want you to die."

"Oh, he doesn't have to worry about that." Anseri pulled him down the hallway and out of sight.

Leraine hastened up the stairs to join the other warrior. She held a swordstaff, a reminder that Leraine herself was unarmed at the moment. "Who are you?"

"Little Slip." A muscle in Little Slip's cheek twitched. "From Joyous Bell's hold. What is going on?"

They entered the hallway side by side, illuminated by a couple of mage lights resting on little shelves between some of the opened windows.

The maneuver bought Leraine a moment to think. What to tell her? Joyous Bell was an ally in name, but a restless one. The shame of Anseri's crimes was bad enough when only Leraine knew. If it spread outside the family, it would do irreparable damage. But was it a question of if, or when?

"I can't help but think you're not taking me seriously, sister," Anseri said. "Do you really think I won't kill your new toy?"

Leraine stopped, and so did Little Slip. "No, I think you're not above murdering someone by your own hand," Leraine said.

Anseri glanced out the window and backed away farther down the hallway. "Please. This boy might be the child of People, but he's not one himself. You can't murder an outsider."

"Says the scaleless bitch that happily worked with one." Her teeth clicked as Leraine cursed her quick tongue. Too quick. Little Slip's gasp told her the other woman had put the clues together.

Anseri looked out again, stopped, and Leraine knew they'd run out of time. She didn't stop to think, to call out, she charged forward and everything happened in the blink of an eye.

Rock twisted and elbowed Anseri, Anseri sliced and pushed Rock. A line of blood splattered over the waxed floor. Rock fell, Resting Python stumbled back.

Leraine snarled and almost impaled herself on Misthell as her sister brought the living sword back up. "You're not—"

Resting Python struggled with her breathing, but her fingers were sure, her limbs steady. She drew a dagger and threw it, but not at Leraine. Little Slip had stopped to check on Rock, crouched on one knee with the swordstaff for extra support.

"I'm all right," he said, pushing her away.

Little Slip looked up just in time to catch the dagger in the throat. She stumbled back and collapsed. Turning back to her sister, Leraine caught her vaulting out the window and into the darkness of the night.

Chapter 30

At an End

EURIK CAUGHT LITTLE Slip as her weapon slipped from her grasp and clattered to the wooden floor. Her wide eyes stared into his, asking if this had happened. He batted away her attempt to touch the blade still stuck in her throat. "Don't touch that." He wanted to promise that she'd be fine, but he didn't know if he could make good on that.

"Is she . . .?"

"I got this," he said to Silver Fang. "Go after her." Resting Python had Misthell. But he couldn't think about that right now. He needed to focus on this.

"Right. I'll get him back."

He heard her follow Resting Python out the window, but didn't look away from Little Slip. She fought for breath, tried to go for the dagger again. He stopped her with his left arm, and lightly touched the dagger with the other. The earth *chiri* within would let him explore the damage it had done.

Missed the arteries. Obstructed airway. Point buried into the spine bones. They had an official name, but he'd never bothered to learn those. Much of the medical treatises he'd read didn't seem to pair with what his own senses had revealed. *Didn't puncture the bone. Obviously. She can still use her limbs. I can help her.*

He smiled. "You're going to be okay."

But would Leraine?

The smile died and he got to work quickly. He'd built up the *chiri* in his body already, and now he sent it flooding into Little Slip and the dagger. *Move the dagger, repair the bone, slide it out farther so that air can pass easily to the lungs again.* Little Slip's breathing grew easier. Now came the hard part, sealing the wound. *Separate the point of the dagger and leave it in the wall of the windpipe, remold it so that it forms a seamless part of the pipe. Not too fast.*

He sat back and cast the dagger aside. Both took a deep breath, and he didn't stop her when she felt at her throat. She wasn't going to die. That left Silver Fang and Misthell. Relief forgotten, Eurik scrambled to his feet.

"I sealed it. You should be fine for now. But go see a shaman," he said as he let go of earth and switched to wind. "I'm after her!" He went out the window after Silver Fang.

Leraine spared Little Slip one last look. A wound like that, no shaman nearby. Maybe Rock could do something. It was her only chance. For a moment, just a moment, she thought of calling him away from Little Slip's side. To not try and go after her sister right away. To let her die. Her and her knowledge.

Leraine looked out the window. That thought was something her mother would approve of. Not the thought of an honorable warrior.

She had heard her sister land on something hollow and she quickly found the source. An overhanging roof of a stable a mere step below the window and slanting down. It ran on to the right of her and she could see a figure running along the roof, something metal flashing.

Misthell should have seen her, but did not call out. Had said nothing when he'd almost killed Rock either. Very unlike Misthell.

A little worried how her sister had managed to get the living sword to shut up for once, Leraine jumped onto the roof and chased after Resting Python. Every step thundered through the night, but only three were needed to get her sister to look back.

Resting Python redoubled her pace. The stable had an L-shape, with a short, enclosed section built at a right angle to the Great Hall itself. Her sister ran up and over that roof, disappearing into the darkness.

Reaching the peak of the roof herself, she stopped and looked around. A mess of buildings had grown up around the Great Hall, and only a couple were a little taller than the stables Leraine stood on. Here and there a mage light shone from an open window or rested in an iron basket.

Movement from the corner of her eye—a figure darting from behind one building to another. The blade in their hand reflected the light of a nearby mage light. Leraine took off after, trusting Rock to catch up.

Leraine jumped from one roof to another, ran along its length and jumped down. She rolled with the impact and sprung to her feet. The figure jumped over a couple of barrels as Rock landed next to her. "Where?"

"Follow me!" He'd been quick. Did that mean saving Little Slip had been easy, or impossible? But that could wait, they had a thieving, murdering sister to catch. Leraine ran after Resting Python, Rock at her heels.

Over the barrels, the flash of someone holding a sword rounding the corner, another glimpse of the figure diving into a tavern. Though something was off. Leraine ran over as a scream erupted from the building and the sound of wood furniture crashing and splintering heralded the return of Resting Python.

Leraine came to a stumbling halt as she got her first good look at the person she'd been chasing and Leraine found herself staring at Rock.

What? How?

The second Rock gave her a nasty grin and quickly sidestepped away from the cloth curtain as others stormed out. All had weapons in hand, ranging from daggers to swords, and the first one out pointed her blade right at her friend. "Murderer!"

What?

Eurik struggled to keep up. With the last of the wind *chiri* already slipping away, his thoughts felt like they'd slowed to a crawl. He met Leraine's gaze as she looked from one to the other. But she didn't ask him if he was the real one.

Breathing in, he listened to the earth. He didn't know exactly how he'd feel through the *chiri* from the point of view of another, but the other 'him' felt wrong still. She didn't move with Rise of the Mountain or Dance of the Whirlwind; it wasn't any of the Ways.

I'm dumb. This is an illusion. But there is a person in there. I can feel them. But why is Misthell helping her?

A group of women charged through the door with weapons drawn. One of them brandished their weapon in his direction and shouted something about murder before leading them in a charge.

"He's not the one you're looking for," Silver Fang said. "Look. Behind you. Listen to me!"

They didn't look like they were about to, so Eurik took a step forward and stomped on the ground. Pillars of dirt and pebbles shot up, impeding their charge. "You should li—" They barely lost a step as some scrambled over the barrier while the ones in the back ran around it.

Eurik drew some of the sand to his wrists, but didn't have enough time to set it into place before he had to deflect the first swipe. The sand exploded away and the steel whacked him on the wrist. But it had lost enough energy that it couldn't cut into his toughened body anymore.

Beside him, Silver Fang went on the attack with a series of quick jabs. Someone else cursed.

His opponent hesitated at the lack of blood, but Eurik couldn't afford to do the same. He felt the rest coming closer.

Step forward. She brought her blade up but couldn't ward off the clod of earth that smashed into her chest and knocked her away.

Sweep the ground. The ground rippled away to trip the closest attackers. Others jumped over it and they kept coming.

Push and rise.

Leraine cursed. At her sister, at the living blade, at her fellow tribeswomen who couldn't spend a moment to think things through. It didn't help that these women were from Uthamac, they didn't want to listen to someone from her own sept. And they rarely wanted to think.

Shouldn't think like that.

She jabbed with her broom handle, aiming for the warrior's face. Her advantage was reach, her enemy's was that she had a proper weapon. "Look at him! He's unarmed!" Leraine chanced a retreat, to give the other an opportunity to look.

Instead, she darted forward and grabbed the end of the stick to wrench it to the side. Snarling, Leraine went with the motion. She slammed the other end into the idiot's sword arm to thwart the stab with one hand, the other she slammed into her enemy's face with an open palm. Her hand came back bloody as the Uthamac warrior stumbled away.

No time to catch her breath; more were coming. *This is useless. This fight serves only her. We have to get out of it.*

The next warrior gave a heedless charge with a swing she could see from a bowshot away. Leraine sidestepped and struck her on the back as she came past. Rock raised more pillars out of the ground but they were catching on, already evading.

But that can still work.

Leraine leapt to Rock's side. "Pillar." She stomped one end of her broom handle on the ground and hoped he'd catch on.

A single blink. "Right." He moved his arms in and up, the ground moved. In moments they towered over the buildings, the wind tugging at her ruined clothes. One of them actually struck the base of the pillar. The clang and the cursing afterward put a smile on her lips.

She took the time to catch her breath before calling down. "You ready to listen?"

"You bring that murderer down here or you'll both die!"

Leraine grit her teeth. *Remember, not the enemy. Just from Uthamac. Keep it simple.* "Idiot, did you forget about the face stealer!"

Things went quiet down on the ground. "It's here?"

"Yes! And it got away thanks to you!" She could feel Rock's look. Leraine took a deep breath and shrugged. "Best to keep things simple. We don't have time to explain," she told him.

"I don't even understand what's going on," he said. "Your sister locked you up? And Misthell is helping her now too."

Leraine laid a hand on his shoulder. "He may not have a choice. You've been treating him as a person, but Misthell is a sword in the end. And weapons were made to be used. But that can wait, lower us down. We're already drawing more of a crowd than I want."

"And your sister?"

Leraine looked out over the quarter. "She was the raven. Helping the face stealer. She calls it a mirror demon. Which is still here. We need to find them."

"I see." The pillar sank down again. Nobody attacked them again, thankfully. But she did spend some time fending off questions. A waste of time, but she couldn't have them accompany them when they went after her sister.

It was selfish, but she wanted to be the one to confront Resting Python. If others knew to look for her, that might not happen.

Finally, they got away as the others spread out to look for the face stealer in small groups. "Can you use your powers to find her?"

He stood still for a moment and closed his eyes, then shook his head. "No. Too many people are running around and I don't know her that well. You, maybe I could. But not your sister . . . you said it was a mirror demon?"

"Yes," Leraine said slowly. "You've heard of them?"

"It's not in Volfangen's Compendium. But the name is interesting. We've been wondering how it got in. You said it killed Tense Coil in a room that contained a magic mirror. What if it entered Chappenuioc through that mirror?"

Leraine frowned. "If it could do that, why not leave the same way? It had a clear run last night, but it didn't even try. No, it tried. That was the sound that day. But the mirror is dedicated to the Great Spirits. It couldn't get past that."

It didn't explain how it could enter the sanctum if that were the case, but she wasn't a shaman. It explained some things. "But how does that help us?"

"When I met your sister, she was with a group carrying a flat object containing silver. And silver is used to make the best mirrors."

"And you heard where it's going?"

Rock shook his head. "No, but I don't need to. That much silver, I can track. As long as it hasn't been brought into the Inza structure," he added in a quiet voice.

"Then you better hurry."

He wasted no more words and closed his eyes. Leraine considered the broom handle. If she was going to confront her sister, she'd need a real weapon. Looking around, she took stock of where she was. An armory was nearby.

Chapter 31

Trust to Steel

HIS MISSING FINGERS itched; missing extremities always did for the first couple of days. Slyvair barely noticed, though. His scalp felt tight as the tension hung heavy in the air. Some of the humans looked at everybody with a wary eye. Others had a hunger. Young fools.

Next to him, Perun was quiet. He noticed the mood as well. But he'd still insisted they went after that boy, Eurik.

"He's probably not there," Slyvair said. He eyed the armed party standing around the entrance of one of the camps. Judging by the markings, it belonged to their Boar tribe. Some had armor, others had shields. Clearly, some had had to scrounge around for the gear. Others looked like they'd been expecting trouble when they'd packed. Slyvair wished he'd had the foresight. "They're not letting anybody but Mochedan into their camps."

"But we have to find out where they are. If I don't watch his back, somebody will steal him!"

And of course his worry was for the living sword, not the boy who carried it. Not that Perun was indifferent. Just blithely sure he'd be fine. Slyvair didn't share that confidence. Not with how Eurik threw himself into danger.

"We'll ask. But you'll let me do the talking."

Perun got that stubborn look again, but it crumbled when it met his own. Only when he got a sullen nod did Slyvair relax. Not much. Not when he himself had nothing but a knife if things went wrong.

They reached the Snakes' camp and he hailed them. Fortune was with him, a few spoke Irelian. "Greetings." She eyed his metal arm, then Perun. "What you want?"

"We're here for Misthell," Perun said. That got a raised eyebrow. "He'd be with Eurik."

"He's speaking of a living sword." And these people went for shield names. Sensible enough, you had to ward off the evil eye. Though expecting it to strike at any moment was taking caution too far.

Eurik hadn't followed the custom at all, but he had adjusted to their expectations. Something Perun hadn't learned yet. "It's being carried by a boy called Rock. He's supposed to have come here looking for Silver Fang."

A fierce one, and as reckless as her friend. Mate, maybe. Human practices were strange, most of the time. Even after living among them for so long, he still found himself baffled from time to time.

The names, at least helped. Recognition rippled through the group, followed by worry. "Yes," one said. "He came, went in looking."

"He did?"

"Yes. With one of us."

Perun charged into the conversation. "Can we?"

"No. He . . . proved he was who he was. I—we—do not know you."

"Ya don't know who Captain Slyvair is?" Perun pointed back at him. "He's the leader of the Gored Axes! He'd have won your competition if it weren't for Eurik and Silver Fang needin' his help!"

"That's enough out of you." He dragged the boy back. "They need to be careful. You should be careful too. That thing can look like anybody." Slyvair turned to the warriors. "Apologies. If you see either one, let them know we came by."

Someone left the camp, passing them by and barely earning a look from the women guarding the entrance. She clearly was Mochedan herself and wore a light cloak to ward off the evening's chill.

"We will."

"Thank you. Come, we best get you to bed." Then Slyvair frowned as Perun gave no protest, barely seemed to hear him as he steered the boy away. "Don't worry about them. They'll be safe inside that camp."

"Not sure. I think that lady had Misthell under her cloak."

"What? Are you sure?"

His nod was slow at first, then picked up speed. "Yeah. I met his eye. But he didn't say so much as hello to me. Maybe he's on a secret mission?"

Slyvair surveyed the crowd, it wasn't hard to spot the woman. Not many wore a cloak and she didn't have her hood up. "Perhaps." But as he studied the woman, he could feel the memory of a flame lick his stump. His right hand went for it, but he lacked the fingers to squeeze it proper.

"Can you find your way back without me?"

"I'm coming with ya. Misthell's my friend." And the boy laid a hand on his dagger too.

Breath rumbled deep in his throat. But there was no time to argue, and he wasn't that comfortable with having Perun wander about alone. Not tonight. "Fine. But you do as I say, and you stay back. And don't you dare touch that dagger unless I tell you to. Clear? I say, is that clear?"

"Yes, sir."

"Right then. Follow me."

Leraine stepped out of the armory, adjusting the gambeson again. Moths had nibbled on the left sleeve, the smell of mold and stale sweat tickled her nose, but it was better than nothing. The same sentiment went for her spear, its shaft ending halfway in a splintered point and its narrow head pitted by rust. Six throwing spikes, but no poison for them. At least the buckler was in decent shape, and so was the cloak she'd thrown on to hide how she was kitted out for a battle.

And one of these days I'll go into battle prepared and in possession of my own high-quality gear.

Rock ran up to her. "I found them. They're not going too fast, but they're a ways away." He pointed in an easterly direction and didn't wait for her response. He began to run.

Hurrying to catch up to him, they jogged through the quarter. "Then it's not hiding within our quarter. The Outsiders Quarter then."

"No. They've already passed it."

Some made to stop them, but once they caught sight of Leraine they hesitated. But Rock's news was a problem. Were they heading to another tribe's quarter? Even attempting to follow them in could ignite a war. But how would Resting Python get in then? Unless she'd decided to leave Chappenuioc on her own rather than seeing to it that the mirror demon got away.

They finally reached the exit, only to have the warriors guarding it shout questions to Rock about where Little Slip was. Worse, some moved to block their passage. "She's fine!" Leraine sprinted to get in front of Rock. "Get out of the way! We don't have time for your questions."

They wavered, but they weren't deciding. "Rock, move them."

For a moment, he said nothing and she worried he might not want to. "Sorry!" He didn't stop, just leaped and came down with a stomp before resuming his jog. Slabs of packed earth turned up, shoving the warriors out of the way to form a narrow but clear passage out of the quarter.

They plunged into the broad street running between Chappenuioc proper and the quarters. There wasn't much traffic, and most had stopped to stare at them bursting out of Snake's Quarter. A couple of the warriors they'd just dashed past ran after them. To her relief, they were called back. A selfish relief.

Leraine ran faster, but she couldn't go full out. She needed to have enough breath and strength at the end of it to fight. And Rock struggled to keep up as it was. He could go a lot faster with his wind power, but if he was using his stone power to track the mirror than that wasn't an option. Unless he'd figured out how to use both and didn't tell her?

"Oh no," Rock suddenly said, looking at Chappenuioc. "They turned west. Going into Chappenuioc. I'm about to lose them."

"Then we'll cut through here and aim for their last known position."

"All right, but can you stop for a moment? And give me one of those spikes?"

"Why?" But she did slow down to a halt right in front of one of the portals of Chappenuioc and handed over one of the asked-for spikes.

"I don't want to go in unprepared." He snapped the spike in two like a twig, then the iron pieces screeched as they were squashed into small beads. Which he proceeded to pop into his mouth one by one, swallowing them.

Leraine worked her mouth, then shook her head. "No, forget it. My questions can wait. Come on."

Slyvair grew increasingly certain that Perun had been right. He hadn't caught a glimpse of the living sword himself, but that woman was fleeing from something. She was in a hurry, kept looking back, but didn't take the time to make sure she wasn't being followed.

That was the only reason why he hadn't been spotted yet. He'd done his best, used all the tricks he knew, but he stood out. Even the night couldn't hide him if she'd really looked. It did help that she'd ducked into the Inza's stoneworks the first chance she'd gotten. It had been an issue when she'd ascended one of the staircases to the buildings placed on the Outer Ring of the Creator structure. Hard not to make noise on them, but up here it was easier to follow.

Mage lights wouldn't work here. Here and there were a couple of oil lamps and braziers that did nothing more than ruin the night vision of anybody who looked right at them.

Could have done with a weapon.

Perun followed, quieter than him, in truth. He'd always had a knack for sneaking about, right from the start. His lip curled into a smile as he remembered the little snot almost getting away with Ceran's supplies. But Ceran would never cook for anybody again. And Perun could die too if he wasn't careful.

"If I tell you to run, you don't question me. You run," he said, not looking back at Perun.

"And leave you alone? I can fight. Gerd and Hanser have been teaching me."

"And you didn't learn much. What's the first thing a man needs to learn to be a soldier? Well?"

"To obey orders."

"So when I order you to run . . ."

"I'll run. I'll go find Silver Fang. Then we can rescue you."

"I'll be fine. No, you're going to find that priestess, the one with the antler stick. We'll need more than one blade if this goes wrong."

When this goes wrong.

Perun stayed silent, but Slyvair was content to wait. "Yes, sir."

"Good." And he didn't breathe out his relief. Slyvair kept his eyes on the cloaked woman. She'd stopped, but not to look back but around. She was searching for something but didn't find it because she set off again. Almost running.

His ears caught it before she did, the noise of several people tromping up one of the staircases. Slyvair froze with his hearts pounding in his chest, they were coming up right behind him. Slyvair risked getting a little closer so he could squeeze himself into a slit between two buildings. Perun had a much easier time of it.

The glow of a lantern heralded their arrival. He shut one eye so not to ruin his own night vision entirely and watched the odd group pass by. The one carrying the light was armed, the rest carried something long and flat between them wrapped in cloth.

None looked in his direction and Slyvair just dared to relax when an angry voice cut through the silence. The voice was not so loud he could hear what was being said and it petered off quickly, but the light didn't move. Not for a good long while.

Perun tapped his thigh. "What's going on?"

"I don't know. I think they know each other. But something didn't go right." In his experience, people rarely started shouting on a dark road if everything was fine. Though what the problem was, he couldn't guess.

Whatever it was, it got resolved. He could hear them move on, the light fading. Only when darkness had returned did Slyvair pull himself out of his hiding place and crack his other eye open again.

He didn't see the cloaked woman right away, because he wasn't looking at the right spot. She led the group and they were moving quick. Slyvair followed, more careful now. There were more eyes to spot him, even if they'd all be half blind from the lantern.

It wasn't for long, about a bowshot from where they'd met, the woman called for a halt. She alone approached a particular building. He saw nothing special about it; it looked as flimsy as most of what was built on the rings. At least they'd taken the time to decorate most of the houses here. He'd never understood the Irelians' preference for plainness.

The thief, if she was that, knocked on the door. Light spilled out as it opened right away and she stepped in as soon as it did. The others hesitated for a moment before following her in.

Send Perun away now? He eyed the boy. *No. He'll argue and we don't know what's going on here. It still might be nothing. But it doesn't feel like nothing.*

Slyvair inhaled deeply of the cool night's air. The scent of wood awoke old memories, though this was the wrong kind. The subtle hints of smoke brought others up, made the skin on his skull go taut. But there was something else there . . .

A plank creaked and Slyvair dropped, leg sweeping the ground behind him. A figure tumbled, but he wasn't alone. Slyvair rolled over the prone human and swung his leg up and down, but they dodged back.

"Captain, it's us," the cloaked figure hissed as the one underneath Slyvair croaked something as well. They threw their hood back and bared their teeth. Starlight reflected weakly off a silver tooth.

"Shouldn't sneak up on me." He got off—yes, that was Eurik. "What are you doing here?"

"I should be asking you that," Silver Fang said, though she spoke in Linesan. Right, Eurik's Irelian was pretty bad.

"I saw a woman with Misthell. Wasn't you, I figured he got kidnapped," Perun said. "We here to rescue him." The boy had been getting better with his Linesan. The sword had helped there.

Silver Fang's head dipped before she squared her shoulders. "That's my sister, Resting Python. She's . . . helping the face stealer. Called it a mirror demon."

"We followed a mirror they're carrying for her," Eurik said. He looked down the narrow street. "We saw them come up here. Did they go into one of the buildings?"

"Yes, that one. And what is that mirror for?" The old burns grew tighter even before he heard their answer.

"We think it will use that mirror to leave Chappenuioc. Maybe mirrors act like a portal for their kind." Silver Fang shrugged. "There's a lot we don't know yet. But we can find that out later."

"Yes." He switched to Irelian and placed a hand on his child's head. "Perun, time for you to find that priestess. Tell her what we know and where we are. Hurry."

He saw the rebellion grow on Perun's face, but he was smart boy. He just nodded, then turned to Eurik and Silver Fang. "Ya better save him or ya'll regret it." He didn't wait for their reply and ran off, silently disappearing into the dark.

Slyvair let out a breath. "I don't suppose either of you have a spare weapon for me?" Eurik, of course, shook his head. That one relied too much on his unarmed combat techniques. And his weapon had gotten stolen. But Silver Fang only offered a knife, which he turned down as he drew his own. At least that was steel he knew, steel he could trust.

Chapter 32

Breaking Down

THEY CLOSED ON THE building that held Misthell, and the mirror. Eurik could barely feel it through the *chiri*-starved wood. They stuck to the shadows as mice fought in his stomach. Neither Slyvair nor Silver Fang looked anything but calm, but Eurik couldn't help but be concerned.

"They've set the mirror down, ground floor." He could hear people moving inside, but not sense them. There was just so little here, like he was underwater. Except this sea had no floor.

"And they're coming out," Slyvair said.

"We don't have time to wait for them to leave," Silver Fang said. She took out her buckler and shortened spear. "They're men anyway, they'll get out of the way when they see us."

"Will they?" Slyvair smiled a little. "They'll still be in the way. Even if you are right. And going in the front is not the best approach anyway. Follow me." He ducked into a narrow alley, not looking back.

Silver Fang seemed torn, only to relent when Eurik passed her and followed Slyvair into the passage. "We don't know how many we'll be facing. I can't sense much." There was steel in there, but there were hints of steel and iron everywhere. It could be pots, nails, or swords. No way to tell from this distance in this place.

"Fine. But hurry."

They reached the back of the building and found a narrow door there. No lock, but it simply rattled in its frame when Slyvair gave it a little shake. "Barred. It's around here, I think," he said, tapping the door about a hand above the rope loop that functioned as a handle.

All of them could hear a door open, the sound of men talking grew louder. The group that had delivered the mirror was leaving.

"Right. We'll have to go in loud, then. Get ready." Slyvair took a few steps back, then ran forward and punched the door.

Leraine had barely had time to grasp the sun-man's meaning when he charged at the door and punched right through it with his metal arm. She felt the impact reverberate under her feet. The sound of splintering wood shattered the night. But Captain Slyvair wasn't done.

Pulling back, he tore the door of its leather hinges and cast it away. Rock reacted faster than her, already slipping past the sun-man and into the building. Biting back a curse, Leraine followed with Captain Slyvair right behind.

She could hear the alarm inside, but also confusion. They hadn't realized yet what was happening. Leraine stormed through the dark kitchen, hanging spoons clacking against each other in Rock's wake. This had to be a feasting hall; the kitchen was too big for a simple house and a larger dwelling would not be so empty as this building felt.

Rock neared the door, but didn't slow down. Instead he took his lead from Captain Slyvair and sprang forward, kicking the door open with both feet. Something broke as the door swung away and light spilled in.

"Yes, they did follow you," someone said. A familiar voice, an impossible one.

She and Rock fanned out into the room, but there was no immediate opposition. Days-old straw lay on the floor, with dark stains in the wood beneath it. Long tables and benches stood on the sides, leaving a large space in the center free for dancing or brawling—or to set up a large freestanding mirror.

The last of the men took one look back and fled into the night through the front door. That cleared one escape route. Captain Slyvair had stopped in the door opening, effectively blocking that off. Leraine barely took notice, most of her attention was on the three in the center of the hall.

Resting Python was one of three, with Misthell still in her hand. She'd already discarded her cloak on one of the tables. Still Pool, not a surprise to find her sister's retainer here. Hand on the blade, but not yet drawn and her eyes bounced from them to the last member of their little conspiracy. Tense Coil smirked as she looked them over. She stood closest to the mirror and had a bundle under one arm.

"You are an idiot," her sister said to Leraine. "Every chance to walk away and you just walk to your death." She grabbed the handle of her segmented sword with her free hand and whipped it out.

Leraine released the clasp of her cloak and let it fall to the floor. "Someone has to uphold the honor of our family." She took a couple of steps to the left, hoping to lure Resting Python away from her allies.

Her sister rolled her eyes. "This act grows tiresome, little sister. Our family has always strived for power. Because that's what matters. Honor is something you can afford to affect later." She turned enough to keep an eye on Leraine, but wasn't moving farther.

Eurik called out from across the hall. "Give up Misthell. Surrender. Please."

Resting Python just laughed. "Give up a living sword?" She admired the blade. "After sampling its power? I can see why you like him, little sister. He's as great a fool as you are."

"Python," Still Pool said, her blade rasping from its scabbard. "We don't have all night."

"I can stand to hear more," Tense Coil said. It had to be the mirror demon. But who did it think would be fooled by that guise? Or was it just its way to twist the knife? "How about you, *oircaid*? What is your stake in this?"

Captain Slyvair growled softly. "You speak my language."

"Yes. Comes in handy when you visit Ainchang Ystoil," the demon said. "Yes. I've walked the silver streets of Telleiproap, watched the Crimson Empress appease Yellow Smoker."

None of it meant anything to Leraine, but it obviously did to Captain Slyvair. "Enough. I don't care what you do with your sister, Silver Fang. But that one," he said, pointing at the mirror demon, "I want it alive. It will answer my questions before it dies."

Leraine didn't acknowledge his words. Something felt off about this. *Where is her confidence coming from? It's three on three, she knows what Rock can do. And Resting Python isn't that good herself. Is it Misthell?*

That thought didn't feel right. The living sword was a peerless blade, but its illusions lost a lot of their power if you knew they couldn't hurt you. Then again, she had killed a blooddrinker with exactly that power. But Resting Python didn't think that way. She thought in moves, get at her enemies from behind, from hiding.

The floor vibrated as Captain Slyvair stomped into the room. He'd drawn his knife and had grabbed a pan from the kitchen. Her sister's posture shifted, a tension left. But Captain Slyvair joining the fight only improved the odds. Unless . . .

Ambush.

Leraine looked about, then realized this was a hall. It had a high ceiling.

Eurik bounced on his feet, kept his arms moving. The wind *chiri* running through his body urged him on, to it stillness was death. Something the demon said, it niggled at him. Ystoil. He'd come across the name before.

Not relevant right now. He's not closer to the mirror. Silver Fang is facing her sister. I should handle the demon. Leave the other to Slyvair.

He was ready, but Silver Fang wasn't. Eurik drew deeper into the winds. He'd act as soon as she would. But she was taking her time. He sensed his own breath, quick but deep. Slyvair's was a gust. Silver Fang's breathing gained speed; she'd move soon.

But there were more breaths stirring the building's air. Many more. Not just in front of him. Eurik looked up at the same time as Silver Fang did.

He saw nothing, just empty rafters cloaked in deep shadows. But he could sense their breathing, hear clothes rustle and bows creak. Eurik whirled his arms around, and the wind picked up the discarded cloaks and sent them flying into the rafters. A curse, cloth ripped, someone fell out of thin air, and everything rattled as the body hit the floor.

The room exploded into chaos. Silver Fang and her sister leaped at each other, arrows flew, and so did a pan. Slyvair grunted when one arrow found him, but the pan he threw smacked the woman with Resting Python right in the face and sent her reeling.

Three arrows were meant for Eurik. They flexed in flight; his shoulder dipped just underneath one, his hand slapped one away, the third ripped his pants and caressed his skin. But the wind carried the pain and the fear away. The wind didn't let itself be held back by anything.

Eurik danced through the room. He still couldn't see them, but he didn't need to. A flick of his hand sent a gust of wind through the rafters. Someone stumbled around up there and nobody loosed another arrow. Nobody got knocked to the ground either.

If the fish don't come to you, you go to the fish.

He bounced off the wall and up into the rafters. It was like plunging into the sea. From in the boat, you couldn't see much between the waves and the sun reflecting of the water. But once through, another world opened up. A gloomy one of wooden beams and armed warriors.

They'd seen him come, two already aiming for him, but he wasn't stopping. He couldn't. An arrow *thunk*ed into the beam next to his head, the other hit the slanting roof behind him. A hop, bounce, jump, and he was among them.

"Kill him, kill him!"

Fervent's here. Why's she here? No. Question later. Focus.

One fighter had drawn another arrow, but rather than putting it on her bowstring she tried to stab him with it when he landed next to her. Eurik spun and swept her legs out from under her. The beam shook as she landed on it and her fingers scraped the wood when she slid off.

But they weren't the only ones on that particular beam. The other one had also drawn another arrow and shot him from four steps away.

Leraine's arms blurred as she stabbed out with her shortened spear, caught an arrow on the buckler, then fell back as her sister lashed out with her segmented blade. She held Misthell in her left hand, and Leraine had to keep an eye on it. She knew how sharp the living sword was; her gambeson wouldn't stop its keen edge.

Can't stay away though. They can't shoot me so easy if they risk hitting their leader.

"Do they know what this is about?"

"They know enough," Resting Python said, then she jumped back and Leraine's gaze darted up. She still couldn't see a thing, but she heard a commotion up there. Rock had jumped up there and had not come back down yet, alive or dead. The arrows had ceased as well.

"Looks like your plan isn't going so well," Leraine said. She risked a look around, things didn't look so bad. Her liver shrank at the sight of Still Pool, blood dripping from her shattered nose, a knife buried in her chest by Captain Slyvair. At least the one that had fallen from the empty air had been a stranger, a warrior from another sept of Snake. This conspiracy involved members of the entire tribe, then.

"That's your mistake, little sister. You imagine victory. While I, I plan for success." She advanced, flicked her segmented blade out, which Leraine easily deflected. But then she followed it up with a crude stab with Misthell and Leraine could barely sidestep it. Her counterthrust almost cost her her weapon as Resting Python chopped at the wooden haft just behind the steel head of the spear.

Another warrior fell out of the rafters, not dead, but not getting up either. Another stranger. Ropes now fell from the ceiling, more warriors rappelling down to meet Captain Slyvair. They were all familiar, all from Urumoy. But the sun-man could handle them. Were they fleeing from Rock? "Really? Funny," Leraine said. "Success looks like defeat from where I'm standing."

"Look again." Resting Python pointed at the front door. Which was the moment another couple of warriors came in. These ones were more than familiar. But they couldn't be! Irelith's daughters had remained in Urumoy.

They drew their weapons and charged her.

Chapter 33

Shatter

THE ARROW ARRIVED IN the blink of an eye. Eurik grabbed it, but the shaft slid through his grasp and seared his fingers. The point came to a rest against his shirt and no farther. His relief was the thing of a moment, before that too was swept away with the currents.

He slid the arrow through his grasp a second time, held the end of it in a three-fingered grasp, and threw it over to another section of the rafters where another archer aimed for Slyvair. The projectile sank into the meat of her behind. He'd aimed for her back. But it messed with her aim enough, and her own arrow hit nothing but straw and wood.

Eurik didn't forget the one who had tried to shoot him. Four steps between them. He needed only two to close the gap. He slapped her half-drawn short sword back into its scabbard and drove her back with a rapid barrage of punches that ended with her slamming her head against a wooden beam.

Then he jumped and spun, more arrows passing him by. They'd come from other beams, a large gap between the two he'd crossed with ease. Rather than landing directly on the beam he aimed below it, catching himself he spun under and over. Another arrow whizzed by, tearing through his shirt before thudding into a table.

He'd barely found his footing when he had to pedal back as one fighter had ditched her bow in favor of a pair of single-edged short swords. She was a whirlwind of slashing steel, and Eurik spotted three throwing ropes down so they could lower themselves back to the ground. Two aimed their bows at his friends down below, trusting their comrades to keep Eurik occupied.

Slyvair kicked up the fallen sword so he didn't have to bend down so much to grab it. The mirror demon—the one who'd claimed to have visited his homeland—just watched everything like it was a play put up for its sole entertainment.

The first girl to have fallen from the sky pushed herself up, arms shaking. A solid kick sent teeth and blood flying. Maybe dead, definitely out of this fight. Good enough. "What are you smiling about?"

"I am gratified to be proven right. Again," the disguised demon said.

"*Tch.*" But Slyvair hesitated. The creature was too relaxed. Too sure of itself when it had no weapon that he could see. When he took a step forward, though, the demon drew back. With a half-smile, Slyvair's steps picked up speed.

But the demon only fell back until it stood beside the mirror. Then it picked up one half of it and pivoted the mirror so that it was aimed at Slyvair. The demon said something in its hideous tongue, light spilled past the wraps of the thing it carried, and the mirror's surface flashed and wobbled.

Slyvair choked as something slipped past his lips and flew toward the mirror. Heat, perhaps, for a chill grew in the pit of his third stomach. He stumbled to a stop, not easy when the room tilted toward the mirror. Except nobody else was bothered by it in the least. He planted the tip of the sword into the floor and braced against the pull.

The demon sneered. "What's the matter? Feeling . . . less? Don't worry, that will soon be over." It chuckled at its own joke.

In the mirror, his reflection stirred. Taking a deep breath, it straightened out even as Slyvair's own legs threatened to collapse.

"It's not a pretty death," the demon said. "No blood, no guts, no pain. Those will have to come after, from the others. When I have some help I can count on to see the world as I do."

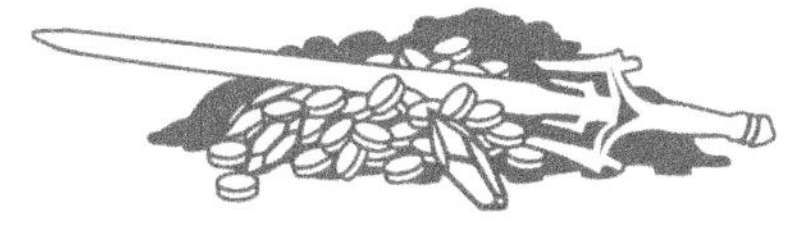

Leraine fell back so she could keep all her opponents in her field of vision. That also allowed her to see Captain Slyvair on one knee not far from the demon. No injuries that she could see, but clearly not doing well.

Like I am doing any better?

Resting Python lashed out. Leraine caught the attack, but couldn't even think of a counterattack before Irelith's daughters joined Resting Python's side.

"What are you two doing here?"

"Revenge," White Gale said.

"For our mother," Flashing Reed added.

Leraine shrank back. "But helping her? Do you even know what she's done?"

White Gale snarled. "There you go, hiding behind others. No, Silver Fang. You will pay for what you did."

Her instincts screamed something was wrong and she barely caught her sister lunging at her from the corner of her eye. Instinct took over and Misthell sliced a sliver off her buckler. Irelith's daughters lunged forward but stopped when she turned to face them. And her own sister tried to sneak out of her field of vision again.

"I did not kill her. The blooddrinker did," Leraine said, twisting to face her mentor's daughters, then back to keep an eye on her own sister. "I avenged her."

"She'd still be alive if not for you."

"I—" She only lost track of Resting Python for a moment, but it was enough. She jumped at the opportunity and thrust with both blades. It was a crude thing, her attack, and that was the only reason Leraine didn't end up on the floor bleeding out.

She lashed out with the broken spear, catching the segmented blade and tangling it with Misthell. The follow-up was more instinct than a plan, pushing Resting Python's weapons down with her buckler she stabbed forward.

Resting Python flinched, but it wasn't necessary. The head of the spear flopped about as her sister's sword had bit deep into the shaft. It threatened to fly off completely when Leraine brought it back.

Her sister let out a long breath and confidence returned to her limbs. "Guess the great Silver Fang's not so dangerous without her magical sword." And she raised Misthell higher. "You were always the spoiled one."

Fast. Leraine Fast. Running out. He saw one starting to slide down the rope. *Time too.*

The world was a strange place when you had wind *chiri* running through your body. Everything moved slow, yet you were moving so much faster. You had time to consider, but your mind couldn't stand still. For to move with the wind, you had to be like the wind, think like wind.

Not time for wind. This will hurt.

Everything happened all at once. His opponent seemed to speed up, the world got simpler. Wind fled as Eurik took his stand and dug deep within himself. Strength poured into his arms, his legs, his skin toughened. But not enough to prevent two blades from carving into him.

The pain was a muted thing, bouncing off the diamond planes of his mind as he pulled at the earth *chiri* in those blades and they came to a jarring halt. She didn't hesitate, tried to pull them out. But that just gave him the time to seize her and throw her into the enemies balancing on the other beam. Occupied with sliding down their ropes, they barely saw their comrade before she slammed into them and all three plummeted to the straw-covered floor below.

There are still two here. He plucked one knife out of his arm and sent it toward the woman who had decided to shoot Slyvair instead of Eurik. It sank into her back. If that didn't kill her, the way she landed headfirst with a sick crunch certainly would. He ignored the weakness, the pain, the nausea. *Fervent's left.*

The beam under his feet groaned as he pushed off and leaped over to the other beam. Fervent turned with the jump and shot him in midair, the arrowhead sinking into his thigh. A grunt escaped past his lips as Eurik landed and a fresh lance of pain ran up and down his leg, chasing the first.

But the arrow gave him more than a wound, it replenished the earth *chiri* he'd just expended. Another arrow, it would have taken out his eye if his hand hadn't been in the way. A third skidded off his neck. Half the knife still stuck in him snapped off, its very essence expended to keep Eurik alive long enough to get to grips with her.

Fervent recognized it too. Switching to her sword, she threw her bow at Eurik which he didn't even bother to bat away. "Why are you working with a demon?"

"I'm not. I used Resting Python and that thing to get you here."

"But I'm already ordered to pay you. Why break your own people's laws?"

"Shut up." Her sword flicked out but it veered out of Eurik's reach when he tried to grab it. How much did she know about his abilities?

"You're just like your mother. You run when things get hard." She swiped at his leg, but it barely scratched his skin. Fervent grimaced as she saw how little that light touch of the blade had done.

Eurik took a step forward and Fervent slid back. "That's why I needed to lure you in. It turned my liver, but for my mother I'll do it. And after that, I'll take care of that traitor down below and her pet demon. Then I'll be the hero who saved Chappenuioc!"

Fervent placed her palm on the flat pommel of her sword and put all her power and weight into her lunge.

Eurik's hand brushed against the sword and he seized control of it. Taking inspiration from the wind, he didn't stop it. He deflected the blade down into the wooden beam, Fervent's hold slipped, and she slammed into it belly first.

While she gasped for air, Eurik took a hold of her arm and threw her off the beam. Then—after drawing as much of the earth *chiri* as he could from the blade—he jumped after her.

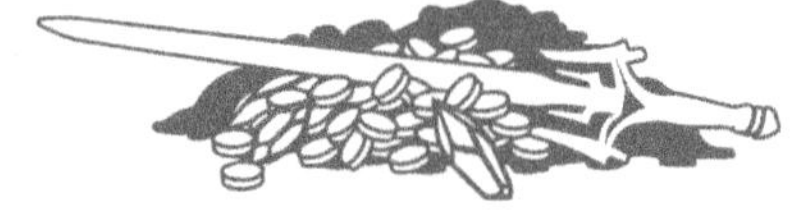

Something isn't right about this fight.

Beyond the fact that she faced family. Family who hated her enough that they wanted her dead more than to preserve the sanctity of Chappenuioc. No, the rhythm of this fight didn't make sense. Irelith's daughters and Resting Python kept alternating their attacks instead of attacking all at once to overwhelm her. And Flashing Reed and White Gale didn't really attack, they'd only feinted.

Her eyes widened as her attention turned to Misthell. *It makes sense. He can do it. But if I'm wrong . . .* Then she noticed Captain Slyvair, on his knees, hand on his chest as something seemed to flow from him to the mirror. The demon raised the heart it had stolen into the air, the picture of triumph.

"You're wrong, sister. It's not the living sword that brought victory. It is my allies." She snapped off the head of the spear, since Resting Python had done most of the work already. Then she threw it. But not at her sister. Her aim true, she knocked the demon heart right out of the mirror demon's hands.

With a wordless snarl of anger, her sister and Irelith's daughters attacked. Leraine focused on the one attack that mattered. She blocked Resting Python's segmented blade and left herself fully open to those who had once been as close as sisters. Their blades did not even stir her clothing.

"And you are running out of those," Leraine said.

His vision had narrowed to the point that he only saw the rippling surface of the mirror and the thing that looked like him on the other side. The first thing that penetrated that small, narrow world was a sound. Something hitting the floor, a curse in a language that scratched at his ears.

The world shattered, a connection snapped, and Slyvair could breathe again after what felt like an eternity. Thought returned. The ice in his chest thawed slower, much slower. *Accursed fool. Finally have two good arms again and you step right into it like you're a hot-blooded kid. I thought I'd left that behind with my left arm.*

The demon had left the mirror unattended, chasing the wrapped demon heart rolling along the floor. Slyvair clambered to his feet. It was slow going and interrupted by the sight of his reflection setting a foot inside the hall. Its fingers curled around the frame and it looked like it was pulling itself into reality.

Slyvair had kept a hold of the sword, he'd managed at least that much. His arm drew back and threw the blade as if it were a spear. It was a weak throw with a weapon not meant to be used like that. It still sent the mirror wobbling as a web of cracks ran through its surface. A howl erupted from the mirror that gave everybody in the hall pause.

All the life and warmth, little pieces of his soul, flooded right back into Slyvair. His gasp was loud in the sudden silence. With renewed strength, he stood proud.

"Fine," the demon said, snapping the silence. "The fun way, then. Python, stop trying and finally kill someone." The demon didn't even give the demon heart a glance, leaving it abandoned as it strode over to Slyvair.

Slyvair looked around for a weapon but saw none within easy reach. The knife would have to do, then. It should be enough.

That confidence took a hit when the demon shifted form. One moment, a human woman with all the frailty and tininess that implied came at him. The next, a fully uniformed guard of the Amber Empress charged him.

It had been decades since he'd been south. Decades since he'd seen the lands from which his people had sprung. First time he'd seen a Ribbon Guard, he'd sneered at their garb. He hadn't believed the stories. Good thing someone even stupider had challenged one before Slyvair himself had had the chance. He'd left impressed shortly afterward. Very shortly. The Ribbon Guard had not respected his opponent either.

All of that came flooding back now, even as he knew that the being coming at him was not truly a Ribbon Guard. He didn't have a drop of mortal blood in his veins. That was hard to remember when he recognized the technique as he blocked and evaded. Classic Bladed Hand, as taught in the shadow of Red Fountain.

Before that flurry of jabs, strikes, and snapping ribbons, he had to give way.

"The fun way, then. Python, stop trying and finally kill someone."

"Yes, Python. Do as it commands. If you can," Leraine added.

Her sister's glare transferred from the demon to Leraine. "I had hoped it wouldn't come to that. You are family. But you're as stubborn as Mother." She struck out and Leraine fell back. "Don't know when to take a step back and let someone else take over." Another blow that Leraine could only deflect.

"At least we're not traitors to our people," Leraine said.

With a wordless snarl her sister attacked. Possessed by fury, there was little room for proper technique. The segmented blade was easy to stop, but every hew of Misthell took a piece off her shield or another finger off the length of what had once been a spear.

Then the moment came. Leraine only recognized after her arm had already moved, after Misthell spun through the air as Resting Python cradled a bloodied hand to her chest, hissing as the splinters dug in with every twitch of her fingers.

"Yes, freedom! Your sister is a horrible person," the living sword cried out. Then he hit the table. "Hey! Couldn't you have aimed me at the soft straw! It's everywhere."

Leraine didn't answer, though she couldn't stop a sigh of relief. It was good to know Misthell was back to his old self. For a little while, anyway. Instead, she pressed the advantage.

A segmented blade's strength lay in surprise, in the first few moments when the opponent didn't realize they were facing armed opposition. Most fights didn't last much longer than that. All Leraine had was a stick and a third of a shield, but it was more than enough.

It was her sister's turn to retreat. Resting Python chanced a look back, looking for allies perhaps, but all she saw was Rock taking out the last of the traitorous warriors of their tribe. And behind him, the crumpled form of Fervent.

Why? No, that can wait. The thought skidded through her mind as she took advantage of her sister's distraction to smack her other weapon out of her hand. "Surrender. I have no desire to kill you either."

"Surrender?" Their fight had taken them halfway through the room, ending right next to the mirror. Rock's heavy footfalls told them both that the net was closing around Resting Python. Her sister took another step back almost stepping on a shard of the mirror as long as a dagger. Resting Python glanced down and quickly picked it up, fresh blood welling up as she held it in a firm grip. "Never. I am a warrior of Snake. I have lived as one, I shall die as one. Kill me, sister, if you can."

Leraine had no reply. For she'd barely heard those last words as she watched in horror as the piece of mirror flowed like water. First, it absorbed the blood. Then it slipped into her sister's body through the wound.

Resting Python gave her suddenly empty hand a bewildered look, then the screaming started.

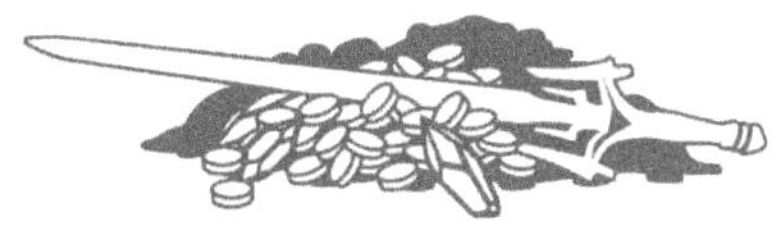

His surprise nearly cost him an eye. Slyvair twisted his head and felt the hand rip the flesh off of his cheek. But rather than take advantage, the demon hopped back and took a look at the source of the screams now filling the hall.

Silver Fang's sister knelt before the broken mirror. At first, he'd thought the arm had been lopped off. But no, it now resembled the mirror behind the human. And the transformation was sliding up her arm.

Silver Fang approached her sister, only to be thrown back as Resting Python opened her mouth and spat green lightning.

"Unexpected," the demon said. "Perhaps I'll have something to present after all." He ran toward the transforming woman.

Eurik tried to stop him. He did better than Slyvair expected. For several heartbeats they exchanged strikes, blocks, counterblows. Then it happened. Eurik faltered and the demon's fingers buried themselves in his chest. Not too deep, but the boy was smart enough to retreat.

Before Silver Fang could circle around to try her own luck, the demon had scooped up Resting Python and touched the mirror. The cracks in its surface didn't disappear, but the scene it reflected changed a great deal.

Gone was the small hall with its wooden floor covered in straw, blood, and bodies. Gone were the benches and the simple tables. Instead, Slyvair saw stone and rugs, a shelf with expensively bound books, and out a window he saw an Irelian city instead of Inza architecture.

"Now hush, little one. All change is painful. No use crying about it. Embrace it," the demon said before its words were cut off as it passed through the mirror.

"You don't get to take her," Silver Fang cried out, leaping after them. But she hit a solid surface, the impact toppling the mirror, and both went down.

Chapter 34
A Story to Tell

WITH THE RUSH OF BATTLE gone, and with the last of his reserve of earth *chiri* left, Eurik shuffled over to where Silver Fang lay. He passed the broken remains of the demon heart; it looked so very plain. The wind carried the sounds of an approaching group, too many and too loud to be anything but the city's guardians. Perun had found someone to listen to their warning, then. It was over.

He collapsed to one knee beside her. "Are you all right?"

"No," Silver Fang said. She rolled over, but made no move to stand up. Eurik could see no serious injury. "My sister . . . Something happened to her at the end. And her crime now falls on us."

"But we didn't do anything. We tried to stop her."

Silver Fang closed her eyes briefly. "No, not you and Captain Slyvair. I mean our family. My family." She let out a long breath. "Perhaps it was a fool's hope that this dishonor could remain quiet."

"I see." He didn't, not quite. It still made little sense to him that one could be held responsible for the actions of another. Even when that person tried and somewhat succeeded in stopping the wrongdoer. Especially in that case. But it was clear Silver Fang believed it to be so, and she would know her people best. But did she think so herself?

Silver Fang gave him a searching look and pushed herself to a seated position. "But you are injured."

"I've stopped the bleeding. I'll live." It hurt. He felt lightheaded. But that was unimportant right now. "Still . . . It occurs to me that in all the years on the island I only got two scars. Six months with you and I have a collection." He fought to give her a smile, but she did not answer it.

"Perhaps it is a good thing then that our paths are separating again. You, to find the memory of your father. Me, to find my cursed sister."

"I only caught a glimpse at the end. But . . . she was changing."

"Then maybe what I have to do will be a mercy," Silver Fang said so softly Eurik barely caught it.

"Could somebody please pick me up from this filthy floor?" Misthell conjured a rough sketch of a hand hanging in the air and pointing down at his position. "Over here. Hurry."

"So I hear Misthell has recovered from his ordeal," Silver Fang said. "You'd best go fetch him. Before his complaints grow in volume."

Eurik hesitated to leave Silver Fang's side right now.

"Yes, get him to shut up," Slyvair said. The orc was covered in two shades of blood, but his wounds had already scabbed over.

"I'd better." Eurik raised his voice as he got up and left Silver Fang in Slyvair's care. "I'm coming Misthell. Don't worry."

"Finally. Do you know how horrible that was? She wouldn't let me talk. She used me to try to kill you guys. And she banged me against everything in sight like a clod. I think I might have a nick. You need to check. But tomorrow. I don't trust the lighting conditions in here."

The sword didn't really stop talking when Eurik picked him up. Just stopped shouting the words.

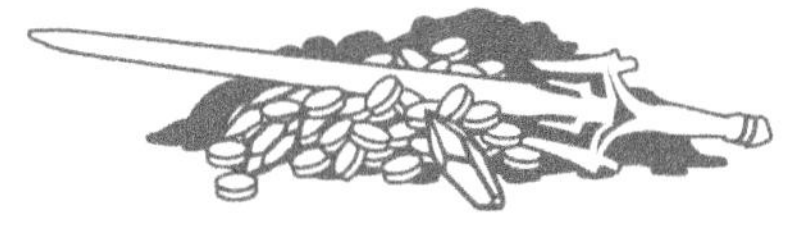

Slyvair lowered his voice, though he was sure it would do any good if Eurik wanted to hear what he had to say. Then again, his Irelian couldn't have improved that much in the last couple of months. "When you're going after your sister, I'm coming with."

"I thank you for the offer," Silver Fang said. Now she pushed herself up. First, into a seated position, then to stand as she continued to speak. "But this is a family matter."

"And you can have her. But I got my own questions to ask that demon." The skill that thing had shown couldn't be acquired in a week or two. Slyvair had spent but a single season on the slope of the Mountain of the Blooming Baichyao while they waited for the winds to turn north again. He'd learned much, but most of all humility.

That demon would have had to spend years in the south. Years among what were his people, despite all that stood between north and south. Slyvair needed to know what the demon had been up to, what its plans were. It might no longer just be a human problem.

"Besides, do you know where to start looking?"

"I . . . I think I saw something in the mirror. An Irelian city. Perhaps a member of the Oathfellowship."

Slyvair grinned, though his torn cheek protested the motion. "Then I got a better look. You need me, girl. If you hope to find them before the trail grows cold." It might anyway, if that demon could just move from one mirror to another one anywhere else. But no, there had to be limits.

Further discussion was interrupted by the arrival of a group of the city's guards, spearheaded by several shamans and followed by Perun. They brandished questions and weapons, but Slyvair ignored them for the moment in favor of his son.

"You did well, soldier." He squeezed Perun's shoulder.

Perun's face reddened a little and he did his best to look him up and down. "You a'right?"

"I've hurt myself more hunting crabs. You aren't rid of me yet." He could point out Perun's lack of proper armor or weapons. But initiative and boldness were things to be treasured. Proper caution, only time could really teach that to hotheaded youths.

Then again, it never sank in with me.

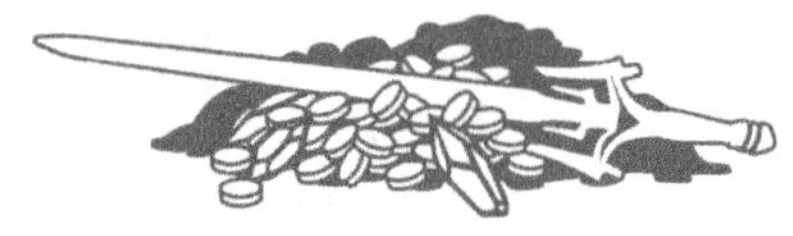

Leraine watched as chaos turned to order. The dead and wounded were sorted, and so were the guilty and the innocent. The guardians took care of the former, while Sharp Prong and Sated Resting Panther led the effort to wring the truth out of the survivors.

She'd thought herself tired at the end of the fight, but now she knew better. Leraine had had to reveal her family's shame. Her failure to stop her sister. It was made all the worse by their quiet understanding.

Sharp Prong let out a long breath. "Then it is over. We have that, at least."

"Is it?" A Boar shaman said. "The Traitor-Mage's mirror is still in storage. What's to stop more of those mirror demons from coming through?"

"Obviously it will need to be secured," a loreteller to Sated Resting Panther's right said. He stroked his chin as he continued. "But that might not be so hard. Why didn't this mirror demon slip in at an earlier time, when nobody was around? It might only work if there are people around, or light. If we remove those, that just might do the trick."

"Might? You would chance the sanctity and safety of the very—"

"An argument for tomorrow," Sated Resting Panther said. His hair was silver, his face like a carved mask of walnut wood, but his voice still carried the power of a trained loreteller. "One of many. That both a True Warrior and a Traditionalist were involved in this will silence some, inflame others. Let us therefore savor these few hours of peace that are left to us. We will need the memory in the days to come."

"And we can all use some sleep," Sharp Prong said. "Including these four." She indicated Leraine, Rock, Captain Slyvair, and his charge. "And since you might not hear it from anybody else: thank you."

The shaman bowed, not too deep to shame Leraine, and walked away. A few inclined their heads, murmured some praise, but all quickly left. Only the Bear loreteller assisting Sated Resting Panther remained behind, since the old Puma himself hadn't moved.

Only when all had left and the sounds of their discussions died away did he speak. "I knew your father, a little," he said to Rock.

"You did?"

"Oh yes. One Claw is a rare name, but there's no mistaking it," he said, giving the living sword in Rock's hands a look. "He earned his name. To this day, I've never heard of anybody else to be so passionate about our craft, while also being utterly unsuited to become one."

Leraine frowned. "How do you mean?"

Sated Resting Panther huffed, a single heave of amusement. "The man could not carry a tune to save his life, and memorizing a tale always ended up in farce. Certainly, he had an imagination. But loretellers do not make up stories; we are the living memory of the People. And yet, every year he would apply. Every year, he was rejected. He'd try other crafts, I heard, but it never lasted. He always came back to stand before us and audition."

"But he did give up." Rock looked down at Misthell. "Instead, he learned how to make living swords."

"Oh, you think so? I've heard of your sword too, these past few days. A memory of steel that can remember even the most obscure tale, and the ability to bring those stories to life like no loreteller can. No, young man, he finally found a way to make his dream a reality. After a fashion. A good way to end his story. I think I will tell it when I return home."

The other loreteller hovered nearby, but Sated Resting Panther ignored him entirely even as he leaned heavily on his walking stick with every step.

"Honored elder," Leraine said before the loreteller left. "What sept did One Claw belong to?"

Sated Resting Panther paused for a moment. "He resided in Uschathevaiuc. It's a small sept downriver of Thevoy."

"Thank you."

"Try to restrain yourself, Silver Fang. The People may have need of you for many more days. And perhaps before I return to the pack of mist and moon."

Leraine did not know what to say to that, and barely remembered to bow her head before Sated Resting Panther thumped out of the hall.

"I knew it," Misthell said. "I wasn't made for war, for fighting. I'm a work of art."

"Perhaps we should put you in a chest again," Rock said. "Only bring you out when we want to hear a story after dinner."

"Let's not go overboard here. I've done enough of that. I do enjoy the outdoors. You know, when it's not raining. Or misty. And you two would be lost without me to solve all your problems. Though maybe for once without stabbing me into something. That would be nice."

"There shouldn't be any of that on your way to Uschathevaiuc," Leraine said. "I don't know the place. But by Sated Resting Panther's description it must be on the Baelar, and the road to Thevoy is well-traveled."

"That's nice, but we're not going there. We're coming with you. Uh, right, Eurik?"

"Yes. We are."

"But you've found out where you can learn more about your father. And he's not . . . well, it doesn't sound like he had enemies there. I cannot ask you to follow me on yet another task that has nothing to do with you."

"I'm pretty sure we've been over this before," Rock said. "You are my friend. What matters to you matters to me. More importantly, I think I finally understand something my *sesin* told me when he said I had to leave the island."

"And what is that?"

"That I needed to find my own path. And my path isn't following in my parent's footsteps. I think they will always be strangers to me. But you," he said, looking Leraine in the eye, "you are not. I'm going to help you. That's where my path is going."

Leraine inclined her head and held it there until she could trust herself to speak. "I am honored. Thank you, Eurik."

"Now if only you knew where to go," Captain Slyvair said, startling Leraine. She had actually forgotten for a moment that he and Perun were still here. "I can help you there. Or should I say, I'll let you come along. Under the right conditions, of course."

She shared a look with Rock, who shrugged after a moment. "Name them," Leraine said. She could say no if they were too onerous.

"We are not killing the demon. Not right away. I have questions it needs to answer first. And you two—no, you three will be part of the Gored Axes for the duration of this expedition. I'll not have you two running around doing your own thing, like during our journey through the Neisham Hills."

"But you will vow to see my sister meet her rightful end as well?"

"Of course."

"I don't have a problem with it if you don't, Silver Fang," Rock said when she turned to him.

"And I hold you to be a man of honor," she told the sun-man. "Very well, it is agreed. We'll join your mercenary company for this quest. So I swear on the Great Serpent. Now, what did you notice that I did not?"

"A moment. I did not hear your friend's oath. Or that of his sword."

"I'm thinking about it," the living sword said.

"I'm not," Rock said. "As the mountain stands, the sun rises, the river flows, and the wind dances, so I will swear. I will be a Gored Axe until you have your answers, and Leraine has her sister."

"Still thinking about it," Misthell said when all eyes turned on him. "Fine, fine, I solemnly swear that I will join your mercenary company for the duration of this adventure. Hey, wait, does that mean you're going to pay me?"

Captain Slyvair opened his mouth, then closed it as if he'd bitten into a spoiled apple. "Yes. I suppose it does."

"Back to important matters. Where is my sister, Captain Slyvair?"

The sun-man's grin showed a hint of teeth. "There were banners flying from the castle in the background. Hard to see, even when they were illuminated by mage lights, but I recognized them. I saw them only a couple of months ago. That mirror demon took your sister to the one hundred-thirty-third emperor of all Irelians, Duke Griffenhart."

THE END

Acknowledgments

The Living Sword series has been an ongoing project now since 2013. The original idea, this setting, is even older than that, but only that year did it come together enough for a story to emerge. That story is not over yet, but we're approaching an ending now.

I would like to take this time to thank my family for their support and love. Those who are still here, and those who are not. My father, for kindling my love of history. My mother, for giving me the confidence to write. And my brother, for showing me the value of not giving up.

I also want to thank Lynda Dietz, the editor of Living Sword, for all her work to turn my writings into a product that I'm not embarrassed to publish.

Then there are the beta readers for this book. Without their advice and generosity, this story would be far less. So thank you, Peter Sagefjor, Bennett Alterman, Gareth Duggan, and many more for your contributions.

James, aka Humble Nations, who designed all the covers for the Living Sword series, is another vital part of the success this series has had. The cover truly is the first argument for a reader to try out a story, and thanks to him I have a good opener.

Then there is Tiffany Munro, who turned my sketch into a real map that fleshes out the world of Living Sword in a way that not even a thousand words could hope to do.

And finally, I want to thank you, the person reading this. It's because of readers like you that I've kept writing.

So until the next adventure,

Pemry Janes